# A Touch of Spleen

The new sequel to 'The Trouble with Wyrms' trilogy

## Mike Williams

MIKE WILLIAMS

Copyright © 2019 Mike Williams
All rights reserved.
ISBN: 9781671659193

# DEDICATION

To Simon Nick, for his love and support.
Dedicated to my friend of over 45 years, Mike Willis.

# MIKE WILLIAMS

# ACKNOWLEDGMENTS

A very big thankyou to Tony Fyler of
Jefferson Franklin Editing for polishing the final manuscript.

MIKE WILLIAMS

# Preface

There is nothing so beautiful as the sea; the smell of it, the sound of it, the way it goes on forever - stretching out to the horizon, then down and around till it surprises you from behind. It's just a pity it's full of fish. I've nothing against fish, especially a nice piece of battered cod sizzling in a pan, but I'd like them far better if they blinked and had eyelashes. There is something about the look of them that makes me shiver, and they don't help themselves by having teeth. Nothing good ever came from a fish with teeth. Nothing good ever came from a fish with an expandable stomach and a name like the Black Swallower too, but that's another story.

This story begins in a small ocean on a distant planet, a little to the left and a sideways cough below the buckle on Orion's Belt. Here the fish are purple with orange spots and eat mermaids for breakfast, which quite frankly, is how it should be. Shed no tears. Mermaids may be all wobbly and voluptuous on top, but downstairs they're all haddock. Pity the sailor on his honeymoon faced with a bathtub of fish eggs and strict instructions to fertilise them, each and every one. No, mermaids deserve all they get.

But this story has nothing to do with what swims in the sea but what floats on it. This story begins with the greatest battleship in the world, the Emperor Spleen's pride and joy - the SS Behemoth. Until it sinks, that is, and then it's back down to Earth and the quiet little town of Grubdale. Grubdale - where witches roam, and dragons roar, and where the mysterious Felicity Merryweather, best-selling author of sickly-sweet romances, has decided to visit for a holiday.

MIKE WILLIAMS

## Chapter One

Commander Crillock was a happy man. It was a glorious day to be a sailor; a fabulous day to stand on the deck of the SS Behemoth and dance a little gig, which he did from the knees down. From the waist up he was as still as a statue, the very essence of authority in his blue serge uniform and gold lace. 'What say you, Mr Flume, should we get the men to sing?' he asked. But the man standing next to the commander was not happy at all. From the knees down or the waist up, it was all the same – it was breakfast.

'Sick again, Mr Flume.' It was not a question but an observation, and the poor man nodded. 'Then stay downwind, or you'll have me heaving like a new recruit. Good heavens, I've never known a person so ill.'

'It's the nerves, sir.'

'I'm sure it is,' the commander said, looking the unfortunate lieutenant up and down. 'Many a sailor gets sick before a battle, just never in such spectacular fashion. Get yourself cleaned up and be quick about it. There's a war to be won, as if you didn't know.'

Lieutenant Flume dashed away to his quarters, trying his best not to look at the ocean but to keep his eyes focused at the level of his shoe buckles. The sea was full of ships, lots of ships, but today there were only two that mattered. The thought of what they were about to do to each other had the lieutenant's digestion spilling over like a kicked bucket. The smell of the SS Behemoth's engines and the slow, relentless roll of the ship had the lieutenant's digestion spilling over too, but then stepping over a puddle would have done the same. Poor Mr Flume was a terrible sailor with an awful stomach, on an awful ship with a terrible cook. It was a wonder he could stand up at all.

It was a wonder the SS Behemoth could float. The battleship was as far from a wood and canvas man o' war as you could imagine. It had all the timeless grace and beauty of an iron brick. Above the waterline was metal plate and below the splash of the waves, the blades of the paddle wheels drove the beast forward at frightening speed. The prow of the battleship, designed to look like some hungry shark with its mouth open, seemed to chew up the ocean as it steamed through the waves, spitting out foam and pilchards on either side. But teeth are one thing, and iron shot another, and great sea battles are not won by dentures alone. It's the guns that count, and the SS Behemoth was as pumped up with cannon as a porcupine with wind.

There were five massive cannon on either side, each capable of sending a 30 pound iron ball spinning across the waves, but on the deck of the ship was a nastier surprise: Big Bessie, a gigantic revolving cannon like an enormous soda bottle ready to spit out its cork, a terrifying 16inch shell. Less deadly perhaps than the real Bessie, especially when she realised someone had named a fat cannon after her, but dangerous all the same.

Filthy black smoke belched from two tall funnels to complete the image. The SS Behemoth - a black monster of a ship, the pride of the Emperor Spleen's navy, ploughed its way through the water as it chased its prey.

'SWING HER AROUND, MEN!' the commander shouted through a copper megaphone. 'BRING THE CANNON TO BEAR!' he bawled. 'WE HAVE THEM NOW!'

The entire length of the ship seemed to rattle with activity. Men dashed across the deck to turn big wheels and pull big levers. Chains snapped tight and cogs, black with grease, slid silently against each other as the giant paddles of the battleship churned the waters to foam. Slowly at first and then with deceptive ease, the monster ship swung sharply to port to bring its target into range.

A pair of doors slammed back on their hinges and from somewhere behind the commander came the sound of rushing feet. 'Welcome back Mr Flume,' the commander said as a figure, noticeably cleaner and sweeter smelling, appeared by his side 'Feeling better?' he asked.

'I am now,' came a voice that caused the commander to feel the opposite immediately.

Some voices are evil. They start viciously in the diaphragm, turn nasty in the nasal cavity and by the time they spill out over the tongue, they're fairly dripping with menace. This new voice was all of these but more - the sort of voice that could whisper sweet nothings to a sphinx and make its nose drop off. It was a voice the commander knew only too well.

'Your Imperial Majesty, I didn't realise...'

'Don't turn around, you needn't look at me,' said the voice. 'Look to the sea. I want this nonsense finished.'

Commander Crillock was relieved by the order. He hated looking at the Emperor. Everyone hated looking at the Emperor.

# A TOUCH OF SPLEEN

'I want no splinter of those ships left,' continued the voice. 'Destroy them, send them to the bottom.' The voice would have said more but for a sudden fit of coughing that suggested all kinds of horror in the lungs. Commander Crillock waited patiently for it to finish. He looked up at the sky, the ships ahead, his fingernails, even the manufacturer's name on the megaphone - anything rather than look to his right at the terrible Emperor Spleen.

'The rebellion,' said Spleen finally, catching his breath. 'It ends today. See to it.' And with that, Commander Crillock heard the footsteps disappearing into the distance. He heard two galley doors swing open too, a little squeak of surprise and then what sounded like a groan and a bucket of porridge hitting the floor. Poor Lieutenant Flume had met Spleen halfway and, even though the Emperor went nowhere without his mask, the thought of what lay behind it was enough.

'Bloody Emperor,' swore the commander under his breath. He'd been in a fine mood that morning till Spleen had appeared, and now the whole pleasure of the chase was ruined. He snorted in disgust and raised the megaphone to his mouth. 'MARK YOUR TARGET WELL, LADS!' he shouted. 'LET'S SEE WHAT A DOSE OF IRON WILL DO TO BREAK THEIR SPIRIT.'

The SS Behemoth had swung around to face the enemy fleet, a ragtag collection of galleons and frigates that were trying to make the best of the wind to manoeuvre. It was going to be a slaughter.

One ship had caught the commander's fancy and was the first on his list. It was a black and yellow galleon bedecked in ever-changing flags as though its captain had no idea what to signal. Commander Crillock could only guess, but it was a fair bet a few of the flags meant 'Oh bugger!' with the rest providing a more colourful accompaniment.

'We'll take that one first, don't you think?' Crillock asked his green-faced lieutenant, the sickly Mr Flume now back at his post. The poor man could only nod. There had been a hint of hairy nastiness about the Emperor, of creatures that climb out of plug holes, and the more Lieutenant Flume thought on the matter, the more he wished he hadn't.

'I shall let you do the honours, Mr Flume,' the commander announced, handing over the megaphone and rubbing his hands with glee. He would make a sailor of the young man yet. 'I think the word you're looking for is "FIRE". Shout it loudly mind you, and time your call well.'

The lieutenant raised the megaphone, and despite Commander Crillock stepping back a pace for fear of being sprayed, Mr Flume's face turned from pale green to red as he shouted his order. 'FIRE!' he screamed.

The five cannon roared each in their turn, lurching back on their chains with the force of recoil. Five balls of spinning iron cut through the air to pound into the ship, and like a terrible, inevitable game of skittles, they powered their way forward down its whole length.

'MAKE READY WITH THE CANNON! ONE MORE BROADSIDE SHOULD DO IT!'

Commander Crillock was impressed. The young man's blood was up. Smoke from the engines and cannon masked his view, but he could sense victory. It was time to unleash Big Bessie, the giant gun now turning slowly on its axis, ready to deliver its terrible cargo in one ear-shattering roar. The commander tapped the lieutenant gently on the shoulder and pointed to the cannon. 'What do you think, Mr Flume?' he asked. 'Should we give the old lady a go?'

The lieutenant nodded excitedly and puffed out his chest, although to be safe the commander took a further step back and pushed the mouth of the megaphone gently away. It always paid to be cautious where Flume was concerned.

'FIRE!' came the order, and the whole length of the battleship lurched sideways with the force of the cannonade. Sheets of flame tore through the smoke as the spinning iron did its ruthless, killing work.

'And that my fine young man, is how we win a war,' laughed the commander giving his lieutenant a playful slap on the back. 'Scratch one ship and on to another. What a glorious day to be alive, and a miserable one to be dead, what!'

The smoke cleared as a smart breeze struck up, allowing the commander to survey the death and destruction his cannon had brought. He peered through a telescope and hummed a little tune as he searched for the sinking ship. A kind man would have felt pity, an honourable man would have raised his hat in salute to his enemy, but the commander was neither of these. In a one-sided battle, there was no pity at all, just a job to be done, hands to be washed before dinner and then to bed. Commander Crillock felt no more for the dead than he did for the fly now crawling over his lens.

Lieutenant Flume cared for the dead. He cared very much. He cared that there weren't any - not a single, solitary cannon-cooked sausage. 'I don't understand!' he muttered to himself, peering through the telescope then shaking the contraption and looking again. 'It can't be, it's an illusion!'

It was too much to take in. The ship and its crew were unharmed. Instead of death and destruction, there were people with not a bruise or scratch about them, waving and jeering. What was more, they appeared to be drinking and having a fine old time. Some were pointing at the lieutenant from across the water then showing off their backsides and slapping their cheeks. 'How rude!' he thought. The cook had warned him about sailors like these and the strange things they got up to; his mother had warned him too, but mostly about the cook.

It was as though the brief battle had never happened. The galleon looked as good as new, and the ever-changing flags seemed more about music and dancing than orders for the fleet. There were sailors in line, kicking out their legs as they paraded around the deck, singing what could faintly be heard as 'Let's all do the Conga!' There were even rockets spiralling upwards into the sky, exploding into glittering starbursts of coloured ribbons.

Commander Crillock was furious, his hands trembling with anger as he focused his telescope on the galleon. 'FIRE!' he screamed.

'Oh yes, FIRE!' shouted the lieutenant, not sure if he should have given this second order earlier or not.

The deadly cannonade rocked the battleship once more, sending the iron balls screaming through the air. It was a perfect shot, with every cannonball on target.

But nothing happened.

Nothing ordinary, that is. In the space of a second, the laws of physics had packed their bags and taken a holiday. The ship disappeared; one moment it was there, the next gone and now, to rub the crew of the SS Behemoth's noses in the dirt, the ship appeared again with louder party music, more dancing and the delicious smell of barbecued chicken everywhere. It was like dropping a stone into a pond and seeing your reflection shatter apart and reassemble a second later, doing the Conga and holding a sausage on a stick.

'Witchcraft,' muttered Commander Crillock, and spat on the floor. 'Why must it always be witchcraft? Doesn't anyone fight fair anymore?'

'It's these waters, sir,' interrupted Lieutenant Flume. 'They're cursed. Ships disappear.'

'I don't mind them disappearing, Mr Flume. It's their coming back that worries me. All I ask is for one of our cannonballs to hit home.'

The commander was about to say something more on why magic had to poke its nose into everyone's business and turn things on their head when one by one the other ships began to shimmer, vanish then reappear. Where they appeared was starting to worry the commander. They were forming a wide circle around the SS Behemoth with all their guns pointed at his ship.

'Well, of all the sneaky tricks! Take a tight hold, young man. We need to force our way out of here.' The commander dashed to the wheelhouse and pushing some of his crew aside began to turn the monster of a ship towards the galleon. If he couldn't hit the damn thing, then he sure as hell could ram it.

'FIRE AT WILL!' shouted the lieutenant, seeing the urgency of the moment and both sides of the SS Behemoth spewed flame and iron into the circle of ships.

'THAT'S THE SPIRIT, MR FLUME! KEEP UP THE PRESSURE!'

The lieutenant was rather enjoying himself. The ever-present urge to be sick had vanished to be replaced by feelings of mastery and a strange desire to conduct an orchestra. He lost himself in the moment. Happy in Commander Crillock's praise, he waltzed around the deck, waving his arms in time to the cannon fire till the figure of Tarantulus Spleen, all stern, disapproving and standing tall in front of the galley doors, brought him back to his senses with a start. 'You haven't hit a thing!' he said.

'HOLD TIGHT!' warned the commander, shouting from the wheelhouse as the SS Behemoth approached the galleon at full speed, and with this, the Emperor Spleen retreated to the safety of his cabin and the security of steel plate. The lieutenant braced himself for impact as the prow of the battleship tore through the wooden hull, yet it was as if the galleon was nothing but a design embroidered on a pair of curtains. The battleship steamed on and out the other side with nothing so much as a splinter chipped loose to betray its passing.

'Damn and blast!' cursed Commander Crillock, throwing down his hat and kicking it through the wheelhouse door. 'What sort of trickery is this?'

None of the crew knew what to say as, like Mr Flume and the others on deck, they stood there in silence, their mouths open in shock.

'Someone tell me what to do! How can I fight these...these phantoms? I can't blow them up. I can't split them in two - what sort of warfare is this?'

The lieutenant wasn't sure if the question was addressed to him, but he ventured an answer. 'It's just magic, that's all. It's these waters. Strange things happen in these waters.'

'No!' shouted the commander, running out of the wheelhouse and pointing towards the galleon. 'It's not these waters. It's her! Look!'

The crew turned to where the commander was pointing, their mouths so wide open with surprise they could catch fish. High on top of the ship's main mast, sitting happily in the crow's nest and conducting the music was the scourge of the Coral Seas, the Pirate Queen herself - Bethesda Chubb. Her bare feet swung this way and that as she took big gulps of who-knows-what from a bottle. Oblivious to everything but the music, her eyes closed as she waved her left arm in the air, looking for all the world like an overweight flamenco dancer down on her luck.

'You sea-witch! You harpy!' cursed Commander Crillock at the top of his voice.

'Sea witches,' the lieutenant said, correcting him, for it was now possible to see where the music was coming from; a brass band of women all dressed the same in tweed and sensible shoes.

'Damn it, man! Don't just stand there! Hand me a rifle!'

# A TOUCH OF SPLEEN

The commander stood with his hand out as he examined the infamous Bethesda Chubb through his telescope, then scanned beneath the main mast to look at the band.

'Urgh,' he said as a rifle was passed over. 'I hate brass bands.' He handed the telescope to his lieutenant. 'But not as much as I hate the sisterhood, say what, Mr Flume?'

'Aye aye, sir.'

'Then let the gods grant me this shot - one lead ball to hit its mark.'

The commander checked for sufficient powder in the pan, pulled back the flint till the lock clicked into place, then bringing the rifle to bear on its target, steadied his aim. 'Quiet back there,' he warned as he adjusted for wind and trajectory. 'The next man to speak gets twenty lashes!'

He squeezed the trigger and felt the kick of the rifle on his shoulder. The woman stumbled as though she'd been hit.

'Quick, load the damn thing!' the commander shouted, throwing the empty gun to the nearest sailor on deck, and snatching the telescope back from Lieutenant Flume, he peered through the smoke. The sailor seemed pre-occupied, making no attempt to catch the rifle.

'Quickly man, quickly!

'Aha! There you are,' Commander Crillock said on seeing his target, but the tone of his voice changed to one of disappointment. Bethesda Chubb was looking straight at him with an expression on her face that could curdle concrete. It was as though the considerable distance between them was nothing but a punch-throw away, and Miss Chubb had the look of someone who could slap a whale and make it cry. Someone had smashed her bottle of rum, which to a thirsty Bethesda halfway through a party and ready for pizza, was just about the worse crime a person could commit; that and looking at her through a telescope with not so much as a 'hello.' Commander Crillock felt decidedly exposed.

'Well, that shot worked,' he said. 'Let's see what a second one can do.' There was a note of desperation in his voice, as though the infamous Miss Chubb would appear on deck and put him across her knee, which according to the latest rumours she did to any officer she caught. That was the trouble with the sisterhood; they didn't play fair. It wasn't enough that they used magic. Now they pulled you up by the sideburns, boxed your ears and if they didn't like you it was ten of the best on the backside with a carpet beater. It was beginning to sap the moral of the Emperor's men. No one likes their dirty laundry aired in public, especially if it's around your knees as you shuffle back along the corridor to obscurity. Where was the honour in that?

'Quickly man, quickly! Hand me the rifle! Hurry, hurry, hurry!'

No one was handing anything to anyone. The galleon's brass band had stopped playing and, save for the sound of the engines and the paddle wheels churning the water, it was far too quiet on deck. It was the kind of quiet that follows an ill-judged joke or the squeak of air in a lift; the type of silence that accompanies a tumbleweed or two rolling across the desert. It was embarrassing and fidgety and made Commander Crillock fear the worse. He turned slowly around to face his crew, and rather wished he hadn't.

His crew were looking elsewhere; even his loyal lieutenant had his backed turned to him. They were hypnotised, for sitting on top of Big Bessie, the giant deck cannon of the SS Behemoth, was something far bigger, far more deadly and definitely of the old world. It was a great wyrm, a golden beast of jewels and sunlight, sitting and licking its claws as though it were a cat in front of a cosy fire.

The creature looked the commander over and licked its lips, the weight of its body forcing the barrel of the cannon slowly downwards till the mouth of the gun rested on the wood panelling of the deck. The wyrm had a horrid purple tongue that reminded the commander of leeches and strips of raw liver. Half of his brain was recoiling from the horror of the tongue, while the other half was screaming for him to leap over the side and take his chances with the fish. The bit that couldn't count had him rooted to the spot.

The wyrm stretched its wings, flapped them a couple of times then leaned forward and sniffed the commander's jacket. 'Boo!' it said, before spreading its wings, pulling the lanyard to the cannon and flying back up in the air. The single 16-inch shell tore through the timbers and out through the steel keel below.

'Shite!' swore Commander Crillock. He could have said more. He could have stormed off into the galley, snapped his sword in two and said very bad words to the Emperor. But 'Shite!' was as good a soliloquy as any, given that the ship's magazine was about to cut further conversation short. He wasn't scared of death. Death to him held the promise of a new beginning; of reincarnation and a chance to be one up on your neighbours. But death can be messy and karma's a bitch, and at the precise moment his old life ended with a bang with bits of him spinning through the air for seagulls to snatch at, his new life began with a sizzle. Someone had cracked him open on the side of a pan and whisked up an omelette.

# Chapter Two

There is never a shortage of things to do in Derbyshire. One can visit Buxton and take the waters or visit Bakewell and take the pudding. But only in the market town of Grubdale, nestled high among the sheep and turnips, can you sample Nadin and Sons' Gold Medal Pork Pies and take to your bed. Grubdale, the mini-metropolis of the peak; brown and grey and glistening in the rain, looking for all the world like a seaside town without the sea. There are the Belle Vue gardens at one end, the Alpine Palace hotel at the other and sandwiched in between, two high streets and as many pubs as you dare visit without waking up married.

Grubdale is one of the highest towns in England and despite annual festivals of this and that, it is largely ignored by the rest of the world. A few tourists brave the train journey to visit, stumbling out of the station with their towering rucksacks balanced only by the size of their boots. There is the daily struggle with the wind and rain as maps the size of picnic spreads are unfurled and examined. A first glance at the market town, a second glance at the map, a third glance at the vista before them and a look of general disappointment with all. Grubdale has a rugged beauty that rewards further scrutiny, but more often than not the tourist map ends up in the bin in a mad scramble to catch the 9.45 back to Manchester Piccadilly.

It may be the weather. Grubdale is used to the rain, and despite their oilcloth jackets and thick cloth caps, the tourists are not. But then Grubdale rain is relentless, shaping and colouring the buildings with time. Winter rain can pummel an army into submission better than any English archer, and mixed with the soot and tar of three hundred chimneys, Grubdale rain has dissolved the carved lions of the Town Hall into four giant slugs that frighten no one but the petunias.

It could be the Great Fire too. Nothing puts off the tourist trade more than smoking timbers and a ravaged Co-op, but that was over twenty years ago. Now, in 1932, most of the damaged buildings have been replaced. Besides, no one will speak of the fire, the school or the Great Mystery. Even the Great War and its terrible cost to the town have not dimmed the sadness of that night when the town was set on fire, the school fell to rubble, and no trace of the boys was ever found - orphans all, with no one to mourn their passing. No, it is best not to speak of such things, best not to travel up the hill and walk around the ruins. There is a new beginning, and the town has a spring in its step. There's a new brass band and new boats on the lake, and if people would only learn not to walk on the tracks, a scenic railway to frighten the ducks. Perhaps now the Great Fire will be forgotten and the tourists return, and if they do, what new treats they will have to enjoy. There is a little bit of England at the top of the high street that is forever California. Where once stood the Alhambra Music Hall, with more fleas in its carpet than Professor Mars' Circus in a Briefcase, stands now a very picture of modern design and entertainment - the Galaxy cinema, with two shows daily and no peeing on the seats.

The Galaxy cinema - it is all the town can talk about this spring. 'The Biggest Screen this side of the Viaduct!' boasts the giant poster, and so it is. There's a Wurlitzer organ that can rise through the floor and a sound system so loud it can shake the moss from the surrounding shop roofs whenever Destry Rides Again, which he does, quite often. Hollywood has come to Grubdale and has enthralled the town. Tom Mix, James Cagney and Greta Garbo are popular topics of conversation.

Particularly Greta Garbo.

No one in Derbyshire ever looked like her. No one in Derbyshire ever looked like Jean Harlow either, but at least with Greta Garbo, you didn't have to rush to the chemist for bottles of peroxide and a big hat to disguise the damage. All you had to do was say 'no' and look sophisticated, and Derbyshire women had been saying 'no' for generations. Sophistication was taking longer to master.

As for the men, well, anyone of any importance seemed to be suffering from too many years in the saddle, walking bowlegged along the high street and forever on the lookout for Cochise. Some racier characters preferred a Chicago outlook to life until whatever they did with half a grapefruit at the breakfast table spilled out onto the streets, with their wives taking the upper hand. Sometimes it is safer to let fantasies stay where they are, half spoken in the cinema. But if this were true, we would have no story to tell. For on this particular spring morning with the first of the snowdrops daring to poke their heads above the leaf mould, and the last of the winter snow banished to the hills, Grubdale was in love with Hollywood and in love with itself. Everything seemed normal. The postman walked past the milkman and nodded gruffly to the greengrocer, and all three said, 'yup' and spat on the ground and gazed out over the purple sage. The town had a new beginning, and all was right with the world. But that was before a certain film arrived in all its aluminium cases, with all its posters and placards to pin up. And that was before a certain ship washed up on the shore of a sleepy North Wales village.

Percy Bamforth sat on the wooden stool in the projection room of the cinema and surveyed his two pets with pride – Mutt and Jeff, the new Western Electric and Ross film projectors, with the all singing, talking and shooting sound system attached. 'Modern science,' he thought as he opened his lunch box to check what delights were in store, 'was truly a wonder.' What his wife had packed for him, unfortunately, wasn't so much a wonder as an abomination. There were three deviled eggs and a stuffed cabbage leaf at the bottom of his box, and it didn't bode well for the evening meal. His wife had been experimenting again with various magazine recipes for what she had read in Woman's Own were the perfect 'Hor's d'oeuvres'. Most of them featured curry powder, dyspepsia and bloater paste. Percy wasn't sure what 'horse's doovries' were, but he wished the local butcher would keep them out of the shop window and stop encouraging his wife to buy them. Horses were horses and meat was meat, and that was an end to it. All this preparation for the mayoral reception was getting out of hand, and he needed to have a stern word in her ear. Two stern words, possibly. He was the manager of the Galaxy cinema, not the owner. Cheese and crackers and a freshly tapped barrel of best would do just fine. He closed his lunchbox and made a mental note to nip over to the pub for a pint of stout and a cheese sandwich later. It was only ten in the morning, and he was starving. But then the awful Mrs O'Reilly might be there, full to the brim with gin and bitterness, and that wouldn't do at all. Ever since she'd 'retired,' the woman had gotten worse, blaming Percy for everything and throwing vegetables at him when no one was looking. She was large at the best of times, but 'retirement' had filled her out even more. Not even the local rugby team would take her on in a fight. No, it would be better for all if he braved the deviled eggs, rather than the devil herself. Not that he was a coward. Percy prided himself on a measure of social authority in the town; a member of the civic trust, always dressed neatly in a pressed suit, polished shoes and a Baratthea coat whatever the weather. It was just that Mary O'Reilly was a force to be reckoned with, and her language was frequently worse.

Since the fire, the old picture house had been Mary's career. She was an orchestra, sound effects, commentator – everything rolled into one as she pounded away at the piano keys in accompaniment to the films. But like every great artiste in history, she had a past, which in her case was two hours at the bar before every performance. A few empty beer bottles would clink at her feet as she stamped on the pedals, and as the film progressed, the few became a few more, till, as predictable as a burp after a half pint, her emotions would get the better of her. Mrs O'Reilly had a lot of emotions and brown ale seemed to set them free. She was a very emotional lady. She would be in fits of laughter to Chaplin, her large frame shaking like jelly till she fell off her stool, the heady mix of Whitbread and The Gold Rush taking its toll. The Wind, starring Lilian Gish was a terrifyingly apt title, more so after thirty minutes, when the tears and wailing would stop for several mesmerising seconds, only to continue with equal passion after the gas had escaped. She would cry like a wet whale at any love scene, shout 'Bashhterd!' and make rude gestures to any villain that dared appear, all the time rattling out tune after tune.

As reel after reel progressed, the beer would take its toll. Mary would become confused and shout 'No Pets Allowed!' at Rin Tin Tin, throw empty bottles at Montagu Love and alas if her spirits were up, would hurl her voluminous bloomers at Rudolph Valentino. The audience loved her. She was more entertaining than most of the films, and terrifying ballistic bloomers aside, she was harmless. If there was one criticism of her music though, it was that it lacked variety. Mary O'Reilly was fond of the hymns, Gilbert and Sullivan and the hit musical of the Great War, The Maid of the Mountains. But far from these detracting from the action on screen, in certain circumstances, the drama was improved. It is surprising how many crises in life can be underscored with a few bars of Abide with Me, I Have A Little List and A Bachelor Gay Am I. For the duller moments though, anything from the Methodist chapel played with one hand would suffice as the resourceful woman swigged from a bottle with the other.

It wasn't the drink that had finished Mary O'Reilly's career but VITAPHONE. By linking gramophone records to film, sound cinema had arrived, and with it The Jazz Singer. At its world premiere in Hollywood, as the end titles flickered on screen and the music came to a close, all that could be heard from the audience were scores of squeaky voices saying 'Shite, there goes my career!' It wasn't a perfect system. The gramophone played 16" shellac records on a turntable the height of a comfortable stool, and on more than one occasion Al Johnson's Mammy was brought to a sudden close with shouts of 'Ouch, my bleedin' arse!' coming from the projection room. Perfect or not though, VITAPHONE was a revolution. The talkies had arrived, and with them the end of many a Hollywood legend's career, many a small picture house, and in all cases, the pianist at the front of the screen. Mickey Mouse had arrived too in the first synchronised sound cartoon. It was all too much for Mary O'Reilly.

# A TOUCH OF SPLEEN

'Steamboat Willie?' she shouted on seeing the poster on a shopping trip to Manchester. 'Steamboat bloody Willie! My Jack had a touch of that in the navy, and it's no feckin' musical, I can tell you!'

The old picture house closed shortly after. With no money for a new-fangled sound system, there was no audience. The larger cinemas in Manchester were equipped with sound, so people took the train to the city instead, and Mary O'Reilly took it all to heart. When the new Galaxy cinema opened at the top of the high street with Percy Bamforth as manager, it was the last straw. 'I can play that big organ in the Intermission,' she had offered, but the mental image proved too horrible to forget. Percy declined; the vacancy had been filled. Lots of men are possessive about their hobbies. Uncle Jim wouldn't let anyone near his penny blacks, Uncle Jack was the same about his tuppeny blues, and Aunt Flo', god bless her, thought philately was something entirely different before she was told to put her teeth in and go home. Percy Bamforth's hobby had nothing to do with stamp collecting. Percy's pride and joy lay beneath the stage of the Galaxy cinema. Percy had installed the very latest in big, electric, theatre organs and only the very fortunate were allowed to sit in the special chair and gaze in wonder at all the knobs and buttons. Mary O'Reilly was not one of these. Percy would rather die than let the woman anywhere near his Wurlitzer. Mary O'Reilly wasn't a musician. Mary O'Reilly was just a hack.

The Reverend Ainsley Cross breathed in the crisp, spring air of the morning and felt refreshed. Spring was his favourite time of year, snowdrops and daffodils and the noisy, busy sounds of ducks in the park. He had survived another miserable winter in Grubdale and all the soups, stews and boiled rhubarb the charity home could throw at him. It was time to celebrate, which at his age meant slices of bread for the ducks, a hip flask of brandy and a push around the Belle Vue gardens in his bath chair. He had a slight touch of gout, and a briefcase stuffed to the handles with gold sovereigns, but that part of his story he kept to himself. He was an ex-vicar of an ex-village, that village now being 40 ft. under water with only the church spire appearing on summer days when the water in Grimspittle reservoir was low.

'Over there please,' he instructed his helper for the morning, pointing to his favourite spot by the boating lake with a few waves of his walking stick, then steering the bath chair uncertainly forward.

'Left rudder, Mr Cross. We don't want you in the water.'

'Blasted contraption, has a mind of its own it does,' he complained.

'There now, how's that? Are we happy? I'll make sure the brake is on so we can wait here for your friend. He did say he was coming this morning?'

'Absolutely, first Monday in March, he's bound to be about, brushing away the winter cobwebs.'

Captain Hilary Dashing had brushed away more than the winter cobwebs. He had polished all his buttons, buffed up the wool of his old army coat and had trimmed and combed his moustache with military precision, such that no white hair was out of place. He clung to his military identity far more than the military wished to be attached to him. Whitehall had retired him early in 1913, and not even the Great War had made the army change their mind. Considering the quality of many of his contemporaries, this told an observer almost all they needed to know about Captain Hilary Dashing. He was an excitable fellow, but about as bright as a lemming on a clifftop. He was the worst sort of lemming too – the sort of lemming that smiled and waved as it jumped feet first into the raging torrent. He had been a liability back then, but now he was just an old man with strange stories to tell, when he dared to share them.

Today he was wearing his medal ribbons and a large French beret with more badges pinned to the front than gravity would advise. 'Forward!' he said as he steered his own bath chair through the park, his progress hindered by the beret slipping over his eyes at regular intervals, requiring the carer to lean over and pull the hat back. 'Can't be late, not for Mr Cross, not on Mad March Monday!'

The carer smiled and kept at her usual pace, pushing the iron and wicker contraption past the bandstand and onward to the lake. 'You look after the steering and I'll take care of the time. He'll be there, don't worry. Just like every week. You two are as predictable as the weather.'

'It's Mad March Monday though, iced buns, coffee and...' He was going to say brandy but thought better of pressing the point. It was his and the vicar's little secret. Feeding the ducks and swigging the hard stuff, and today the vicar had promised a very select vintage from Greece, seven star Metaxa brandy and a couple of cigars thrown in too. They would toast the new season in style and sleep all through the afternoon.

'Morning, Vicar!' he greeted as he spied his companion by the bench. 'Hey ho! Spring is here!'

The captain managed to steer his chair with some difficulty alongside his friend's. He allowed his helper to fuss over him, arranging the rug around his legs and pulling the beret back from his eyes. He smiled at his friend and pretended it was all a slight annoyance.

'Right you two,' said the helper, an attractive young girl from the retirement home. 'We're going to leave you here for half an hour and get a cup of tea. Don't get into trouble, will you?'

'Not staying to hear our stories?' asked the vicar. The two helpers laughed. 'I think we know them backwards, Mr Cross, in all their silly detail. Witches and

## A TOUCH OF SPLEEN

dragons indeed. And don't upset the children with them, either. Mrs Froggat's young one is still having nightmares.'

At the mention of witches, Captain Dashing shivered as though someone had walked over his grave. His beret slipped over his eyes, and he stabbed out with his stick as though fighting off a beast.

'And don't be upsetting your friend. Be good, that's what I say.'

The vicar sighed. 'Being good is what I do,' he said. 'It goes with the collar. A few stumbles on the way, but no one's perfect.' It was said almost with regret, as though more stumbles were both possible and, in the heart of his hearts, desirable.

'And butter wouldn't melt, I know. Right, we're off. Come on Joan, before these two offer us one of their sandwiches.' The two young helpers walked arm in arm along the path, laughing and waving as they went, up past the rhododendrons and on to their favourite café, where pilchard sandwiches were never heard of.

Captain Dashing had taken off his beret and was looking across the lake. 'I thought it was iced buns and coffee; a celebration of spring and all that, not those bloody pilchard sandwiches of yours. Have you forgotten?' he asked.

'Care for one?' asked the vicar.

'You must be joking, not on your life. Let the poor ducks have them.'

'They are horrid, I must admit. The kitchens have a love affair with tinned pilchards. I love fish, but something evil happens inside a tin with tomato sauce. Opening one of those tins is like opening Tutankhamen's tomb. It's a wonder we're not surrounded by seagulls from the stink.'

'Speaking of seagulls...'

The vicar reached out and squeezed his friend's arm. 'Perhaps we shouldn't,' he said. 'Not today. Today is for spring flowers, Madeira cake and Greek brandy.'

'And perhaps a film?'

'Always a film, my dear friend, it's Fu Manchu, after all.'

'Bless you, here's a hanky,' came the expected retort. It was an old joke, but then the captain liked old jokes, though not as much as the vicar loved the despicable Dr Fu Manchu. It was a passion.

'The Return of Fu Manchu, it's the second feature at the Galaxy. Evil genius, Chinese concubines, Nayland Smith and a bag of chips at the end. Sounds just the ticket.'

'Think I've seen it, dear chap,' said the captain.

'Nonsense, that was The Mysterious Dr Fu Manchu. Evil genius, Chinese concubines, Nayland Smith and...well, you might have a point. Just a thought, Mad March Monday and all that.'

'It's an excellent idea, don't worry.'

The vicar smiled. He had seen The Mysterious Dr Fu Manchu a number of times, mainly because he kept falling asleep and losing the thread. It didn't help that films were shown with a second feature, and at his age, nodding off halfway through Fu Manchu and waking up during a musical made for a confusing storyline. The acting was as bad as a church hall pantomime on a Boxing Day afternoon, with the cast still drunk from the night before. But the character of the evil genius had fascinated the vicar's excitable brain so much that he had ordered a few of the Fu Manchu novels from the local bookshop. He was now an expert on the devious plots of the master criminal, although the captain was never sure if the vicar thought them fiction or fact. 'You do know those stories are just rattling good yarns, no truth to them at all?'

'Absolutely,' said the vicar, but the faraway look in his eyes seemed to suggest the opposite.

'They're just a bit of fun.'

'Yes, I know.'

The captain wasn't convinced. Once or twice in the past, his friend had used the words 'yellow peril' and 'the threat from the East' and he hadn't been referring to English mustard. 'Perhaps we've had our fill of evil geniuses,' suggested the captain. 'But not so the Chinese concubines, what?' he joked, nudging the vicar in the arm.

'Now then, a man of the cloth, vicar present, eyes above the parapet.'

Suitably chastised, the captain turned his attention to the boating lake and watched the ducks chase each other up and down the water. It passed the time for a minute or two, but it served to remind him of other feathery beings with sharp beaks and bad tempers.

'I had that blasted dream again. Clear in every detail it was,' he said.

'Not the birds and bees again, dear chap. Really my friend, unchain yourself from the beast. Think of higher things. We are both of a golden age, no point in running a race neither of us can win.'

'It was those blasted seagulls, all over my bed, pecking at me like I was a rubbish heap.'

Captain Dashing grabbed hold of the vicar's arm and stared at him with bloodshot eyes. 'I'm deadly serious. There were seagulls everywhere. And when I woke up with my heart going twenty to the dozen and my chest fit to burst, I flung aside the curtains and what did I see? Those bloody birds, strutting about the lawn as though they owned the place. I tell you Mr Cross, it means something. It's witchcraft; it's a sign. Those women are coming back!'

At the mention of 'those women,' the two gentlemen shifted uncomfortably in their chairs. 'Those women' had vanished years ago, but the mental scars were red and raw.

'My dear Hilary,' said the vicar, trying to reassure his friend. 'It was twenty years ago, all in the past.'

'But is it? Don't you ever think of the past, of what happened? The memories have me tied up in a knot, I don't mind telling you.'

'Well,' said the vicar, gently patting the captain's hand and loosening his grip at the same time. 'If we are both in the confessional, then I suppose I shall have to come clean. If you dream of seagulls, then I dream of giant rats.' They both shivered at the thought. 'It's a constant nightmare and look, I still wear bicycle clips, just in case.' The vicar stretched out his right leg and there it was, a black cycle clip pressing the leg of his cream-coloured trousers tight against his ankle.

'Rats?' inquired the captain with a knowing look and the vicar nodded.

'I think I can beat that.' Captain Dashing threw aside his tartan rug and showed off each of his legs as though they were dressed in silk stockings. Below each knee were gaiters wrapped tight against his calves. 'They're not for the puddles, just in case you were thinking.'

'It was twenty years ago, such an age. We should be past this nonsense by now.'

'Well, I'm not. Retired in disgrace from the army, sanity questioned, four years in a special home surrounded by loo-lahs and dribblers. And because of that, I didn't get to fight in the war and defend king and country. How do you think that makes me feel? I'm no coward by jingo, no coward at all!'

'Here my friend, don't get yourself into a blue fit. Take a sip of the old medicine.'

The vicar handed over his silver hip flask and the captain drank from it deeply, far too deeply. To the vicar's dismay, he could hear all the seven-star smoothness of his velvet brandy being gulped down with not a breath. 'That's my good deed for the day,' he muttered as the empty flask was handed back.

The brandy had loosened the captain's tongue. 'They've marked us,' he said, spluttering spittle down his chin. 'Those damned witches have scarred us for life! You see before you only half a man.'

'There, there. Have some cake.'

'Half a man I tell you, denied the chance to fight with my regiment, to die with honour on the field of battle, branded a madman and worse, and all because of those....those harpies!' He plunged his head into the Madeira cake and made quick work of that too. 'Why, if I ever met one of them today, I would shoot them dead, bang, bang – and I would go to the gallows a happy man, a very happy man!'

The vicar folded up the large square of greaseproof paper in which his delicious cake had been wrapped and with a sigh, took out a smaller parcel from his jacket pocket. 'Care for a pilchard sandwich?' he asked.

A TOUCH OF SPLEEN

## Chapter Three

The Alpine Palace hotel stands overlooking the town like a proud mother hen. It is neither Alpine nor a Palace, having an architectural style uniquely its own; a heady mix of Brighton Pier and correctional institute, with so much wrought iron filigree as to suggest the architect was a dab hand at the crochet. It is Grubdale's finest building, boasting Grubdale's finest cuisine, with Grubdale's finest teatime orchestra playing all the bloody time.

'Here you are madam, a pot of Earl Grey and a plate of sandwiches. Is there anything else I can get you?'

Miss Elsie Tapp looked at the neat, white squares of meat paste sandwiches and shook her head. 'No thank you. These look lovely,' she said. 'Very delicious, I'm sure,' and with a sweet smile she placed the plate on the floor beside her feet and sat back in the wicker chair to pour a cup of tea.

'Would you like me to make some room?' the waiter inquired, seeming puzzled as to why the adequate table in front of the guest was apparently not adequate enough.

'No, honestly that's fine. Thank you.'

The waiter showed no desire to leave, darting his eyes to the plate on the floor.

'Please don't fuss. I dislike people fussing. The tea is lovely, and the sandwiches look delicious. For anything else I shall ring this little bell, like so.' Elsie Tapp shook the tiny bell that sat between the sugar dish and the milk jug on her table. She waved it in such a way as to dismiss further comment.

She was sitting in the 'Palm House' of the hotel, as the top of her tea menu announced, although from the look of the various-sized potted plants scattered around, it had been a harsh winter in the tropics. There was an aspidistra with delusions of grandeur, and an agave or two with corks stuck on the end of their spines as a health and safety afterthought. The rest of the plants looked temperate and as far removed from the rainforest as a bucket of daisies could get without arousing suspicion. Only a mynah bird in a small wicker aviary gave a hint of the exotic. It was talking at speed in a Sheffield accent and betraying a tendency for Tourette's and the dark side of the Oxford English Dictionary. The sheer number of millet branches and pieces of cuttlefish bone sticking out between the bars was evidence of the bird's popularity.

'How quaint,' Elsie thought and popped two cubes of sugar into her cup before opening a small carpet bag nestled tightly against her. Princess Peaches of Pontefract poked her head above the handles and licked her mistress's hand. 'Din dins,' cried Elsie in appalling baby talk, and lifted her pride and joy out and onto the floor to gobble up the sandwiches.

Princess Peaches of Pontefract was a pink toy poodle; her femininity in perfect counterbalance to Miss Tapp's rather formidable appearance. The poodle had a diamond collar, trimmed and polished claws, fur shaped and bobbed as though she were wearing pom-poms on each of her legs, and sleek, trimmed ears on either side of an excitable face. She was the kind of toy poodle that would break the heart of a duchess but make the chauffeur reach for a bucket. Miss Tapp, on the other hand, was the kind of woman that would break the heart of a Turkish wrestler, and from the look of her, mostly with her fists. But appearances can be deceptive. Beneath the harsh weather-beaten exterior of calico, cotton and Scottish twill was pure goo, for Miss Tapp had a secret. To her adoring fans everywhere she was Felicity Merryweather, 'Queen of Romance', and never were there gooier tales of love, villainy and tight-fitting Regency uniforms than between the covers of her books. There were pretenders to the throne, even imitators, but through her twelve novels set among the chalk hills and villages of the South Downs, Felicity Merryweather ruled supreme. To her readers, she was a slender silhouette on the back sleeve of her books. There was no photograph or portrait, just a head and shoulders image of someone as unlike Elsie Tapp as could be imagined. It was how Miss Tapp liked it to be.

Miss Tapp was a private person. Let her publisher deal with the public, what Felicity Merryweather required was peace, isolation and a ream of good quality paper. When Felicity Merryweather ceased to be, when with the final words of each book were typed onto pale pink paper, the quiet and unassuming Miss Tapp took over. There was a ritual to follow. The Remington typewriter was locked away, pencils and foolscap hidden, all evidence of her writing career removed from view before the holiday suitcase could be lifted down from on top of the wardrobe. Only total escape would do, to relax the calloused fingertips and wash away the embedded ink, to bathe in perfect anonymity. Usually, this involved a night train to Dover, a rough channel crossing and a quiet fishing village in France. But not this year. This year Miss Tapp had grown tired of France. This year she had decided to hide away in the market town of Grubdale for no other reason than the stab of a pin, a map of the British Isles and blind providence. If only she had sneezed, she would have been safe in Scotland.

Princess Peaches of Pontefract had finished her sandwiches and was now standing on her back legs, scratching at her mistress's skirt to be lifted up.

'Ups-a-daisy,' cooed Miss Tapp and let the pink toy poodle jump on her lap and sniff at the milk jug for pudding. 'No, no you naughty thing,' she said, opening her carpetbag so the poodle could climb in. 'Pop into your kennel like a good little girl.

'Well, what do you think, should we stay in Grubdale, do we like the town?' The poodle yawned and settled down to sleep. 'Yes, that's what I thought. Interesting architecture, beautiful countryside, lovely little shops. If only the people would stop staring.'

Miss Tapp disliked being stared at. It made her uncomfortable and uncertain what to do. The habit appeared so commonplace in Grubdale that once or twice during the day Elsie had checked to see if her slip was showing, or worse. In fact, now she came to think of it, she was being stared at again. Even the mynah bird had stopped swearing and was looking in her general direction.

One figure, in particular, was making Elsie feel uncomfortable; a gentleman more at home in a hospital than the sun lounge of a grand hotel. He was dressed in a smoking jacket and fez, and from all the bandages wrapped around his body, had the appearance of someone who'd recently lit a cheroot in the local gasworks. He had the face of an Egyptian mummy before the lid slammed shut, with the added sophistication of a pair of ink-black spectacles pinned to the webbing. His companion, far shorter in stature and dressed in a white coat and facemask, was helping him to drink from a glass jug of what looked like the largest martini with olives Elsie had ever seen. Occasionally the bandaged man would nudge his companion to mix the contents more thoroughly, or change the paper straw for a fresh one, but as he drank he stared continuously in her direction.

'Maybe he's blind,' she thought trying to be charitable, but the greater part of her thought otherwise. She had the distinct impression of being studied, and not in a flattering way; of being measured for some task and found wanting. It was not a situation she could tolerate. 'Well, dear,' she said, standing up and snapping the carpet bag shut. 'I think we may have outstayed our welcome.' And with as much pride and dignity as she could muster, Elsie Tapp sprinkled the necessary coins onto a saucer, then swept out of the Palm House, oblivious to the tablecloth dragging behind her and the sound of best Grubdale china dropping to the floor.

Captain Hilary Dashing was in a better mood for seeing his friend. His morning panic had melted away with the brandy, Madeira cake and the calming influence of throwing crusts at the ducks; the Chinese concubines on the silver screen had played their part too. Now he was resting in his favourite armchair in the front lounge of the Ashgrove Nursing Home; not as grand as The Beeches, where the vicar stayed but then beggars couldn't be choosers. It was warm, friendly and smelled of ginger, and bread and butter pudding. Most important of all, it was the only nursing home in Grubdale that would take him in. Captain Dashing tended to scream at night whenever he had a particular dream. In between these periods, he was as mild-mannered as any ex-soldier in the winter of his life.

He was fond of a warm coal fire and a drop of the hard stuff. If there was more than a drop on offer, he was fond of recounting his days in the 1st Grubdale Rifles - far too fond. It was during such periods of wide-eyed storytelling, with a glass of scotch as the infantry square and a scattering of boiled sweets as the charging forces of the Mahdi, that he would forget where he was. He would introduce new characters into the battle, like the walking dead, giant rats and fire-breathing dragons. This would usually be followed by the landlord of the Pig and Shovel making a friendly phone call to the staff of the Ashgrove to come and collect their star performer. On a good night, they could get him home before he mentioned women in tweed and used his tobacco pipe as a literary device. On a bad night, he'd get a slap.

The lovely young woman with the hostess trolley handed him his special mug full of strong, sweet tea. She placed a copy of the local paper by his side - The Grubdale and District Advertiser, a quiet little paper for a quiet little town. It was a comforting ritual. Captain Dashing sat up in his chair and opened the Advertiser to the most important page first, the obituaries. It was all very morbid, keeping the grim reaper at arm's length and playing the odds, but it had become an addiction. He scanned the names and noted at least one person in the room who was in for a shock when he woke up, or not as the case may be.

Death was a frequent visitor to the Ashgrove and made a game of dominoes a chancy business. Where was the fun in slamming down your second to last domino only to have your opponent jump out of his skin, keel over and deny you your rightful winnings? It was worse playing bridge. Many a 'three heart' contract could be down by two by the end of a cold winter's evening, and it didn't pay to make any sudden noises. Still, a healthy turnover in guests made for interesting conversation, and what the captain had lost playing dominoes he usually made up for on the sweepstake.

# A TOUCH OF SPLEEN

Captain Dashing turned to the sports page and an account of Grubdale FC versus Barton's Bakery. Once again Grubdale were on winning form, helped by playing at home and entertaining the visiting team the night before with a barrel of Danglers' Best. It was to Grubdale's advantage that their football ground was the highest in England. There's no better feeling for a Grubdale man than to march onto the pitch and be met by a wheezing opposition still green about the gills and having difficulty tying up their boots. It's what football is all about.

The usual injuries at the local darts match, read the captain. An everyday occurrence in the Pig and Shovel with the dartboard nailed to the lavatory door, but what was this – vandalism on the crown green? In contrast to Grubdale FC, the local bowling club was having a terrible year. The article seemed to suggest a nearby village was responsible, having introduced half a dozen sex-starved moles onto the green under cover of night - one at each corner and two at the sides. Two days later and the bumpiest of union jacks was there for all to see.

The captain sighed. 'All's fair in love and bowls,' he thought, and turned to the front page for the news of the week. Mayoral elections, a new sweet shop, local man steals lead off church roof, sheep found mutilated on a nearby farm. It was the sudden brutality of the headline that caught his notice.

'Police are warning farmers to be on the lookout for stray dogs after a number of sheep were found butchered on Wormhill Moor. This is the second incidence of sheep kills this month.'

The article went on to warn people to keep their dogs on a lead when walking in the hills and to check they were safely kennelled at night. What struck Captain Dashing as more than peculiar was the description of the sheep carcasses found - drained of blood like empty sacks. It was all very lurid and very, very strange.

Someone else was reading a paper in the lounge and had started coughing, which made the captain uneasy at the best of times. It was like Pavlov's dogs: as soon as one gentleman started then, sure enough, one by one the whole lounge-full of guests joined in as though they all had consumption. The captain sank back into his chair, pulled the front of his jumper up over his nose, and carried on reading.

In the Palm House of the Alpine Palace, a solitary gentleman was coughing too, the tassel on his fez jumping this way and that with each violent jerk. The noise of his coughing echoed around the tables, but apart from his helper, the room lay deserted. There were no other guests, no one to see him cough up a fur ball the size of a tomato and for his assistant to hide it in his pocket.

The following morning brought the return of spring rain to the town and the familiar drumming of raindrops on canvas awnings. Not to be daunted by the typical Grubdale weather, two bath chairs were pushed along the high street by two happy-faced young helpers out for a feed. Two happy-faced occupants steered the Victorian contraptions past stalls of fruit and vegetables and as far away from Mac Fisheries Fish Shop as they could. Fresh fish was on Mondays, Wednesdays and Fridays but this was a Tuesday, with only the ugly fish left. Not that they smelled any different, but ugly fish had a habit of jumping into your lap crying 'buy me', and whatever qualities deep trawled fish had, looks weren't top of their list. It was so dark in the depths, they didn't bother with makeup at all.

The morning's treat had been the vicar's suggestion. A promise of breakfast and a walk in the fresh air had coerced the two young helpers to provide the push power for their excursion. 'Two big breakfasts mind, and some money for the pictures,' they had insisted. So, smiling sweetly, the vicar had squeezed the necessary coins into their hands and instructed one of them to skip along to the Ashgrove and pick up Captain Dashing.

'Heaven's above, you'll have me bankrupt,' he joked as he and the captain were steered through the doors of the Regency Cafe and shown to a large table by the window. 'Two big fry-ups for the girls and two teas over here, thank you very much,' he ordered and saw to it that Joan and Agnes, lovely company though they were, sat at another table. He wanted a quiet and serious word with his friend.

Captain Dashing was in an irritable mood. 'We don't need these bath chairs,' he said. 'It's an affectation. We should be getting exercise, not sitting in these damned things. People are suspecting I'm an invalid, and I'm not at all.'

'Neither am I,' whispered the vicar, popping a sugar cube into his mouth and crunching loudly. 'But hey ho, isn't it fun. These wonderful contraptions are the nearest thing to a car we can get. I brought a horn with me today but haven't the courage to use it. Let's give it till tomorrow, how about that? Then we can have a miracle. I'll make a show of limping happily with my walking stick, and you can make a perfect recovery. Drum up business for the church, what?'

'Isn't that rather dishonest?' the captain asked, shocked at his friend's suggestion.

'Pffft, it's all show business really. The feeding of the five thousand? People brought their sandwiches, simple as that. The secret's in the telling.'

'Well, if there is to be a miracle, then don't make a fuss, please. I intend to walk down the high street as though nothing has happened.'

'Nonsense dear chap,' joked the vicar. 'I shall make you a star. Your name will be in the church magazine in big letters.'

'Don't talk rubbish. You know only too well they wouldn't print a word. You're persona non grata with that magazine. It's a wonder they let you through the door after that crossword you submitted.'

'Sensitive souls dear Hilary, sensitive souls. I was being creative. The Kingdom of Sodom didn't fall because of a little bit of slap and tickle.'

'Well, perhaps Sodom and Gomorrah wasn't your best choice for the puzzle, and being honest Ainsley dear chap, perhaps the good people of Grubdale could have done without sixteen across and twenty one down, to say nothing of six, seven and eight.'

'Pish tush, Hilary. They were perfect examples of the compiler's art - anagrams, homophones, double meanings...'

'Exactly,' said the captain. 'I rest my case.'

The vicar popped another sugar cube into his mouth and sucked at it slowly. 'Hilary,' he said, the tone of his voice more strict than before. 'I didn't call you here to chat about crosswords. We have more serious things to discuss than word puzzles. Something sinister is happening under our very noses. I take it you've read this week's Advertiser?'

'I have, and what of it?'

The vicar drummed his fingers on the table, obviously annoyed. 'What of it, you ask. I'll tell you "what of it." Baa, Baa, Woof, Woof, that's exactly "what of it." The article about the sheep, it has me quite shook up. Surely you've read it?'

'Oh yes, the sheep. Sucked dry to the bone and left to flap about in the wind. Very morbid.'

'Absolutely, although I'm not so sure of your description, but sucked dry they were and how peculiar is that? It doesn't take an expert to realise the police have it all wrong. Dogs indeed, pfft!'

The vicar was fond of using 'pfft', it was his latest expression. 'Tssk, tssk,' had been another, and so had 'brrrrp,' but 'pfft' was as concise and effective as the other two and had the bonus of blowing away anything stuck between the teeth.

'If it had been dogs there would've been an unholy mess. Have you ever seen a spaniel eat? Good heavens, the biscuits fly everywhere. It was not dogs that killed Mr Pursglove's sheep; oh no, it was something far more sinister. Here, read this.'

The vicar took a rolled up copy of the Liverpool Echo from his jacket and gave it to the captain. The entire front page was devoted to an account of the wreckage of an old warship found washed up on a beach in North Wales and the discovery of a body tied to the ship's wheel.

'Oh my, I don't believe it,' said the captain studying the page. 'This is terrible, this is...'

'Exactly!' interrupted the vicar. 'Vampires!'
'Civil war!'
'What?'
'Civil war! I knew it would happen. A pleasure steamer with cannon, such a devious trick! It's Owain Glyndwr all over again. They'll be taking back the castles and closing down the border, mark my words. The Scots will follow. No good came from signing that treaty across the water. It's given them ideas! Free Staters are going to pop up everywhere!'

The vicar looked aghast at his friend. The shared horror of twenty years ago was a strong bond between them, but as fond as he was of Captain Dashing, the man could spout some awful rubbish. Had he not read Bram Stoker's infamous novel? Had he not watched the alarming Max Shreck in Nosferatu a few years back with old Mary O'Reilly playing the piano and shouting out what an ugly bugger he was? All that was different was the geography. Instead of the ship running aground in Whitby, it had chosen a different beach. It was far too close to the novel for comfort.

'My dear chap, have you read the article?'

'I don't need to. It's all there in the photo. A paddle boat with cannon - last time I'll be spending my summer holidays in Colwyn Bay. I knew they were plotting something. Closing their pubs on a Sunday and not letting me know. Despicable! They were making plans behind the curtains!'

'Well, it's a ghastly affair all the same, that poor man tied to the wheel.'

'Brave man, steering the ship to the last, have to admire the sacrifice if not the cause.'

'But cannon, dear chap, cannon. Don't you think it strange? This is 1932. A steamship with cannon? I think boat design has progressed somewhat since the American Civil War.'

'That's my point! It's the colonists stirring up trouble again with their second-hand goods! Devious tricks they play!'

Sometimes it was the better option to allow the captain his say. He had a knack for seeing things differently to other people, and his was a suspicious world. The vicar's world was full of dark things too, especially at night after a large cheese sandwich and a story from the Brothers Grimm. As usual, the vicar waited for his friend to take a breath, then butted in.

'But doesn't the story give you the shivers? I mean, think about it, a ship that appears from nowhere, from a time long past with the only crew member on board dead and tied to the wheel. A ghost ship from a bygone age, the SS Behemoth, deserted but for rats...'

'Where does it say that? Show me!' snapped the captain. 'Where does it say anything about rats?'

## A TOUCH OF SPLEEN

'Oh my!' said the vicar, his face white. 'Oh dear, oh dear, I didn't think!' He slowly pointed with his finger to the single sentence. 'But all ships have rats, don't they? Surely that can't be important?'

Captain Dashing put down the paper and looked his friend straight in the eye. 'It's beginning again,' he said. 'Whatever they were, wherever they went, it's beginning again. I tell you I can feel it in my bones; they're coming back - the witches, the dragons, the dead things! And we're the only two alive who remember. Everyone else is dead, the war saw to that. No one will believe us until it's too late!'

'Dracula,' whispered the vicar.

'What?'

'Dracula's coming; it's a sign...look!' The vicar was pointing to a figure across the street, a bill sticker pasting the latest poster for the forthcoming attractions at the Galaxy cinema. There in bold letters were revealed the words:

**The story of the strangest passion the world has ever known!
Carl Lehmle presents The Vampire thriller
DRACULA
A Todd Browning Production**

'It's a sign I tell you, a message. The seagulls, the sheep, the ship, that poster - these things are more than mere coincidence. Fate is trying to warn us.'

'About what though?'

'Vampires, dear chap. Black magic, things that go bump in the night. We need to keep our eyes open and make our case.'

Thoughts of living through the horrors of twenty years past were too awful to think, but think them they did. A sane man would have dismissed such ideas as nonsense, but neither the vicar nor the captain had firm hands on the tiller. Strong winds and choppy seas could sweep them easily off course. The two sat in silence behind the front window of the Regency Cafe, the cogs and wheels in their minds working overtime. They were holding their tea mugs the same intense way, and taking the occasional sip in unison.

'I see Tarzan's showing again,' said the captain after a good few minutes of staring at the bill sticker's work, his voice expressionless, as if he were in a trance.

'That's nice. I like Tarzan,' said the vicar, his voice equally non-committal as they both thought on the horrors of the past, and on the possibility of new ones to come. Anyone walking past would be forgiven for stopping and staring through the window as the two friends opened and closed their mouths in harmony, imitating in their mind the call of the ape-man as he swung through the trees.

'Of course, it could all be stuff and nonsense,' the vicar said after a while. 'Two excitable chaps fearing the worse. There may be a perfectly innocent explanation for everything.'

'And what would that be?'

'Haven't a clue dear chap, haven't a clue. I was trying to be positive. I don't like to dwell on the past, but now I've planted this seed of suspicion I find myself coming back to it and watering the damned thing every day.'

'Bugger the seed, we have a bloody big beanstalk now, look!' and as the two of them stared out of the window, Miss Elsie Tapp walked briskly past with her poodle, dodging the puddles. Elsie had decided on her best Donegal tweed jacket and skirt for the morning walk, and the effect was obvious.

'Oh no!' cried the vicar, his face white with shock as he grasped the captain's arm. 'It's true! Those damned witches are back!'

# Chapter Four

Harry Renfield was a jovial fellow; it went with the job. You couldn't be a miserable sourpuss and sell novelty gifts; you had to live the product and Happy Harry, as the large balloon letters painted on the side of his van advertised, lived life to the full. It was why he was sporting a black eye and driving rather fast through the back lanes of North Wales. Not everyone shared his love of the whoopee cushion, especially husbands coming home early and hearing wind and giggles from the bedroom. Popguns were his favourite too, painted wooden tubes that shot corks across the room, but they were, as he'd discovered, useless in self-defence.

He'd had a busy morning selling saucy postcards and games of blow football, and had flirted with both to great effect. But now he was suffering the consequences. It was another Welsh market town to cross off the list and another bumpy road to shake the rust from his old van as he slammed his foot down hard on the accelerator.

His poor van. It had seen better days, just like its owner. It wasn't meant for speed. It wasn't good for anything other than delivering turnips - and pre-bruised ones at that. The suspension was a distant memory. The seats technically still had springs, but it took an act of faith to notice them, and whatever was stored in the back rattled and crashed like a fist fight in a dustbin.

'Bugger!' shouted Harry as he suddenly remembered, but the tell-tale smell was enough - he'd remembered too late. He applied the brakes, then cursed again as an almighty crash sounded from the back. He eased off the pedals and coasted slowly to a stop, covering his nose and mouth with a handkerchief. Passers-by might have suspected pig smuggling or worse, but the truth was far simpler. There was a box of 'Happy Harry's Stinkers' in the back, leaking their contents to horrendous effect.

'Happy Harry's Stinkers' were the ultimate in stink bombs. They could make grown pigs cry in shame, and entire villages check their shoes for something nasty. They were a benzene ring short of chemical warfare, and three of the bombs had 'exploded' in the back of Harry's van. 'Bugger, bugger, bugger!' he swore. There were other goods in the back; party balloons and streamers, Chinese lanterns and novelty crackers.

'No one will want to buy them now,' he thought. 'Not if they stink to high heaven.'

The only thing to do was unpack the van and air the goods on the side of the road. He was in luck. A slight breeze had struck up to make the task easier, and the van had stopped on a quiet coast road with a track that led down to the sand dunes and sea. Harry shifted the engine back into gear and drove, gently this time, towards the beach.

It didn't take long to open the boxes and let the cool breeze do its work. The damage wasn't as bad as he'd feared; just a box or two of streamers and paper hats that reeked of the sewers. He sighed with relief, but rather regretted taking a deep breath. He reached over the front seat and retrieved an old biscuit tin and thermos flask, then walked a few yards upwind of the van. It was time for a very late lunch.

Harry was particular when it came to lunch. It was the best meal of the day. Breakfasts were hurried, and he was often too tired in the evening to cook a meal, but a packed lunch was a delight. Today's lunch was as delicious as ever; a cheese and onion pie, a slice of ginger cake and a flask of strong 'Scottish' coffee - the sort of coffee that comes from a bottle showing an officer in a kilt, his orderly in a turban and the word 'Camp' printed above. It's still a mystery as to what happened to the man who thought up the name, but rumours persist of a faint voice in the dungeons of Edinburgh Castle crying out 'Is anybody there?'

It was a joy to relax after the panic of the day, and there was nothing more soothing for Harry than the gentle sound of the waves and the fresh, salty air of the sea. He sat in quiet contemplation, eating his lunch and digging a trench in the sand with his feet. He'd brought a packet of Digestive biscuits - gloriously crumbly biscuits that you could dunk only once. After scoffing a quarter of them, he repacked the tin and lay back to rest.

Harry's happiness was complete. There was no greater joy than sitting on the dunes, watching the waves roll in and remembering past holidays as a child. He closed his eyes and listened to the call of the seagulls, and like a key turning in a lock, a door was opened on precious memories. It was as though he were ten years old, running barefoot along the beach with his kite in tow. He could picture his beloved springer spaniel chasing after him, the dog barking excitedly, snapping at the waves, and if he concentrated hard enough he could imagine his parents calling as they unwrapped the picnic lunch. Cheese and onion pie and a mug of Camp coffee - it was his photograph of heaven from thirty years past.

## A TOUCH OF SPLEEN

Time passed slowly for Harry as he lay there on the sand, looking up at the clouds with his hands behind his head. He loved seeing the shapes in the sky, pink and white goldfish in the evenings or billowing faces in the day. It made him happy and sleepy, and hungry for spiders.

What? Harry shivered and sat up quickly, as though a seagull had squawked in his ear. Spiders? Why on earth had he thought about them? He hated spiders; he hated anything that lacked a backbone and scuttled about, and on a scale of six legs to eight, spiders were the worse. Spiders dropped down your neck or ran up your trouser leg and bit what they found. He no more wanted to think about spiders than a bluebottle caught fast in a web. But they were delicious. Spiders that is, with their big fat tummies and elbows and toes.

Harry spat on the sand. 'Yuck!' he said, then spat some more. His imagination was playing tricks, feeding him sickening images of spiders coated in batter. 'It must be the bloody stink bombs,' he thought. 'I've been gassed!' He tried to think of nicer things, of childhood memories again, but the mood was ruined. A tiny sand beetle crawling over his fingers looked enticing. He popped it into his mouth like a single crumb of bread, but spat it out again in disgust.

'What on earth am I doing? The very thought of it!' he cried, but his mind was busy with images of tasty spiders dousing their bodies in olive oil and jumping slapdash into a skillet. It wasn't beetles he craved but nasty, eight-legged monstrosities that hid in your plughole and came out at night to talk. 'I must be going mad!' he thought. Which he was, ever so slowly. Something was speaking to him from far away, a soft, gentle voice whispering delicious words like recipes from a book. 'Take one pound of tarantulas, and a pinch of salt...'

'No!' Harry said, pleading. 'No more, please!' But then it was pudding.

Percy Bamforth tried to look confident as he swung his umbrella and walked towards the front gate to his house, but the truth was he had taken the long way home. For all his standing in the community as manager of the Galaxy cinema and respected member of the town council, someone had thrown a cabbage and had shouted some uncharitable adjectives as the vegetable flew through the air. It had become a frequent occurrence, every market day with the pubs open from early in the morning. The vegetables changed, but the unerring accuracy did not; neither did the pub. Someone in the Eagle had taken a dislike to poor Percy and it was hardly a secret in town as to who it was - the formidable Mary O'Reilly, a dead shot with a root vegetable after three bottles of brown.

Percy had been mulling over the situation all day. Discretion was the better part of valour. He no more wanted to face down Mrs O'Reilly than Theseus did the Minotaur. On quiet reflection, Theseus had the better deal. The only solution was to take the long way home, avoiding the market square and keeping his head down past the privet hedges. But just when he thought he was safe, a cabbage had knocked his bowler hat clean off his head. From the giggles and sound of little feet running away, it seemed the canny Mrs O'Reilly had recruited a following. Things were getting out of hand.

'Still, there is balance in everything,' he thought, for the day was not all ruined. The Galaxy cinema was going from strength to strength. Takings were up, and the distributors had confirmed delivery of Tarzan in Trouble, a jungle adventure filmed in Leeds starring Fred Barnes as Tarzan and Dolores Del Monte as 'Trouble.' The press release promised 'Passion, Adventure and Nelly the Elephant' and for good reason. 'Our Nelly' was more famous than her co-stars and available for rides every day of the week but Tuesday.

Dracula was coming to the Galaxy too, and that was money in the bank, even if the film had been out for a year. Hollywood films took longer to climb the hill to Grubdale. Some only made it as far as Manchester. It was why Yorkshire's very own Tarzan, Fred Barnes, was a star in the Pennines but a nobody south of the Trent.

Percy pushed open the gate and walked briskly up the path to his front door. All things considered, it wasn't a bad day after all. There was a mayoral election soon, and if business continued to improve, he stood a good chance of being elected to office. What was a vegetable or two thrown in anger compared with that? Even the peculiar smells from the kitchen couldn't dampen his mood, although he had to admit as he opened the door and stepped into the hallway, they were the most peculiar yet.

'I'm home!' he shouted as he took off his bowler hat and unbuttoned his coat, 'and I've brought some wine.'

His wife appeared in the hallway. She'd been watering her large collection of houseplants and dusting their leaves. Helping her husband off with his coat, she kissed him lightly on the cheek. 'More wine, dear? That's nice, but aren't we getting a little extravagant? I'm sure we don't need a glass or two with every meal, just for special occasions.'

The truth was, Percy Bamforth needed the wine. Not as an alcoholic needs wine but as an essential tool at the dinner table to help him swallow the food. 'The way to a man's heart is through his stomach' is a common maxim, but recently that well-trodden path had lost all sense of direction and didn't know where to stop. Percy laid the blame squarely at the feet of the editors of Women's Own, Woman's Weekly, Good Housekeeping and just about any other magazine with an advert for Bird's Custard Powder on the back. If only there were titles such as Rabbit Pie Monthly or The Pudding Club. The Bamforth kitchen was going through its own Suet Crisis and poor Percy was

# A TOUCH OF SPLEEN

beginning to suspect an ulcer. 'What's for dinner dear?' he asked tentatively, refusing to be discouraged.

'Fennel and grapefruit soup, Chicken Afghanistan and goat's cheese syllabub for dessert.'

The poor man's heart sank. He didn't need wine, he needed something far stronger, something halfway between a port and a single malt that could power a lawnmower. His bottom lip quivered. He was a simple man with simple tastes. He'd only recently taught himself to say 'dinner' not 'tea', and in his mind, a dessert was where you found camels, not puddings. Heaven only knew what a syllabub was; it sounded like a bloody big beetle. It was going to be a bumpy evening.

'That's nice dear. I'll pop upstairs and get cleaned up. I thought we could go out later, maybe a dance at the Belle Vue Tea Rooms. What do you think?'

Evaline Bamforth looked at once pleased and annoyed. 'That's rather short notice Percy, my love. A lady needs to be forewarned. I haven't a spare dress ready.'

'You'll sweep everyone off their feet, no matter what you wear. You're the prettiest girl in town, and I want everyone to know.'

'Percy Bamforth,' giggled Evaline, 'I'd swear there's an ulterior motive in your words if I didn't know you any better. Hurry up then, din-dins and a dance, how wonderful!' and she tapped him on his bottom as he squeezed past.

Evaline was a bubbly woman in her forties who was trying her best to understand the complexities of Grubdale society. It didn't help that the mayoral elections were ten days away and that her husband was in the running. She was afraid to put a foot wrong, but at the same time, there was an ambitious streak to her the width of Asia Minor.

Every spring, the town councillors elected a new mayor from among their number, and Percy had been a prominent member of the council for two years. Mayors didn't do much other than chair the town council meetings. They had free rein of the town hall drinks cabinet and were always on the first float in the annual summer parade. They could waltz around the streets on special occasions wearing the fake chain of office. The original had been stolen years ago, and the present copy was so obviously chromed tin and cut paste that any self-respecting magpie would think twice before flying away with it. Pomposity though is all in the dressing up, and Evaline liked the idea of being a wife to a mayor very much. She loved it even more if she could be called Lady Mayoress, but the machinations and intrigue of council politics held little interest for her. Evaline's strategy for the mayoral election was to be the perfect host and lend her support to her husband in every way. Her canapés and cocktail evenings had been a success, even if poor Percy had been bent double in bed burping on the bicarbonate. But her next plan required stealth and audacity in equal measure. She had started the process with a few hastily written letters. She was planning a final party for the campaign where all the councillors and their better halves would attend. But it was to be a very special party, with very special guests. It just wasn't the right time to tell her husband. She loved him dearly, but husbands had a silly habit of ruining everything. She would beguile him first and then make a terrible confession. But maybe not this evening.

Happy Harry Renfield was happy no more. He was far from happy; about as far away as Grimsby to put it in medical terms. What began as a sunny morning in a Welsh market town had turned sour by midday and practically poisonous by three in the afternoon. It was a few minutes past four, and Harry was shivering on a beach, listening to voices. These were not giggly, up-to-no-good voices coming from the dunes, but shrill metallic ones tight inside his head. It was as though his brain was a wireless and some cruel surgeon was twisting the dial, scanning all the wavelengths with the volume turned up and with every programme the same.

'Spiders!' whispered the voices. 'Itsy bitsy spiders!'

Harry was going slowly insane. The sand dunes were overrun. He could sense the spiders' presence, and not little spiders either. These were as big as a Christmas pudding; giant spiders, like black poodles on stilts, reaching out to tap him on the shoulder and shout 'You're 'It!'

'Go away!' he cried, even though he couldn't see them. But they were there for sure, a blur of movement in the corner of his eye.

'Tasty spiders!' the voices were saying. 'Squidgy, chewy, yummy spiders!'

'No!' he screamed and struck out with a branch of wood, spinning around in an attempt to hit the creatures for six. 'Horrid' he could cope with, 'tasty' he could not. He wanted to knock the giant spiders to the ground, truss them up in a tight bundle and throw them on the barbeque alongside a few mushrooms and sliced peppers.

'No, I do not!' he shouted. 'Enough with the cooking!'

The very thought of barbequed spider was horrid, racks of blackened legs all tender and delicious and covered in grease. Disgusting! Sickening! Irresistible! He wanted to eat them now, every one of them, and have more for pudding.

'Chase me, catch me, bite me!' whispered the voices.

Harry was delirious, swinging the branch like a golf club, hitting out at the sand as though trapped in a bunker with no hope of the green. In his imagination there were spiders everywhere, giant spiders the size of footballs, spiders jumping out from the dunes and landing on his shoulders, tugging at his trouser legs and pulling him down.

'STOP!' shouted someone from behind.

Harry shuddered as though someone had walked across his grave, someone with far too many feet, each in need of a pedicure. It was a new voice, strict with authority and calling to Harry from across the beach. It was a voice of dark and velvet secrets, but with razor blades attached, a voice better obeyed than ignored.

Harry dropped the branch and spat out a mouthful of sand. The other voices had vanished, along with images of spiders - all that remained was this one echo, enticing him forward. He climbed out of the hollow and looked across the beach, scanning the horizon to see who was there. 'Funny,' he said under his breath. 'I never noticed that before.'

The object lay on the sand, the tide lapping at its base and pushing it this way and that. It was a large red box, like a giant tea chest, but with chains and ropes wrapped around as though what was inside was too precious to lose. There was smoke too, a faint stain of red surrounding the box, a trail of vapour that swirled and wafted towards him.

'Roses,' thought Harry, smelling the delicious aroma. It was as though everything beautiful in the world had been stirred together and sprinkled with petals. Harry was powerless to resist. He walked as a man possessed across the marram grass and onto the beach, seduced by a cloud of perfume so potent as to sweeten the awful memories of the day.

The box was a work of art, Harry could see that now. Every inch of its wooden surface was covered with carvings - forests and birds and mythical creatures, all intertwined into one intricate design. It was large too, far larger than a tea chest; about as large as the old blanket box at the top of the stairs. A few barnacles had made their home within the carvings, and wraps of seaweed had become tangled between the chains and rope. Besides these, the box looked as good as new, as though it had been in the sea for only a short while. Harry ran his fingers across the busy wooden surface. There was something sensual about the way the carvings swirled, spiralled and merged into each other, as though he was sliding his fingers into wet mud. He withdrew his hand at once. Carvings were not supposed to do that; it was the perfume playing tricks on his brain.

'Harry!' purred the most seductive of female voices. 'Take me home.' It was an offer to turn any red-blooded male into a grinning fool, but usually, there was a face. There was usually a body too, draped seductively over the bar of the Pig and Shovel, with a Woodbine cigarette in one hand and a broken-heeled shoe in the other. Today there was neither. Today there was just a voice. 'Come closer!' it urged.

Harry looked around, till it eventually dawned on him that the seductive voice in his head was from the seductive box by his side, and that the seductive smoke up his nose was making him decidedly drunk. It was a sudden realisation, almost as unexpected as his legs giving way and the loud splash as he sat down hard in the pool of water by his feet.

'Bugger,' he said, giggling to himself. He'd heard of tobacco smoke like this, strange, exotic blends from the tropics that made you laugh, cry and become an expert on any topic of conversation except standing up straight and running to the lavatory. Harry yawned, his mouth stretched open as wide as it could, before giggling with the effort and resting his head on the lid of the box.

'It's right rum stuff, this smoke,' he thought. 'I could make a bloody killing.'

'Oi, you in there!' Harry shouted, banging the box. 'Give us a fag and stop being a meanie!' Harry could hear movement as though someone inside was shifting their weight and searching their pockets. 'Only one mind,' he said. 'I'm half cut as it is.'

'Take me home,' came the reply, even more, seductive than before.

'Aye, well I dunno if I'm up to that, you little minx,' Harry said, laughing. 'But I can drag you out of the wet if you'd like. Might take some time though, my legs seem a bit wobbly, to tell the truth.'

To illustrate the point, Harry pedalled his legs as though riding a bike. 'Can't even stand up, can I? Come on love, stop mucking about and give us a fag. Ouch!'

Harry felt a sharp stab in his wrist where it draped over the side of the box.

'Bloody splinters,' he said, making no attempt to move his arm. He felt a sharp stab in his neck too, and for the next few minutes, it was as though he were sitting at the back of the Galaxy cinema, being chewed by a sweetheart as he tried to concentrate on Tom Mix galloping across the screen. It was like being in love.

The Belle Vue Tea Rooms overlooked Grubdale's boating lake and miniature railway and did a roaring trade in buttered scones and tea. You could ask for a dollop of jam and a splodge of cream, but that was considered pretentious. Let the Alpine Palace have their cream teas. The Belle Vue Tea Rooms served drinks in mugs, with cakes and dainties from the local Women's Institute served slightly charred but delicious all the same. They sold love and romance on a Friday and Saturday evening. Here the tables were pushed to the sides, and the floor quickly swept before Albert Buttons and his Cinderella Strings stepped smartly on stage and made a lot of fuss over tuning their instruments. 'Middle C,' Albert would whisper to one of the ugly sisters playing the piano. Without fail, the ugly sister would tap Bb repeatedly or C# if the mood took, but with the added complication of being next to the drummer and hearing only one note in two. This nonsense would last a few minutes more,

## A TOUCH OF SPLEEN

with maybe a hard of hearing couple waltzing around the floor and thinking it all very modern. Everything would stop with Albert waving his baton high above his head and saying the familiar words 'Ladies and Gentlemen, take your partners, please.' The Belle Vue Tea Room dance had begun.

Percy and Evaline Bamforth made a handsome couple as they walked hand in hand to the floor. Dancing was a passion - not that they were good, just enthusiastic. Dressed in their spring finery, they were the very picture of Grubdale glamour, big fish in a little pond and happy with their lot. The other dancers smiled and gave them room. Lots of room. Percy and Evaline were the darlings of the dance floor, but sometimes a little haphazard with their feet.

'Tonight I can refuse you nothing,' cooed Percy, rather tipsy with the necessary wine as he guided his wife to star position opposite the band. 'Chocolate cake, caramel éclairs, anything you wish. There's a lovely lemon drizzle on the counter, say the word.'

'That's very sweet of you, Percy. You're quite the romantic.'

Percy was quite the bon viveur. He was desperate for something decent to eat. Chicken Afghanistan had taken half a bottle of red to swallow, and Goat's cheese syllabub had tasted like sick. The rescue plan was cake, lots of cake, and he had a sneaking suspicion Evaline was of the same mind too.

'Think nothing of it, my angel. You've made this evening special. Chocolate cake after, I think.'

'Oh goody, the Gay Gordons. Nothing too complicated to start with - are you ready?'

'As ever, Evaline my love, eyes down for a full house.'

The Gay Gordons was a favourite dance in the tea rooms; a lively promenade, with a twirl and a polka, and the occasional Celtic whoop of joy as the couples danced around the room. The dance was accompanied by two violins, a piano and a drum set, hardly the war cry of the Highlands – not the sort of music that would have the French running for cover at Waterloo, unless they were critics – but in the Belle Vue Tea Rooms, Albert Buttons and his Cinderella Strings were a triumph.

'One and two and, one and two and...'

'You needn't count Percy, my love; you're doing fine. Now get ready for the next bit – here we go, spin me around but don't make me sick.'

Percy obliged and, heady with the wine and music, he twirled his wife around the floor in a lively polka before returning to the start, the back and the forth and the twiddly bit in the middle.

'How am I doing?'

'Like a hero my sweet, we haven't bumped into anything. Off we go again.'

And the quick polka steps had them giddy with joy as they galloped along.

'Phew, I'm quite dizzy. I love this dance.'

Percy looked adoringly at his wife and smiled. Her cheeks were flushed, and there was a sparkle in her eyes. She smiled back and giggled.

'Darling,' she whispered. 'I'm not sure what Afghanistan is famous for, but I doubt it's the chicken. Oh, here we are, back to the beginning, one and two, and three and four, and …hic!'

Percy gazed at his wife with even greater affection.

'And I promise,' she continued as they danced back and forth. 'Never, ever to let a goat near the sylillybubble, bubbubble, sillybubble, thingymajig again.'

'Really?'

'Absolutely, and another thing – oh dear, nearly tripped up there – lift your feet up, silly. Now, where was I?'

At this stage of the dance, the ladies were all spinning on the spot, but not as fast as Evaline. 'Wheeeeeee!' she sang before Percy held her close and bounced her around the room in polka fashion. She gave a delightful little burp and winked at her husband. 'I do love this dance. Right, think Evaline, think; one and two and three and four and…'

'And I love you to the stars and back; you do know that?'

'Do you? I mean I do, but you should say it more often. And please don't interrupt, big confession time here. There are two little words that should never, on pain of death, excommunication or whatever comes first, be allowed within a million miles of one other.'

'And they are?'

'The first is Grapefruit; the second is Fennel, oh, and there's a third - Soup!'

Percy laughed aloud and hugged his wife close.

'Does that mean we can go back to good old steak and kidney pudding?'

'Yes!'

'And gravy?'

'Buckets of the stuff!'

'And treacle tart?'

'Absolutely!'

He led his wife off the dance floor and sat her safely on a chair by the large French windows overlooking the lake. He held her hands and kissed them. 'I do love you my sweet, every inch. You wanted to help and your cocktail evenings were a great success, but I think more so for the drink.'

'I know!' she giggled. 'They were gulping down the stuff. One plate of my canapés and they turned into raving alcoholics!'

'It was the stuffed cabbage leaves.'

'Ghastly!'

'The samosa surprise.'

# A TOUCH OF SPLEEN

'Pure poison!'

'But I did like the cheese and pineapple.'

'My darling, everyone likes cheese and pineapple. I was aiming for sophistication but missed by a mile.'

'We don't need sophistication. We need pie and peas, a barrel of beer in the kitchen and a bowl of fruit punch in the lounge, with you, of course, my darling as the perfect hostess.'

'I was trying my best.'

'Of course you were, it's what you do all the time, and I need to thank you more often.'

His tummy gave an enormous rumble.

'Bloody syllabub,' laughed Evaline, and her tummy rumbled too.

'We need cake, lots of it and orange squash.'

'No, my handsome man, we don't need cake. We need a waltz.'

Taking his hand, Evaline led her husband unsteadily past the front of the stage and onto the floor, apologising to any couple she bumped into on her way.

'Ladies and gentlemen, take your partners please for the St Bernard's Waltz.'

'There you see, excellent timing. Now hold me properly and let's steal the show. Are we ready?'

Percy Bamforth was, and with a gentleness of touch that promised more than a slice of lemon drizzle, he swept his darling wife around the floor, taking particular care not to stamp, clap or waltz out of place.

Their enjoyment was infectious. The other couples laughed, twirled and danced in unison and the Cinderella Strings rose to the occasion with perfect harmony. It was like the final scene of a Maurice Chevalier romance; the camera pulling back and out through the French windows as the orchestra played to the full. But this was real life, the French windows shut, and something far more peculiar than a slow fade to credits was happening outside. Oblivious to a few puzzled faces pressed tight to the glass, a bandaged man in a wheelchair was being pushed, pulled and spun in a circle, and all in time to the music.

## Chapter Five

It was market day in Grubdale. The sun had set its hat early, warming the damp streets and wet corners of the town, elbowing aside the grey clouds till they slipped off the edge to Yorkshire. Stalls were set out and the first shoppers of the day, eager for a bargain and with wicker baskets gripped tight, huddled together, ready for the start.

'Good morning,' said Mr Nadin to each passer-by as he arranged the many pork pies on his stall. 'Can I tempt you with a scotch egg?' It was hardly original, but the patter served him well and given the knowing looks and giggles of the housewives as they walked past, not just on his stall.

'Best Staffordshire crockery!' shouted Mr Hardwick, not to be outdone. He was dusting pile upon pile of dinner plates whose authenticity appeared lost somewhere south of Nanking. 'Willow pattern plates, come and get your willow pattern plates!' he cried. 'Hot off the kiln, don't burn your fingers!'

Willow pattern was a loose description at the best of times, and it was never more loosely applied than on Mr Hardwick's stall. Koong-She and Chang, it seemed, not only escaped from the evil Mandarin but found time to visit Buckingham Palace, the Eiffel Tower and a field of cattle grazing by a windmill.

'It's blue, there's a bridge, and it's foreign - what more can I say? You're getting a bargain.'

Bargains there were, and plenty to be found on the other stalls, from ironware to woollens and with cheeses in between. Always the cheeses; Derbyshire was famous for its cheeses. Some were still so wet you could suck them from a spoon while others were so mature they had hairs and a bus pass.

'Bloody 'ell mate,' swore a rather uptight Mr Persimmon. 'I'm trying to sell soaps and bath salts here. Can't you keep those damned things in a box? It's like someone's died.'

The owner of the cheese stall dismissed Mr Persimmon's complaints with a shake of his cloth. 'I've every bit as much right to be here as you', he said. 'And cheeses are meant to stink; it's what they do. You don't hear me going on about your bloody French soap.'

'And what's wrong with my French soap?' Mr Persimmon asked.

'It's like a pig in a field of lavender - nothing but posh muck.'

Before the conversation got out of hand, which it often did, this being as regular an argument as a talk about the weather, commerce got in the way, in the form of a formidable looking woman with a poodle.

'Such lovely soap,' said Elsie Tapp, leaning across the display of bathroom goods. She picked up a slightly grey-looking example and, putting it to her nose, took a long hard sniff.

'Handmade, you say?'

Politeness stopped her from saying more, from asking the significance of the colour or the reason for the peculiar smell. There was lavender in there somewhere, but you would be hard pressed to pinpoint its location. It was as though a few seeds had been added as an afterthought, the main thought being 'I'll kill that bloody cat.' She placed the soap gently back on the stall, as though it were a grenade.

'Oh look, Princess, these are far prettier!' Elsie lifted her poodle so she could see the various soaps on display. 'Let's choose this one, shall we?' she said, picking up a pink bar of soap.

Mr Persimmon was pleased. 'The finest rose oil from Turkey,' he said. 'You can't beat the quality.'

'We love roses, don't we Princess?' But from the expression on Elsie's face, as she took another long sniff, her love affair was short-lived. It was all she could do to stop coughing into her handkerchief. Even her poodle was having a sneezing fit all over the produce.

'Turkey, you say? Such a long way to travel.'

Elsie picked up a dainty bottle of bath crystals and shook it to see the colours. It made the sound of nails rattling in a jar, and promised more than a nasty accident.

'We have hard water here; it's the limestone,' explained Mr Persimmon, sensing some excuse was required.

Elsie Tapp handed back the jar and smiled sweetly. 'Such a charming stall, such pretty things,' she said. 'But maybe some other time. Oh wait, can I smell cheese?'

It was hardly the most tactful of comments, but Miss Tapp loved cheese. Princess Peaches loved cheese too and at the mention of the word started to bark and wag her tail twenty to the dozen. Mr Persimmon hated cheese and mumbled something under his breath about how people could smell it in bloody Bakewell, let alone here in the market, but Miss Tapp wasn't listening.

Breakfast had been slivers of toast and marmalade, and she fancied something more substantial to eat. Saying good day to Mr Persimmon, Elsie placed Princess Peaches back on the ground and moved along the row of stalls to the Maypole Dairy stand and the source of the delicious smell.

A few yards behind and on the other side of the street, Captain Hilary Dashing and the Reverend Ainsley Cross were trying their best to look inconspicuous. The excitement of playing detective was lost on the captain. He was in a particularly bad mood that morning, pushing the vicar around in his bath chair.

'I thought you said we were both to have a miracle, not just me.'

'God works in mysterious ways Hilary dear friend, mysterious ways. My time has yet to come. You get to walk; I get to sit, and my foot gets to give me grief all day. Hey ho, what can we do?'

'We can lay off the port and pork pies before bedtime, that's what we can do.'

'Alas dear Hilary, I'm a slave to the savoury.'

The captain ignored the excuse and stopped the bath chair opposite the fish shop in front of a particular smelly box of kippers at nose height to the vicar.

'Well, there she is. What do we do now?'

The 'she' in question was across the street and showing great interest in tasting various cheeses. Her pink poodle was doing the same and with equal enthusiasm.

'We shall do what any budding Nayland Smith would do, my friend. We shall sit awhile and wait, but perhaps not here if you don't mind. These kippers are giving me the evil eye.'

'Here's as good a place as any,' said the captain, smiling and showing no inclination to move the bath chair.

The vicar shrugged his shoulders. 'As you wish,' he said, then reached inside his coat and retrieved a set of opera glasses. 'Good heavens, how many cheeses is that woman buying?' he asked as he studied Miss Tapp closely. 'It's not natural. Mark my words Hilary old chap, there's something strange going on in this town and that woman is at the centre of it. She's buying enough cheese to feed...'

'The five thousand?'

'Exactly, I bet there's a damned coven of witches in town, and none of us the wiser.'

'Perhaps she just likes cheese,' suggested the captain

'Nonsense, not the cheese she's buying; wrapped in nettles and full of maggots? One scoop of that and you're in the cottage hospital for a week. It's filthy stuff. No, my friend, she's up to no good, I tell you.

## A TOUCH OF SPLEEN

'Quick! She's making a move. After her, tally ho!'

The captain made heavy going of negotiating the bath chair off the pavement, across the cobbled street and up onto another. Cars were not as common in town as they were in the city. The age of the Austin 7 was spreading out from Manchester and Sheffield, but Grubdale was still a safe place to cross the street if you gave the traffic fair warning - something both the vicar and the captain refused steadfastly to do. The bath chair had brought the morning's traffic to a halt; one pickup truck and a small group of cyclists, and what the truck's klaxon lacked in volume was more than made up for by the driver's vocabulary. Even the cyclists gave vent to their feelings in similar fashion.

'Close your ears Hilary, rise above it,' was the vicar's sage advice, and as the two followed Miss Tapp they could hear a squeak of rusty wheels from behind.

'Do we need a drop of oil, old chap?' asked the vicar.

'It's not our chair that's making the noise.'

'Really? It sounds like it to me. Damned annoying too.'

The captain looked behind but could make nothing out from the crowd.

'There it is again, are you sure we don't need a touch of lubrication?'

'I could do with a whisky and soda if that's what you mean.'

'All in good time. We must see out the chase first, tally ho! Good heavens, is it your shoes making that peculiar din?'

'I tell you, it's not me, and it's not this chair. We can change places if you'd like.'

The vicar didn't 'like'. He was getting very fond of being pushed around the town and steering the bath chair as though he was competing at Brooklands. He had taken to making the noise of a car engine too, but quietly, under his breath. 'No need for that,' he said in a placatory tone. 'I believe you.'

So the 'chase' continued; Miss Tapp stopping and starting, seemingly at random as she visited the various stalls on the market square, and the captain and vicar close behind. Another two figures made up the rear - a man in a wheelchair with his face hidden from view and a smaller gentleman wearing a scarf as though it was the middle of winter. 'Vroom, vroom,' went the man in the wheelchair and 'squeak, squeak' went the wheels as he was pushed along.

Evaline Bamforth enjoyed her mornings. She enjoyed them even more now she had a shower installed in her bathroom, but if only she could get the damn thing to work. She sang as she soaped her hair, shrieked as the temperature of the water plummeted to that of a frozen puddle, then purred with delight as the pipes rattled and tropical conditions were restored. She was particularly happy with herself and for a good reason; today was the day to tell her husband the good news.

She got dressed in her best morning clothes; a lively print dress sprinkled liberally with parrots - a pandemonium of parrots if the dictionary was to be believed - so many parrots as to suggest she'd driven helter-skelter through a rainforest with the windscreen down. Matching blue shoes with sensible heels finished her outfit, along with a silver budgerigar broach that seemed to shout 'style', 'panache' and 'Polly wants a cracker', but only very quietly.

For the final touch, there was perfume, expensive perfume from a department store in Manchester. 'An Evening in Paris' read the label in ornate Victorian lettering, although the shape of the bottle suggested more a dirty weekend in Amsterdam. The lingering aroma was undoubtedly exotic, and if words could be found to describe its allure, they would be French and whispered with giggles under the counterpane.

'Darling you look delicious, scrumptious even,' commented her husband as he kissed her lightly on the neck. 'But aren't we a little overdressed for breakfast?'

'Hollywood and kippers dear,' she laughed and kissed him back. 'Glamour and porridge, I've decided to spring clean our mornings.'

Percy Bamforth smiled and sat back down at the breakfast table. 'Well, I think it's a smashing idea,' he said. 'No kippers for me though. It doesn't seem right. Not with you all dolled up and spectacular. Save them for tonight with chips and brown bread. Coffee, toast and boiled eggs will do this morning. Although champagne would be nice, and freshly squeezed orange juice too.'

It was Evaline's turn to smile. 'Don't let the perfume rush to your head, my love. It's a pot of tea and cereal this morning; you had bubble and squeak yesterday, and it gave you indigestion.'

'I love bubble and squeak.'

'I know, but it doesn't love you. It's as the doctor said, one day on and one day off. Today is a day off breakfast.'

Percy sighed. He wasn't too upholstered, but the bits of him that were, wobbled, which was hardly flattering for a man in his forties. His had been a very comfortable winter. That was the kindest way to put it, but now spring had arrived and with it a doctor's warning.

'Do you think Dr Pickering knows what he's talking about?' he said. 'He looks well fed to me, definitely a bacon, sausage and grilled tomato man if ever I saw one. I bet he hasn't had a bowl of wheat flakes in his life. And as for this Lucky Jim character...'

Percy Bamforth was looking with disdain at the box of breakfast cereal on the table, FORCE wheat flakes with a picture of a lanky gentleman with a pigtail on the front.

# A TOUCH OF SPLEEN

'If ever there was a man in need of a hearty fry-up it's this skinny bugger, all jolly and depressing of a morning. Listen to this,' he said, reading from the side of the box. "Vigor Vim, perfect Trim, FORCE made him Sunny Jim." I'd say a steamroller, more like. The poor chap looks flat as a pancake. Pancakes, now there's a thought, sprinkled with sugar and dripping with lemon juice.'

'Here's your tea dear,' Evaline interrupted. 'And you can have as many sugar lumps as you want.'

Percy looked at the broad smile on his beloved wife's face and her eyes shining brightly. He was never allowed free rein of the sugar bowl. Two lumps per cup were the enforced maximum, even for the pint mug he liked to sip from when listening to the radio. Smart clothes, sensuous perfume, and now sugar lumps a-plenty; something was definitely afoot.

'You have something to tell me Evaline, don't you?' he asked.

Evaline sat down beside her husband and poured herself a cup. 'Yes, I do, but I want you to hear me out before making any comment,' she said, squeezing his hand.

Perhaps the squeezed hand was a mistake. Thoughts of biology raced through Percy's mind, but remained hidden beneath his calm but slightly perspiring countenance. Some were of birds, not the sort that peppered his wife's dress, but the kind that appeared on christening cakes and made nests on chimneys. He loosened his collar and focussed straight ahead, looking out into the garden at row upon row of gooseberry bushes. 'I'm all ears,' he said.

'We're going to have a party – a fancy dress party. Not here but in the cinema. We shall invite all the town council, their partners and friends, our friends too, and we'll hire that Mr Buttons and his Cinderella Strings. It will be the party of the season.'

'Will it be a ...' Percy struggled to find the right word. 'Will it be a celebration of some kind?' he asked.

'I do hope so, my love because we shall be celebrating your election as mayor. There, I've said it,' laughed Evaline. 'The cat is out of the bag. Your beautiful wife is a scheming busybody.'

'Oh, I see...' said Percy, his voice betraying little of the firework display going off in his mind - of big rockets exploding in the sky and storks plummeting to the ground like so many dead pheasants. 'Isn't that a little presumptuous? I mean we don't want people thinking I'm confident of getting their vote.'

'No silly, it's not presumptuous at all because you will win, I promise you. Trust your wife's intuition. And you're being naughty. No interruptions until I've finished, I said.'

'You're not finished?'

'No dear, I'm not. There's something else I have to tell you, something very, very important.'

Images of fireworks gave way to thoughts of static electricity, of sparks and flashing lights, and mad scientists shouting 'It's alive! It's alive!' as one by one the dead storks sprang to life.

'Fire away,' said Percy.

'We shall have a special guest, someone everyone will want to see. Someone people would sell their mothers for to get a ticket. That's why I'm all dolled up and smelling of Paris, my love. So tell me, do I look a million dollars?'

'Every cent and more, you know you do.'

'Good, because today I need to look every inch the wealthy wife of a very wealthy businessman. You, my love need to look the part too, the businessman that is. Oh, you know what I mean.'

'We're not poor, dear,' urged Percy, feeling somewhat aggrieved.

'Of course we're not, but neither are we dripping with cash, and to net our prize that simply won't do. Your best suit is on the bed, although it pongs of mothballs. Hurry now; we haven't all day. We have a train to catch for Leeds.'

'Leeds?'

'We're hardly going to meet our Tarzan in the sheep fields of Grubdale, are we?'

'Tarzan?' Percy was now thoroughly confused. The storks had gone, trampled underfoot by herds of wildebeest.

'Fred Barnes - elephant caller, crocodile wrestler, friend of the chimps.'

'Fred Barnes the film star? Our very own Tarzan?'

'Please try and keep up darling, you're not very bright this morning. Yes Percy, Fred Barnes the film star. He's the nearest thing we have to Hollywood, even if his films are made in Yorkshire. The important thing is that he looks good in a leotard.' Evaline winked and pinched her husband's cheek. 'Never underestimate the allure of muscles my love - muscles, good legs and something mysterious in the shrubbery.'

'I'm not at all sure what you mean by that.'

'Nor am I darling,' said Evaline, kissing Percy on the forehead. 'But it's why women flock to his films, mystery or not, and it's why I've been writing to him, persuading Mr Barnes to be our special guest.'

'And he's agreed?'

'Well, he's agreed to see us, but that's a start. Although I did tell a white lie, a pretty big one. I said you were a producer.'

'Evaline!'

'I said you had links to Hollywood, which you do in a way. 'Now don't look so cross. He's even thinking of bringing Nellie, the elephant.'

'Our Nellie?'

'Exactly. And who wouldn't vote for my darling husband, knowing you'd persuaded Tarzan to pay a visit. The election is in the bag if we can persuade him to come, and he's already agreed to see us. You'll be mayor.'

'And you'll be mayoress; we mustn't forget that,' Percy said, his eyes bright with love for his mad, impulsive, whirlwind of a wife.

'I know,' she smiled. 'How thrilling is that!'

## Chapter Six

The pursuit of Elsie Tapp was getting out of hand. Despite her appearance, the lady had proven herself a whirlwind of activity; not a description you could apply to the Reverend Ainsley Cross, whose bath chair had come to an abrupt stop on the high street, its 'engine' wheezing and coughing and refusing to go any further.

'I need to sit down,' complained Captain Dashing. 'Those last bloody shops were all uphill. I've never known a person to buy so much stuff. Anybody would think it's Christmas.'

'Aha, exactly!' cried the vicar scribbling away in a notebook. 'It isn't Christmas, and there's the mystery.'

'It's no mystery at all. It's bloody March, of course it's not Christmas.' The captain was getting fed up of the vicar's notebook. The man had been scribbling away all morning and muttering obvious phrases like 'how interesting,' 'I see,' and 'the plot thickens.' The entire day was beginning to feel like a chapter in a cheap detective novel. 'What are you writing down now?' he asked rather testily. 'The mileage?'

The vicar sighed and tucked his notebook into his jacket pocket. 'Evidence, dear Hilary,' he said, tapping his pocket. 'The vital clues to our case. While you've been so good as to provide the horsepower, I've written down everything that woman has purchased. There's a pattern here if only I could fathom it.'

'Maybe she likes shopping. She's certainly got the stamina for it, if not the shoe leather.'

'Nonsense, no one likes shopping. It's a horrid necessity, that's all. Show me any man on the high street at Christmas with a smile on his face, and I'll show you a drunk. No, people shop for a purpose; although what the purpose is with that woman I have no idea. We must study the evidence closely and probe the mystery.'

# A TOUCH OF SPLEEN

'I'll say one thing for her,' said the captain, interrupting the vicar's train of thought. 'She's more money than sense. Did you see how much she paid for that silver goblet in the jewellers or those candlesticks from that antique shop on the corner? It was daylight robbery. They'll be welcoming her back with open arms. And who uses a paperknife nowadays, especially one shaped like a Turkish dagger?'

'You see,' said the vicar. 'That's my point. There's no reason to this list, no reason at all, unless I've missed something important.'

Elsie Tapp was smiling. She had made a decision, and for someone who prided themselves on order and meaning to life, decisions were important. Decisions kept chaos at bay and fate in the broom cupboard. That it contradicted her choice from the day before was irrelevant; even though she had tossed and turned and mulled over the question till the early hours of the morning, it was a new decision, and that made her happy. She had decided to stay in Grubdale, the people here were just too odd to ignore. The more Miss Tapp thought about the town with its peculiar ways and its strange people, the less she thought about Miss Merryweather; and the less she thought about Miss Merryweather, the better she felt. What Elsie wanted was to parcel up her alter ego and enjoy a well-earned holiday. Felicity Merryweather had been getting out of hand and far too boisterous of late. Where one book a year would previously suffice, she now demanded two, and fresh ideas were as difficult to catch as a trout in a stream. No, she would purge herself of Felicity for a few days more and explore the surrounding countryside; besides, Fred Barnes was starring in Tarzan in Trouble at the Galaxy. If there was one actor who could make Elsie Tapp feel less like Felicity Merryweather, it was this beefy young man in the poster. He could carry her away to his banana leaf mattress anytime, and from the look of his physique, he had the legs to do so too.

Elsie was sitting in the corner of the lounge bar of the Cheddar Cheese, surrounded by her parcels. It was a charming little pub with pictures of cows and sheep on the walls, and strange brass contraptions hanging from the ceiling that resembled more the contents of a veterinary's car boot than anything to do with brewing. No matter how hard she pictured them drilling holes for spigots, or retrieving stubborn corks from dusty bottles, the more obvious image of a happy calf entering one door and a sad bullock leaving by another came to mind.

'Here you are love, your milk stout, poured to perfection. It's almost a shame to sup,' laughed the landlord, handing Miss Tapp a glass filled to the brim with cool, dark beer and with a perfect creamy head on top. 'A dish of water for your poodle, and as ordered, a salt beef sandwich with the crusts cut off,' he added, placing everything down on the small table in front of her. 'Is that everything?'

Elsie nodded and thanked the landlord most warmly, aware that once again she was being stared at, this time by an old man sipping hot whisky from a mug and giggling to himself.

'Now don't you mind old George over there, he stares and laughs at everyone, don't you mate?'

George raised his mug and toasted them both.

'Ee's 'armless, just a bit thin on sense if you know what I mean, aren't you, me ole duck.'

George toasted them again and pointed at Princess Peaches.

'Baaaa!' he said and laughed to himself.

'No George, it's not a lamb, now that's being rude. It's a poodle and a charming one at that.'

The barman bent down and tickled the Princess under her chin. 'I used to have one myself. Very affectionate she was, broke my heart when she died.'

'What happened?' asked Miss Tapp politely. 'Was it old age?'

'Not really, my other dog ate her. That's him in the window.'

A shocked Elsie Tapp glanced around expecting the worse, only to see a stuffed bull terrier in a glass dome with an expression of surprise on its face.

'It's like having the two of them in a way,' the barman said, the light shining through the window highlighting the tears in his eyes. 'He choked on her bones.'

Elsie found it difficult to know what to say. She clutched her beloved Princess Peaches closer to her breast and tried not to think of the dead terrier with the dead poodle inside. It was as if she half expected a whimper and a tap on the glass. She shivered and placed Princess Peaches in the safety of her carpet bag before sipping her milk stout and chewing the beef sandwich.

A copy of the Grubdale and District Advertiser lay on the red leather couch beside her. Having nothing better to read other than the various pub posters on the wall, Elsie reached over, picked up the paper and glanced through its pages. It was a treasure trove of the macabre. From blood-drained sheep to skulduggery on the bowling green, the various articles and advertisements were a delight. Elsie's view of country life came distilled, second hand as it were through the pages of Country House and Gardens, a magazine where the only excitement was dry rot, carrot root fly or a photo of a wedding. The pages of the Grubdale and District Advertiser told a different story - a wonderful, eccentric story of muck and brass and dark deeds; of sheep dips, bile pills and recipes for rabbit jelly. It was fascinating; Grubdale appeared quainter by the minute. Miss Tapp had made the right decision, a sideways look at life and all was well. She would stay in Grubdale, bathe in its eccentricities and to hell with Felicity Merryweather. Miss Merryweather could remain at home for the duration. Miss Tapp downed the milk stout in one, and staring right back at the old man in the corner, gave a loud and most indelicate burp.

'Baaaaa!' he said and winked at her with admiration.

Elsie smiled and feeling adventurous, decided to order another drink. She was on holiday after all, and her shoes pinched.

'To hell with it,' she thought. 'No one will bother if I make myself comfortable.' So feeling liberated and just a little flirtatious, Elsie slipped off her shoes and rested her stocking feet on the floor. 'Landlord!' she called, twiddling her toes in delight. 'Another milk stout if you please.'

The old man in the corner seemed transfixed at the sight of Elsie's feet and began making the noise of donkey braying.

'Now then George!' shouted the landlord from the other bar. 'Leave the poor woman alone, or it's out you go!'

Elsie, feeling not only adventurous, but liberated and flirtatious, added irreverent to the list and blew a loud raspberry at the old man. Whether it was the passion of the delivery or the threat from the landlord, George shrunk back into the corner and sipped his pint, whimpering like a puppy.

It was neither; the door to the lounge bar swung open, and an 'emotional' Mary O'Reilly swept in from the street. George had sensed her presence like the change in the weather, retreating to the shadows for safety.

Mary was a force of nature - a brown ale-fuelled, tornado of emotion, with occasional bursts of port and lemon logic. She smelt of cod, chips and tomcat - a pungent aroma that made your eyes water or mouth dribble depending on the wind, and today there seemed to be a lot of wind.

Mary smiled at the landlord, or tried to, then rummaged about in her handbag. She was swaying ever so slightly, sufficient to take three steps backwards to regain her balance, and trying her best to look sober. 'A bottle of brown ale, please,' she said, placing the correct number of pennies down on the bar with one hand and holding onto the back of a chair for support with the other.

'I'll be with you in a minute,' the landlord said, lifting the corner of the bar and sending the pennies sliding down to the other side. He walked over to Elsie and placed her milk stout on the table. 'Enjoy,' he said, taking the price of the drink.

Princess Peaches stared at the landlord from the safety of her carpet bag, and still thinking of his unfortunate bull terrier, the landlord's emotions got the better of him. He tickled the poodle under the chin and wiped back a tear. 'I've got a budgie now, but it's not the same,' he said. 'Still, he keeps me company and rings the bell at closing time.'

Elsie looked over the landlord's shoulder and saw the outline of a bird cage in the next bar.

'Bobby's his name. He's a great little talker but rubbish at catching a stick.'

Elsie wasn't sure what to make of this but nodded all the same.

'Right then Mary,' said the landlord, remembering his other customer and walking back to the counter. 'One bottle of Dangler's Nut Brown, coming up.'

Mary O'Reilly's smile seemed to have frozen on her face. She was lost in thought; her mind heaven knows where but her eyes focussed well and truly on Miss Tapp. Usually, there was no stopping the woman. Silence was never golden with Mary O'Reilly - silence was a gap in conversation needing to be filled.

'There we go, shall I pour it for you?' asked the landlord, placing a beer glass and a bottle of ale on the counter, but Mary merely stood there, staring at Miss Tapp. Not even the noise and commotion of a bath chair being manhandled into the pub interrupted her concentration.

'Oi, you can't bring that thing in here!' complained the landlord.

'Now then,' said the vicar. 'What sort of talk is that? I'm not a "thing," Mr Furness. I'm one of your valued customers.'

The vicar was being bumped and bruised in an attempt to fit his bath chair through the door. 'Heavens above, Hilary!' he complained. 'You're making a pig's ear out of this! Why dont you do as I ask? You need to pull me over the step not push, then you wouldn't be chipping the paintwork and upsetting the good Mr Furness now, would you?'

Captain Dashing was having mutinous thoughts, and tipping the vicar out of the bath chair and pushing that wicker monstrosity under the nearest steamroller being top of the list. The final straw had been his friend's insistence they should overtake a nanny pushing her pram along the pavement. The vicar made such loud and ridiculous engine noises as they swept past that the baby woke up screaming and the nanny, having taken the best part of the morning to get the little dear to sleep, had expressed her frustration by striking the captain smartly on the head with an umbrella. It was now a furious but persistent Hilary Dashing that manhandled the bath chair through the door of the Cheddar Cheese, pushing and pulling the contraption as though he was mowing a particularly stubborn patch of thistles.

'I said you couldn't bring that bloody thing in here; it won't fit!'

'Fine!' shouted the captain, breaking his silence. The bath chair stopped moving, and its confused occupant sat there, half in and half out of the pub, trying his best to look behind.

# A TOUCH OF SPLEEN

There was the sound of footsteps disappearing past the front window of the pub, and then, after an exchange of confused looks between the vicar and the landlord, the tap-room door opened and in marched Captain Dashing and sat himself down at the bar. 'A very large whisky, my good man,' he ordered. 'And a bag of pork scratchings for that idiot over there.'

The vicar ignored the insult. 'Are you just going to let me sit here stranded?' he asked, surprised.

'Why not, it seems a good idea to me. You can step out of that bath chair and walk. You can pay for this drink too, after all the work I've done.'

The captain made the sign of the cross. 'There, see - abracadabra, you're cured.'

It was then that Mary O'Reilly, ex-pianist of an ex-picture house, finally realised who the stranger with the poodle reminded her of. 'You!' she said, pointing her shaking finger at Elsie Tapp. 'It's you!'

Elsie looked behind but saw only the unfortunate bull terrier, stuffed and alone under its glass dome. 'Are you referring to me?' she asked.

'It's you!' seemed the only sentence Mary could say, and she repeated it over and over again with increasing passion.

'Now then Mary, don't you be upsetting my customers. I'll have to ask you to leave if you don't behave.'

'It's her, don't you see,' Mary protested. 'It's her. She's come back!'

'I beg your pardon!' snapped Elsie. 'What do you mean by that?'

But Mary O'Reilly was in full flow, her mind focussing on memories from years past, horrid images she had buried under gallons of brown ale, memories of her previous life as cook at Grubdale Towers, of that terrible night where the school caught fire. 'J'accuse!' she shouted, pointing her finger once more at the unfortunate Miss Tapp. 'J'accuse!' Not that she knew what the phrase meant; just that it sounded posh and sophisticated, the only posh and sophisticated subtitle from a posh and sophisticated film she knew.

'Right, you've had your warning. Here's the money for your drink and I'll take that off you now.' The landlord returned the few coins to Mary and poured her glass of ale down the sink. 'I won't have people upsetting my customers. You'll be getting no more drink from me today.'

Having failed at the posh and sophisticated, Mary resorted to her normal vocabulary. She rearranged her bonnet, hitched up her skirt and with as sufficient dignity as she could muster, managed to climb over the vicar and his bath chair and step down to the street.

'Well, I never!' exclaimed Elsie Tapp, surprised, shocked but secretly thrilled. Grubdale was getting more eccentric by the day. She chuckled to herself and took a deep draft from her glass.

'Isn't anyone going to help? I seem to be stuck.'

It was the voice of the unfortunate vicar, still sitting in his bath chair and blushing with embarrassment. The indomitable Mary O'Reilly had hoisted her skirt and scrambled all over him, and he was feeling a little confused.

Elsie sighed and got to her stocking feet. 'Is there anything I can do?' she asked, walking towards him. Apparently there wasn't - the sight of another woman about to invade his personal space had provided the cure. The speed at which he managed to extricate himself from the chair, pay for the drinks then stumble out of the pub was matched only by the time it took for Captain Dashing to gulp down his whisky and run for the door.

'Curiouser and curiouser,' exclaimed Miss Tapp, delighting in the mystery. 'I do believe those gentlemen are scared. Tell me, Mr Furness, do I look like the kind of woman a person should run away from?'

The landlord shook his head. 'Don't mind them, love,' he said. 'They live in a world of their own. As for that Mary O'Reilly, well, she lives on a different planet. It's a sad story. She was the cook at the school up the hill. It burnt down, years ago now, long before the war - they never found a trace of the boys, not a single button.'

'How terrible.'

'Aye, well, a thing like that can turn a person, I suppose. She's harmless really, just fond of the gargle. She can play a decent tune on the piano though, I'll give her that.'

'The poor woman seemed to think I was someone else, someone...significant.'

'Don't let that bother you. Mary's probably talking to a lamp post by now. It's a terrible thing, drink, when it gets hold of you. She shouldn't be pointing and saying bad things, though. It's not right.'

'I don't mind. I'm not offended. It takes more than a finger and a bad French accent to upset me, it's just that the poor woman was so insistent. There's a mystery here, and I hate mysteries. I shall never sleep till I get to the bottom of it. It's like that unfortunate gentleman in the wheelchair. There must be a reason why he's chewing your ornaments.'

The landlord looked at Elsie, puzzled, so she leaned over the counter and whispered to him quietly. 'I don't want to alarm you unnecessarily,' she said. 'But that peculiar man in the bandages over there, behind you - he appears to be eating your stuffed animals.'

'This is posh, Evaline my love,' said Percy Bamforth, sitting back in his chair and admiring the decor. 'I'd hate to think what they charge for a night. A pretty penny, I bet. I'd be bankrupt before breakfast.'

## A TOUCH OF SPLEEN

'You don't need to worry. I've booked us in at a pub down the road. See what a clever wife you have.'

Percy and his clever wife were sitting in the grand foyer of one of Leeds' most magnificent hotels - The Royal. They were trying their best to look like regular guests, as though all the grace and opulence on display were second nature to them if not all rather boring, but Percy had his mouth open and was ruining the effect. He was a simple man with simple tastes. He was used to the Alpine Palace back in Grubdale with its dinner dances and pie suppers. The ballroom there was full of antlers and oak beams, with a few fancy things pinned to the walls or else hanging from the ceiling, but that was as nothing compared with the decor of The Royal. Here the chandeliers went on forever, like columns of ice crystals almost touching his head; it was like a different world.

'Don't look so awestruck, dear,' said Evaline. 'Remember, you're an important businessman - try to appear underwhelmed, as though something nasty's just plopped in your drink.'

Percy looked at his drink, as though he was Sherlock Holmes checking for lipstick, then tasted it carefully and pulled a face that was far from complimentary.

'It doesn't need anything plopping in,' he said. 'It's nasty from the start. Good grief Evaline, what is this muck?'

'It's a Gin and It - very sophisticated. Everyone drinks them. I read all about the cocktail in this month's Good Housekeeping.'

'What does the "It" stand for? Don't tell me, I think I can guess,' said poor Percy, placing the glass down on the table in front of him and pushing it aside. 'It smells like your mother's embrocation - very medicinal.'

'A Gin and Italian - it's all the rage in Hollywood. People gargle with it for breakfast. Here, let me try.' Evaline picked up the drink and took a healthy swallow, then rather wished she hadn't. The face she pulled was one of disappointment, as though a window on a brighter life had been closed for good. 'It's like sweet sherry and turkey stuffing. Waste of a good gin.'

Percy smiled. 'Hollywood cocktails, whatever next?' he said. 'I hope I'm not supposed to be an American, besides a successful businessman. I'm rubbish at accents.'

'No silly, I just thought it would help. The young man will be expecting sophistication, not a pint of brown and bitter. Oh, and another thing - you'd better leave the talking to me, just at first. We don't want to confuse him from the start.'

The 'him' in question entered the hotel. He was a well-built young man with brown hair and cheeks red from scrubbing and fresh air. But for all his confidence and youthful swagger, his suit seemed odd and ill-fitting, or, as the women in the foyer seemed to think as they looked him over and blushed, tight in all the right places. Evaline Bamforth recognised him at once.

'Here he is, but my, how different he looks without the leopard skin. Don't stare, dear; pretend you're saying something profound and important so I can laugh and look adorable.'

'If he touches your leg, I'll flatten him,' replied Percy, jokingly and Evaline laughed daintily but uncertain, and for far longer than she had planned.

Fred Barnes looked across the foyer, trying to make out from the many people, the most likely candidate for a Hollywood producer. He had pictured someone dressed garishly, probably talking in a loud voice and smoking an over-sized cigar, but no one seemed to fit the bill. Everyone was talking loudly; no one appeared to be dressed in anything other than a dull charcoal grey, and there was not a single cigar in sight. As for attractive secretaries, the best that could be said of the women on view was a bus trip to Blackpool.

'Mr Barnes?' asked a young hotel porter. Fred smiled. 'Yes, that's me,' he said. 'Who wants to know?'

The porter tried to appear not the least bit interested. His girlfriend had compared him unfavourably to the Yorkshire Tarzan during a moment of lukewarm passion. 'Mr and Mrs Pricklewood have a table in the corner if you'd follow me, sir,' he said, trying his best to sound underwhelmed.

'Righto, lad,' said the cheerful Fred Barnes. 'You lead the way.'

The young porter made his way through the crowded foyer, weaving himself between tables and guests, trying his best to look more important than the gentleman that followed, and more sophisticated than the word 'lad' would suggest. 'Here we are, sir,' he said and pointed to three large comfortable armchairs, with Percy and Evaline Bamforth seated in two of them. His hand was extended dramatically, and with an open palm, but to no avail. Fred Barnes was as accustomed to tipping as Tarzan of the Apes was to paisley Y-fronts.

Evaline stood up and pressed a coin into the porter's hand before shooing him away. 'Fred Barnes,' she said, greeting the young man as though she'd known him for years. 'How wonderful to see you, and my, how you've changed. You're dressed, for a start.'

Fred laughed, his cheeks blushing as Evaline offered her hand to be kissed. 'Sam dear, this is our little Freddy I've been telling you about. Hasn't he grown?'

Percy was about to look around the room to see who on earth this Sam character was before the penny dropped. He got to his feet and in as Hollywood an accent he could manage greeted the young man and beckoned him to a chair.

## A TOUCH OF SPLEEN

'Are you feeling fine?' asked Evaline, flashing a brief, stern look at her husband. 'Your voice went funny there for a moment.

'Honestly Fred, my husband's like a big child. He's taken to speaking like an American. I haven't a clue why. He's as Yorkshire as they come. Now dear, sit close and tell me all about your poor mother. It was such a shock when I read the news, and with her and me as thick as thieves. Such a sad business.'

Percy sank back into his armchair and looked on incredulous as his wife began to dab at her eyes with a handkerchief. She reached out and squeezed Fred Barnes' hand.

'Poor, dear Barbara,' she said with much emotion.

'Florry,' corrected the young man.

'Yes, poor, dear Florry,' Evaline said with even more emotion. 'It was all so sudden.'

'It was a number 10 bus.'

'That's very sudden.'

'It was last year.'

'Our post is terrible. The business we've lost. As soon as we heard we rushed here, didn't we Sam, all the way from the States.'

'We sure did, honey. I mean, yup, I mean yee hah, I mean...I don't know what to say.'

Evaline held Percy's hand and squeezed that too. 'I know darling, it's hard to think of the right words, but we're here for little Freddy now, and that's the important thing.'

Fred Barnes shivered at the description. No one had ever called him little, and certainly never Freddy. You wouldn't call a budgie Freddy, not even a green one. He shifted awkwardly in his seat.

'Are you sleeping?' Evaline asked, her motherly voice pouring over the young man like a warm, reassuring blanket. 'You look a little pale.'

'I'm fine. Couldn't be better.'

'There you go, always the brave little boy. I remember the day you fell into the nettles, not a scream out of you, and your face and legs covered in bumps.'

Fred was feeling uncomfortable. He hated fuss and bother, and there was something not right about a stranger fawning over him as though she was his aunt. 'I don't mean to be rude,' he said, 'but I don't remember you at all, I'm sorry.'

'And why should you? You were nothing but a little cherub when I left, wobbling about in the altogether. Such a cute little boy.'

Fred was feeling more than uncomfortable now; he was feeling exposed. It was as if the lady had x-ray vision the way she kept chattering on about him being naked. It was like being verbally tampered with, and all in public.

'Mrs Pricklewood, I have to be honest, I can't remember mum ever mentioning your name either.'

Evaline laughed and gave Percy an affection nudge. 'Well she wouldn't have, would she? I'm married to this lovely man now. I had a different name back then.'

Her laughter continued but changed subtly to tears as Percy looked on in admiration. Whatever came next was bound to be nothing short of a Sarah Bernhardt performance with extra sprinkles, and Evaline was not a woman to disappoint. The poor man didn't stand a chance. In the time it took the waiter to approach the table, take an order then return with the drinks, Evaline had convinced Fred Barnes of just about everything other than her being a fairy godmother. Percy Bamforth didn't know whether to kiss his wife or refuse to believe her ever again.

'If only I'd known how ill poor Florry was,' Evaline whispered, her voice breaking with emotion.

'But she wasn't ill, she was flattened.'

'If only I'd known the number of the bus...'

Percy coughed and spluttered. His whisky sour had crept up on him unawares, being mostly sour and very little else, but it was the sheer audacity of his wife that had taken him by surprise. He needn't have worried. Fred Barnes was like a small boy being told a bedtime story and believing every word.

'Geography,' Evaline said, looking into the young man's eyes and making him long for a glass of warm milk and a motherly embrace. 'It's just folding maps when you think of it, isn't it? Distance can be as short or as long as you want.' She tapped his hand daintily as though to say she was finished, then sat back in her chair and took a long sip from a Brandy Alexander. She'd said something important, but what it was she wasn't sure. Still, if this had been the Paris Opera House there would have been cheers, bouquets of flowers covering the stage and cries of 'encore,' and 'show us your leg.'

'When are you coming to pay our town a little visit?' she asked, and Fred Barnes was powerless to refuse. 'You'll have to take us as you find us, mind,' she added, smiling and stirring the rest of her drink with her finger. 'We've not let the money go to our heads. We hardly spend a thing, do we dear? Just enough to get by and be happy.'

Percy choked on his cocktail again. 'Aye,' he said, desperately thinking of something profound and fiscal to add to the conversation. 'You get nothing but trouble flashing the cash nowadays. Might as well keep it under the mattress for a rainy day.'

# A TOUCH OF SPLEEN

'Not that we're misers. We do have our hobbies, don't we Sam, the movies being one.' Evaline said no more on the subject but Fred's face lit up with interest.

'You're in the movies?' he asked.

'Not in a big way, mind,' interrupted Percy. 'You can lose your shirt if you're not careful. But yes, we dabble a bit. I've even got my own cinema.'

Fred sat back in his armchair and smiled. 'You have a cinema as a hobby?' he asked.

'Yup, I certainly do. Mind you, some days it seems more a full-time job than a hobby. Doesn't it, dear?'

Evaline nodded in agreement and winked at her husband. It was hardly a lie, but then neither was it entirely the truth. Not that it mattered, the little fib had done its trick, for young Mr Barnes was making himself comfortable in his chair and looking every inch the sort of chap who'd dress up in costume and ride into Grubdale on an elephant. All Evaline had to do was put the idea in his mind, and for a sophisticated Derbyshire lass like herself, that was child's play. 'Who's for another cocktail?' she asked, after downing the last of her Brandy Alexander and placing the empty glass daintily on the table. 'I rather fancy something big and hairy, like a coconut.'

The Reverend Ainsley Cross was thinking of something big and hairy. He was thinking SASQUATCH. But then if SASQUATCH was right, six across was wrong and probably five and six down too. He couldn't for the life of him think of a five-letter word beginning with X, ending with Q and having a C in the middle, and he wasn't too sure of X neither. 'Oh bother!' he said before crossing out the entire word and writing BLACK BEAR instead. 'That'll have to do.'

The vicar was hopeless at crosswords, and this particular puzzle seemed more difficult than most. The lateness of the hour didn't help and neither did the stilton cheese and pickled onions he'd wolfed down for supper, or the glass of port by his bed. He rattled the pencil between his teeth as he studied the crossword, trying to make sense of the clues. Now he came to think of it, perhaps ORANGE HAG was wrong, and HARRIDAN too. In fact, on closer inspection GINGER TOM and HANDYMAN seemed far more plausible. He sighed and crossed out the words TOOTHLESS, CRONE and BROOMSTICK for good measure, then giving up on the puzzle, threw the newspaper on the floor.

'I should try and sleep,' he thought, looking at his watch, although sleep was difficult at the best of times, and since the peculiar Elsie Tapp had arrived, nigh on impossible. The woman weighed heavily on the vicar's mind, along with all the terrible memories of twenty years past. Things had been going so well for him recently. The nightmares had stopped. The painted dragon above The Chu Chin Chow Chipper no longer winked at him. He could walk past a pet shop window without screaming at the mice, and apart from the occasional mishap, he hadn't felt the urge to sneak into the local funeral home and knock loudly on the coffins for months.

Perhaps the bottle of port would work. He'd sipped two large glasses while attempting the crossword and maybe, just maybe, this delicious plum soup of a drink would smother his thoughts and let him slide into sleep. 'How lovely that would be,' he thought, 'to slip into delicious slumber, rather like a happy seal falling 'plop!' into the sea, except the sea would be freezing and the barnacles would catch on his pyjamas and rip his knees and...

'Oh, for heaven's sake, Ainsley - get a grip of yourself!'

He pulled the bed covers up and over his shoulders and fell back on the pillows, his eyes closed tight as he tried to will himself to sleep.

Wherever the Sandman was that night, he wasn't in The Beeches nursing home, Grubdale. Poor Ainsley couldn't get comfortable. He was hot and bothered with his head full of questions, and to make matters worse, the pillows were flat and at all angles to each other. Thumping them helped, and although the vicar was not a violent man, there was more than the usual vigour in the way he set about the task. 'That should do it,' he said after a knockout and two stopped fights. He stacked plump pillows one on top of the other, buried his head into the pile and closed his eyes.

'Oh, bugger!'

He'd forgotten to switch off the light.

'Damn and blast!' he swore as he got out of bed, but more choice words followed when he stubbed his toe on the way back and, as bad luck would have it, on his gouty foot too. He limped around the room, losing a fortune to the cuss box, then trying too hard to hop on his good leg, tripped and grabbed at the large velvet curtains for support. Slowly Ainsley swung around as the curtains drew apart till he was hanging, half standing up, half not, like some peculiar fan dancer of a troubled persuasion looking down on his audience. His audience stared back; a solitary figure on the pavement below, a short, hunched man dressed in a mask and tatty cloak. The vicar felt his heart race. This was no ordinary gentleman late from a party. No ordinary gentleman would bring fog - sweet smelling, red and billowing around their feet. And as for the gentleman's feet... The vicar stifled a scream as he let go of the curtain and fell to the floor. Two feet were enough for any man. Three legs had their benefits, but to be in possession of six? The vicar pulled himself closer to the window and peered outside. No, he wasn't mistaken. Six legs there were, and now he came to think of it, a multitude of arms too. 'Demon!' he hissed before falling in a faint and ruining the pattern of his Indian rug.

## Chapter Seven

The flagship of the rebel fleet, the Emily P, struck a colourful silhouette against the evening sky, although being a few hundred light years away and a tight turn to the right, no one on Earth noticed. Not even the inhabitants of Fish Gut Bay, a few hundred light years away, one turn to the right and a quick swim across the pond noticed until it was too late.

Silas Churn, Master of the Watch and Keeper of the Tinderbox, looked out from his office and spat out a large piece of sandwich. 'Ye Gods!' he swore, seeing the Emily P away in the distance. 'She's back!'

That was the trouble with the Emily P, she had a nasty habit of appearing 'poof!' as if from nowhere, and heaven help a master of the watch who was ill-prepared.

Silas shook off the tight-fitting office chair, grabbed his frock coat with the hat and feathers, and hurried outside. 'Come on, you scurvy-looking lads,' he cried as he dressed on the move. 'We've rockets to fire and bells to ring!'

Various scurvy-looking lads scrambled to action, running along the harbour wall with armfuls of the largest looking fireworks a child could imagine; big tubes of painted cardboard with names like Wall-Blaster, Ship-Sinker and Dragon-Belch stamped on their sides.

'Pack them tight! Trim those fuses!' shouted Silas, slipping on the wet cobbles as he hurried to catch up. 'And ring those bells, goddamn you! Shake up the town!'

Two burly lads rolled up their shirt sleeves and spat on their hands, then with a cry of 'Geronimo!' leapt from the harbour wall to swing on a giant rope suspended from the bell tower. From high above their heads, and with a skull-shaking clang that could rattle the teeth from a crocodile, the great bell Buddunng-Buddunng sounded its voice loud and clear. From further along the wall and less impressive, its companion Ting-Tong-Ding-Dong rang out a tune, sounding more like an insistent door-to-door salesman than a call to arms.

# A TOUCH OF SPLEEN

The bells did their work; the sleepy harbour came to life with doors flung open and people shouting in panic and excitement. Dogs barked and cats screamed. Hastily-dressed soldiers tumbled out of houses with muskets thrown after, and sailors in striped vests dropped their tankards and rushed to the bathroom.

'Keep your hand steady, boy, and wait till I give the signal,' whispered Silas Churn. 'Let's give the Emily P the welcome she deserves.'

The boy nodded, smiling with enthusiasm. He blew on his match, a length of slow burning rope that had ceased to spit and smoulder.

'You're not going to launch anything blowing like that now, are you? What's the matter with your lungs? Blood rot?"

Silas clipped the lad around the ear and snatched the match from him. 'Keep it lit like this, see?' he said, puffing at the end of the rope as though it was a hot chip from Thompsons the Fish Shop.

'Good heavens, there's no heat in this at all. Here, hold the damn thing!'

The poor lad held the match in his fingers as Silas brought out the Royal Tinderbox from his coat pocket. 'If a job's worth doing, it's worth doing well,' he said, trying to pry open the lid with shaking fingers, dropping the contents of the box on the damp stones.

'Oh bother and blast!'

Silas was all nerves. He could see the Emily P clearly now, as the ship sailed towards the harbour. Bending down as far as his girth would allow, Silas fumbled for the flints and fire steel on the ground. 'Right, let's try that again,' he said, struggling to his feet. 'Now keep it steady.'

With a burst of activity that belied his profession, Silas managed to get the match smouldering once more, but not without ripping his thumbnail, bruising his knuckles and setting the poor boy's lace cuffs on fire. 'You'd better blow on both,' Silas said with a sense of satisfaction. 'And quickly now, quickly!'

The boy did as he was told, puffing away madly till the end of the smouldering match glowed bright red.

'Well then, what are you waiting for? Light the bloody fuse!' shouted Silas, looking out over the harbour wall. 'And that goes for all of you! Fire, damn you! Fire, before it's too late!'

All along the wall stood tube after tube of rockets, each with their fuses lit and each with an excitable lad now running as fast as he could for cover. Discretion was the better part of valour, particularly where trigonometry and gunpowder were concerned, for no matter how many times an angle was measured or a calculation checked, the fickle finger of fate could fly up anyone's frock coat and rattle the buttons.

Bethesda Chubb, Scourge of the Coral Seas and captain of the Emily P, stood at the helm of the ship and spat in a bucket. She was chewing tobacco, not the nicest of habits for a Pirate Queen, but then neither was snatching dentures from her victims and wearing a string of them around her neck as a prize.

'Ungrateful swine, not even a string of bunting to welcome us home. You'd think we'd lost the war, not won a great battle!'

Bethesda was about to say more, much, much more and none of it charitable, when the sky above the harbour exploded into light. Firework after firework whooshed overhead, showering the deck and sails of the ship with streams of sparks. Some flew higher than most then exploded into starbursts of purple, white and green, while others released words of welcome in short-lived, fiery letters.

'Someone's been busy!' Bethesda said, her face illuminated as though standing in front of a giant stained glass window. She pointed to a string of letters now glowing sulphur yellow and laughed. 'Look, my name in lights! How wonderful!'

The spelling was hardly perfect. Parachute letters had a mind of their own when floating back to the ground, and for one uncertain moment, Bethesda was sure she could read 'BAD-BUTCH- BITCH,' through the smoke. Far from being insulted, Bethesda seemed to warm to the idea and smacked a member of her crew a little too forcefully between the shoulder blades. 'Someone likes me, what?' she cried, pointing at the letters. The unfortunate crew member managed to stop himself from falling. 'Everyone likes you, ma'am,' he said. 'Even the prisoners.'

'Oh yeth, we love you to bitth!' shouted a few of the prisoners from below deck. 'Three cheerth and all that thtuff.'

Bethesda smiled and rattled her necklace of dentures. 'And so you should,' she shouted, then burst into laughter. 'Wait, listen, I can hear bells!'

'They're ringing your praise, ma'am,' shouted a sailor from the rigging. 'The whole town is out.'

'Really? Do you think so? How lovely! Break out the bubbly and let's have a party! Oh, it's nice to be home!'

'While we're still moving, ma'am?' asked a sailor at the wheel.

Bethesda frowned. 'No, of course not. Drop the big thingamajig, or whatever you call it, into the water and roll up the canvas. We need to buy mince pies. You can't throw a good party without serving mince pies! Send the dainty Miss Carp out to get them. She's done nothing in the war so far.'

Bethesda looked around. 'Speaking of our high and mightiness, has anybody seen her? She is on board, isn't she? She hasn't flown off?'

# A TOUCH OF SPLEEN

Her high and mightiness, Rowena Carp, was feeling even less a sailor than when buying her fashionable outfit from Damsels of Pond Street. She was sitting below deck in her silks and feathers and trying her best not to think of dinner. Of all the sisterhood of witches, Rowena was the most glamorous, but the most unseaworthy. She felt sick at the sight of a seashell. Let the other witches tie knots and swig rum, all Rowena wanted was her two feet on solid ground, and the air to smell of something other than armpits and salted cod.

To take her mind off the endless swell of the ocean, Rowena had taken to spending most of her time beneath deck, not daring to peer out of the porthole. She ordered her meals through a speaking tube on the wall and, being a curious sort of witch, listened in on conversations. Today's dialogue seemed to be all about her.

'Oh, where is she?' asked a deep female voice that could only be Bethesda Chubb.

'Miss Carp is where she always is; in the scuppers being sick or else poring over those damned maps of hers.'

This second voice was thin and reedy. Rowena frowned. 'Florentine Trout,' she muttered.

'Well, couldn't someone go below deck and get her? I want her here.'

'You'd be wasting your time. Madam Uppity would rather be where she is, sketching away with her pens and pretending to do big sums in her notebook.'

'Or nattering on about the wyrm,' interrupted a third voice.

'Oh yes, that too. Madam Uppity is very fond of nattering on about the wyrm. As though no one else here has kept a pet. She's become an expert on everything. To be honest, it's a godsend when she's clutching the bucket.'

Rowena held the speaking tube to her ear and tapped her foot angrily on the floor. 'Well, I never!' she said. 'There's sympathy for you. Come and hear this, Demetrios. Little Miss Florentine is complaining, again.'

A pink, podgy creature, best described as a bizarre poodle looked up from what he was doing and snorted smoke from his nose. It was a single snort, but worth at least three pages of translation if one was polite and preferred to go round its linguistic and scatological houses.

Rowena smiled. 'Exactly,' she said. 'Couldn't have put it better myself. If they want a party, they can jolly well have one without me.'

Demetrios snorted again.

'Us,' Rowena said, hastily. 'Anyhow, they know what I think on the matter.'

Another snort, this one sharp and to the point and scorching a hole in a wooden beam.

'WE - they know what WE think on the matter.'

Demetrios seemed satisfied and returned to the more critical task of hunting down a flea, one that had dined à la carte in his fur.

'What's there to party about? It's not as though the war's over. We blew up Spleen's ship, that's all, and what sort of a stupid idea was that? Is he dead? Do we know for sure? Can you blow up an evil sorcerer? The very least an evil genius would do would be to pull on a pair of iron underpants, just in case. Take Slithertwist the Wart, his outfits were half steel at least, and you don't read about him being blown to pieces now, do you? Stands to reason, not even a thunderbolt could get inside his trousers…'

Rowena lost her train of thought, but Demetrios, as tactful as ever, chose to ignore her comments and continue chasing his flea.

'We should have captured Spleen and paraded the traitor through the streets. We should have shown the world how silly he was…then we could have blown him up. Now we don't know if he's alive or dead, just disappeared.'

Rowena held the speaking tube close to her ear but continued the conversation. Spleen's disappearance was a constant topic with her and one that bored the crew of the Emily P to frustration. 'Thanks to our wyrm and his trigger-happy snout,' she said, 'we've blown the Behemoth sky-high. It's Bethesda's fault, and the silly sisterhood to be honest. Together they've spoilt the beast something rotten. Not that those fools upstairs want to listen. Oh no, they "ooh" and "ahh," as though the wyrm can do no wrong, as though setting fire to any poor soul is acceptable behaviour. Well, it isn't. That creature's so free and easy with his flames you'd think he'd sprung a leak.

'And,' Rowena continued, standing up and waving her finger at Demetrios, 'it will only get worse, you mark my words. He's a drake without a newt, a young drake.'

Demetrios stopped rummaging in his fur and looked at Rowena, puzzled.

'Remember when you were all bump and grind? Nothing was safe; scorch marks everywhere. But at least you didn't burn down the street; not something I can say for our young Mr Firestarter upstairs. I wouldn't trust him with a pine forest, let alone a pile of sticks. And if he's not burning up the countryside, then he's eating his way through half the cowsheds in the district. I tell you, nothing good can come of this. A drake without a newt? It's not natural. He needs a companion, or else a trip to the…'

Rowena put her hand over her mouth to stop the terrible words escaping, but it was too late. Demetrios knew exactly what she meant. He raised his lip and growled. There were two types of 'trips' in his world, and the one Rowena was hinting at had little to do with a corner shop.

'Oh stop being such a grouch. I don't know what's gotten into you recently. You're as moody as a hen on a hedgehog.'

Demetrios grumbled again, then buried his nose in his fur. He had a sense of something missing, a sixth sense made all the more real as he searched for the flea. It was ever the same at times like these; a good sniff and a lick, and then an overwhelming urge to hunt down any damn silly fool with a name like Doolittle and stop his singing for good.

Rowena was about to say more when a burst of conversation from the speaker tube caught her attention. The talk on deck was getting loud and heated. 'Honestly, will that Trout woman ever shut up?' she said. 'I've a good mind to go upstairs and tell her what I think.'

Miss Trout was doing precisely that, telling everyone what she thought of Madam Uppity Carp, and from the look on Rowena's face, she was making a meal of it too.

'Well, I never!' Rowena said, hanging the speaking tube back on the wall and dusting off her hands. 'If people can't say nice things about a person, then they should jolly well shut up. That's what my mother used to say, if she said anything at all.'

Demetrios raised his eyes. The chance of Rowena being quiet for anything other than a glass of champagne was hardly worth considering.

'And listening to all that blather upstairs won't find our egg now, will it? We've wasted enough time already.'

Demetrios sighed. This infatuation with eggs was becoming a bore. Not that there was anything wrong with eggs. Breakfast was all the better for omelette and chips, it was just that Rowena seemed to talk about nothing else, and one egg in particular. It was like living with the Easter Bunny. 'Still,' he thought, 'a plate of delicious bacon and eggs wouldn't go amiss, especially with a spoonful of grated cheese. Life was all the better for a spoonful of cheese.'

'Oh no! Please!' cried Rowena. 'Not on the maps!'

Spread out on a table were many maps and charts, each of them covered with calculations written in red ink, and with arrows and circles highlighting various points of detail.

'If you've slobbered over my sums, I shall be very cross! Come on, off with you!'

Rowena lifted her pink, podgy companion from the table and dabbed at a pool of dribble left behind.

'See what you've done! I can't tell if that number there is a four or a seven, it could even be an eight! Damn it all, Demetrios, how are we supposed to find the egg if I don't know which wyrmhole to choose? We could end up on the wrong planet, let alone the wrong town. I mean, look at all the trouble we had trying to get home.'

She sighed in frustration. 'It's no use. I'm going to have to check all these figures again. I'm not even sure if it's the right map.'

Rowena stumbled against the table as the ship lurched to the left, then fell back into a tatty looking armchair. There was a sharp 'crack' as though someone had snapped a chicken leg.

'Oh bugger!'

Rowena eased herself out of the chair and gazed in dismay at what lay broken on the cushion: a slide rule and a set of measuring sticks given to her years ago by a love-struck young student with a tickly moustache.

'Well, that's torn it! I'll never finish the calculations now!'

A keen ear would have sensed a note of relief in her voice. Arithmetic was never Rowena's strong point. She was far better at mixing balms and lotions than twiddling about with a pair of dividers. Now she came to think of it, a slide rule and set of measuring sticks was a pretty rubbish present for a man to give the woman of his dreams.

'There's only one thing for it,' Rowena said, brushing the broken pieces onto the floor and flopping back down into the chair. 'We shall have to take the wyrm with us. He can make his own holes!'

Demetrios, none the wiser for the explanation, cracked the flea between his teeth and lay down by Rowena's feet.

'Cheese,' he thought as he fell into a deep slumber. 'Fleas taste better with cheese.'

## Chapter Eight

Happiness is as fleeting as a game of tennis with a pickled egg. In the words of Mr Micawber - annual income twenty pounds, annual expenditure twenty pounds, two shillings and thruppence - happiness is a half-crown coin in the middle of the street. Misery on the other hand, is the number 61 bus from Glossop thundering towards you as you bend over to pick the money up. In the words of Harry Renfield - annual income cash only, and none of your bloody business - there is no such thing as happiness, not since fate had intervened in the shape of a large oblong box.

Some things in this world are better left where they lie; large oblong boxes covered in busy little carvings being top of the list, especially when they're found washed up on a beach, resemble more a coffin than a crate of bananas, and sing like a boy soprano. These are the worst of the lot. Harry Renfield's box was all of this and more. It leaked sweet-smelling red smoke, was as demanding as a diva, and had a nasty habit of biting anything that sat on it. Not, you would think, the ideal piece of furniture for number 42 Coal Pit Lane, but then poor Mr Renfield had no choice. The box had insisted on coming home, and that was that. It had insisted on talking too, all the way from Wales to Grubdale, criticising Harry's driving and shouting terrible things to any car that passed.

Poor, pathetic Harry - if he'd been a stronger man he would have pushed the van over a cliff. If he'd had the gift of foresight, he would have leapt into the sea after it too, but he was weak and easily led. Even if the better part of his character had forced the van back towards the sea and pressed down on the accelerator, his weaker side would have slammed on the brakes and bought ice cream. There was no escape. He was a slave to the voice as a fly is to a spoon of sugar. And speaking of flies there was a particularly fat and delicious one on the dashboard.

Harry's alarm clock went off, shrill and painful; an unfortunate reminder of how little he'd slept. It was a cheap imitation of a Mickey Mouse souvenir, except the manufacturers had painted the wrong figure on the dial, and in the wrong colours and Harry had a stack of them, unsold in his attic. To be honest, 'Mickey' looked more like an ink blob with a black belt in semaphore, but the clock kept time and could wake the very devil, and that's how Harry was feeling that morning. He reached out with his hand, groping among the rubbish on his bedside table, but managed only to knock his dentures on the floor. There was a 'splash' as his upper set fell into something best pushed under the bed, and his heart sank, as did his teeth. 'Typical,' he thought. 'Another horrid start to another horrid day.'

It didn't help Harry's mood, toothless or not, that the house was in complete darkness. It had been like this for three days, with all the curtains closed and secured with clothes pegs. The box had insisted, and the box was always obeyed. So each morning Harry had stumbled down the stairs, stepped gingerly across the parlour with his arms outstretched in case of breakages, had tapped three times on the kitchen door, and then like a dutiful husband, had made himself tea and jam sandwiches in the dark.

Harry was fed up with the dark. Not even a candle or the strike of a match was allowed. He had foolishly used a torch to look for a tin of beans in the kitchen, but the beam of light had shone straight into the face of something so horrid that he had dropped the torch on the slate floor and smashed the bulb. There had been screams and shouts, and the slamming shut of a lid, and then nothing more was said. Breakfasts were taken in the dark with Harry sipping quietly on his tea, while whatever was up and about slurped and munched on heaven knows what. Lunches were the same and dinner too, until the thought of another jam sandwich had poor Harry itching with hives. It was all very polite and all very English, but Harry was a prisoner all the same. Any time he tried to sneak out of the house, something big and bristly growled in his ear. He couldn't even use the outside loo.

'Dammit!' Harry swore. 'Anymore of this nonsense and I'll have rickets! It has to stop, right now, today, this week!'

It was brave talk, but muttered from the safety of the bedroom. Tiptoeing down the stairs brought the usual change of heart and a depressing trudge across the floor to the kitchen.

'Is it safe to come in?' Harry asked, but this time there was silence; this time the kitchen door opened on its own accord, flooding the parlour with light. Harry had to squint, his pupils the size of pinpricks, but he could see well enough. The kitchen was a mess.

There were empty tins and broken jars everywhere, the entire contents of his larder sampled, chewed and drank, except the pickles scattered carelessly

# A TOUCH OF SPLEEN

across the floor as though thrown away in disgust. In the middle of this mess lay the large oblong box, now on its side and with its lid wide open.

'Are you there?' Henry asked, stepping slowly into the kitchen and nearly doing the splits as his feet slid on a pickled gherkin. 'Coo-eee?'

The box was empty, but for a thin yellow cloak, like the remains of a giant cocoon shredded and kicked to the corner. Harry prodded it with his finger then shivered and wiped his hands on the side of his trousers. 'The greedy bugger!' he said as he looked around the room, for someone had made a meal of the tinned salmon, a leg of ham and all of the cheddar cheese. The pork roll had vanished too, along with poor Harry's goldfish.

This was the cruellest blow. Harry could put up with the stolen food and the terrible mess on the floor, but to lose Betty Boop, his prize fantail fish was unforgivable. She was his confessor, gladly listening to all of his problems as he made his cocoa at night. The ghastly image of the fish pressed between two slices of bread was too much, and Harry kicked out at the box in frustration. 'Damn you!' he cried, then thought better of it as the door to the backyard swung slowly open. Harry's heart was in his mouth, along with just about every other organ in his body. 'And relax,' he whispered, letting out a slow, deliberate breath as he realised there was no one there. 'The door must have opened of its own accord, that's it,' he thought.

Harry took a few steps outside then wished he'd stayed put, for the backyard was far worse than the kitchen. The contents of the box had progressed from tinned food to meat on the hoof - or paw if you were grammatically correct. There were flat, dead hairy things scattered everywhere, mostly with collars around their necks and with names like Tinkerbell and Mr Fluffybutt. 'Oh my god!' Harry said, recognising the chewed corpse of next door's cat. 'What will the neighbours think?'

There was little time for anyone to think, let alone Harry standing there in his pyjamas. Someone flushed the outside loo and rattled the bolt on the door, and in a flash poor Harry ran back in the house and up the stairs to safety.

Grubdale police station was as busy as a fish market on a Friday morning. Twenty or more townsfolk were huddled together in the lobby of the building, forming as orderly a queue as possible. At the front stood a distressed Mrs Froggatt, explaining everything to the desk sergeant as he tried to look suitably concerned. There had been no burglaries to speak of, no spate of 'knock-a-door run' or trampling of the daffodils in the park; something far more critical had occurred. Tiddles had failed to appear for her morning kippers, and Mrs Froggatt was in a terrible state.

'Missing, one tortoiseshell cat,' the desk sergeant read out as he scribbled down the particulars. 'Answers to the name of Tiddles. Property of Mrs Froggatt, 16 Limekiln Road.'

'It's all so worrying, Sergeant,' insisted Mrs Froggat, dabbing at her eyes with a handkerchief. 'You see, she's not one of those common gad-about-town cats. Tiddles hates the outdoors. She spends most of the day looking out the kitchen window and swatting bluebottles. The only time she sets foot in the garden is when nature calls, and then only as far as the rhubarb. It's not like her to go missing, not like her at all. Oh dear, I'm in such a tizzy.'

She was not the only one; old Jack Bell was in a tizzy too. His ginger tom had gone missing. 'Although he answers to Charlie-fart-arse most of the time,' he pointed out. 'Or Dirty Bugger. You can take your pick what to shout out.'

'Shout out?' asked the desk sergeant.

'Well, you bobbies are gonna need to shout something to call him back, aren't you? Might as well be his name.'

The mystery continued. Miss Robinson's Siamese had been missing for two nights as had Penelope Grunt's Caesar Augustus. The three kittens from Number 25 had vanished along with Mr Gregory's Jack Russell, and to add spice to the commotion, two otherwise gentle old ladies were taking swipes at each other with their handbags and arguing over precisely who owned Truffles McSnuffles.

'He's mine. I've had him nine years from a kitten. He sleeps in my armchair all day!'

'Rubbish! He's been sleeping on my bed for eight years at least. And he's not Truffles; he's Albert!'

'Truffles!'

'Albert!'

'Truffles!'

'It's just like you, Connie Stevens, to try and get your hands on my cat! You've been trying to get your hands on my husband ever since you moved next door. You trollop!'

'Well, I never! Trollop indeed! You should tell your dirty old man to keep his hands to himself. It's not safe to queue for stamps with him around. He should be sent to the vet, the dirty old goat!'

'Tart!'

'Witch!'

'Knicker Dropper Glory!'

This last insult took a few moments to sink in. Connie Stephens wasn't sure what had been said, and Sue Cathcart was surprised she'd said it at all. Either way, it proved the catalyst for some heated umbrella action and much kicking of the shins.

'Now then ladies, stop that at once!' snapped the desk sergeant. 'It doesn't matter who owns the bloody cat. It's gone missing, right?'

The two ladies ceased their fighting and with bottom lips quivering with emotion admitted that yes, the cat had been missing for two nights now and they were at their wits' end.

'Name?'

The two ladies looked at each other. There was a bond, an acceptance of grief.

'Albert...' said one with tears running down her cheeks.

'Albert Truffles McSnuffles,' corrected the other, and not being able to hold back their emotions any longer, the two women sobbed and wailed in between describing their cat's distinguishing features, right down to the smell of its breath.

'Shocking it is, like the black hole of Calcutta. But he won't let me brush his teeth. He gets very cross.'

'I find a peppermint helps. He's especially fond of mint imperials, Len is. I mean Truffles, I mean the cat. I mean....goodness, is that the time?'

'NEXT!' shouted the desk sergeant, dismissing the two ladies before they could resume their fight. He had hoped for a quiet Thursday morning, a time to catch up on paperwork or the cryptic crossword in the Daily Record, but his plans had come to nought. He had marched purposefully to work to be met not with his usual mug of hot, sweet tea but with a crime wave of feline proportion, and if there was anything he cared less about it was cats. Cats made him sneeze, and that was the best he could say about them. 'NEXT!' he cried, ringing the bell on the counter for attention.

A little girl's head appeared over the desk. 'Please sir, my Tommy's gone missing.'

The desk sergeant placed his pencil carefully down on the report book. 'And I suppose your Tommy is a cat?' he asked.

The little girl nodded. 'He's mine and my sister's, but mostly mine. He pees on the bed. Daddy said he'd kick him out the window if he did it again. He's very naughty. He pooed in Daddy's slipper yesterday, and Daddy said some naughty words.' She shrugged her shoulders. 'Now he's gone missing.'

'Your daddy?' asked the desk sergeant, secretly hoping it would be the case, only to bring some purpose to his morning.

'No silly,' said the little girl, giggling. 'Tommy's gone missing, not Daddy.' It seemed wrong to laugh, so she paused, gave the policeman a stern look and said in a serious, little girl's voice, 'We're very sad.'

The desk sergeant didn't look sad at all. 'EXCUSE ME!' he shouted in an attempt to get attention from the other people in the room. 'IS THERE ANYONE HERE WHO HASN'T LOST A CAT?'

A single hand waved at him from the back of the room. 'That would be me I suppose,' and the owner of the gentle voice pushed himself through the queue to stand opposite the desk.

'Well?' asked the sergeant.

'It's about my poor cow.'

The desk sergeant felt a twitch of pain coming from his stomach. 'I take it we're talking farm animals here?' he asked, looking at the gentleman and making a mental note of his appearance. From the dishevelled coat and trousers, and state of the man's footwear, 'farmer' was as safe presumption as any.

'Aye, I've come about Betty, my best milker.'

'And what's happened to her? Please don't tell me she's gone missing. Ever wake up in the morning longing for a bank robbery? I do.'

'What?' said the gentleman, scratching his head. 'Oh no, she's not missing. I know where Betty is alright, she's by the side of the road. She's dead. Ripped to pieces, she is, and not by any dog, that's for sure.'

Elsie Tapp stood on the front steps of the Alpine Palace hotel and pulled on her gloves. 'How beautiful!' she said, looking out across the town to the woods and fields in the distance, but then Elsie was a city girl brought up on city sights and city smells. A hotel maid brought up on nothing but Grubdale shook her duster from an upstairs window and came to a different conclusion. 'No chance of putting the washing out in this,' she complained, loudly. 'It's as grey as my old man's spit!'

Elsie shuddered at the image, but not to be disheartened, thrust a large umbrella under her arm and pulling her beloved poodle behind her, set off at a brisk pace down the hotel steps and out through the main gate. This was her happy time, the best part of the day – a morning walk spent in the fresh air away from London; her little bit of exercise between breakfast and lunch. Princess Peaches loved her walks too, but not as much as breakfast, nor as much as lunch. In fact, now the little poodle came to think of it, and particularly so after being dragged through a muddy puddle and with an east wind blowing where it shouldn't, perhaps she didn't like morning walks at all.

'Come on, poppet – don't dawdle,' Elsie said, giving the lead a sharp tug. 'We don't want to waste the day now, do we? Not with a mystery to solve.'

Princess Peaches made a token gesture of defiance by sitting down on the pavement. It made little difference. Miss Tapp was in such good, bouncy humour that she dragged the poodle behind her, greeting each early shopper

## A TOUCH OF SPLEEN

she passed with a hearty 'Good Morning!' Elsie was a force of nature, a one-woman band of enthusiasm marching lively through the streets, and even if Grubdale townsfolk could be sullen and moody, her cheerful manner shocked them into a response. 'Isn't it just?' they would say, before looking once more to the pavement and making their escape.

One particular gentleman was so intent on looking at the pavement that Elsie had to step out of his way for fear of being knocked over. 'Well, I never!' she cried as he hurried on past. There was a mumble of apology, but nothing convincing. A large, ill-fitting cloth cap was pulled so far down on the gentleman's head that staring at the pavement was probably the only thing he could do. 'Why don't you look where you're going?' Elsie snapped.

The rebuke was enough to make the man stop and change tack, or it may have been the streetlamp appearing suddenly ahead. He zig-zagged along the street, not keeping to the same direction for more than a few seconds.

'How peculiar!' Elsie said, stepping back on the pavement and looking back. It was as though the gentleman was trying his hardest to avoid the cracks in the pavement or else dodge imaginary snowballs but to no avail. A perfectly thrown cabbage hit him squarely on the back of the head.

'Damn it all!' he cried, throwing the cloth cap to the ground and shaking his fists in the air. 'I know it's you, Mary O'Reilly, wherever you are!'

Elsie stared in surprise as the man stormed off along the high street towards the cinema. 'How I love this town,' she said, hugging herself with pleasure. 'Far more fun than our usual holidays, don't you think?'

Princess Peaches was unimpressed and pawed at her owner's leg to be picked up.

'Oh, don't be such a lazy bones, the exercise will do you good. What say we have a little adventure?' Elsie pointed with her umbrella to the woods in the distance and the ruins of the old school behind that. 'You never know our luck; we might catch a rabbit.'

Rabbit, there was that word again. Princess Peaches loved this short, sharp collection of syllables. It had the same effect every time – a rush of blood to the head and an uncontrollable urge to bark and chase pigeons in the park.

'There, you see,' laughed Elsie, patting her poodle on the head. 'I knew you'd agree. Now, off we pop – no dawdling mind, we've got a long trek ahead.'

A gust of wind caught Elsie off guard and blew her carefully combed hairstyle all over the place. 'Oh damn and blast, I knew I should've brought a hat!' But Elsie hated hats; they made her head look two sizes too big or else her nose far too small. It was why she took the greatest of care in her hairstyle, an intricate design held in place with pins, clips and a net at the back.

'Needs must, I suppose,' she said and taking a headscarf from her pocket proceeded to wrap it around and tie it under her chin, a task made all the more difficult by having an umbrella under one arm, and the dog lead held tight between her teeth. Elsie made use of the nearest large window she could find instead of a mirror. 'Oh well, I suppose it will have to do,' she said, tucking the last curl of hair behind her scarf and blowing a kiss at her reflection. 'It's not like anyone cares, is it?'

The Reverend Ainsley Cross cared. He cared very much. He cared so much as to push away the café table he was sitting at, point at Miss Tapp through the large front window and say something entirely out of character for a man of the cloth.

'I say, steady on old chap,' whispered Captain Dashing, trying to stop the milk jug from toppling over. 'Ladies present and all that.'

But the vicar was far from steady. He was a bag of nerves; a sleep-deprived powder keg of emotions with the fuse still fizzing, and all because of the strange spider-like creature he'd seen through his bedroom window.

'For heaven's sake, sit down before you get us both thrown out.'

The vicar did as he was told, but fumbled in his jacket pocket for a large crucifix which he held tight with both hands.

'You saw what she did there, Hilary. She mocked the church!'

'She blew you a kiss, that's all. Nothing more than that.'

'Nothing more, you say? Here, hold this while I find my notebook. I'll show you what "Nothing more" amounts to. Witchcraft and devilry, that's what, and I have the proof!'

The vicar pressed the crucifix into the captain's hand then spent a few moments rummaging through his own pockets. 'Here we are. I knew I'd brought it,' he said, throwing the book onto the table with a flourish before snatching the crucifix back. 'Read the last two pages and then tell me it's nothing. It's black magic, that's what it is, plain and simple. She's a witch, just as we suspected.'

Captain Dashing brought out a pair of thin wire spectacles and adjusted them with difficulty onto his nose. 'I hope you're mistaken,' he said, opening the book and reading the vicar's small, neat handwriting. On each page was a list of items Elsie Tapp had bought, with the most peculiar ones circled in red crayon and underlined three times for good measure. The captain was unimpressed. 'Damn it, man, this is a shopping list - nothing to get skittish and nervous about, and to be honest, Ainsley, if I can speak my mind - you're just wasting money buying this rubbish.'

'It's not my shopping list, you idiot; it's hers. My, but we're a little challenged this morning.'

# A TOUCH OF SPLEEN

'No need to be rude, old chap; just because you didn't get any sleep. I can't see what it proves anyway, other than a terrible taste in souvenirs.'

'Souvenirs be damned!' cried the vicar and proceeded to point to each item on the list as though he was stabbing peas. 'Candlesticks, dagger, pewter goblet, ram's skull, chicken giblets!' he shouted. 'Do I have to spell it out? The only piece missing is chalk for the floor!'

The captain stared at the words but was none the wiser.

'Chalk to draw a star with?' suggested the vicar. 'A pentagram?'

'I'm hopeless at crosswords; you know that. Stop being clever and come to the point.'

'Sexton Blake and the Creature from Hell?'

The captain dropped the notebook as though it was alive. 'You don't say!' he cried, his eyes wide open in surprise.

'I do dear friend, very much so!'

'She wants to summon a demon?' he asked. 'Like Morgana Threep in the book?'

'Exactly!'

'Crikey!'

Captain Dashing reached inside his jacket for a small piece of cloth and rubbed it against his cheek. 'But summoning a demon, isn't that a bit far-fetched?'

'Hilary, dear friend, I wish you'd think before you speak. We've had zombies and dragons before. What's so far-fetched about a demon? And I've seen it; you forget that. A mockery of a man.'

The captain pressed the piece of blanket closer to his cheek. 'You saw it?' he asked, his face draining of colour as the old fears returned. 'But are you sure it was a demon? It could have been the fog. There was a nasty bit of fog last night; it could have been anybody - the lamplighter, perhaps? He's an ugly bugger in the daylight, let alone the dark. I don't think my nerves could stand chasing demons.'

'It was a demon, I tell you - grinning at me with a face like death. Look, I can hardly keep my hands from shaking.'

The captain's hands were shaking too. Images of Lon Chaney in The Phantom of the Opera had come to mind, and what a terror of an evening that had been. There weren't many films that made the captain drop his egg sandwich and scream for mother, but the infamous unmasking of the phantom in the fourth reel was one. Even Mary O'Reilly playing 'I do like to be beside the seaside,' hadn't remotely dulled the horror.

'A face like death, you say? Oh dear, I don't like the sound of that.'

85

'It was terrifying. I screamed like a baby, and I'm not ashamed to admit it. I thought he was a policeman at first, standing there under the streetlight. But then he turned his head to look up at me and…'

The vicar tried to think of a suitable metaphor. 'You know that film we never talk about?' he said. 'The one that made you…'

The captain nodded. He was well ahead of the vicar, about two reels to be precise, where the phantom was standing on the roof of the Paris Opera House with his cloak blowing in the wind.

'Well, it was worse than that, far worse. This creature was like some giant insect.'

There was a moment's silence between the two gentlemen as the captain tried to imagine the scene. 'A giant insect you say, a giant insect with a man's head?'

The vicar nodded.

'A giant insect with a man's head, trying to get inside your bedroom?'

The vicar frowned. The tone of the captain's voice was not as sympathetic as he would like. 'Yes, that's what I said – a giant insect with a man's head, wearing a mask and dressed in a cape.'

'And trying to get inside your bedroom?'

'Yes! Yes! Yes! And trying to get inside my bedroom. Why these questions all of a sudden, don't you believe me?'

The captain put away his piece of blue blanket and started to drum his fingers on the table. 'You've been at the bloody port and stilton again, it's obvious.'

'I beg your pardon?'

'Look at the state of you, all excitable after one of your cheese and pickle nightmares. You had me going with the shopping list, I'll give you that. But as for this demon – well, take a glance at that poster over there. You've described its appearance in every detail.'

'I don't know what you mean. Are you suggesting I made the whole thing up?'

'I'm suggesting your imagination may be more cheese and wine than common sense – too much port and stilton before bedtime. Remember when you thought the postmistress had designs on your inheritance? You had me buying stamps and posting parcels for weeks. You confuse fantasy with reality, and never so often as after the cheese and pickles. It's happened before, don't deny it.'

'Well, you're quite the Sigmund Freud today, and no mistake. I suppose what happened twenty years ago was my imagination too, and yours.'

## A TOUCH OF SPLEEN

'I'm saying no such thing. I'm just hinting that maybe, just maybe mind – you've had another one of your vivid dreams and woken up thinking it real.'

The vicar dismissed the idea with a loud sniff and edged his seat noisily around so as not to look at the captain. 'Never been so insulted,' he mumbled. 'Port and stilton nightmares, my foot! Are you suggesting I have a problem with the drink? What I saw was real, as real as any…'

His voice faded to a mere whisper. On the far wall of the café, where once hung a lithograph of a Scottish terrier in a Tam-O-Shanter, the proprietor had stuck the latest film poster for the Galaxy cinema. The image was unmistakable – a giant spider's web with Dracula's head and arms in the middle.

'Oh dear,' thought the vicar and took a large but secretive sip of brandy from his hip flask. There was no escaping the obvious, the more he stared at the poster, and the more the image of Dracula stared back, the more familiar it all seemed. There was an annoying possibility that the captain had been right all along. 'Oh dear!' he mumbled. 'Oh dear, oh dear, oh dear!'

'What's that you say?' asked the captain, smiling like a Cheshire cat, but his triumph was short-lived. A police car sped down the high street with its alarm bell ringing and all thoughts in the café turned to gangsters, bank robberies and hoodlums being sprayed with bullets - except this was Grubdale, where reality never failed to disappoint. The door to the café opened, and a red-faced Mrs Cathcart of Truffles-McSnuffles fame stumbled in. 'Hey Martha!' she called, her best friend serving cake behind the counter. 'You'll never guess what's happened. Some monster's eaten half of Old Potter's cows! Taken great lumps out of them! Blood and guts everywhere!'

The vicar turned to look at his friend and offered a comforting squeeze of his hand. 'Now do you believe me?' he asked, as the captain searched for his piece of blue blanket and whimpered like a frightened child.

## Chapter Nine

Two of Grubdale's constabulary stood in the middle of the lane and contemplated the finer things in life; gardening, football, fishing for pike in the local canal - anything they could put their mind to as long as it wasn't breakfast. A fried egg and a greasy rasher may have been delicious earlier, but now they were standing in front of a dead, smelly cow.

'It looks worse under that tarpaulin sheet,' said PC Wiggery. 'Poor thing's head's uncovered like it was tucked up in bed. Can't we do something?'

PC Drudge rocked back and forth on his heels, all thoughts of his prize geraniums gone in an instant. 'Mustn't tamper with the evidence,' he said, trying to keep words to a minimum. 'Don't look, if it bothers you so much.'

'Can't help it. Head and tail on show, and not much left in the middle. It's a bloody horror film. I mean, what sort of animal chews up a cow – a stray dog? Must be a fat one, if it is. And what about those empty sheep on the moor? Nothing but woolly handbags they were, drained to the last drop of raspberry jam.'

'A tiger.'

'Yeah, right. This is Derbyshire, not India. There're no big cats around here. Mind you, after this morning, it seems there're no little cats neither. Rum times we live in, George, and that's a fact.'

'Vampires, then.'

'Now you're being daft.'

'Pink fluffy vampires in tartan coats.'

'What are you talking about?'

'Legs together and a hand on your crucifix – here's one of the bloodthirsty killers now.'

PC Drudge nodded in the general direction of the town as the jolly figure of Miss Tapp appeared at the bottom of the lane with her pink poodle in tow.

## A TOUCH OF SPLEEN

PC Wiggery laughed. 'God help us, look at the size of that beast. We're in for it now. The creature's come back for pudding. One bite from that, and we'll be as dead as this cow.'

'Why do they do it, though?'

'What, kill cows?'

'No, women of a certain age dying their poodles pink. Small and fluffy is bad enough, but dipped in paint? She's dressed that one in tartan like a tin of Scottish toffee. Poor bugger, no wonder it's turned out wrong. I'd be biting sheep if I looked like that.'

Elsie was striding purposefully along the lane, humming a march and swinging her bag in time to the beat. It was a lovely day, and from what she could see over the top of the walls, the countryside looked beautiful too. It was just that the walls were very high, the gates and breaks in the stonework few and far between, and the way the lane twisted and turned, it didn't seem she would reach the top of the hill before sundown. Seeing the policemen in front, Elsie slowed down and pulled Princess Peaches close to her.

'Good day,' she said, her jolly enthusiasm constrained by a sense of guilt. Not that Elsie had done anything wrong, but the way the two policemen were staring suggested a master criminal at least.

'Madam,' they said, nodding their heads slowly.

Elsie saw the unfortunate body of the cow as she walked past and stopped short. 'Oh my!' she cried. 'Oh, how terrible, the poor thing! What happened?'

The policemen looked Elsie and the poodle up and down, trying their best not to smile. 'An accident, madam. A nasty accident…with a motorcar.'

'Oh dear, have you called the vet? Is there anything we can do?'

'No ma'am, far too late for that.'

To make their point, the two constables took one step away from each other so that Elsie could get a better look.

'Heavens above!' she said before the constables stepped back and blocked the view.

'Yes, ma'am, a very nasty accident. Move along now; there's nothing more to see.'

Elsie wasn't sure she wanted to see anything else; one glance had been enough. 'Absolutely, I'll be on my way. Life can be horrid at times, can't it.'

'Yes ma'am, it can - especially if you're a cow.'

PC Wiggery smiled and nudged his companion. There was a little bit of fun to be had, harmless fun to break the monotony. 'A word to the wise, ma'am,' he said, 'if you don't mind me saying. We have an upset farmer back there who'd think nothing of shooting an elephant let alone a dog. Best keep that beast of yours on a lead. The safest thing for it.'

It was PC Drudge's turn to smile and join the fun. 'Aye, safest thing, especially seeing how it's Scottish an' all. He's not too fond of the tartan. It was a milkman from Glasgow who ran off with his missus. Have you a Union Jack to wrap the wee beastie in? Don't want to provoke the old bugger.'

It took a few moments for Elsie to realise the constable was referring to her precious Princess. 'She's not a beast, young man, she's royalty. She's a toy poodle and one with a pedigree as long as your arm. Her father was none other than King Bootles III, breed champion and best in show for five years – Peckham Dog Show that is, none of your mongrel parades.'

'All the same, ma'am. Keep it on a lead. Best to be safe.'

Elsie frowned. 'Good day to you both,' she said before scooping Princess Peaches up in her arms and setting off along the lane. 'The cheek of the man, calling you a beast. Probably keeps a cat!' This was Elsie's ultimate insult. She would no more keep a cat than buy her clothes from the Co-op. She mumbled sweet nothings in Princess Peaches' ear as she walked briskly away. Her beloved poodle, rather pleased at being referred to as a beast, looked back over Elsie's shoulder and curled her top lip - except it made her sneeze loudly, which ruined the effect.

Percy Bamforth's day had started poorly and was showing no sign of improvement. Breakfast had been healthy, with not enough marmalade to cover a stamp. He'd been hit on the head by a cauliflower on the way to work, and now, with an empty cup in one hand and a flask of tea that rattled suspiciously when shook in the other, he listened carefully to what Sid Bottle, the Galaxy's handyman had to say, and groaned.

'It's fleas, Mr Bamforth. The cinema's crawling with them.'

Percy's heart sank. This was not what he wanted to hear. The Grubdale premiere of Dracula was just days away, and his wife was already posting invitations to the special viewing at his party.

'"Crawling" seems a bit excessive, Sid. Is it as bad as that? We've hardly been open six months.'

Sid Bottle shrugged his shoulders. 'A splash of paint and some curtains means nothing to the little buggers. You can get bitten in the Paramount just as well as here.'

'Pffft!' snorted Percy, not appreciating the comparison. The Paramount cinema in Manchester was a palace, overshadowing any pretence the Galaxy had of Hollywood glamour. It boasted Greek statues that towered over the pavement, each holding torches that flickered with electric light. Film posters so large they could paper a ceiling advertised each show, and everywhere you looked were queues of people eager to be entertained. In contrast, the Galaxy had an art deco overhang that kept people dry in the rain, and pigeons – lots of pigeons, but Percy loved the place, and that was all that mattered - and it housed his Wurlitzer organ

'You can catch more than fleas from the Paramount Sid, and the least said of that bordello the better. This is Grubdale, and we're a clean, godly folk.'

'Aye, some of us, maybe, but those that ain't have brought critters, and if I find out who they are they'll be hell to pay.'

Percy couldn't help notice a certain discomfort to Sid's conversation, a definite scratching and chasing the enemy around the underclothes.

'Ah Sid, don't tell me you've caught one.'

'I have and no bloody wonder. I dare anyone to run up and down the aisle without scratching like a monkey. It's like the trenches out there.'

'Aren't you exaggerating, just a little bit?'

'No I ain't, look at this!'

Before Percy could stop the man, Sid had yanked up his shirt and exposed the evidence – a red weal that looked more as though the poor man had been fighting with a giant octopus than a speck of dust with teeth.

Percy was horrified. 'Holy crap, Sid! What sort of flea did that?'

Elsie Tapp brushed away the clumps of damp moss from the seat, then sat down on the bench to rest her feet. It had been a hard trek up the country lane, dodging potholes and puddles and with nothing much to look at but stone walls and the body of a dead cow half-hidden under a tarpaulin sheet. 'Well, that was hardly Constable's The Hay Wain,' she said, stretching her legs out in front and admiring the way her walking shoes shone in the sun. 'More like a butcher's basket. What say we take a different path home, somewhere a little less visceral?'

The question was addressed to Princess Peaches, who far from living up to her name, was nurturing thoughts and emotions worthy of a lesser being. Wet, cold and grumpy, Princess Peaches was ready to snap at anything – especially rabbits. Rabbits made the great outdoors bearable. You could chase rabbits. Pigeons were good fun too, but full of feathers, while sticks were …well, sticks were just sticks and best not talked about. They made you do silly things like run headlong into clumps of thistles or jump into ponds. Princess had been promised rabbits, and rabbits she wanted. She curled her top lip and growled, but very quietly and behind her paw so no one could see.

'And what's got into you? We're on holiday aren't we, not getting pushed and trampled in a big city. Now sit by me and stop moaning. Anybody would think you're hard done by, you silly sausage.'

Princess Peaches was in no mood to sit next to anyone. She lay down beneath the bench and shivered. There was a brisk breeze blowing through her fur, her paws were muddy, and all she wanted to do was jump in a warm basket and snuggle down for the day.

'Suit yourself,' Elsie said, making herself comfortable and enjoying the scenery. 'Stay there and be grumpy, see if I care. You'll be wanting food soon enough.'

Elsie took a deep breath of the country air and sighed. It was a warm, comforting sigh of contentment, yet short-lived. The beautiful vista of the Derbyshire hills lay before her, but try as she might to be one with nature, it wasn't enough. Constable would have been happy, but then any old dollop of England did the trick with him; a few trees in the background with a few cows in front and he'd paint away for days. Elsie was a more sensitive soul. She liked her countryside washed, combed and devoid of the red stuff. It was no good; she couldn't settle. All Elsie could think about was the poor unlucky cow, half-hidden under a tarpaulin sheet, two miles down the lane.

'They were quick to move us on, weren't they?' Elsie said, after sucking noisily on a lemon sherbet. 'The police, that is,' she explained. 'The way they were acting it was like a murder had happened, not some cow getting run over. I half expected a line of chalk around the body and some photographers. All very peculiar.'

Elsie popped another boiled sweet into her mouth and thought some more, crunching it between her teeth as her mind worked overtime. She was having a Dorothy L Sayers moment, seeing intrigue and whimsy everywhere. But this was the countryside, not the Bellona Club, although you could still tread in something unpleasant.

'Who would run over a cow? It doesn't seem possible. Not unless it was a very big car and the cow was very obliging. No, I'd say the police were fobbing us off with an excuse. Something mysterious happened back there, and not with a Bedford Truck.'

Princess Peaches felt a tug on her lead as Elsie lifted a thermos flask and pack of sandwiches from her bag. 'Of course,' she said, continuing her analysis, 'the poor thing could have been shot – put down like a wild beast. Perhaps that's what happened. But then, where was the blood? I would have expected a drop, more than a drop – a bucket of the stuff, even. Oh dear, I do hate a mystery.'

Princess Peaches hated only three things in life - cats, the rain and a wet country walk to the top of a hill. She barked to make her feelings known then carried on sulking.

'Exactly, my point entirely. Would you like some soup?'

## A TOUCH OF SPLEEN

A saucer of delicious broth appeared by Princess's nose and succeeded for a brief moment in cheering her up.

'Goodness, that didn't last long. You're supposed to be a sophisticated lady of fashion, not some scruffy mongrel. Don't blame me if you're sick afterwards.'

Princess Peaches sneezed, more from the pepper in the soup than the cold, then sniffed around the saucer for more.

'There's another possibility I suppose. The unfortunate cow could have died from old age - it was thin enough. What sort of farmer keeps a cow till it keels over and then calls the police? It doesn't seem right to me.'

Another thought came to mind, this time more Agatha Christie with daggers attached.

'Oh, my!' Elsie cried, remembering the newspaper article the day before. 'Do you think the death of that cow had anything to do with the sheep? I mean the dead, flat ones found on the moor?'

Princess Peaches' ears pricked up. There was a rustle of greaseproof paper, and that meant one thing, or so she hoped - roast chicken sandwiches. She stuck her head out from under the bench to make sure. Sometimes life could be disappointing, sometimes life delivered nothing but jam sandwiches or fooled you with the noise of someone unfolding a map. Today, though, life was good. The poodle's bad mood vanished in an instant as Elsie waved an entire chicken leg in her hand and tapped on her lap. 'Come on then, misery guts,' she said. 'Din-dins!'

Elsie's attention strayed from the question of flat sheep and flattened cows to the vast expanse of shrubbery behind. If her ears weren't deceiving her, someone had screamed – a short scream, more a shout of frustration, as though someone had landed headfirst in a bunch of nettles. Elsie turned to where the noise was coming from and stared at the ominous plants – vicious-looking nettles, each chest high and ready to pump poison into any unfortunate cyclist. But what was this? If Elsie's eyes weren't deceiving her, the nettles were now tropical ferns, or was it a jungle of rhubarb? Something very peculiar was happening. The vegetation appeared in two minds as to know what it was, the stems twisting and coiling around each other and with the leaves getting fatter and softer by the second.

Perhaps it was a trick of the light, or else the wind causing Elsie's eyes to water. Plants didn't move like that, not in the daytime, not when people were looking, and neither did they play gramophone records or speak in a loud voice. Elsie pinched her nose and blew, but the noise was still there. Somewhere from deep within the vegetation, someone was listening to ballroom music and shouting at the same time.

'Grubdale calling, Grubdale calling!' boomed the voice. 'Come in Wellington Boot!'

There was a crackle of static and then snippets of other music, as though the dial of a giant radio was turning back and forth. The opening bars of a Viennese waltz lasted all too briefly before being replaced by the clipped tones of someone very posh reading a recipe for onion soup.

'Grubdale calling Wellington Boot! Grubdale calling Wellington Boot! Come in Wellington Boot, Over!'

The recipe for French onion soup lasted as far as the cheese. The booming resonance of a Russian choir was next, The Song of the Volga Boatmen making Elsie's teeth rattle.

'Grubdale calling! Grubdale calling! Ah come on, Wellington Boot, will you get a move on!'

The Russian choir morphed into an American jazz band then back to the palm court orchestra playing The Blue Danube.

'Damn and blast!' swore the voice, before extolling in words of amazement the discovery of a big red button marked 'press.' 'I wonder what this does?' it said.

There was a noticeable 'click,' a burst of white noise and then a different voice, equally female and equally exasperated, shouting back over the airwaves.

'Wellington Boot calling Grubdale! Wellington Boot calling Grubdale! For heaven's sake Rowena, will you press the bloody button!'

There was a polite cough, a rustle of paper as though someone was leafing through the pages of a manual, and then the original voice continued, less agitated than before. 'Grubdale here. Keep your hair on. No need to be rude. The Budgie has landed. I repeat, the Budgie has landed. Over!'

'This is Wellington Boot. Good to hear we have splash down!'

'Yes, well there wasn't much of a 'splash,' just a lot of nettles. Over!'

'Wellington Boot calling Grubdale. Any sign of Cuttlefish?'

There was a pause in the conversation, and then evidence of violent movement in the shrubbery. It was as though instead of leafing through a manual, various instruction books were being thrown all over the place until whoever was operating the radio had found the right one.

'This is Grubdale calling. Could you run that question by me again? Who exactly is Cuttlefish? Over!'

'You know bloody well who Cuttlefish is!'

'No, I don't. That's why I'm bloody well asking. Heaven's sake Bethesda, what manual are you using? There's no mention of Cuttlefish here, just Mirror, Ladder, Little-Bell and Tinkle. If I knew who Cuttlefish was, I'd tell you. Over!'

# A TOUCH OF SPLEEN

'Wellington Boot calling Grubdale. Cuttlefish is missing. Suspect Grubdale knows where Cuttlefish is. Suspect Grubdale has Cuttlefish. Over!'

Elsie cupped her ear with her hand and listened carefully, but for some reason the conversation had stopped.

'Wellington Boot calling Grubdale! Wellington Boot calling Grubdale! Do you have Cuttlefish? Over!'

There was another pause in the conversation, an embarrassing pause – someone was purposefully not answering'.

'Rowena, are you there? Is Cuttlefish with you? Plum-face is very angry. Over!'

'Broadsword calling Danny Boy! Broadsword calling Danny Boy! Come in Danny Boy!'

Elsie smiled. The last voice sounded very much like the first, but with a thick Welsh accent. It was as if the first voice was pretending desperately to be someone else.

'Well, there's another mystery, Princess. What do you think of that? AAHHHHH!'

Elsie hadn't meant to scream, it just came out, and now that she'd started, it felt rather silly to stop. Sitting by her side and with not a care in the world, was an altogether bigger and meaner looking pink poodle than her delicate Princess. Elsie wasn't sure if it even was a poodle. Poodles, as far as she knew, were soft fluffy creatures incapable of blowing smoke rings or growing teeth like alligators. They most certainly never crunched chicken legs sideways in their mouth or had eyebrows that wiggled up and down. 'Get away from me, you ugly brute!' she shouted, then jumped to her feet and threw the half-eaten chicken leg down the lane. If it wasn't for the collar around the creature's neck and the way its tail flapped twenty to the dozen, Elsie would have been hard-pressed to think the creature a dog at all.

Princess Peaches had no such doubts. She sat in front of the bench and stared at the pink monstrosity in awe. She was having thoughts, thoughts that years of being pampered and whisked off to the poodle parlour every second Monday had pushed to the back of her mind; thoughts of running in slow-motion through fields of carrots and with rabbits banging tambourines and throwing streamers in the air.

'Go away, go on! Shoo!' shouted Elsie, fearing for her Princess's honour. She stamped her feet and shook her fists, but the strange-looking dog just scratched its ear and sneezed. A small burst of flame shot from its nose, causing Elsie to jump back in fright and scream again.

'Do you mind?' interrupted a loud voice from behind. 'I'm trying to have a conversation here! If you will insist on screaming, then at least do it quietly!'

Elsie turned around. 'I beg your pardon?' she said, both frightened and confused.

'You can beg all you want, dear. But I still say shut up!'

The voice came from a gap in the shrubbery as the figure of what looked like a substantial aunt fought her way through. 'Honestly, I thought you were being attacked.'

Elsie looked on, hardly believing her eyes. It was as though the woman had stepped out of an Edwardian fashion magazine and had brought all the feathers.

'I know, you don't have to say a word. I can see from your face. I look gorgeous, don't I?'

The lady struck a pose as though she was hailing a cab and skating on the ice at the same time.

'It's all the rage in Paris, you know – the dress, I mean.' She looked Elsie up and down, sighed then gave up the pretence of posing for a photograph. 'Hardly suitable for here, though, that's obvious.'

Elsie wasn't sure what the woman meant, but being a positive person and not one to judge, rather hoped it was the weather.

The fashionable lady smoothed down her clothes and tried her best to keep her large hat from blowing backwards in the breeze. 'Look,' she said, pointing dramatically at her coat. 'Three buttons missing, and heaven knows what I look like from behind. It won't do; it won't do at all. They should have sent someone else, someone better prepared.'

'I'm sorry?'

'Of course you are, and nice of you to say so. But really, the noise you made was like a stuck pig.'

'I'm sorry?'

'Yes, so you've said. No need to go on. Now, can I rely on you to be as quiet as a mouse, not a dicky bird and all that? I'm halfway through an urgent phone call, and the line is bad enough as it is. Oh, and another thing…'

The strange lady lifted her rolled umbrella and pointed at the bench.

'Stop feeding my dog. He'll get sick, and when he's sick, he's impossible.'

The conversation was over. Seemingly there was nothing more to say - nothing by the lady of fashion. Elsie, on the other hand, had plenty to say if only she could stop shaking and think of exactly what it was. 'Excuse me…' she managed after a few moments of clenching her fists and concentrating hard, but it was all too late. The shrubbery parted like the Red Sea, and the mysterious follower of Edwardian fashion stepped through and out of sight. The strange pink creature stayed where it was.

'Shoo!' Elsie shouted. 'Away with you! Go and follow your mistress!'

# A TOUCH OF SPLEEN

The creature yawned, winked at Princess Peaches then blew a smoke ring towards the poodle, the soft, blue circle growing ever larger till it rested around her neck like a collar. Princess Peaches barked excitedly then stood on her hind legs, pawing at the air and hopping on the spot as though she were a star performer in a circus act.

'That's quite enough of that!' Elsie shouted, giving the lead a sharp tug, so the poor dog fell back on all fours. 'You're flirting like a trollop!' She scooped the poodle into her arms for the second time that morning and placed the small dog safe and secure inside her bag.

'Demetrios!' called the voice from the shrubbery. 'Stop showing off and come back here!'

Elsie baulked at the name. 'Demetrios? Well, that settles it, no hairy gladiator is getting anywhere near my Princess.' So saying, she pushed her beloved poodle's head back inside the large bag and fastened it shut. 'And as for you,' she said, pointing at the horrid pink creature. 'Gladiator or not, you can leave this arena now! Go on, away with you! I know very well what you're after!'

Someone whistled and Demetrios' ears pricked up. There was a hint of chastisement and 'no dinner for you if you don't come back this instant,' about the call. Deciding that discretion was the better part of valour, and snorting a last sooty smoke ring in Elsie's direction, Demetrios jumped off the bench and trotted off in the direction of the call.

'Why, you spiteful beast!' Elsie exclaimed, discovering the smoke ring stain on her best coat. 'Just wait till I catch you…' She rushed after the creature but stopped short at the shrubbery. The tall foliage had separated, and there stood the strange woman in the Edwardian dress, her arms folded and one of her feet tapping the ground repeatedly in anger.

'You leave my Demetrios alone,' she said, the threat in her voice obvious from the slow, clear pronunciation of her words. 'Otherwise, McTavish here may get upset.'

A shadow fell across both Elsie and the elegant woman of fashion as something large and most certainly not Scottish poked its head out from the shadows.

'Well, perhaps McTavish isn't his real name, but it's far better than Cuttlefish, don't you think?'

Elsie stared at McTavish and felt her knees give way. She screamed…

'Heavens above dear, not that awful noise again!'

…ran as fast as her clothes would allow…

'I don't know – not as much as a goodbye or a shake of the hand. Not our sort of person, McTavish, dear, is she?'

…and stumbled down the lane to town, stopping only to catch her breath as she rounded the corner where the two constables stood on guard. 'Up there,' she tried to say, pointing first at the cow and then back from where she'd come. 'Big! Yellow! Lots of teeth!'

'Beg your pardon, ma'am?'

'Teeth! Yellow! Big!'

Elsie set off again at an uncertain pace, half stumbling, half jogging but making good speed for her size.

'Well, Jack – did you make any sense of that? She's scared of something.'

'Aye, a bloody big tiger from the sound of things. What do you reckon? Should we take a look?'

PC Drudge stared in disbelief at his colleague. 'Take a look? Us two? Go up there and be pounced on by a tiger?'

'Everything but that last part – what do you think?'

'I'll tell you what I think, Jack. I think we've got a brace of truncheons between us, that's what I think. I might add that I'm three years off a very nice pension and a quiet life with me missus and the garden.'

'So, that's a yes then, is it?'

'Aye, bugger it. Anything's better than standing guard over a dead cow.'

The two constables retrieved their bicycles from the ditch and began the slow but steady pedal up the lane.

A TOUCH OF SPLEEN

## Chapter Ten

Evaline Bamforth sang as she danced around the house, her mood as sunny and cheery as the numerous vases of flowers in every room, gifts from a loving husband in appreciation for all she had done. She stopped by each bouquet and read the message on each card. 'Oh, how wonderful!' she said before setting off again around the house, her eyes half-closed as she imagined being swept across a dance floor by queues of strong young men, all dressed in leopard skins.

She could be forgiven her fantasy. The weekend trip to Leeds had been a great success, the final act in a gentle deception. Fred Barnes, the local film star of very local films, had agreed to be the guest of honour at a very special party, one that would secure her husband the chain of office and the position of mayor of Grubdale. The handsome Mr Barnes had even promised to arrive in costume. Hopefully, the one he wore in Tarzan the Brute, a three-reel adventure which had half the women in Manchester swooning in the cheap seats, and a few men from the racier parts of Stockport too.

Evaline smiled to herself. She had taken the liberty of choosing her costume with Fred Barnes in mind. She had decided to go as 'Jane.' Not the Jane from the Tarzan movies, where modesty and jungle leaves wrestled each other in gay abandon, but a more demure and sensible Jane in jodhpurs, riding boots and a suitably tailored jacket - the sort of Jane that looked like she wouldn't, but gorillas rather thought that she might.

The telephone rang in the hall, snatching Jane out from the Congo and back to reality. It was Percy, and a very nervous Percy at that.

'Darling, did you receive the flowers?'

'Yes, I did, my love. And they're very beautiful. We must treat ourselves to more weekends away if this is what I can expect, especially the cocktails. But my darling, all these flowers? A simple bunch of roses would suffice with a bottle of bubbly of course, and a big box of chocolates.'

'I can buy those if you'd like.'

'Don't be silly, Percy. You've spent enough already, you bad, bad boy.'

The giggle in Evaline's voice was misplaced. There was a pause, an embarrassing silence on the phone that suggested her husband was not alone. Evaline made a mental note not to woof like a dog.

'Evaline, dear – you know those invitations you wrote out so nicely and left on the kitchen table?'

'Of course, I do, Percy – all one hundred and twenty-six, why?'

'Nothing to worry about, my angel. You haven't by any chance posted them, have you?'

'Yes, every single one. Just as we discussed.'

Another awkward silence, broken, Evaline thought, by the sound of someone swearing.

'Percy?' she asked. 'Is anything a matter?'

'No, my sweet. Everything is fine. I was just making sure you'd remembered. Bye…'

Evaline held the receiver for a moment, staring at the black Bakelite contraption as though seeing it for the first time, puzzled as to the abrupt end to the conversation. Surely Percy wasn't having second thoughts, not now, not after all the work they'd put in together?

Percy was having more than second thoughts; he was well into double figures by now. 'Bugger! Bugger! Bugger! She's only gone and posted the invitations, every damn one of them! What are we going to do, Sid? The party's in three days.'

Sid took off his cap and swept his hand through his hair. 'There's nothing much we can do, boss – except tell her. Best come clean and hope for the best. Honesty's the best policy, as the saying goes. It's better to be slapped with the truth than kissed with a lie.'

'Blimey, Sid, - and where did you read that little gem? From a Christmas cracker? Whoever wrote those words was never slapped by anyone, particularly my wife. She'd kill me if she found out. No, Sid; honesty is not the answer. Disinfectant is, and buckets of the stuff. Let's drown the bastards.'

'If you say so, boss. But I fancy we need more than Jeyes fluid for what's in the cellar.'

Sid put his cap back on and looked Percy straight in the eye. 'I fancy we need a mallet.'

Harry Renfield held the claw hammer tight in his hand and tried to stop his whole body from shaking. It had taken three-quarters of a bottle of cheap

# A TOUCH OF SPLEEN

whisky to pluck up courage, and the rest of the bottle to open the kitchen door, but he had made a decision. The horrible smoke-belching chest with its horrible smoke-belching contents had to go – today, right now, for the sake of the poor man's sanity, if not the entire pussycat population of Grubdale.

Poor Harry; he wasn't sleeping. He was a prisoner in his own home, and if he had to bury another flat cat by the dustbins in the backyard, he'd scream. He'd been screaming a lot lately; screaming at the slightest noise behind him or the feel of something not quite human brushing against his legs in the dark. And it was always dark in the house, with the curtains closed and pegged together and the gas turned off at the mains. Sometimes Harry would forget and foolishly light a candle, but then he would catch a glimpse of the chest and its horrid contents, and he would scream the loudest. Today though, all this nonsense would stop. The Jolly Highlander had said so, and who was Harry to argue with a bottle of ten year-old, cask-conditioned turnip juice that could peel the stripes off a zebra? Harry burped, swallowed back the sharp taste of creosote and branch water, then conjuring all the courage he could muster into two or three footsteps, strode purposefully into the kitchen with his arms outstretched.

'Ouch!' he cried as he stubbed his toe on a table leg in the dark and fell sideways into a pile of plates on the floor. The mysterious lodger had re-arranged the furniture again.

Harry waited a few moments to catch his breath, crossed himself and whispered some words of encouragement to St Jude and St Gregory, the patron saints of hopeless causes. He mentioned St Eligius too, to be safe. The patron saint of horse jockeys had been very good to him the year before, and there was no harm in nudging the fellow awake for the second time.

Harry turned over on his front and started to crawl, slowly and carefully around the room, feeling his way forward with his hands and keeping the noise to a minimum. The chest had to be somewhere, he thought. Unless the beast inside had decided on a holiday and what a lucky turn that would be. But no, the patron saint of gambling had let his eye off the ball and torn the betting slips into pieces. Harry felt the tell-tale carved wooden surface of the chest in front of him and sighed. The job was at hand, and there was no escape. He drew his legs up beneath him and placed the hammer in his jacket pocket. He had taken what he thought were the necessary precautions – drowned his cowardice with whisky, stuffed his ears and nose with cotton wool against the voices and red smoke. All he had to do now was close the lid and nail it shut. All he wanted to do was rest his head against the box and dribble. That was the trouble with Dutch courage; it was short-lived, and made your tired and as dizzy as a Chihuahua on a merry-go-round.

Harry took a deep breath and tried to focus. 'Come on, you idiot,' he whispered. 'Get a grip!' He reached out with his free hand and touched the intricate carvings on the chest, following them to the top till he could feel the gap where the lid lay, half-open. Now came the disturbing part, checking for contents. The last thing he wanted after hammering the nails home was a gentle tap on the shoulder and a face full of frying pan. 'Here goes,' Harry said before taking a deep breath and pushing his fingers carefully through the gap. 'Just think of it as playing the piano.'

Harry's brain refused, deciding upon images of gin traps and toads with razor-sharp teeth instead. He screwed his eyes tight shut and tried to think of beautiful things, of pretty kittens playing with balls of wool. But the kittens changed to hungry pike, and the balls of wool grew thorns like giant conker shells. Harry began to regret drinking cheap whisky. There was a better class of paranoia at the bottom of a bottle of single malt. All Jolly Highlander had to offer were flashing lights, tunnel vision and burps that could burn holes in a carpet.

'Argh!' he screamed. Something warm and covered in bristles had moved beneath his fingers. With a burst of activity that surprised even him, Harry pulled his hand back, slammed the lid shut, and then flung himself on top. 'Got you!' he cried, and for one brief moment, as he sat down on the chest and made himself comfortable, Harry smiled. He would have been better shouting 'yee-haw!' and leaping out the window.

There's a reason cowboys are bow-legged and yodel with the coyotes. It's the same reason Tom Mix stares into the distance and spits. It's called a saddle. Plumped up with stuffing and sprung like a mattress, a good saddle could win you the West; a thin and splintered one, though, could lose you the Little Big Horn. Poor Harry had neither a plump nor splintered saddle; all poor Harry had were pyjama bottoms and a nasty case of piles.

The first kick from the chest sent Harry's ever wandering dentures spinning across the room; the second made him suck in air so deep he swallowed cobwebs from the ceiling. There was hardly time to breathe out before the carved chest was at it again, leaping around the room like a bucking bronco with poor Harry determined to stay on top. Rodeo had come to Number 42, Coal Pit Lane, but only in the kitchen. 'Owwww!' Harry cried. 'Jesus, Mary and Joseph!' It was as though a kangaroo was trapped inside and trying its darnedest to get out. There was no question of sitting astride the chest and riding it like a cowboy. Cheeks together and hanging on for dear life was the answer here. Well, that and keeping your head down low to avoid pots and pans.

'Ow! You vicious bugger!' swore Harry. 'Don't you ever give up?'

## A TOUCH OF SPLEEN

The chest had no intention of throwing in the towel. It raced around the kitchen as though it was the odds-on favourite at the Grand National and with every fence a Becher's Brook.

'Steady, boy! Steady!'

Harry had had enough. He reached into his pocket and brought out a hammer and a couple of two-inch nails, then quickly, in between sudden bursts of Aintree activity, drove the nails down hard through the lid. It was as though he'd branded the woodwork with a hot iron. The chest screamed like a stuck pig then, forgetting the Grand National, decided to spin around in a circle and body slam the linoleum. It took all of Harry's strength to stay on top, but for every bounce, spin and stab of pain, Harry gave double in return. Nail after nail he hammered through the lid, trapping the creature inside. 'And this is for Betty Boop!' he cried, striking the last one home with a single blow.

The chest came to an abrupt stop, throwing Harry forward with such force that his nose squashed flat against the lid. It was the final straw. Being splattered like a jam sandwich would test the patience of a saint, and Happy Harry Renfield was a long way down from there. 'Ha!' he shouted, rolling painfully off the chest onto the floor. 'See if you can get out of that!' The chest stayed where it was, silent, as though the creature inside had been struck through the heart. 'I said,' insisted Harry, kicking out with his foot, 'see if you can get out of that!'

There was no response, no noise from the darkness, and the silence made Harry uneasy. Could the creature be saving its energy, building up its strength for one last push? What if the wood was rotten and the nails failed to hold? Harry was about to kick the chest again when a saucepan fell to the floor.

'Oh, Jesus!' Harry cried, before crawling as fast as he could towards the kitchen sink. A lid from a saucepan was next, rattling on the floor as it landed, the noise going on and on till it came to a stop. Harry was sweating, his heart beating faster than a drum solo.

'Don't say there's another creature in the kitchen!' This new thought made Harry forget his pain, leap to his feet and tear down the kitchen curtains. 'Burn in Hell!' he screamed, as the light from outside flooded the room.

'Good heavens, whatever made me say that?'

Harry covered his mouth, shocked at the language and his stupidity. The last thing he needed was a fire. There was enough wood scattered about the kitchen to send the house up in smoke. And why was he even thinking of fire? It was a picture that had come suddenly to mind, an image of a carved wooden chest smouldering then bursting into flames as the sun's rays danced on its surface. Harry filled a bucket with water and threw it over the chest to make sure, then, suspicious of the silence, stamped his foot down hard on the floor. The chest stayed where it was,, even when Harry tiptoed closer and gave the side panel a hefty kick.

'Well, I never,' he said, rather pleased with himself. 'I think it's dead! I think I've killed it!'

Back at the Galaxy cinema, Percy Bamforth and Sid Bottle had succeeded in killing nothing but their sense of smell. They had followed to the letter a recipe Sid had found in an old farming magazine, but now as they stood over a large enamel bucket and stirred the peculiar mixture with a broom handle, Percy wasn't sure if they hadn't added a few letters of their own.

'Sid, I'm not sure about this. Looks very yellow to me.'

'My dad used to swear by the stuff. Bloody wonderful it was for ticks and fleas. He used it on his roses, and for treating the garden fence.'

'That's as may be, but is it supposed to fizz like that? I'm sure this broom handle was longer when we started. You should have let me buy a few gallons of Jeyes fluid.'

'Waste of money. What we have here is Tobacco Jones' Coal Tar Drench, or as near as dammit. They'll be no fleas in the cheap seats now, Mr Bamforth. Not after I've squirted it about.'

'I'm worried they'll be no cheap seats, neither. I'm not convinced. Having fleas is one thing, but I reckon this stuff could rip the shell off a turtle.'

'Go on, let me splash it around in the basement,' Sid said, rubbing the bite marks on his stomach. 'I reckon it's more than fleas we've got down there. When I switch the lights on, the dust moves.'

'Good heavens, Sid. You're making the Galaxy sound like some Victorian slum. We've only been open a year. The place should be squeaky clean. What are you trying to tell me? That fleas are the least of our troubles?'

Sid Bottle looked his boss squarely in the face. 'All I know is that it ain't mice. Mice leave droppings. What's down there leaves pellets, and that's not natural. I've heard things, Mr Bamforth, scratches and rustlings in the shadows. If we don't do something now, who knows what might happen.'

'They'd better not be nibbling away at my Wurlitzer, Sid. I'm warning you. You go down there and kill anything that moves!'

## Chapter Eleven

For the lucky few who could afford the adventure, driving a car through the Derbyshire moors in the early 1930s was like playing Russian roulette with nature. Roads vanished into tracks and tracks disappeared into bogs, and everywhere there were sheep; ragged, rain-drenched sheep that rewarded unwary drivers with bumps, bleats and tufts of wool in the radiator. There was thick fog too, and tumble-down gritstone walls, and to add to the fun, a new piece of legislation allowing cars to be driven at any speed. Chance meetings with sheep were now more colourful affairs, involving the squeal of brakes, broken windscreens and a less than Golden Fleece splattered across the upholstery. Chance meetings with pedestrians were worse.

At least in Grubdale, you were safe. You could count the cars passing through on two hands, or two hands and a foot on market day. Most were of such an age that speed was a fantasy, a hearty swipe with a handbag being enough to bring them to heel, but today was an exception. A large sign on the outskirts of town boasted 'Grubdale Rewards Careful Drivers,' but whatever the reward offered, the driver of the small green van seemed unimpressed. He sat hunched at the wheel; his nose almost pressed to the glass as he thumped the klaxon. He drove through the town square, swerving to avoid the busy shoppers, his language betraying the words 'Happy Harry' painted in balloon lettering on each side of the vehicle.

'And the same to you!' shouted a certain Mrs Froggat, shocked at the profanities and hitting out with her umbrella as the van passed. 'You common little man!'

'What are you trying to do? Kill us all?' shouted a Mr Peabody, banging his fist on the bonnet. 'And learn some bloody manners!' he swore, throwing his bag of eggs at the driver. 'Idiot!'

Harry Renfield pressed hard on the klaxon. 'Get out of the way!' he cried, and as for being called an idiot, Harry let the insult fly over his head, much like the eggs now splattered on the cobblestones. He'd been called many things in the past, and 'idiot' wasn't half bad in comparison. Harry pressed his foot on the accelerator and drove the van around the last of the angry shoppers. He needed to be far away from Grubdale, and sooner the better. No one, not even a stupid pedestrian stepping out into the street, was going to get in his way, and as if on cue, Elsie Tapp appeared from around the corner.

Elsie Tapp's timing was terrible, worse than a mayfly who'd decided to sleep in. She was all pinched feet and flapping arms as she stumbled into view, still mouthing the words 'Big!' 'Teeth!' and 'Monster!' at the top of her voice. She'd seen something terrifying in the shrubbery, and scared for her life, had fled as fast as her roly-poly figure could manage - down the hill, around the corner and into the street.

'Look out!' someone screamed, and the unfortunate Miss Tapp found herself pulled backwards by the collar of her coat. 'You could've been killed!' the voice said, as Elsie tripped and sat down with a bump on the pavement, watching in horror as a green van sped past, only inches away from her toes.

Bruised, confused and embarrassed from the fall, Elsie kept a tight hold of her shopping bag. She tried to mouth some suitable reply but could manage only a squeak and a sob as she burst into tears. It wasn't like Elsie to cry; the emotional stuff she usually saved for her books. Her characters sobbed and swooned to order, but the most Elsie would allow herself was an occasional snuffle and a squeeze of a hand. Now she felt as fragile as one of her heroines; used, abused and thrown to the streets, and with no sight of a highwayman for three chapters at least. Princess Peaches pushed her head out of the bag and licked Elsie's cheek, making her cry even more.

'Give me your hand. Come on, love. Up you come. You've had a nasty tumble.'

Elsie stared at a pair of polished black shoes and the spotless turn-ups of a woollen suit.

'Hope I didn't hurt you,' the voice said. 'Don't know my own strength, that's my problem. But you would've been squashed flat. That idiot was stopping for no one. Bloody motorists think they own the place. Give me a horse and cart any day. You know where you are with a horse and cart.'

Elsie raised her eyes and looked at the smiling, rosy-cheeked face of the landlord of the Cheddar Cheese.

'Well I never, it's the lady with the pink poodle. Bob Furness, remember? Good Samaritan, publican and purveyor of salt beef sandwiches.'

The kindly Bob offered his hand and managed to pull Elsie to her feet. 'There,' he said as if completing some massive task. 'No damage done.' He was about to brush the pavement dirt from her coat but thought better of it. There was a look in the woman's eyes that wrestlers shared, just before the forearm smash and a half-Nelson. Bob flourished the pocket handkerchief in the air as though it had been his intention all along. 'Flies,' he said. 'Can't stand them.'

Elsie stared at Mr Furness, not sure if she should thank the man or give him a piece of her mind, but still in shock, Elsie could only snuffle and sob.

'Oh dear, this won't do, this won't do at all. Let me buy you a brandy. I insist, best drink I can think of for calming the nerves.'

The horse looked over the wall and snorted in disgust. She was of a respectable age with the madness of youth behind her, and apart from a brisk trot around the thistles and the promise of a peppermint, her days were slow and reassuring. Outside of her field, life ran to a different clock, one wound up tight and with the alarm set for every half-hour. If only it weren't so noisy. The horse stamped her feet in frustration. How was she to get any peace with all this fuss and commotion? Noisy cows and police cars, excitable women, and now this - a green box with wheels hurtling along the country lane as though being chased by all the horseflies in Derbyshire. The horse flicked her tail and shook her head. Let the world dash about, but let it happen away from her field, and without this horrid red smoke billowing around her feet.

Harry Renfield coughed and spluttered, his eyes smarting from the red mist filling his van. The wooden chest had started to leak smoke, and this time the smoke smelt sour, no longer sweet and entrancing, but like chicken soup on the turn. The creature was awake and upset.

'You can stop that nonsense!' he shouted, wiping the condensation off the windscreen with his sleeve. 'I'm not letting you out!'

Harry had nailed the chest shut back at the house, and had wrapped some old rope around the box for good measure. 'Consider our friendship over!' he'd whispered, manhandling it into the back of the van. 'I'm taking you back to the sea.'

The creature knew different. It could read Harry's mind and picture the can of fuel by his feet. The smoke turned from red to deep brown, and the voices in Harry's head changed.

'It's no good; I'm not listening!' Harry shouted, and took a swig of whiskey for courage. 'You can witter on all you like. You took advantage of my good nature, and…'

Harry gulped down some more whisky.

'…you killed my goldfish!'

The voices in his head were far from apologetic. They spoke of many things, of knives and cleavers and what Harry would look like on a butchers slab. Harry pressed his foot down hard on the accelerator, urging the van to go faster.

'You're wasting your time. I told you, I'm not listening!'

But Harry was and took the third swig from the bottle to stop shaking.

'She'll be coming 'round the mountain when she comes!' he sang. 'She'll be coming round the mountain when she...'

The voices added new lines to the song, making Harry swerve wildly on the road.

'Filthy, dirty beast!' he swore. 'I'll be well rid of you!'

Harry dropped the bottle by his feet and gripped the wheel with both hands. He needed all his concentration to steer the van back on course. 'God save our gracious king. Long live our noble king. God save our king!' he sang and swung the wheel to the right, but bad luck stuck to Harry like toilet paper to a shoe. The van skidded around the corner and sped down the lane to where half an hour earlier the two policemen had stood on guard.

There was hardly time to scream.

It is said that death takes many forms, although drunks say the silliest of things, especially the tearful ones with photographs of their wives. For poor Happy Harry, death was the body of a cow in the middle of the road and with what looked like an Egyptian mummy sitting on its back. Harry stamped on the brakes, but it was all too quick and all too late. The van careered into the side of the cow and threw its unlucky driver out through the windscreen and onto the bonnet.

The horse strolled up the field to the source of the terrible noise, and looked over the gap in the wall. That's what happens when people rush and dash about; they get bent into all sorts of shapes. Being a curious horse, she pressed close to the wall and stretched her neck over the stones to get a more unobstructed view. How terrible, and such a pity. One man was in such a rush he'd dressed in bandages, just in case. And as for the other…

The horse stepped back, deciding some shapes were better left unseen. The green box with the spinning wheels was still alive and sounded very angry, leaking smoke and making the noise of a stallion kicking down a door. The old mare twitched her tail and shivered. The last thing she needed was a stallion, let alone one stuck in a box, and definitely, quite definitely and never to be told otherwise, not one that snorted smoke. She whinnied loud in protest, then turned tail and trotted away to the safety of the blackthorn bushes at the bottom of the field. There she could spend the rest of the day in peace, leaving all this terrible excitement to others.

'Here, drink this.'

Bob Furness placed the largest glass of brandy this side of a bottle into Elsie Tapp's hand and made sure the coal fire in the room was stoked and burning. It was the least he could do after pulling the unfortunate woman to the ground, but then he had saved her life. Bob prodded and stirred the fire with a poker, rattling the metal against the grate. 'A thank you wouldn't go amiss,' he thought, 'for the brandy at least.'

The two of them were in the snug bar of the Cheddar Cheese, a small but cosy back room popular in the evening with the various widows and spinsters of the town or, as Bob Furness had christened them, 'the gin and bitters.' Here gossip flew back and forth with the excitement of a Wimbledon final. Reputations were won, dissected and thrown to the floor, but only after much consideration and studying of the evidence. During the day the room was empty, the lunchtime trade limited to the lounge and saloon bar at the front.

Elsie was in shock. Her hands were shaking, and conversation was proving so fraught with tears that silence perhaps was the better option. She sat in a battered leather armchair, her beloved poodle on her lap, staring at the large measure of brandy in her hand. Princess Peaches, feeling light-headed and ready for a song, stared at the drink too – all three glasses of the strange liquid and all out of focus.

'I'll walk you to the police station when you're ready,' Bob Furness said. 'The missus can take over here till I'm back.'

Elsie managed a smile and a nod, but at the expense of spilling a good measure of Grubdale's most excellent brandy down her sleeve. A ruddy-faced woman leant over the counter of the serving hatch and smiled. 'Bob's told me what happened,' she said. 'The big lump. Walk you to the police station, my eye. Take no notice of the silly bugger; he can go on his own. You stay there love, for as long as you like. And I've another brandy here when you've finished that one. You look like you've seen a ghost.'

Elsie found her voice. 'It wasn't a ghost I saw,' she cried, then downed her drink in two gulps. 'It was a dragon!'

There was silence, all the chat and commotion of the pub stopped in an instant as though someone had thrown a switch.

'It's true; I saw a dragon. There, I said it.'

A few faces appeared behind the ruddy-faced woman, all looking over her shoulder and into the snug. Elsie glanced at each of them in turn, from the landlord to his wife and with the nosey customers in between

'You can stop staring at me like that,' she said. 'I'm not mad.'

Bob Furness took the empty glass of brandy from Elsie's hand and passed it to his wife.

'Of course not. No one's saying you are.'

'I know what I saw, I tell you. It was a dragon.'

There was a collective sigh, as though everyone but Elsie had the same idea, one that involved strong coffee, pats on the back and knowing looks where Grubdale's finest brandy was concerned. It wasn't everyone who could drink the amber liquid, as many a charge sheet in the police station could prove. Even alcoholics preferred furniture polish given a choice, especially when the choice was Grubdale's Special Reserve in a bottle shaped like a turnip.

Elsie was handed a new glass, this time full of sparkling clear liquid and a slice of lemon. Elsie took a sip, shivered and placed it back on the table.

'What on earth am I doing? I can't sit here; I must warn the police.'

Elsie tried to stand but came over all peculiar.

'Oh dear,' she said, falling back on the leather couch. 'What must you think of me?'

'I think you shouldn't be going around the town talking about dragons, that's what I think.'

Elsie looked around the room to see who'd spoken and noticed an untidy-looking woman sitting in the corner. 'I'm sorry?' she asked. 'What did you say?'

The woman leaned forward out of the shadows and pushed an empty glass aside. 'I said you shouldn't be talking about dragons, not 'ere. Dragons are a sore point, for those that choose to remember, that is.'

Elsie recognised the face immediately. It was the excitable lady with the pointing finger from the day before.

'Remember what?' she asked.

The woman stared at Elsie for a few seconds then stood up and walked somewhat unsteadily, over to her table. 'I never forget a face,' she said, pulling a stool away from the table and sitting down in front of Elsie. 'Or a pink poodle.'

'Really? Well, other than you poking a finger at me the other day and shouting "J'accuse!" we've never met. You've mistaken me for someone else.'

'Pffft!' The woman tapped her nose with her finger and tried to wink, but not sure which eye should be closed, or which should be open, merely looked as though she was about to sneeze. 'The name will come to me in a minute,' she said, before picking Elsie's drink up and knocking it back in a single swallow. 'Bleaugh! What muck is this?'

'Lemonade. You need to be run over in the street before they give you brandy.'

The woman stared at the glass, first with one eye and then the other, turning the glass around in her hand as though hunting for clues. 'It needs gin, preferably a bottle,' she said before staring at Elsie with renewed interest. 'Big and butch, it's coming to me now.'

'I beg your pardon?'

'I'm getting warm, aren't I? I can tell from your face.'

'I hope you weren't referring to me with that last comment.'
'Aha!'

The strange woman clapped her hands and rocked back on her stool, almost falling off in her excitement at guessing the name. 'I know it! I have it now!' she cried. 'Demetrios!'

'What!'

'Demetrios! It's Demetrios, isn't it? There, I told you – I never forget a face!' The woman folded her arms in triumph, pleased at proving her point.

Elsie stared back, her mouth wide open in shock. She'd met some rude, unpredictable people in her time, but this drunken virago was the worst. Temporarily lost for words and contemplating a brisk slap across the woman's face with her shopping bag, Elsie snatched the empty glass and slammed it down on the table.

'Well,' she said. 'You're hardly a goddess of spring yourself! Demetrios? Really? I've never been so insulted!'

Elsie struggled to her feet and pushed the table forcibly away. 'And just for the record,' she said, trying not to shout her words. 'I prefer the name I was christened with…Elsie!'

The strange woman burst into laughter.

'A good day to you, too!' snapped Elsie and holding her shopping bag tight to her chest she walked unsteadily but with purpose, across the slate floor.

'Not you, you idiot! I meant your bloody poodle!'

Elsie stopped and checked to see if her beloved poodle was in her bag. Two bright eyes stared back and a small wet nose sneezed. 'You're mad, completely mad!' she cried. 'Demetrios is a ridiculous name for a Princess!'

'That may be so, I never said it was proper, I just remembered it, that's all.'

Elsie reached for the door then thought better of leaving the pub without thanking Mr Furness and his wife. She turned her head and trying not to look at the rude woman, called out to the landlord.

'You've been very kind, both of you, but I really must be going.'

'Are you sure you'll be alright?' asked Mrs Furness from behind the bar. 'Bob can walk you to the police station or wherever you're staying. It'll be no trouble.'

'It's quite alright. I'm not an invalid. You've done enough, really you have. Here, I think this will cover the drinks.'

Elsie placed a handful of coins on the nearest table.

'Haven't you forgotten something?' asked the strange woman.

'I have no wish to speak to you, thank you,' snapped Elsie.

'Hark at Miss High and Mighty. Well if you're going, you might as well take your dog…'

'That is precisely what I'm doing.'

'…before he sets fire to the curtains.'

Elsie froze, not daring to turn her head, knowing only too well what creature sat on the battered leather sofa, wagging its tail. She looked inside her shopping bag and tried to smile at her beloved Princess, now struggling to peer over the top. 'There, there,' she whispered, trying to calm the excitable poodle, but Princess had only one idea in mind and one that reeked of nature and convivial pursuits.

Demetrios barked and, for the brief moment that Elsie looked his way, decided to impersonate a dragon and scorch the upholstery. Elsie tried to scream, but all she could manage as she fell in a faint to the floor was a tiny burp from the lemonade.

Smoke billowed around Harry Renfield's van, thick smoke that crept over the top of the doors till even the brightly painted panels vanished from sight. It was as though Harry had driven headfirst into a pit of red candyfloss and had stayed to eat the lot. Only the roof remained uncovered, bleached and rusting but providing the perfect table for two inquisitive crows to strut around and peck at the paintwork.

Wiser crows kept to the branches of an old elm tree. Smoke meant kippered wings, a racking cough and boiled eggs if you were unlucky; but this smoke was different. Besides its peculiar colour, the smoke smelled of toffee, and every bird from here to Frogwallop knew the dangers of toffee. One peck of a discarded caramel and that was your beak glued shut for a month. No, the general opinion was that ruby red, toffee-smelling smoke was best left alone unless you were a few feathers short of a duster.

The two crows on the roof of Harry's van were more than a few feathers short; when it came to common sense, they were as bald as a plucked chicken. They hopped from one rusty patch to another, pecking at flakes of paint but oblivious to the red smoke lapping over their feet, or the warnings squawked from a nearby tree.

Something pecked back.

The two crows raised their heads, then being the intelligent, inquisitive creatures they were, continued as though nothing had happened. But there it was again, tapping from the underside of the roof, a constant noise as though a giant chick was trying to hatch from an enormous egg. The two crows cocked their heads and listened as the tapping grew louder and faster. This was a new puzzle, but over in the corner, there was a new flake of paint to peck and pull at.

## A TOUCH OF SPLEEN

The wiser crows, high above the van and from the safety of the old elm, squawked even louder. They jumped from branch to branch, desperate to catch the other two's attention. They could see shapes in the red smoke, quick, slithery forms like eels in mud.

A hand smashed through the roof of the van and snatched the first crow, pulling it down into the depths before the poor creature knew what happened. The second crow was next, guilty of looking into the hole and saying 'Hello' before being grabbed by the neck and snatched out of sight. The wiser crows looked on in shock, wide-eyed and open-beaked. They were no strangers to death. A crow's life was short at the best of times, and mostly punctuated with shot. If the toffees didn't get you, the farmer would, and if by some strange twist of fate a crow survived, there was always the cold, the sneeze and the long drop down. But this? This was something new. This was a 'snatch and grab,' and a 'munch and swallow,' for whatever hid inside the clouds of red smoke was making short work of this little snack.

The sweet smell of the smoke grew worse, with whatever it covered losing shape or disappearing altogether. There was no trace of the van, or the dead cow or the unfortunate gentleman in the bandages. All that remained was a swirling red column, like clay on a giant potter's wheel, moulded into the vague outline of a man. It was all too much for the crows.

The vague outline roared in anger. It was a cry so loud as to scatter the remaining birds in every direction, a cry half human and half fingernails on slate; a cry typical of evil sorcerers everywhere, especially ones drenched in guano so fresh you could sieve out the pips.

'Make way!' shouted a voice in the distance.

'Can't stop!' shouted another.

'Tiger in pursuit!'

Two constables sped past on bikes, their legs pumping vigorously in an attempt to escape.

'Don't stand in the middle of the road! You'll cause a crash!'

If only they'd looked more carefully, they would have seen something far more deadly than a tiger in pursuit. Tigers, after all, are just pussycats fed up with drinking milk. Evil sorcerers, on the other hand, are maniacs fed up with life, other people's mostly and witches' in particular.

The tall figure stepped out of the smoke and brushed away what he could from the folds of his cloak; a task made all the easier by an excess of hands. Two were too few; four not enough but six were ideal; just the right number to clean, polish and pick feathers from his mouth. Any more and it was impossible to get three cardigans to fit.

'Spleen!' whispered a fashionable woman in silks and feathers, hiding behind a wall for cover. 'I knew he was still alive!'

## Chapter Twelve

Light years away from the hustle and bustle of Grubdale, on a small planet a touch to the left and a jiggle down from the buckle on Orion's belt, the flagship Emily P lay at anchor. It was the second day of celebrations, but only just. The morning had brought a change of wind and with it a change of heart. It was the fermented fish. Fish Gut Bay was famous for its fermented fish, but no matter how delicious the taste, there was no escaping the smell. There are few words to describe the overpowering stench of a barrel of fermented fish; most are unprintable, and a few are punishable by death. Some sailors swear by the stuff, swallowing bowl after bowl and shouting for more, just not the sailors on the Emily P. The sailors on the Emily P could hardly face a greasy egg, and now the morning breeze had put paid to their festivities quicker than a knock on the door and a shout of 'Police!' Even a small boat sent out for provisions was making poor headway, the allure of the open ocean seeming a far safer bet.

Back on board the flagship, a few of the younger members of the crew were feeling worse for wear. A pirate's life may be preferable to school, but the endless swell of the ocean and the salty sea air were taking their toll.

'More beer, Mr Mildew?' asked a pale-faced Mr Squint, the two youths hanging onto the edge of a large table as though someone had pulled away their chairs.

Mildew studied his companion closely, very closely; the sort of close examination that precedes a burp and a rush to the rigging. The young lad shook his head slowly and covered the top of his tankard with both hands.

'It's a bit chewy,' Squint said, pouring a splash or two into his own mug, but mostly over the floor.

'Who would have thought it; you, me and green-face Pursglove over there, as pirates! This is a proper education, innit! All the same, I ain't a clue where we are. It's hardly Bognor-bloody-Regis.'

Squint had adopted a cockney accent, thinking it more grown-up and suited for a life at sea. Distant memories of reading Treasure Island had coloured his vocabulary, although far from being considered a jolly sailor, frequent chants of 'yo-ho-ho and a barrel of rum' had him marked down as an alcoholic.

'It's not Bognor, and it's not bloody London neither. Who do you think you are, the Pearly King? Talk proper like we do.'

The green-faced Pursglove had woken up to a pounding headache and was in no mood for Squint's silliness. He raised his head from the table, took one sniff of the morning air then turned noticeably green. 'I hate being a bloody pirate!' he said before trying to get back to sleep.

'No you don't, you love it. That's just the grog talking. Get some breakfast down ya!'

At the mention of breakfast, someone slid a plate of cold fried eggs down the table. Squint looked at the floppy whites, and greasy yolks and all thoughts of being Cockney vanished like the mist.

'Oh god, that's me for the bucket,' he said in a broad Derbyshire accent before sliding the plate back to the other end of the table. 'Worse than school dinners.'

Mildew braved a word or two. 'I miss school dinners.'

Pursglove hit the table with his fist. 'Give it a rest, Mildew! You miss school dinners, you miss the school cook, and you miss your boring life at boring Grubdale Towers! But we're not at Grubdale Towers, are we? We're not even on the same planet. We're on a ship parked outside some rotten fish factory in some grotty harbour at the arse end of nowhere. So quit your bellyaching, accept the fact you're a pirate and let me get some bloody sleep!'

Squint winked at Mildew and mimed drinking from a tankard. 'One pint wonder,' he whispered, conveniently forgetting he was a two and a half pint genius himself.

A thin sparrow of a woman skipped past, her jacket and dress covered in crumbs and wine stains. 'Sleep?' She said and smiled at the three, her happy nature as much sweet sherry as personality. 'Who said anything about sleep? You should be singing and dancing. My, but you sailors are a dull lot. Spleen's dead, the war's nearly over, and we haven't even started on the sandwiches.'

Bethesda Chubb, scourge of the Coral Seas and a bad woman to know in a paddling pool, thumped the big box of lights and switches. 'SPLEEN'S

# A TOUCH OF SPLEEN

ALIVE?' she cried, trying to return the dials to their correct setting. 'WHAT DO YOU MEAN SPLEEN'S ALIVE?'

A faint voice spoke out of the brass funnel on top, a voice so soft as to make Bethesda wonder if she'd smashed the volume control as well.

'Grubdale to Wellington Boot,' whispered the voice. 'There's no need to shout, over.'

'THERE'S EVERY REASON TO SHOUT!'

The lights on the box flickered and changed colour. It was as though Grubdale had panicked at the other end and was flicking every switch and twisting every knob.

'Damn it all, Bethesda, are you trying to get me killed? I mean Wellington Boot, I mean…Oh honestly, do we have to talk like this?

'The truth is Bethesda, if you insist on shouting and making this horrid machine buzz and squawk then Spleen's going to hear, and if that happens, I'll be as dead as a dodo, or whatever the name was of that delicious bird we had for dinner.'

'Polly,' Bethesda said, before sitting back in her chair and taking a series of deep breaths. She'd been warned about stress. She'd been warned about drinking like a hippo and eating meat with no vegetables, but what could she do? She was a pirate and lived a pirate's life, however short.

'Grubdale to Wellington Boot, are you there? Over.'

Bethesda tried counting to ten but at five she was fit to burst, and at seven she'd kicked a plate of bacon sandwiches flying across the room.

'Yes, Rowena. I'm still here.'

'Thank heavens; I thought this stupid machine was on the blink. Listen, we have to whisper. Spleen's close by and I'm hiding in some bushes. Honestly, you wouldn't believe what's happened to the school. It's just rubble and nettles. I've had to wave my wand about just to sit down.'

'It can't be Spleen. It's impossible. You saw the Behemoth blow up. Not even a ship's biscuit could survive that explosion.'

'I tell you it's him! He's got six arms, hasn't he? Who else do we know with six arms and a face like a bluebottle, apart from those naughty gods in that temple at Kumquat!'

'Shhh!'

'Don't you shush me, Miss Chubb! I'm the one hiding in the bushes, not you! And I'll tell you another thing; you'd better come here soon 'cos I'm not tackling Mr Spleen on my own. No sir-ee, not even with this wyrm.'

Bethesda sat bolt upright and breathed deeply, very deeply - a ritual her doctor prescribed for moments like these: deep breaths, a large glass of liver salts and a choir outside the window singing the love song of the blue whale.

'So, Grubdale has Cuttlefish,' she whispered, the anger in her voice freezing each syllable.

'Stop calling him Cuttlefish; he's a royal wyrm. Of course Grubdale has Cuttlefish. How else do you think I got here, by my own calculations? I can't even time an egg, let alone find one.'

'You and that bloody egg! I told you it was a wild goose chase!'

'It's nothing of the sort. The dragon's egg is here, just buried by rubble. It was in a display case in the school, and I can distinctly remember a bird sitting on top of the egg, reading a newspaper. It's so obvious now I come to think of it - like the old books say; a wyrm's egg leaking magic. Just a pity I didn't realise the significance at the time. I bet there are flocks of birds around here bored of something to read.'

'You could always ask them.'

'Oh very funny…mind you, now I come to think of it.'

'Rowena, forget the egg! It's Spleen we need to worry about.'

'I've brought the wyrm to sniff out the egg; simple really, like pigs and truffles. I know the dragon's egg is around here somewhere. I need to find my bearings.'

'Rowena, listen, this is important. Keep the wyrm out of sight till we get there.'

'And it's a female egg, I'm sure. Male eggs wouldn't be that clever, leaking magic and teaching birds how to read.'

'Please Rowena, enough about the egg!'

'And a female wyrm is just what our young drake here needs; keep his mind off everything flammable.'

'Wellington Boot to Grubdale! Wellington Boot to Grubdale! Will you jolly well shut up!'

'Beg your pardon, I'm sure.'

Bethesda drummed her fingers on the side of the table then gulped down a jigger of rum. Conversations with Rowena improved with alcohol. 'There'll be time enough to find your egg,' she said. 'But we have Spleen to deal with. Everyone here thinks he's dead.'

'Well he's not, is he. I told you as much, days ago. Now we've got proof.'

'You'll have to follow him.'

'What?'

'You'll have to follow him till we get there. Otherwise, how do we know where he is?'

'I don't like the sound of that. You should see what he's done to a cow. There's hardly as much as a hoof left, and he's had two crows for pudding!'

'We'll be as quick as we can.'

## A TOUCH OF SPLEEN

'Quicker than that, please. I don't fancy being the cheese course.'

'But there is a slight problem; the wyrmhole. Where is it?'

'Oh, I don't know. I can't make head nor tail of the professor's charts. There are hundreds of holes; it's a wonder we don't drain away. I just got the wyrm to make his own; it seemed the easiest thing at the time. I pointed at the stars, shouted 'giddy-up!' and hey ho, I landed in a bunch of nettles. Simple really.'

'But how do we know which hole to use?'

'Well you can hear me, surely that means something. If I'm talking through a hole, then why not follow my voice and crawl through. Isn't that how physics works?'

'Don't ask me. I'm strictly potions and pills.'

'So am I, and hopeless with sums. I tell you what, I'll squirt some of my best perfume, and you can follow the smell. There, see; I'm not just a pretty face.'

Bethesda looked around for a second glass of rum. If Rowena was fishing for compliments then only alcohol would do.

The fashionable Miss Carp flicked the main switch on the talking machine to 'off,' then pushed the contraption back into the bushes, hiding the various wires and fiddly bits as best she could. 'Well,' she said, muttering to herself as she dusted her dress clean with a handful of bracken. 'If Bethesda thinks I'm going to follow Spleen like some amateur detective skulking in the shadows, then she's a bigger fool than I thought. Two arms against six, and each of them as sharp as a sickle; I don't think so.'

She rubbed the bracken against a stubborn smear of soil, then seeing how she'd made it worse and added a smudge of chlorophyll, Rowena decided to trust to magic and colour the whole of her outfit an emerald green. Rowena took pride in her appearance. She was a senior witch, and there were standards to be maintained, and as her physical looks started to droop and wrinkle with time, her wardrobe followed an opposite path, one rich in feathers, furs and unfortunate creatures pinned to her hat. 'Oh, to hell with it,' she said, looking down at the green silks and ribbons on her skirt. 'I look like a tatty cabbage!' With the second click of her fingers, the green turned into stripes of pink and cream, and Rowena stepped out of the shrubbery and into the sun, the very image of an Italian dessert.

'DEMETRIOS!' she called, then winced, realising she was supposed to be quiet. 'Dammit,' she whispered as loud as she could. 'Where are you now?'

Instead of her small pink companion, a giant yellow one trotted out of the bushes and nudged her from behind.

'Careful, McTavish! You'll have me over on my face!'

For some reason known only to herself, Rowena had christened the yellow wyrm McTavish, a term of affection for when he was good. When the wyrm was bad and setting fire to the countryside, she called him other Celtic names full of phlegm and invective. But today the wyrm was on his best behaviour and worthy of the plaid.

'It seems our little pink friend has disappeared, and today of all days. What is it with him?'

'Him!' repeated the wyrm and rested his head on Rowena's shoulder.

'You don't think he's run off after that floozy, do you?' Rowena asked, scratching the wyrm's chin. 'She was no bigger than a ball of fluff!'

'Fluff!' repeated the wyrm.

'I shall be very annoyed if he has. I was counting on him being useful today. I was relying on his nose.'

'Nose!' purred the wyrm, enjoying his chin being scratched.

'Hey, don't you fall asleep. I've a job for you, too.'

Rowena patted the wyrm on his snout then retrieved a map from the bushes and unrolled it on the ground. 'Hey ho,' she sang as she placed a stone at each corner. 'Now, where do we start?'

Rowena stood staring at the map and then out across the moss-covered bricks and stones where the school once stood. Three years had passed. The prince was in his teens and shaping up well to his duties; even Squint had matured into a reasonable human being, but compared to the ruins of the school, they had hardly aged at all. It was as though a generation had passed. She closed her eyes and tried to visualise the layout of the buildings, to see the school again as she had for the first time, in all its horror.

The wyrm nudged her from behind.

'McTavish! Stop that! I'm trying to think! If I'm not mistaken,' Rowena said with a flash of inspiration, 'I believe the main steps are over there.'

'Steps!' repeated the wyrm.

'And if those are the steps, then that means the main tower should be behind and to the left.'

'Left!' said the wyrm.

'The museum below and to the right.'

'Right!'

'And that means somewhere beneath that pile of rubble lies our egg!'

'Bacon!' cried the wyrm.

'No, silly. I said "egg."'

'Bacon!' repeated the wyrm, with some insistence.

'Please, don't tell me you're hungry. You've already eaten your sheep.'

# A TOUCH OF SPLEEN

'Sheep, bleaugh!' protested the wyrm and spat out a few clumps of wool at Rowena's feet. 'Bacon, yum!'

'Surely you can wait a while? It's not as though you're dying of the hunger now, is it?'

The wyrm placed a claw to his brow and closed his eyes. 'Dying!' he said in a voice faint with hunger but rich in amateur dramatics. 'Dying, nearly dead! Bacon, yum!'

'Really?'

'Dying, need bacon!'

'I'm sure you do, but bacon is strictly off the menu, as are, and look at me when I'm talking to you, policemen on bikes.'

The wyrm started to giggle and covered his mouth. 'Ding, Ding! Arrrgh!' he said, then gave a near-perfect rendition of two policemen on bikes meeting a dragon for the first time.

'Yes, very funny, I don't think,' said Rowena setting off in the direction of the stones. 'No one's supposed to know we're here, and those poor policemen will be back with reinforcements, mark my words. We haven't much time.'

'Ding, Ding! Arrrgh!' repeated the wyrm, then still giggling like a schoolgirl, the creature followed Rowena, scrambling across the stones and broken brickwork to where she stood.

'There,' she said, pointing with her parasol to a large pile of slates and stones. 'That's where we'll start. Let's see what's under all this rubble.'

## Chapter Thirteen

The Reverend Cross was standing in the doorway of the Pig and Shovel, a witness to the commotion in the high street and feeling more uneasy by the minute.

'There goes another police car with its bell ringing.' He said. 'I knew they'd be trouble.'

It wasn't every day that Grubdale's finest were put to the test, and the count so far was two police cars and a few pale-faced constables on bikes struggling to keep up.

'All that for a half-eaten cow? I don't think so.'

He took a sip from a large whisky and soda and licked his lips. 'It's started, Hilary; the old black magic, and we're in the thick of it.'

'Tigers!' shouted an excitable mother from the other side of the street. She was pushing her pram as fast as she could along the pavement. 'Mr Possett from the fish shop says its tigers!'

The vicar dismissed this call to panic with a raised eyebrow and a raised glass of whisky in salute.

'Thank you, Nancy,' he shouted. 'Safe trip home.'

Captain Dashing looked over his friend's shoulder. 'Tigers my arse!' he said, feeling a little cavalier on the drink. 'That's just to shut us up.'

'I'm sure it is Hilary dear, but the word 'tiger' may explain the frightened looks from those poor constables. Fancy facing one of those man-eaters with just a truncheon and a bell on your bicycle. Doesn't bear thinking about.'

'They'll have guns.'

'I should certainly hope so, and a crucifix and the good book. Still, there's nothing we can do. Might as well have another drink, what? Steady the nerves. Look how brave we are on the Scottish juice. I feel as though I can take on the world and that dreadful woman myself.'

## A TOUCH OF SPLEEN

'I'd need another bottle,' interrupted the captain, and vanished back into the pub to see about doubling his courage.

The vicar turned to follow, but curiosity held him back. Something peculiar was happening a few yards down the street outside the Cheddar Cheese. 'Well fancy that,' he said, clipping his spectacles onto his nose and squinting through the greasy finger-marks. A group of excitable women were laughing and jostling each other as they tried to squeeze their way through the front door of the pub.

'Hmmpff! I don't like the look of that. Always a bad sign if a place is popular with the ladies. Have to mind your manners and worse.'

The vicar shivered, remembering groups of ladies in the past, particularly ones wearing tweed and flying through the air. 'It'd better not happen here,' he said. 'Not in the Pig and Shovel. Not in this last bastion of the free man.'

The vicar rather liked this speech, standing in the doorway and thinking of Henry V, but it was a quiet rebellion, and hardly Shakespeare. 'Witches!' he said, then gulped back the last of his drink and retreated to the safety of a quiet game of dominoes. 'Why does it always have to be witches?'

Elsie Tapp had said something. She wasn't sure what she'd said or who she'd said it to, but she'd definitely said something.

'Felicity Merryweather, who would believe it,' whispered a kindly voice.

'Oh dear,' thought Elsie. 'Did I say that?'

It appeared she had, and more besides, and all in her sleep. Elsie opened her eyes to find herself lying on an old settee in an unfamiliar room, surrounded by smiling, unfamiliar women. 'Ouch,' she said, rubbing the side of her head, and as she gazed at the kindly faces staring back, the room seemed to shrink as more people crowded in and gathered around.

'We've all your books,' said one. 'Haven't we girls, and every edition from The Goose Girl and the Highwayman to The Countess and The Hussar.'

There was a sigh of pleasure at the mention of the Hussar. Mr Darcy was fine for a pleasant afternoon, and Heathcliffe for a wintery evening with the radio switched off, but for passion, damp shirts and tight cherry breeches, Felicity Merryweather's Hussar had them all licked.

'I've your recipes!' shouted someone from the back, waving a copy of Good Housekeeping, then apologised and promised to shut up.

'Could you sign my book, Miss Merryweather? Just a sentence will do – To my very special fan, with thanks, Felicity.'

'Oh yes, could you sign mine!'

'And mine! Hey, stop pushing and let me through. I've been a fan of Miss Merryweather since before you were born!'

Elsie wasn't sure what to make of this last gesture of affection; successful romance author she may be, but child prodigy at the age of four she most certainly was not.

'Ladies please, let poor Miss Merryweather breathe! Come on, out you go the lot of you. There's room in the snug to chat. And guess what, ladies. You can buy drinks there too.'

'At last some sense,' thought Elsie, although the kind lady giving the orders seemed permanently attached to her hand and rather too fond of wafting the smelling salts around to make a point. Elsie sneezed and pushed the offending bottle of ammonia aside. 'Take that awful stuff away, I'm not an invalid,' she managed to say, before feeling quite the opposite and laying her head back on the settee. 'Oh dear, where am I?'

The landlady smiled and squeezed her hand. 'You're still in the Cheddar Cheese love,' she said. 'But you took an awful tumble. I thought it best you lay down, especially after talking in your sleep. My, but I had no idea what an important guest you were. Felicity Merryweather indeed!'

'Tapp, the name's Elsie Tapp.'

The landlady winked and squeezed Elsie's hand again. 'Of course dear, so you said – "nom de plume" or however you pronounce it. But to be honest, as one friend to another, I'd stick with Felicity. You look more like an author with Felicity. And where do you think you're going?'

Elsie was struggling to get off the settee.

'I need to get back to my hotel. Really, I should. You and your husband have been very kind.'

'Don't be silly. This is Grubdale. We're a friendly lot here. My husband's phoned for the doctor. You've got a nasty bump on your head.'

'I'll be quite alright, honestly. It's just a scratch.'

The landlady was insistent. 'Nonsense, think of your career. My brother-in-law's not put pen to paper since bumping his head. Mind you, he never wrote much beforehand, but that's a different story. It's the thought that counts and you can never be too careful.'

Elsie shrugged her shoulders and lay back on the settee. There was little point in arguing. The landlady had set her mind to be the perfect host, and as much as it embarrassed Elsie, there was sense in what she'd said. She did feel dizzy, and one read such horrid things in the Daily Mail, of blood clots and brain fever and collapsing dead in the street.

'Can I get you something while I'm here? Another brandy, perhaps? On the house of course.'

Elsie shook her head, a little too vehemently perhaps, for politeness' sake.

'A cup of tea then, and a biscuit?'

'No thank you,' Elsie said, somewhat distracted by the hustle of commerce coming from the next room. Someone was selling tickets for a raffle, and to great success by the sound of it. Excited shouts and ringing of the till - the atmosphere was more like the floor of the London Stock Exchange than any pub Elsie knew.

'Oooh, they do make a noise,' the landlady said, closing the door with the back of her foot, but not before Elsie heard the words 'complete set', 'each copy signed' and 'none of your cheap stuff.'

There was an embarrassed silence, Elsie looking closely at the landlady and the landlady looking closely at her watch.

'I'm sure the doctor will be here soon. He's normally very prompt where the pub's concerned. He's seeing a nasty case of something or other up the road.'

Elsie wasn't convinced. She waited for the inevitable question.

'Of course, if you really want to know, I love your books too.'

'Really? That's kind of you to say,' Elsie said, smiling.

'I haven't read all of them, mind.'

'Well, I wouldn't expect many people have. I do seem to have written quite a lot.'

'I've all the 'The Princess in Pink books. I must have bought them ten times over as presents.'

The landlady's struggle was all too clear; she was fluffing up a cushion to place behind Elsie's head and getting carried away in the process. 'I hate to appear rude, and I know it's an awful cheek,' she said, twisting and thumping the cushion as though it had disgraced itself behind the settee, 'but you wouldn't mind signing them, would you? There's only six.'

There was a look of horror on Elsie's face, entirely out of proportion to the question asked. She struggled to her feet and searched frantically for her bag. 'Oh no! This is terrible!' she cried.

'Well, fair's fair; it's just a few scribbles I want. Not a bloody essay.'

'No! You don't understand. Princess Peaches, my poodle! Where is she?'

The Reverend Cross stared at his fifth whisky and soda and thought of food.

'Hideous invention, these pickled eggs,' he said, dipping a long spoon into a jar by his bed and fishing out another. 'What we need is a pork pie.'

What his friend the captain needed was a white flag. He sat slumped in an armchair and tried not to think of meat products. Thinking was bad, thinking was responsible for him being three-quarters full with drink and nursing a revolver in his lap.

'A touch of the dodo about this one,' the vicar said, dropping the shiny white object back into the vinegar and reaching for his drink. 'Not sure if I'm supposed to eat the damn thing or send it to a museum.'

Captain Dashing remained silent, his eyes fixed on a spot on the far wall as his imagination skipped merrily from meat products to pickled eggs, then back again. He was suffering the digestion of the damned with a stomach that threatened to tell the world he was on the Big Dipper at Blackpool.

It was the afternoon's fault, and much of the evening; a good many hours spent in the Pig and Shovel at the mercy of drink, cheap cigars and dry sandwiches. There had been dominoes and cards, sulks and harsh words, and all before six o'clock. The evening was much the same, perhaps a little louder and with the spots on the dominoes more difficult to count, but with each game played and each hand won, the prospect of an uncertain walk home had weighed heavily with the two friends. The vicar had broached the subject first.

'Hilary, old chap,' he'd said, grabbing the captain by the sleeve with some urgency. 'You see before you a fraud, a hollow man, a mere veneer.'

'Oh, I wouldn't say that. You're a swine with the cards, playing the two of trumps when I knew you had a heart, but I wouldn't say you're a fraud.'

Such mention of sharp practice had thrown the vicar off track. 'I did no such thing!' he'd said.

'You most certainly did!'

'I most certainly did not! And who are you to call foul? You're hopeless at whist. You shouted "rummy" in that last game and tried to hide the evidence with a cough!'

'Did I? Well, to be honest, dear boy, it's a wonder I didn't shout "Snap!" There were two Queen of Hearts played, one after the other, and don't tell me she was a diamond.'

'I won't; she was nothing of the sort. She was a Jack.'

'Then she was a damned peculiar looking fellow. Jack of Hearts my eye. I know a second pack of cards when I see one.'

'Are you accusing me of cheating?'

'Nothing of the sort, I'm pointing out a few peculiarities. Damn it all, Ainsley, but you're a prickly fellow tonight.'

'Well? Wouldn't you be? I'm a marked man I tell you, a marked man!'

It was time to pour oil over rough waters, especially those mixed with 40 per cent proof.

'Look, take no notice of me, Ainsley. I don't know what I'm saying. I doubt I could tell the difference between the King of Clubs and a beermat. That last scoop did it for me. I'm holed beneath the waterline. Tiddly as a stickleback.'

## A TOUCH OF SPLEEN

The vicar had accepted the apology with good grace, nodding in agreement as though absolving sins in a confessional, his face a picture of perfect concentration as his thoughts returned to their original tack. 'Damn it Hilary, but I'm scared to go home,' he'd whispered as only drunk people can, loud and with much moisture. His grip had tightened on his friend's arm. 'I'm petrified. There, I've said it. I'm nothing but a coward!'

The captain had stared at the vicar, shocked and touched with the emotion of the moment. 'There, there,' he'd said, tapping the poor man's hand. 'No need to be scared, dear chap. Captain Dashing of the 1st Grubdale Rifles here.'

The vicar appeared less than impressed. He was sweating with fear at the prospect of walking back to The Beeches on his own. Dutch courage had all but scarpered to Amsterdam, leaving the poor man half stupid with worry. What if the monster was waiting, hiding in the shadows ready to smash through the bedroom window and do… whatever vampires did with gentlemen of the cloth? Strewth, he was even scared to go to bed.

'It's no use, Hilary. You're going to have to stay the night.'

It had taken some persuasion, but in the end, the captain had agreed. For one night mind, that was all. Any more requests like this and the vicar would have to get a dog, a small dog, preferably a terrier and one called Measles.

'Why on earth should I call it Measles? Strange name for a dog, if you ask me.'

'Because it's better than calling it Spot,' the captain explained with all the logic of an evening on the drink.

'DAMN IT ALL, HILARY! ARE YOU ASLEEP!

The captain shuddered and opened his eyes.

'You're no good to me asleep. We could be murdered in our sleep.'

The fog of drink took a little longer to clear, but slowly and with some disappointment, the captain remembered where he was, in a large leather armchair in the vicar's large, carpeted bedroom. He wiped some dribble from his jacket and looked to his side where the vicar, sitting on top of his bed, was tapping an empty glass against a jar of pickled eggs.

'Come on slow coach,' the vicar said. 'How about another snifter before we call it a night?'

The captain chose to ignore the request and rising unsteadily to his feet, walked across his friend's bedroom to a large bay window. He peered through the curtains to the street below. 'No sign of your demon yet,' he said with much difficulty, as though each word had to be pronounced slowly and perfectly and preceded by burps.

'He speaks!'

The captain gave his friend an annoyed 'officer-in-charge' look, then made a great show of snapping open his Webley revolver, checking the bullets and closing the weapon. He was on guard duty after all.

'It's so good of you to stay the night. Much appreciated,' the vicar said.

The captain mumbled a sullen acceptance but chose to peer through the curtains rather than make conversation. He was a reluctant bodyguard at best and was regretting the whole situation. What had seemed an excellent idea in the Pig and Shovel was now, by the soft light of a bedside lamp and with the vicar in his silk pyjamas, turning bizarre indeed. The damned fellow was lying on his bed, and a very big bed it looked. Friendship was one thing, but touching toes in the middle of the night was quite another.

'I hope you don't mind sleeping by the window,' the vicar said. 'The armchair's more than comfortable and there's a couple of blankets to keep you warm.'

The captain sighed with relief and clicked his heels. 'God's in his heaven, and all's right in the world,' he thought.

'I feel terrible for asking,' the vicar continued, 'but you're the old soldier. I wouldn't know what to do with a gun.' The vicar knew what to do with a bottle of whisky though, and helped himself to the last drop. 'Make every bullet count,' he joked, before feeling the need to rest his head on the pillow and snore very loudly.

Across the park from The Beeches nursing home and in the smart but spartan bedroom of Number 78 Macclesfield Road, a good night's sleep was out of the question. Percy Bamforth had opened a cardboard box with the dreaded words 'FANCY DRESS COSTUME,' printed on the lid, along with a picture of a huge gorilla fighting a large man wearing a tiny loincloth.

'Isn't the costume wonderful?' shouted his wife from the next room. 'I couldn't resist when I saw the picture on the box.'

Percy stared at his reflection in the mirror and sighed. It was the sigh of a man staring disappointment in the face; a sincere, heartfelt sigh that spoke of yak hair, mothballs and a chest like two dinner plates.

'You'll be the toast of the party. Just think of the publicity, my love.'

Percy closed his eyes and thought of nothing else; front page, banner headline publicity with newspaper boys shouting 'Read all about it!' from every street corner.

'And that nice man from the shop let me have it half-price. Wasn't that kind?'

Percy opened his eyes and looked at the full horror of his costume for the second time. Kindness didn't enter into it. Kindness would have been a loaded revolver thrown in at no extra cost.

'Don't try eating the bananas though, they're papier-mâché.'

There were bananas too? Percy's heart sank. The costume was awful as it was without the need for fruit. His wife had dressed him as a gorilla, and not even a scary looking gorilla.

'More fur coat and slippers than King of the Congo,' he thought.

Evaline walked into the bedroom and rested her chin on his shoulder. 'Gorgeous!' she said and gave one of Percy's large felt ears a pinch. 'You'll have the ladies fighting over you tomorrow night.'

'Hmmmpft! I doubt that. I look about as dangerous as a teddy bear.'

'A hairy teddy bear, dear,' Evaline said and kissed her husband on the cheek. 'Never underestimate the allure of the fur.'

Percy attempted to smile but succeeded in looking even more ridiculous. 'Isn't there a mask?' he said. 'I would have liked a mask.'

'You can't wear a mask, darling; you're the host. You have to greet your guests and advance the cause. It would be pretty pointless me going to all this trouble if no one recognised you. Trust me; you'll look better without a mask. You'll be able to see where you're going, at least.'

It was hard to hide the disappointment. Percy shrugged his shoulders and sat down on the bed. 'Half the fun of dressing up as a gorilla is the mask,' he said. 'Otherwise, it's just this…' Percy flicked the two felt ears with his hands. 'A balaclava with flaps.'

'Don't sulk, dear. A gorilla never sulks.'

'This gorilla does.'

Evaline checked her hair in the mirror, smiled at her husband then walked briskly to the bathroom. She left a trail of exotic perfume lingering in the air.

'You smell nice.'

'Thank you.'

'Not like this bloody thing.' Percy sniffed his costume and screwed his face up in disgust. 'It smells like a wet dog.'

A perfume bottle landed by his side.

'Two squirts tomorrow, dear. But nothing more,' Evaline shouted. 'We want to shake hands, not kiss them.'

'Very funny!'

Evaline appeared after a while, brushed and scrubbed and ready for bed. 'Come on dear, out of those furs and into your pyjamas. We've got a busy day ahead.'

'But what about your costume? Don't I get to see what you'll wear?'

'Good heavens, no. It's a surprise.'
'Well, I bet you a fried breakfast it isn't a female gorilla.'
'Of course, it's not, silly. I'd look ridiculous dressed up as an ape. There's only one beast of the jungle in this house, and he'll be having tea and toast tomorrow, as usual.'
'I should get a medal for wearing this, and a fried breakfast.'
'Come on love, cheer up. If all goes to plan, you'll be getting more than a medal; you'll be getting a chain of office to hang it from.'
Percy smiled and squeezed his wife's hand, but with a little less enthusiasm than required. It was a clue immediately pounced upon and analysed.
'Percy? Is everything alright?'
'Absolutely. Nothing could be better, apart from the costume, that is.'
It was the tiniest of fibs. Percy was more worried about the party than he was letting on. He'd spent the best part of the day spraying the cinema with Tobacco Jones' Coal Tar Drench, and the least said about the smell the better. The least said about that mad O'Reilly woman the better too. She'd switched from cabbages to eggs and her aim was as true as ever. Heaven knows what she'd do if she managed to sneak into the party. Percy shuddered. It didn't bear thinking about. If she ever got her grubby, fat hands on his Wurlitzer, he didn't know what he would do.
'Well,' Evaline said, 'if you're that upset about the costume I can change it tomorrow. Honestly, all this fuss over a gorilla suit. It'll be potluck in the shop, but I'd say there'll be a few Pierrot costumes left, and a giant chicken.'
'I rather fancy being a cowboy.'
'As does every bloke in town, dear; so you can forget about that. The cowboy costumes are gone. If you don't want to be a gorilla, then it's Pierrot or the feathers, take your pick.'
'Well, if you put it like that, I suppose a gorilla suit isn't so bad.'
'Of course not, it's wonderful. And more to the point, you look wonderful, and everyone at the party will think you look wonderful. Now, climb out of those furs and get ready for bed.'
Percy smiled at his wife, winked, then beat his chest like a real gorilla.
'And you can put that idea out of your head too, along with your fried breakfast.'

## Chapter Fourteen

Captain Dashing awoke with a start, and for that brief moment between dropping his revolver and catching the top set of dentures in his lap, had no idea where he was. The room was warm and carpeted, not like his own. Large velvet drapes covered the windows, with large wooden crucifixes nailed to the walls, and to top the religious décor, a large number of porcelain saints looked down at him from the mantelpiece. It was only the absence of flowers and organ music that stopped him from checking his pulse or looking for a cardboard label tied to his toe. That was the trouble with nights out at his age; they invariably led to thoughts of mortality, with headaches to match.

A loud snort and the rustle of an eiderdown brought the captain to his senses. Not knowing what to think yet fearing the worst, he peered around the side of his armchair, only to see his friend the vicar fast asleep. The captain breathed a heartfelt sigh of relief, the prospect of a miserable future with a very religious barmaid consigned to the dustbin, along with other possibilities too terrifying to mention. 'Damn close call, what!' he whispered, vowing never to partake of whiskey and soda again. Not that he was afraid of the fairer sex, just suspicious of evolution and his formidable aunts in particular.

The captain's relief was short-lived. His memory was vague at the best of times, especially after an evening in the Pig and Shovel, but why he was wrapped in a blanket in a large armchair and not asleep in his own bed was a distant memory. He'd been asked to stand guard, that was it, to protect his friend from heaven knows what.

The captain looked at his pocket watch. 'Quarter to two in the morning! Good heavens, anything could have happened!' He glanced around the room for signs of witchcraft or anything else he might have missed, but seeing as his friend was safely tucked up in bed and snoring like a whale, the captain thought nothing more of it. 'Quietly does it,' he said as he bent down to retrieve the revolver from the carpet. 'No cause for alarm.'

Perhaps it was a rush of blood to the head, but images bubbled to the surface and noises too, vivid scenes of crumpled cars and twisted bikes and language that would shrivel a saint. There was a vague recollection of an irresistible police force meeting a large and immovable object, but he couldn't be sure. It may all have been a dream. 'Brrrrr!' mumbled the captain, shaking his head to clear the nonsense.

The vicar turned over in bed, kicking and pulling at the sheets as though fighting some mythical beast, a struggle which succeeded in nothing more than an empty bottle of whisky falling to the floor.

'Tsk, tsk! The evils of drink,' thought the captain, feeling suitably righteous if not hungover and wretched. But there was a job to be done and a promise to keep, so sitting back in his armchair, Hilary Dashing opened a gap in the curtains with his foot and peered out at the pavement below.

It had rained during the night, quite a spring shower from the look of it, and two dogs were running back and forth through the puddles.

'Pfft! Poodles!'

The captain had definite views on dogs, and any creature trimmed like a privet bush was not for him. He had definite views on pink dogs with tartan raincoats too, and ones that breathed fire.

'Heaven's above!' shouted the captain, sitting bolt upright in his chair, for hadn't one of the creatures just toasted a brace of pigeons with a single sneeze?

'Demetrios!'

What was this? A roman gladiator?

'Princess Peaches!'

And royalty too? It was all very confusing.

The two 'poodles' ceased their happy frolics and stood next to one another, each with a roast pigeon in its mouth and their tail wagging.

'Dammit, girl! Where are you?' shouted a female voice, more demanding than before.

'Demetrios? Are you hiding from me! Come here this instant!' bellowed another.

The two 'poodles' shared a knowing look, one that spoke of many things in many languages and all of them involving buckets of water. It was the call of the wild, with the call of domesticity and dog biscuits coming a poor second. Without as much as a backward glance or a wave of a paw to say goodbye, Demetrios and Princess Peaches set off in high excitement, running and leaping over each other as they disappeared in the general direction of the Belle Vue Gardens.

The captain pulled back the curtains and stood with his face pressed against the window. 'Stupid, stupid, stupid!' he whispered, cursing himself for

# A TOUCH OF SPLEEN

forgetting the obvious. There was only one explanation for a pair of fire-breathing poodles in town, a pair of wretched witches to make up the set.

'Demetrios!'

The passion in the voice was unmistakable, and the accent too - a splash of the Scottish moors with a squeeze of the Potteries. It was an accent the captain remembered despite years of trying to forget; an accent that made the brave officer sick with worry and start looking for seagulls.

'DEMETRIOS!'

Hilary Dashing leapt back from the window and scurried behind the armchair to hide. 'The abominable Miss Carp!' he hissed as he cast a quick glance at the street below, for there on the pavement dressed from head to toe in Edwardian fashion, marched a stern-looking Rowena, intent on trouble.

Memories flooded back, humiliating memories of twenty years past when the captain's career had come to an abrupt halt. It had been the witches' fault, that and possibly the school burning down along with most of Grubdale's high street, but these were minor details. In the captain's eyes, the witches were responsible for everything. Up until their arrival life had been quiet, pleasantly dull even, with an occasional brass band. A few autumn days in 1912 had changed all that, days full of dark magic, dark creatures and women in tweed. There had been the pugilistic Miss Chubb with her razor-billed gulls, the flirtatious Miss Carp with her fire-breathing pink poodle, and to complete the trio, the formidable Miss Pike with her monocle and bossy ways.

The captain's hand trembled at the thought of Miss Pike. Middle-aged women weren't supposed to put middle-aged soldiers over their knee and administer six of the best with a volume of the Encyclopaedia Britannica; it just wasn't done. 'Bloody witches!' he shouted, reliving the humiliation and pain, for there was a sufficiency of information between the letters A and D, and every paragraph had hurt.

'Shoot her!'

'What?'

The vicar was standing in front of the chair and struggling to open the window.

'Shoot her! Now's your chance. Save the town!'

'I'll do no such thing!'

'You know it makes sense! Squeeze the trigger!'

The captain stared in horror at the vicar. The drink did many things to a gentleman, most of them bad, but for a retired man of the cloth to propose murder was shocking. The last time he'd seen his friend like this was with a copy of the National Geographic in the library.

'For God's sake Ainsley, sober up! You're talking rubbish!'

'Hilary, you've not seen what these women are capable of! Zombies and dragons were just the beginning. It will be the devil next and all his minions! Here, give me the gun!'

The vicar made a lunge for the captain's revolver, and in the slow-motion struggle that a bottle of whiskey, two bad backs and a festival of arthritis could manage, someone squeezed the trigger, shattered the window and caused Rowena to stop in her tracks.

The silence was deafening, as three ostrich feathers fell from Rowena's hat slowly to the floor.

The two gentlemen stood still, their faces pressed together and their hands interlinked around the one smoking gun.

'Now look what you've done,' whispered the captain. 'You've clipped her wings!'

'It wasn't her bonnet I was aiming for.'

'Well, you're a terrible shot. You've done nothing but catch that witch's attention. Dammit, you fool, what do we do now?'

The vicar sized up the situation in an instant. 'We dance!' he said.

'What?'

'Hold tight and dance. Think of Valentino in that Argentinian film.'

'What!'

Before the captain could protest in the strongest terms, the vicar twisted him around in a circle and proceeded to re-enact the tango from The Four Horseman of the Apocalypse, hoping against hope that the dreadful Miss Carp would think nothing of it and walk away. It was a plan doomed to failure. The dreadful Miss Carp thought more of it than she should and stared at the two men in disbelief. Grubdale had changed, and not for the better.

'Filthy beasts!' she shouted at the top of her voice, then turned around and marched from view.

'Filthy beasts!' mimicked the yellow dragon following in her footsteps, but not before staring through the broken window and raising his eyes in contempt.

There are many types of scream. Some are silent, despite the mouth being open and the eyes tight shut. Some are so high-pitched that glasses full of wine shatter in an instant. Others are so loud a second thrust of the dagger is required to shut the screamer up. The scream from The Beeches nursing home was none of these. It was a duet of excitable panic, a concerto of shrieks and wails and flapping of hands. It was the kind of scream Degas, not Munch, would have painted, and with more ballet dancers and mice.

'Pathetic!' Rowena commented without so much as breaking her stride.

# A TOUCH OF SPLEEN

Elsie Tapp was in no mood for an argument. Clasping a wet and muddy Princess Peaches under her arm, she walked past the night porter and through to the main lobby of the hotel.

'In future ma'am, I suggest you ask for a passkey if you're going to be this late.'

'There'll be no "in future,"' came the curt reply. 'And if you wouldn't mind, I'd like the key to my room. Number 203, if you please.'

The night porter was in no rush and trudged slowly back to the reception desk. 'You have a telegram, ma'am,' he said, handing over the key and a small envelope marked URGENT. 'It was delivered this evening.'

'Thank you.'

'Marked URGENT, mind,' he said, pointing at the red lettering.

'So I see.'

The porter seemed reluctant to let go of the envelope. It was as if he were waiting for a tip or a hint as to what it contained. Elsie gave the envelope a sharp tug and waved it in the air. 'I've no small change,' she said, knowing too well that she had, then turned towards the lift, having no desire to take the stairs to her room.

'The lift's broken,' said the porter, flicking through the pages of the guest book. 'Has been all day. Temperamental machinery at best.'

The ding of a bell and the whir of machinery told a different story, and one the porter ignored. 'I wouldn't chance it if I were you,' he said, running his fingers down a column of names and feigning interest. 'Safer to take the stairs.'

The doors to the lift slid open.

'It tends to do that; lure the guests inside then stop between floors. You could be trapped for hours.'

'Well, really!' snapped Elsie, not wanting to listen to this ridiculous man any longer. 'And you can stop fidgeting!' she said, holding Princess Peaches to her chest as she walked across the hall to the central staircase. 'You've been a bad girl, a very bad girl!'

The bad girl merely wagged her tail and barked in agreement.

'Stop that noise! Honestly, I don't know what the matter is with you. You've behaved worse than a trollop.'

The trollop rather liked the name and barked some more.

'Oh for heaven's sake, be quiet! You're going in your basket when we get to the room, and no biscuits either.'

Princess Peaches didn't like the sound of that.

'Not so much the independent lady now, are we?'

The scolding and speeches continued from the first floor to the second, and all the way along the corridor to Room 203.

'You had me worried sick, you wretched girl. Running off with that brute. Heaven knows what he's done.'

The Princess knew and wagged her tail.

Elsie fumbled with the key to the door. 'I don't know what to say, I really don't. I brought you up to be a good girl.' Pushing the door open with her shoulder, Elsie stepped inside and switched on the light. 'Stay there,' she said, finally putting the poodle in her sleeping basket, and removing the toys. 'And I don't want a peep from you, not as much as a whimper, you understand?'

The Princess tried her sad and adorable face, just in case.

'Not a chance, young girl. You can stay there till I've run your bath.'

At the word 'bath' the Princess's face appeared more sad than adorable, then sullen, then angry, then as a last hope, ill and sick with the flu.

'You can blink those eyes as much as you want, dear, but it won't work. Mummy is very cross.'

Elsie's temper didn't improve on opening the telegram. It was a very curt note from her publisher, Marjorie Whippet, the tone of the text requiring a soft chair and a generous count to ten.

'THE SECRET IS OUT! STAY INDOORS! DENY EVERYTHING!'

Elsie read further. It appeared the news of Felicity Merryweather's true identity had been broadcast the length and breadth of the country. It also appeared that Felicity Merryweather's adoring public deserved nothing less than a glamorous siren as befitting the silhouette on the back of each of her books.

'Well, the cheek of the woman!' gasped Elsie. 'How dare she! I AM Felicity Merryweather!'

These three phrases were repeated with various frequency and volume for the rest of the night, and with much dunking and scrubbing of a poodle. 'Deny everything! Who does she think she is?' Elsie snapped, rubbing more of her expensive soap into Princess Peaches' fur. 'I'll deny nothing! And if she thinks she can dictate to me, Elsie Tapp, the only author who makes Honeysweet Publishers money, then she's another thing coming.'

The question of having to hide irked Elsie the most. 'Stay indoors!' she said, rinsing the poor poodle for the fourth time. 'And what if I did, how would that help? I might as well keep the curtains closed and send out for food.'

'Damn it, but I'm not her prisoner!' she cried after considering all the possibilities, a process that lasted from the bathroom to the bedroom with a shivering Princess Peaches wrapped up in a towel. 'I'm a successful author!'

Just how successful she'd be if Felicity's silhouette were exchanged for hers, she didn't know. The question deserved further thought, even though framed in the most impolite terms by the telegram. 'Oh bother!' Elsie said, vigorously drying the poodle on her lap. What she needed was a decent night's sleep.

## A TOUCH OF SPLEEN

Perhaps things would be clear in the morning. At the moment all she wanted to do was catch the next train back to London and forget about Grubdale forever, sentiments that were shared by a certain Reverend Cross and Captain Dashing as they hammered on the door of the police station, desperate to be let in.

'Dragon! There's a fire-breathing dragon loose in the town!'
'Yellow in colour was it, sir? Answers to the name of McTavish?'
'I'm sorry?' asked the vicar.
'This dragon you saw,' said the desk sergeant, writing the details down in his book. 'Was it yellow and Scottish?'
'I've no idea. Surely it's enough there's a dragon.'
'Well, that would be saying now, wouldn't it? PC Grime over there is convinced he saw a giraffe, and PC Smith standing next to him says it was a grizzly bear. PC Jones though, he thought he saw a rhino. But at least they all agree on the colour and its name, and the fact that it sat on their car and squashed the front flat.'
'It did, sir, crumpled it like cardboard.'
'Put it in the report Jones, just as I said.'
'Yes, sir,' said the young constable, who seemed to be taking great pains in threading a double sheet of paper into an old battered typewriter.
The sergeant continued. 'Now PC Wiggery and Drudge thought they saw a tiger, and I've three more PCs who swear they saw nothing at all but still managed to ride their bikes headlong into something solid. A dragon though, that's taking the game a little too far, don't you think?'
'Sir, it's not a game. Something big, yellow and answering to the name McTavish crushed our car, and probably the bikes too.'
'Write it down Jones, write it down.'
'Yes, sir.'
'So you see, gentlemen, what am I supposed to do? The whole station seems to have lost its marbles. A dragon though, that really takes the biscuit.'
Captain Dashing pushed the vicar gently aside. 'Now look here, Sergeant,' he said. 'You don't seem to realise the enormity of the situation. The last time there were dragons in Grubdale, half the town burnt down and we lost the school. We were there, the vicar and me. We saw it all.'
The desk sergeant stared at the captain for a few moments then slowly closed the book. 'It's a Mr Dashing isn't it, and a Mr Cross?'
'It most certainly is. Captain Hilary Dashing, 1st Grubdale Rifles, retired.'
'Retired but still on active service in the Pig and Shovel, what?'
'I'm sorry?'
'Look you two, if there is a wild animal on the loose–'

'But there is,' interrupted PC Jones as he struggled behind the desk with his report. 'And it's yellow with teeth!'

The sergeant scowled at the young constable, who immediately apologised and continued typing his account one letter at a time.

'If there is a wild animal on the loose, and I'm not saying there is; and if this wild animal answers to the name of McTavish, and I'm not saying it does, then the very last thing it'll be is a fire-breathing dragon now, isn't it? This being England and not some fantasy land from the bottom of a bottle.'

'I beg your pardon?'

'Mr Dashing, you've been drinking. I can smell it on your breath. Please be a good fellow and go home.'

'But you don't understand. It's happened before! Heavens above, Ainsley, are we the only people in town that remember?'

'Remember what, Mr Dashing?'

'The bloody dragons, goddamit!' shouted the captain.

The sergeant took out a large red handkerchief and wiped the spit from his face.

'Mr Cross,' he said, beckoning the vicar to come close. 'You seem a reasonable chap. Why don't you take your friend home and we'll say no more about it. There's no crime in being three sheets to the wind, but your friend's a galleon, if you get my drift?'

The vicar didn't; three nautical terms delivered one after the other had him confused, as did the whisky awash in his scuppers. He was having one of those moments, one of those embarrassing fractions of a second where his brain had stopped and restarted but without telling the rest of his body where he was and what had happened.

'I'm sorry?' he asked.

'I think you should take your friend home before I book the both of you for wasting police time.'

The vicar looked hurt, as though the sergeant had accused him of stealing the church gold. He was about to proclaim his innocence when the door to the street swung open, and a very emotional young couple rushed in from outside.

'There's been a murder!' they both cried. 'There's a body on the miniature railway!'

'And there's a bloody dragon too!' shouted the captain, not wanting to be outdone.

## Chapter Fifteen

It was Grubdale rain at its finest - cold, penetrating and relentless. It was the sort of rain that stung your eyes, rolled down the back of your neck and filled your pockets; a miserable rain at an unfortunate hour in the morning with only fools or policeman up and about.

'The poor bugger, what a way to die; tied to the tracks of a miniature railway and cut to ribbons. It's the stuff of cheap thrillers; no decency at all.'

Two senior members of the Grubdale constabulary were huddled together under an umbrella, waiting for their superiors to arrive from Manchester. They were standing in the middle of Belle Vue Gardens with the body of a middle-aged man at their feet. Morbid curiosity had mixed with professional duty, but only as far as shining their torches on the corpse. A sheet of cloth now covered the unfortunate man, just like the dead cow from the day before.

'Can't see what's wrong with a pistol shot, or a decent knock to the head. All this seems so unnecessary.'

'Who is he anyway, do we know?'

'A Mr Harry Renfield apparently, dealer in toys and novelties. Quite a popular man by all accounts.'

'Not too popular though, obviously, or else he'd still be with us.'

'Aye, you can say that. It's a nasty business this. Just like that cow and those sheep. Notice anything peculiar?'

'Apart from being tied to the tracks, you mean? It doesn't get more peculiar than that.'

'But there's no blood though, is there. You'd expect the ground to be soaked in the stuff. It's like those poor bloody animals. There's a connection here if we can only work it out, but don't mention vampires. We'll be the laughing stock of the whole police force if we do. Were there any witnesses?'

'There's the statement of the young couple who discovered him, but that's no use. They were up to no good in the bandstand and didn't notice a thing.'

'The bandstand is it? Funny how things never change. I used to meet my Gladys there when we were courting. I'd say that place is responsible for half the kids in Grubdale.'

'You would've thought they'd have heard something, though; a scream at least. We're hardly talking a gentle death. I'd be screaming my bloody head off if I was tied to the tracks. No, I reckon he was killed elsewhere, it would explain the lack of blood. I doubt a train ever touched him. I bet our little steam engine's still in the shed.'

'I thought there was another witness.'

'There was, an old drunk sleeping off the effects of cheap booze.'

'Not that dreadful O'Reilly woman, is it? She's three-parts gin at best.'

'No, it was old George Stubbins from across the moors. He says he saw the murderer. The trouble is, he says it's a giant spider.'

'A giant spider! Well, at least it's not a giant dragon. What is it with this town? Why can't we have a nice, normal murder without all these bloody complications?'

Elsie Tapp reached out for the bedside lamp and struggled with the switch. 'Half past five in the morning!' she said, looking at her travel clock and fighting the urge to throw it across the room.

Elsie, for all her tiredness, had barely managed two hours sleep, and now the rain was gurgling through the gutters and downpipes and keeping her awake. Someone was wheeling a cart beneath her window and making poor progress in steering - at least she assumed it was a cart. There were wheels, definitely; she could hear them squeaking and crunching the gravel, and whoever was pushing the contraption sounded as though they needed a squirt from an oil can too.

'Oh, this is impossible!' Elsie cried after the cart crashed noisily into some other garden ornament.

She slipped her bed jacket over her shoulders and threw off the sheets. 'How can anyone sleep with this commotion outside?' she mumbled as she walked to the window and drew aside the curtains.

The cause of the noise was obvious; the mysterious bandaged man had returned in his wheelchair, but his small assistant was making heavy weather of steering the contraption in any meaningful direction save around in a circle.

'Do you mind!' shouted Elsie after struggling to lift the bottom part of her sash window open. 'People are trying to sleep here!'

The bandaged gentleman held up his hand, and the chair came to an abrupt stop, the light from Elsie's room highlighting a pathetic state of affairs. The wheels of the chair were bent and on the verge of collapse, the gentleman's bandages loose and trailing on the ground, while the unfortunate assistant

# A TOUCH OF SPLEEN

looked as though he'd been dragged through a bush backwards then just for the fun of it, gobbled up and spat out by a whale.

'Yes, I'm talking to you! Do you realise the time? It's not even 6 o'clock!'

The strange figure turned around in his chair and looked up at Elsie's window, the ink-black glass in his spectacles making his face look like a skull.

'Yes, well, wheelchair or not, could you please keep the noise down, thank you very much,' Elsie said, then tried to pull the window shut.

Perhaps she hadn't shouted loud enough, or maybe the peculiar gentleman wasn't used to being spoken to in so abrupt a manner. Either way, he remained where he sat, staring up at Elsie for an uncomfortable length of time, the rain soaking further into his clothes.

'You're welcome,' she said after finally managing to close the window.

The strange figure snapped his fingers, and as if rehearsed beforehand, the assistant placed a polished wooden box in the gentleman's lap and opened the lid. A second snap of the fingers saw a large flintlock pistol placed into the gentleman's hand with the assistant pulling the hammer back until it clicked into place.

'What the Dickens is he doing now?' Elsie cried as the peculiar figure raised the peculiar pistol and aimed it directly at her window. But as other pairs of curtains were drawn back, and other windows in the hotel opened, the bandaged figure changed his mind. He barked an order and the wheelchair disappeared, dragged out of the light and away into the darkness.

Elsie breathed a long sigh of relief. Her legs were shaking, her stomach felt cold, and she felt a sudden urge to run to the bathroom. 'This is most definitely the final straw!' she cried. 'We are leaving, Princess! I'm not staying a moment longer in this horrid town!'

The rain had stopped. Not that it made pushing the wheelchair along the street any easier, but such was the assistant's lot in life. He puffed and wheezed, struggling with each yard gained as though the chair was loaded with bags of wet cement. Its passenger, the strange gentleman in the bandages, took no notice of the suffering but urged the wheelchair forward. It was too much for the assistant. The chair came to an abrupt stop outside Nadin and Sons, Pork Butchers, its main form of propulsion collapsing in a heap.

There is a smell to every shop; a smell that seeps into the plasterwork and makes the building its own. The smell from Nadin and Sons was renowned the length and breadth of Grubdale and would make a vegetarian sick - meat with a hint of a galvanised bucket. To the two solitary figures now transfixed and staring at the window, the smell was perfume. They drooled and laid their faces against the glass, staring with intent at a string of rubber sausages and a plaster figure of a pig in a butcher's apron.

A cat fresh from inspecting the dustbins at the back of Massey's fish shop trotted out into the high street and sniffed the early morning air. This was a Hercules of a cat, as big as a badger; a happy cat full of fish heads and shrimp, trotting along with not a care in the world. Being an intelligent and sophisticated cat, it took great pleasure in observing the peculiarities of others, and having nothing better to do that morning, it decided to stop and stare at the two peculiar gentlemen so interested in the butchers' window. It sat a safe distance away and studied the scene with interest. Humans were strange at the best of times, full of baby talk and saucers of milk until you did unspeakable things to their house plants; but these two were stranger than most. The peculiar pair were licking the shop window, one leaning forward from a chair, the other butting in where it could, drooling and slurping like long-tongued dogs chasing food around in a bowl.

The cat growled, its fur standing on end and its tail twitching as though charged with electricity. It could sense trouble. The cat had learnt to avoid four things in life; dogs, buckets of water, peculiar people that looked as though they were carrying buckets of water, and that sultry minx of a tortoiseshell at number 24. People who licked windows though, this was something new. The cat hissed and spat, not so much as a warning as a statement of disgust. It had dismissed the two characters as bucket carriers, the obvious logic being that if they enjoyed licking windows then they probably enjoyed washing them too, and as every cat knows, people who wash windows throw water, often with great accuracy.

The bandaged figure stopped and turned to see where the noise was coming from, its large red tongue still hanging from his mouth. It was too much for the cat. With a final growl of protest the animal made its escape, leaping over fences and squeezing through gaps, dashing across gardens till the safety of its home lay tantalisingly close. It stared straight ahead as it passed number 24, tried to think of higher things as it trotted towards number 26, then deciding that drugs were the better option, leapt into the biggest bush of catmint this side of Afghanistan.

'Tiddles!' called its owner, holding the door to number 28 open and letting light out into the street. 'Coo-ee, Tiddles! Come to Mummy!'

Mary O'Reilly wasn't all beer and bad temper, she had a soft centre that was devoted to her ginger tom. She worried about her poor darling. The news of a cat-napper was all around town, but try as she might to keep her Tiddles indoors, the ginger tom was as crafty as an escapologist with a tummy full of keys.

'Puss, puss, puss!' she called, tapping a spoon against an enamel dish, and sure enough the promise of milk tempted the cat out of the shrubbery and up on the wall.

'Tiddles,' cooed Mary, seeing her beloved cat from across the street. 'Puss, puss, puss!'

A figure emerged from the shadows, a tall figure in yellow robes and with a close-fitting mask that did nothing for its looks. There was red smoke too, peculiar smoke that smelled to Mary of cloves and treacle toffee. For once she was scared. Pantomime villains belonged on stage or in flickering films accompanied by Gilbert and Sullivan, not lurking around the back streets of Grubdale, and certainly not at this hour in the morning.

'Oi! What's your game? You should be ashamed, spying on a poor defenceless woman. I've read about people like you in the Sunday papers.'

Mary had read a good deal about people like 'him' in the Sunday papers. The News of the World was her one source of information and it spared little detail when it came to scandal and titillation.

'And stop staring like that. It's rude. Haven't you seen a lady in a dressing gown and wellingtons before? I'll give you something to look at if you don't clear off. And don't think you can hide behind that mask. I know it's you, Bert Smedley, you're nothing but a peeping tom!'

The figure didn't move.

'I said stop it! Grief, your wife's only gone three months, and you're back to your old tricks. Go on, away with you! Undressing me with your eyes, you're nothing but a filthy beast, Bert Smedley – a filthy beast!'

Filthy beast or not, Mary's husband had been dead and buried for over three years. 'Well, are you going to stand there like a bloody scarecrow or open the gate? I haven't got all day.'

The figure stayed put.

'Then suit yourself,' Mary said. 'No skin off my nose.' But as she bent down to tickle her beloved Tiddles under the chin, the mysterious figure seemed to float across the road, climb over the gate and stand by her side.

'I'll get the kettle on then, shall I?' said Mary, nudging the gentleman in the ribs. 'One hump or two? Mind you, no sugar tongues – not on a first date.'

Someone screamed; a short cry of fear from somewhere over the rooftops.

'Oh for heaven's sake, what sort of town is this?' Elsie said, throwing blouse after blouse into her suitcase. 'The sooner we're out of here the better.'

Grubdale had lost its magic; it was no longer quaint. The Cotswolds were quaint, parts of Devon were quaint; but after all the goings-on these past two days, Grubdale had smashed through quaint and was now firmly in the realm of the bloody peculiar.

'We can catch the next train to London and then the boat train to France,' Elsie said, wrestling with a large woollen jacket that refused to fold flat. 'I need sticky cakes and champagne!'

There was another scream, far away, but near enough for Elsie to hear. She shivered and returned to her packing with renewed vigour. 'Brrr! What on earth made us come here? There should be warning posters at St Pancras station, "Abandon hope all ye who venture north!"'

Elsie rolled the last pair of stockings into a ball and was about to tuck them tidily away when she noticed the stern face of her poodle looking up from under the bed.

'So you expect me to go to the police? Well, I won't go, I tell you, and there's the end of it.'

Princess Peaches barked. The poodle had no interest in the police, nor even any knowledge of what the word meant; she was in a sulk, plain and simple. She hated baths, and she hated baby powder, and she most definitely hated cheap perfume sprinkled over her back.

'Be reasonable, please. I mean, what could I say? "A yellow dragon, yes. Oh, and before I forget, there was a peculiar gentleman with a duelling pistol outside my window. I didn't get a look at his face, though. He was wrapped from head to toe in bandages." No, Princess, we're not going to the police. They'll think I'm mad and who would blame them? I'm beginning to think I'm a little touched myself.'

Princess Peaches barked again and hid under the bed. How could anyone expect her to go outside smelling of lavender soap? Oh, the shame of it.

'Well, really!' Elsie protested. 'Now you're just being mean.'

The desk sergeant checked the nib of his pen, flicked a string of ink drops on the floor, then started to write in perfect copperplate. 'One yellow dragon and one man in bandages trying to kill you,' he said. 'And here's me thinking I'd get a quiet night. Anything else madam?'

Elsie waited until the gentleman had finished transcribing her words, then added 'I heard a scream, a terrible scream.'

The sergeant sighed. 'One terrible scream. Not any old scream, mind but a terrible scream.'

He seemed to be taking greater care than usual, underlining the word 'terrible' many times till the ink bled through the page, then adding an exclamation mark at the end. 'And what time would that be?' he asked.

'Oh I don't know, about 45 minutes ago I think. It was very loud. I'm surprised no one else reported it.'

'Well, let me see,' the desk sergeant said, putting down his pen and leafing through the pages of the report book. 'I've got flat sheep, an empty cow, missing cats, flat cats, Indian tigers, yellow dragons,' the sergeant glanced up at Elsie. 'Three reports of those.' He returned to his report book. 'A dead body on the miniature railway, more flat cats, and now a bandaged assassin in a wheelchair. Not a bad haul for a quiet little town on the moors. I'd say a scream is pretty dull fare nowadays, don't you think? Terrible or otherwise. Hardly worth a scribble in a notebook.'

'You said a body on a railway line?'

'Unfortunately so.'

'Oh my, that's terrible! Still, I thought I was going mad…I mean dragons, in this day and age?'

'Yes, and on my watch too. Now madam, if you wouldn't mind waiting a few minutes, I'll organise for someone to take down a full statement.'

'Oh dear, is this necessary? I'm in such a terrible hurry. I need to check out of my hotel and catch the next train to London. Surely what I told you should suffice?'

'Madam, there's been a murder. No one is going anywhere.'

Elsie stood in front of the desk, not knowing what to say.

'There'll be some questions we need to ask. I'm sure you understand. You may be our only reliable witness.'

Elsie protested. 'But I don't know anything about a murder,' she said.

'But you saw a man with a gun. That's a start, don't you think?'

'Wellington Boot to Grubdale. Wellington Boot to Grubdale. Come in Grubdale, over!'

The machine in the bushes bleeped and flashed and whispered its message, but to no avail. 'Grubdale' was out of earshot, making her two companions regret their bad behaviour from the night before.

'Dig Demetrios, dig!' Rowena snapped, standing over her pink familiar in the morning light, and Demetrios, feeling suitably guilty, tried his best to loosen the soil. 'As for you, McTavish.' Rowena pointed her Parisian parasol at the yellow wyrm. 'Be useful for a change and clear away those stones.'

Demetrios was in disgrace. It had taken Rowena most of the night to find him, lying on his back under a rhododendron bush and blowing smoke rings in the air, and the yellow wyrm had behaved no better – juggling dustbins and hitting them for six with his tail.

'Stay here,' she had told the wyrm, tapping him on the nose and insisting he remained hidden. But the creature was young and impulsive and had followed her into town, merging with the scenery like a chameleon. It had been a long walk back to the school ruins, Rowena carrying a smug Demetrios over her shoulder, and with the yellow wyrm changing from yellow bushes to yellow dustbins, to yellow front doors and back again, with the occasional spout of red flame whenever a stray dog showed interest.

'Don't give me that "but there are no rabbits here," look! You know what we're searching for; it's an egg, a big egg about the size of a bowling ball.'

Demetrios spat out a mouthful of dandelion roots, changed his expression to a "but there are no ostriches here," look, then plunged his nose back in the hole and clawed at the soil.

'And mind where you're throwing those clumps!' Rowena said, stepping nimbly aside to avoid the dirt.

'WELLINGTON BOOT TO GRUBDALE! WELLINGTON BOOT TO GRUBDALE! COME IN GRUBDALE!'

The voice screamed from the machine like a ship's siren, blowing the vegetation flat and making Rowena hold on to her hat.

'Good heavens McTavish, was that you?' Rowena cried.

'ROWENA! PICK UP THE BLOODY TUBE!'

'Oh crikey, Bethesda!'

Rowena scrambled over the stones and bricks as fast as she could, which wasn't very fast, but then anything other than a jump and a shuffle was out of the question in her Parisian skirt.

'I'm coming! I'm coming!' she cried as she pulled herself up into the hedge. 'Keep your bloody hair on!'

The language from the machine was fast deteriorating before Rowena managed to pick up the tube, hit the reply button with her parasol and scream a reply.

'WHAT'S THE PANIC!' she cried.

'WE'RE HERE!' Bethesda shouted, causing Rowena to look around as though being attacked by a wasp.

'What do you mean "We're here!"? I can't see you? Are you sure you're here? Where's "here"? Did you follow the tunnel as I said?'

'We're in Grubdale, that's where "here" is, and you're not!'

'Oh, yes I am! I'm standing precisely where I told you, near the ruins of the school. And if you and your silly pirates had done what I'd asked, then you'd be here, wouldn't you and not there, wherever "there" is.'

# A TOUCH OF SPLEEN

There is a limit to madness, when peculiarity turns so peculiar that even a giant steel shark bubbling up from the depths seems normal. The vicar had reached this stage and beyond; his friend, however, was still on the slopes.

'What the hell is that!' Captain Dashing screamed as the shark broke the surface of the boating lake, its carved mouth full of pond weed and surprised ducks.

'Whatever it is, dear friend, the police will say "drink." We are but a lone voice in the wilderness, Hilary. No one cares to listen. It's the same tale, and I'm tired of the telling. We should head home and away to our beds.'

The two gentlemen had been heading home and away to their beds for the last two hours, but the need to sit down, rest and take stock of their predicament had been great; almost as great as their need to keep to the shadows and hide at the sound of anything more peculiar than the rattle of a dustbin.

'Oi! You two! Is this Grubdale?'

To the captain's horror, one of the shark's eyes had opened like a porthole, and someone was shouting from inside the beast.

'Well, I never! It's a submarine!'

'Keep walking, Hilary. No good will come of this,' urged the vicar.

'Oi!' the voice cried again. 'Is this Grubdale?'

'Yes!' answered the captain, waving his cap. 'And you're welcome to it!'

There was a hiss of steam, and a squirt of oil as the shark's mouth opened, and then the sound of flapping wings and seabirds hungry for food.

'You should have said no!' whispered the vicar. 'Now look what's happened.'

An angry flock of seagulls had escaped from the shark's mouth and was staring at the captain from the safety of a tree; a flock of seagulls that rattled their beaks together as though sharpening them like knives.

'I know those birds!'

'And I know those women!' cried the vicar, for a rowing boat had appeared from the other end of the submarine, and in it were a group of substantial women all dressed in tweeds and sensible shoes, and all waving hats and shouting 'Coo-ee!'

'Run, Hilary!' shouted the vicar, walking very briskly for a gentleman of his age. 'Run for your life!'

## Chapter Sixteen

Bethesda Chubb, scourge of the seas, captain of the Emily P and now big boss of the rowing boat, waved her pirate hat in the air and shouted encouragement.

'Heave ho, Petunia! You're doing a fine job!'

Petunia Mullet smiled and attacked the water with her oars, propelling the small boat forward with as much strength as she could manage.

'Easy with the splashes, Petunia! I'm getting soaked here,' cried a damp and dripping Miss Trout. 'And try and keep to port. Anymore right and we'll be back inside the shark.'

Petunia tried her best, but her technique was more skimming the custard than Olympic champion.

'For pity's sake, keep the boat steady. I'm trying to get a reading, and you're upsetting the ether.'

A studious Miss Cod peered into a glass sphere, at the centre of which a single red needle spun in a circle, making the poor woman feel ill. It was the latest idea from the professor's workshop, and although designed to highlight the presence of evil megalomaniacs everywhere, seemed more inclined to point to items of jewellery, low-flying fish or just about anything it thought interesting at the time. 'Useless piece of junk!' seemed the consensus, but Miss Cod thought the machine wonderful. Only last month she'd found her lost dentures, a biscuit tin full of pennies, and the slugs in her garden eating the lettuce.

'You'd be better off shouting Spleen's name than trusting to that,' laughed Petunia as, in a stroke of luck, both oars hit the water at the same time.

'That's the spirit!' Bethesda cried. 'Straight as she goes! Come on, you lot, try to keep up!'

Other rowing boats appeared from behind the submarine, each one filled to wobbling with ladies in tweed as the peculiar flotilla made its way to the side of the lake.

## A TOUCH OF SPLEEN

'Ooh, look at him, Mr Distinguished over there. Quite the stocking dropper and no mistake!'

'Eyes front, Cecily. You know what the boss said. "No fraternising with the locals." This is supposed to be a quick "in and out" job.'

'Ooh, lovely!'

The object of Miss Roach's admiration was standing by the water's edge, his mouth wide open in horror but not able to say a word. It was Captain Dashing, and his nightmare was complete. Not only had the sisterhood returned, but those dreadful seagulls with their razor-sharp beaks had come with them. It was all he could do to stop whimpering like a baby and falling to his knees.

'Hello handsome!' shouted the amorous Miss Roach, and with a squeak of little magic, magic so small that Bethesda Chubb wouldn't notice, Cecily conjured up a dainty posy of flowers and tossed it towards him as her boat rowed past.

The captain, nervous, highly strung and with a Webley revolver in his hand, shot the posy to pieces as it flew through the air.

'Well, really!' Cecily was about to say before a bolt of green magic hit the captain squarely in the chest and sent him rolling back into the bushes. Bethesda Chubb had spoken.

'I don't believe it!' cried PC Wiggery. 'That wasn't a gunshot. Surely that wasn't a gunshot? Tell me that wasn't a gunshot, Jack.'

'Sounded like a gunshot to me.'

'Ah for heaven's sake, it's getting to be like the Wild West around here! Look lively, blow the whistle, I suppose we have to investigate.'

PC Drudge held out a shaking hand. 'Do we? That's nerves, that is; the tremors. I can hardly hold a mug of tea, let alone a whistle. I tell you, this town's got me spooked.'

'Aye, well spooked or not, it's our job. Come on, follow me. That shot came from over there.'

'Over there' was the side of the boating lake, now full of women in tweed as they stepped onto dry land and made ready with their weapons, a strange collection of brass band instruments that seemed to appear from thin air. There were seagulls too, perching on the ladies' shoulders or flying overhead.

'Witches!' shouted a prostrate Captain Dashing, his thick coat still smoking from the thump of magic to his chest. 'You hags!'

He shouted other words, very bad words which, after seeing the revolver in his hand turn green and sprout flowers, he felt were heartfelt and richly deserved.

'Eyes to the front, sisters!' shouted Bethesda Chubb. 'He's just a silly old man with a dirty mouth, and we've all heard worse from better, have we not?'

They had - far worse and mostly from the cook.

'Now, Miss Cod, if you'd like to lead the way.'

Miss Cod, her shoes and stockings wet from stumbling out of the boat, elbowed her way to the front of the queue. 'This way,' she said, staring into the large glass sphere, and trusting to the red arrow pointing ahead, beckoning the sisterhood to follow. 'The signal is strong here,' she said as she marched along the lake path, 'and it's getting stronger!'

It may have had a lot to do with cake. The sphere was partial to cake, and the Belle Vue Tea Rooms were nearby with all their crumbly goodness. Or it could have been the buttons. The uniform of the Grubdale constabulary fairly shimmered with buttons, and the sphere was partial to a quick tickle of magnetism too. The red arrow swung from left to right as it tried to make up its mind.

'Get ready girls!' shouted Miss Cod, excitedly. 'I've never seen the sphere behave like this before! I'd swear something evil is just around the corner!'

Although it was correct to say that PCs Wiggery and Drudge were no oil paintings, to describe them as evil would be pushing it. Frightening maybe, and indeed, their moustaches didn't help. Neither did their oilskin capes, flapping behind them as they leapt out from the bushes, making them look like two Dr Jeckyls after knocking back the frothy drink. Perhaps blowing their whistles was a mistake too.

'DENTURES!' shouted Bethesda Chubb. 'HELMETS!' cried the others, and all of them rolled up their sleeves and pounced on the policemen like farmers catching sheep.

'LEAVE THOSE POOR MEN ALONE!' screamed Captain Dashing, but then wished he hadn't. The dreaded seagulls, excitable as ever, seemed keen to join in the fun and were eyeing him up with wicked intent.

'Nice birdies,' he whispered and started to walk back along the path. 'Nice, gentle, peaceful birdies.'

'So what you're trying to tell me is that a group of middle-aged women, all dressed in tweeds and sensible shoes, boxed you around the ears then vanished into thin air?'

The desk sergeant was looking in disbelief at the state of PCs Drudge and Wiggery as they wobbled and dribbled before him.

'Thatsh about the gisht of it, shir.'

'But not before stealing your helmets.'

'Thatsh correct. They pinched our helmetsh and just dishappeared.'

'Along with your dentures.'
'Along with our teesh, yesh. But only the upper shet with me. Poor Jack here ish mishing topsh and bottomsh.'
'Bashturdsh!' swore Jack under his breath.
'Oh, and they were shinging the Marshaleish.'
'The what?'
'The Marshaleish. The French shong!'
'La Marseillaise? You're telling me the women were French?'
'I don't know, shir. All I knowsh is they have mushles!'
'And inshtrumentsh. Don't forget the inshtrumentsh.'
'Oh, yesh. I forgot. They were a brash band.'

The door to the police station swung open and two distressed gentlemen staggered in, their clothes all ripped and shredded.

'I demand to see the officer in charge!'

Captain Dashing marched as best he could over to the desk, with a sheepish Reverend Cross in tow.

'We've been attacked, pecked to ribbons!' he said. 'Hijacked in the park!'

The desk sergeant closed his eyes and mumbled something uncharitable under his breath. Any more of these peculiar goings on and he might as well tear up his invite to the Galaxy cinema and return his fancy dress costume to the shop, he'd be going nowhere. 'Captain,' he said, turning to yet another empty page in the large report book. 'Back so soon? Pecked, you say?'

'To an inch of our lives, I tell you,' added a very emotional Reverend Cross. 'Killer seagulls! The spawn of Satan!'

The desk sergeant sighed and shook his head.

'He doesn't believe us, Hilary. I knew he wouldn't. We're wasting our time.'

'Well, someone had better believe us. I insist you do something about these witches and their infernal pets. Look!'

The captain indicated the sorry state of his clothes with a sweep of his hands. 'And I wasn't even shooting at the bloody birds!'

'Shooting?' asked the desk sergeant. 'Are you telling me you fired a gun?'

The captain threw what looked like a floppy cucumber dipped in daisies on to the counter. 'You call that a gun? I call it a travesty! An insult! Go on, charge me with possession of a dangerous vegetable!'

'They ruined his Webley,' the vicar explained. 'He's very cross.'

'Cross! I'm bloody livid! And what's more…'

The captain noticed the other gentlemen in the room.

'Wait a minute,' he said. 'I know you. You two were in the park. I saw you attacked by those witches! You see, officer. You have to believe us now. We're evidence!'

Elsie Tapp sat in the dining hall of the Alpine Palace, playing with her breakfast. The only item on the menu she could face was half a grapefruit, but now the dish had arrived the best she could do was chase the cherry around on top with her spoon. She was scared and eager to leave town, but mostly she was annoyed. Her bags were packed and ready for the porter to collect, but she had missed the morning train. To make matters worse, she had received a second telegram from her publisher, the astonishingly rude Marjorie Whippet, urging her to stay put. It seemed journalists from all over the kingdom were travelling as fast as they could towards Grubdale, and on no account must Elsie talk to them; not until Marjorie was there to tell her what to say.

'Waiter!' she said, a little louder than usual. 'Could you take this away, please?' She indicated the grapefruit with a flick of her spoon. 'And bring me a boiled egg in a cup and two large sausages in a dish. Not those fat, Lincoln monstrosities mind, just two normal sausages fit for a dog.'

'I'm sorry, madam?'

'And a fresh pot of tea, but remember - two spoons of Earl Grey and a pinch of Lapsang Souchong. I haven't a clue what you brought me last time, but it could tan leather.'

'Madam?'

'Make it less Yorkshire and more China. I'm sure you understand.'

'Of course, madam. Right away.'

Elsie sighed. She hated being bossy, but this town seemed to bring out the matron in her. The sooner she was on the train to London the better. Elsie had a holiday to rescue.

'And you can stop whimpering.'

The comment was aimed at Princess Peaches, but such was the stern rebuke the waiter mumbled an apology and hurried off to the kitchen.

The pink poodle looked out from her carpet bag and made 'where's my breakfast' noises.

'I don't think naughty dogs deserve breakfast, do you?'

Princess Peaches did and made her feelings known.

'Yes, well if you were a fruit bat you could've had my grapefruit, but you're not, so there. You'll just have to wait till your sausages arrive.'

On hearing the word, 'sausages,' Princess Peaches became far too excited and started to yap and jump up and down. Elsie tapped her sharply on the nose with her finger.

'Behave yourself! My, but what a common little doggy you are; quite the street urchin today and no mistake!'

Princess Peaches sat down at once and rubbed her nose with her paw.

# A TOUCH OF SPLEEN

'I should think so too. I don't know what these nice people must think.'

The 'nice' people in the dining room seemed very friendly, and not at all bothered by the poodle's behaviour. They were smiling and waving at Elsie with their serviettes. People outside the dining room were smiling at Elsie. People on the hotel lawn peering into the dining room were smiling at Elsie. Everyone seemed to be smiling at Elsie - with more smiling people arriving by the minute.

'There, I told you there was an egg! I knew there was an egg! Well done you two!'

Demetrios and the yellow wyrm smiled, their faces covered in soil as Rowena gave them both a hug. 'What do you think, cake and custard?'

Demetrios barked his approval. The podgy bundle of spite had developed a taste for cake at about the same time Rowena had given up ship's biscuits and bought a hamper from Portly and Fudge. As for the yellow wyrm, anything Demetrios liked, he liked too, except for rabbits; rabbits were a great disappointment.

'Look everyone, an egg!' Rowena cried. She was standing in the middle of a grid of painted white lines, and within each square was a freshly dug hole. Her audience seemed underwhelmed, a huddle of ladies in tweed still annoyed at Rowena for hijacking the wyrm.

'It's a bit dull and dirty for a dragon's egg. Aren't they supposed to be shiny and studded with gems?'

Rowena, never the best at keeping her temper, waited for the laughter to die down.

'You'd be dull and dirty too if you were this old and buried.'

'Well, if it's going to be that old then it's going to be rotten, isn't it? Stands to reason. You'd better not break the damn thing, or you'll stink us out.'

'I'd give it a shake. It might be empty.'

'I'd kick it, more like. It might be a rugby ball.'

Rowena raised her eyes to the sky. 'Go on, have your fun. Water off a duck's back to me. Sticks and stones will break my bones, but names will never hurt me.'

This was so blatantly untrue even Demetrios covered his mouth to stop the giggles.

'It'll be a different story when I've hatched the egg.'

The choice of words was unfortunate. It was impossible to escape the image of a broody Rowena in feather trimmings, sitting on the dragon's egg like a mother hen. It was too much; the mental picture just too absurd. The ladies in tweed collapsed against each other, crying with laughter.

'Oh, for pity's sake grow up!'

Rowena pulled the large egg from the soil but lost her footing and fell back on the grass. 'I don't suppose one of you ladies could lend a hand? When you've managed to catch your breath, that is. I mean I'd hate to be a spoilsport and ruin your fun.'

Bethesda took pity on her friend and pulled her to her feet. 'Try not to be so sensitive. You're a pirate after all.'

'I am nothing of the kind! Let me remind you, Miss Chubb; I stumbled aboard under false pretences. I was promised two hot baths a day and a rather fetching purple uniform with ribbons and lace. You mentioned cake, champagne and a feather mattress, none of which I've seen. So enough of this pirate nonsense; another week on board the Emily P and I'll be sporting a beard, a bad back and breath that could kill a seagull. I'm a lady, Miss Chubb, not one of your tattooed friends with chins like sideboards.'

'Enough!' Bethesda stared red-faced at Rowena, her gaze betraying each turn of a page as she struggled to think of a reply worthy of a pirate queen.

'Save your breath, dear,' Rowena said wrapping the giant egg in a shawl and placing it tight under her arm. 'I've found the egg, that's all I came for. Now if you wouldn't mind stepping aside, I'll say my goodbyes and be off. I'm sure you're more than capable of dealing with Spleen on your own.'

'Nonsense, you can't just go. You can't just decide to be a pirate one day and leave the next. It doesn't work like that.'

'I wasn't aware I was a pirate. Did I sign a contract in my sleep? Don't make me out to be a fool, Miss Chubb or I'll clip your wings. You wouldn't want a senior witch upset now, would you, not in front of your friends.'

Rowena fell silent. It was pointless to continue, for neither Bethesda nor the rest of the sisterhood seemed interested in what she had to say. A sudden movement in the ruins had caught their attention, and even Demetrios and the yellow wyrm were growling under their breath like two angry guard dogs ready to pounce.

Rowena took a tight hold of her parasol. Wizards had their wands and the sisterhood their musical instruments, but Rowena had her parasol; a silk and tasselled accessory with as many gadgets as a plumber's trouser pocket. She turned slowly around, fearing the worse but was relieved to see only a poor gentleman in a wheelchair.

'Stop growling you two for heaven's sake, and McTavish, show some common sense and hide.'

The yellow wyrm did as he was told, crouching low behind the remains of the school wall, but Demetrios growled and muttered, being a 'snort first and ask questions later' sort of creature.

'Morning!' shouted Rowena, then stepped back under the full force of the sisterhood's withering looks.

'What? So it's wrong to say hello? He's hardly likely to be Spleen now, is he? I mean look at him. I've seen fewer bandages on an Egyptian mummy.'

It was an interesting point of debate, but one dismissed as soon as considered. A bandaged gentleman in a wheelchair was precisely how an evil sorcerer should look, especially one so lucky as to survive an explosion as big as the Behemoth.

'Give me that sphere!' Bethesda cried, grabbing hold of Miss Cod's arm so tight she let out a squeal. 'Are you sure it's working?'

The sisterhood stood guard; their brass band instruments brought to bear as Bethesda shook and tapped the sphere, daring the arrow to point at the unfortunate gentleman in the distance.

'Nice day for a stroll, isn't it?' shouted Rowena, making a point of being civil. 'Well?' she whispered, recognising the glass object in Bethesda's hand from the many she had seen in the professor's workshop. 'What does our little gadget predict? Are we in for some stormy weather?'

Bethesda mumbled something under her breath and gave the sphere back to Miss Cod.

'Just as I thought,' Rowena continued, 'an unfortunate invalid out for a push. Come on, stand aside. Show respect for an old soldier.'

Rowena's description of the gentleman seemed to soften the ladies' resolve, and far from blasting the chair and its contents to kingdom come, the kindly ladies lowered their musical instruments and made sympathetic noises as the wheelchair trundled slowly over the rocks and stones.

'Such a shame.'

'The poor, poor man.'

'I've got curtains that colour back home, the very same shade.'

'Ladies, please! Let the poor gentleman pass!'

The wheelchair bumped and skidded through the ruins, as whoever pushed from behind struggled in steering the contraption between the two rows of women.

'Oh dear, war can be hell,' Rowena muttered, shaking her head at the sight of all those bandages. 'Still, you'll know better next time, won't you? Every disaster has a silver lining.'

The wheelchair stopped briefly, the unfortunate gentleman and his helper struggling with Rowena's unique logic, then shaking their heads, the two continued their journey out through the ruins and up to the grassy verge.

Miss Cod stared at the glass sphere, still insistent that something was wrong, even going so far as to shake it violently like a pepper pot over soup.

'Manners, dear,' hissed Rowena.

'Manners be damned, the arrow's stuck! You can pretend to be as caring and sympathetic as you like, but as far as I'm concerned that creature over there is …Well, I don't know what he is. He's just strange, that's what he is!'

'Really, Miss Cod; none of us are perfect.'

The woman was fit to explode. Rowena's contrary, condescending manner was guaranteed to infuriate a saint let alone a quick-tempered, middle-aged woman with hot flushes for breakfast. Even Bethesda Chubb knew when to hold her tongue where Miss Cod was concerned.

'Look!' another of the sisterhood cried. 'He's giving us the finger!'

All eyes turned to the gentleman in the wheelchair who far from insulting the sisterhood appeared to be beckoning them to follow.

'Crikey,' whispered Miss Roach. 'He's got some cheek. All of us and with him in a wheelchair? It must be the fresh air.'

'Shush, Cecily, and get that euphonium out of my face. I can't see what he's saying.'

Bethesda elbowed the lady aside and stood at the front of the group. 'Well, I never, he wants us to follow. How strange.'

Strange or not, the peculiar gentleman beckoned the ladies forward with increasingly wild sweeps of his hand.

'He's very insistent,' said Miss Cod, still shaking the sphere and glancing at the arrow. 'I don't like this one bit.'

'He's just friendly,' Rowena added, then waved at the gentleman. 'Bless him.'

The gentleman seemed agitated. Even his diminutive helper had joined in with the frantic hand signals, the two of them moving in perfect harmony like some new dance from the city.

Miss Roach smiled and began to wave her hands like the peculiar gentleman. 'I wonder what they want,' she asked, shimmying around the ruins. 'Music perhaps, should we strike up the band?'

'We'll do no such thing,' snapped Bethesda. 'We're not here to party; we're here to find Spleen.'

At the mention of the sorcerer's name, the peculiar gentleman sat up straight in his chair and used his hand to cover his face like a mask. There was a gasp of shock and surprise from the ladies.

'Well, I never! He's impersonating Spleen!'

At the second mention of the evil sorcerer, the peculiar gentleman drew his finger across his throat, mimicked being shot, and if that wasn't enough, pretended to be stabbed multiple times in the stomach.

'He lost me on the second bullet. What's he trying to say, that he wants Spleen dead?'

# A TOUCH OF SPLEEN

The peculiar gentleman nodded his head with such enthusiasm that his fez fell off, and as the sisterhood pondered the question of who he was and what he knew of the terrible Spleen, the gentleman's accomplice turned the wheelchair around and started the long trek to town.

Miss Cod squealed with excitement and nudged Bethesda in the ribs. 'Look, the sphere's working, the arrow's spinning.'

'Weapons!' shouted Bethesda staring after the wheelchair as it disappeared down the lane. 'Music!'

'You mean we're going after them?'

'Seems stupid not to. What do you say, girls?'

The ladies were all for the plan, their brass band instruments raised to their lips.

'Well you can forget about me,' Rowena said, beckoning the yellow wyrm to come out from the shadows. 'My days of following peculiar men in wheelchairs are over. Besides, I've got an egg to look after, a very important egg.'

'I don't think so. You're coming with us - and you're bringing the wyrm. We need your McTavish in a fight.'

'Really? Well, I refuse. There, I've said it. Now, what are you going to do, clap me in irons and throw me to the sharks?'

'We're on land, silly. I'll thump you.'

'You'll do no such thing! One more step and I'll put you over my knee and slap some sense into you! Now go away and leave me in peace. As for McTavish, it's up to him what he does. I'm not his boss. He just prefers my company, don't you dear?'

McTavish ambled over to Rowena and rested his head on her shoulder. 'Bllllrppppt!' he said.

'You've not heard the last of this! Mutiny is treason!'

'Oh do shut up and be off with you. I'm far too long in the tooth for fisticuffs and policeman's helmets. You've all your pirates to capture Spleen with; more than enough muscles and magic without my help. What would you need with an old witch like me?'

'Bacon!' whispered the yellow wyrm as Rowena scratched him under the chin. 'Bacon!'

MIKE WILLIAMS

## Chapter Seventeen

For a town like Grubdale, nestled high amongst the sheep and turnips, the arrival of the railway in the late 1860s brought prosperity, tourism and the chance of fresh fish. It brought the Oxford Ragwort, Buddleia and a nasty cough too. For Evaline Bamforth, waiting nervously on the station platform and continually checking her watch, none of this mattered. It was 1932 and Yorkshire's own Tarzan, Fred Barnes, was expected on the 12.15 from Manchester.

A young porter wheeled an empty trolley along the platform. He whistled as he went about his work, turning the contraption around and pushing it in the opposite direction so he could cast a cheeky wink. Evaline smiled. She smiled at the station guard, who deciding the young man was acting the goat had clipped his ear as he'd passed. She smiled at the station clock, the pigeons at her feet, even the couple sitting on a bench and eating fish and chips. She smiled at everyone and everything in her attempt to appear graceful and calm, the very picture of elegant sophistication. But beneath the hastily applied rouge and face powder, the peacock blue coat and matching cloche hat, Evaline was all panic. She looked at her watch then rechecked the time on the large platform clock that ticked so loud and slow above her. The more she willed the minute hand to move, the more she regretted the absence of a welcoming brass band or even some bunting. No one it seemed was interested in her special guest, not even the local press. The news that the mysterious Felicity Merryweather was in town had changed everything. Sugary-sweet romance had won the day and 'Tarzan in Trouble' would have to take second place. Evaline's smile vanished from her face. What if the young Mr Barnes took one look at the deserted platform and caught the next train home? If only she'd thought more about publicity. If only the invitations had the name 'Fred Barnes' written out in large letters, instead of 'a very special, mystery guest.' If only she'd phoned the Grubdale and District Gazette earlier. If only…

# A TOUCH OF SPLEEN

Evaline shivered and stamped her feet. There were too many 'if only's'. There were more 'regrets' here than a songwriter could put to music. 'Damn!' she swore. 'Damn and blast!'

'Excuse me?' she called, trying to catch the attention of the porter. 'Have you any news about the Manchester train?'

The young man rubbed the back of his head, his good humour banished from the clip to the ear.

'Well the last thing I heard, it was black and covered in soot.'

The guard clipped the young man's ear again and pushed him aside. 'Don't mind our lad,' he said. 'He's all fluff and no whiskers. I'll give him what for when he gets home. Now, madam. If I could be of some service? What exactly did you want to know?'

'I asked if there was any news of the Manchester train.'

'News you say. Well…' The guard put his hand to his ear in dramatic fashion and as if on cue a whistle sounded loud and shrill. 'I should say it's here, bang on time as usual. We're nothing if not punctual at the London, Midland and Scottish.'

Evaline thanked the guard and, shielding her eyes from the glare of the afternoon sun, looked in the general direction of the Grubdale tunnel. That was the trouble with Grubdale, it was a town built in a basin, surrounded by hills. The arrival of a train was as much a surprise to the passengers waiting on the platform as for the pigeons pecking at niceties on the track. Hidden from sight by the surrounding hills, then threading their way through the long tunnel, each expected train would burst into view with a blast of noise, an explosion of smoke and, depending on the driver, a squeal of brakes as the end of the line came sharply into view.

The guard checked his watch and nodded approvingly at the first signs of smoke in the distance, and not for the first time that day, Evaline felt her stomach turn cold with guilt. Her little ruse didn't seem so small anymore. It had grown to Machiavellian proportions, outreaching even Lady Macbeth handing out the cutlery.

'Are you alright?' the guard asked. 'You're as white as a sheet. Do you want to sit down?'

'I'm fine, really I am. It's just been a busy morning.'

'Aye, well don't fall over the side or you'll have me as white as a sheet. Best to step back a bit and be safe.'

Evaline did as she was told and waited nervously for the train to appear. She was being silly, she told herself. Last minute nerves, nothing more than that. The preparations for the party were complete. All she had to do was see the young Mr Barnes safely to his hotel, make sure of his costume then escort him in secret to the cinema before the other guests arrived. What could possibly go wrong? Everything, she thought - anything and everything starting from now.

There is something warm and comforting about a train arriving in a station; the cosy smell of grease and soot, the clouds of steam as the large wheels come to a stop. Even the pigeons, nervous of sudden movement, bathe in the smoke and soot till they fall half-baked from the rafters. Evaline sighed. What will be, will be, she mused as the doors to the carriages opened, and the first of the passengers stepped down to the platform. There were the unfortunate tourists and battle-worn shoppers, all the usual passengers thought Evaline on a typical Grubdale afternoon and not a handsome chap amongst them.

'Are you for Manchester?' asked the guard. 'You've ages yet. The next train isn't for forty minutes.'

'No, it's alright. I was waiting for someone. They must have missed the train I suppose.'

The guard tut-tutted in disapproval. His life was measured to the minute by the London, Midland and Scottish, and the thought of anyone being so unpunctual as to miss a train was a sin as equal to Eve biting the apple. 'Unforgivable,' he muttered and seeing that all the carriage doors were closed, went away to his office for a pork pie sandwich and a swig of tea.

Evaline sighed and turned to leave. Fred Barnes had failed to appear, and there was nothing more she could do. She would have to apologise to poor Percy and explain to the guests that…Evaline didn't know what to explain. If only she'd known Felicity Merryweather was in town, she could have invited her instead.

'For heaven's sake Mabel, don't pull the damned thing, just twist it!'

Evaline stopped in her tracks.

'I am twisting the bloody thing, and it still isn't working!'

'Then lean against the door and put your weight behind it. Come on love. I know you can do better than that!'

'I don't know what you mean, Fred Barnes! Shame on you, I'm a good girl, I am!' said the good girl, giggling.

'Ouch! How dare you!'

There were more giggles and then the sound of a carriage door being swung wide open.

'There you see, you just needed a push!'

'You leave my bum alone, Fred Barnes, or I'll whistle for a bobby! Taking liberties with my 'derriere', the very thought of it!'

Evaline turned and smiled at the sight of her special guest standing on the platform. She waved excitedly, but then secretaries to very important people tend not to jump up and down and shout 'Coo-ee! Over here!' Secretaries to very important people don't have to. Secretaries to very important people tend to organise brass bands, bunting and a photographer at least. Guilt returned with a cold grip to her stomach.

'Mrs Bamforth!' shouted Fred Barnes. 'I told you I'd be here!'

Evaline smoothed down her coat and nodded in approval as the young man approached. What a handsome man, she thought. A nicely scrubbed, boy-next-door; fresh faced and free from the usual trappings of fame and fortune. Although, she considered after closer inspection, perhaps too free. Success didn't seemed to amount to much, just a nice suit, a cardboard suitcase and a young lady in tow. A young lady that looked to Evaline's eyes as though she'd one foot on the social ladder and the rest of herself in a chip shop.

'Mr Barnes,' she said and gave the young man her hand to kiss. 'So nice to see you.'

'And it's nice to see you Mrs Pricklewood.'

Evaline looked puzzled for a moment before remembering Pricklewood was supposed to be her name. 'And this is?' she asked, looking at the young man's acquaintance.

'This is Mabel, Mrs Pricklewood. She's the Pudsey Carnival Queen.'

Quite, thought Evaline, mishearing the title altogether.

A small group of not-so-small women huddled together at the corner of the high street, all dressed the same in tweeds and sensible shoes, and all out of breath. Their chase had come to nothing, the pace too fast, and now the peculiar gentleman in the wheelchair had disappeared with not even a strip of bandage left behind as a clue. Flushed and footsore from their dash downhill, the sisterhood leant on each other for support, a poor excuse for a brass band with hardly the strength to blow a note.

'Play us a song, then,' said a small girl sucking a large sweet, and taking great delight in rattling it from side to side in her mouth.

'Clear off!' snapped the very unmusical lead trombone.

'That's rude!' the small girl cried, taking the sweet out of her mouth for better effect.

'And so is this!' replied the lead trombone sending a bolt of green magic fizzing towards the little girl's feet.

'Discipline in the ranks!'

'Oh give it a rest, Bethesda - we're tired.'

All the sisterhood were tired. The poor ladies had run their best, but strong knees and sensible shoes were no match for a fast set of wheels and a steep slope.

'What's that bloody sphere saying now?' Miss Trout asked as the little girl with the big sweet ran screaming for cover. 'If it's pointing back there,' she said indicating the top of the hill with her trombone, 'then I may have to smash it to pieces.'

Miss Cod gave the appearance of looking closely at the glass sphere, but her attention was elsewhere. Being a pirate wasn't half the fun she'd been led to believe. What was the point in amassing a small fortune in gold if the only things you could buy were rum and plug tobacco? Grubdale was a revelation, a Sultan Bazar in comparison, its shop windows full of all manner of baubles and trinkets, each as essential as the rest and every one of them whispering 'buy me, buy me,' in soft, seductive voices. 'It seems to be pointing over there,' she said, ignoring the little red arrow and quickly shoving the sphere back in her pocket before anyone could tell her different. 'Percival Brothers' Department Store. Come on girls, follow me!'

The sisterhood needed no persuasion. Even Bethesda Chubb did as she was told, admiring a beautifully tailored jacket in the window before following the group through the large double doors. The concierge, a thin shrew of a man in a maroon coat and trimmings, stood in their way.

'I'm sorry ladies, but I must ask you to leave. This is a department store not an orchestra pit.'

'I'm sorry?' Bethesda asked, assuming an air of innocence. 'Do we look like musicians?'

The concierge looked carefully at the ladies and shook his head. 'I can't let you in. Not unless you leave your instruments outside. I can't have you knocking our display cabinets over now, can I? Be bad for business.'

'And what instruments might they be, perchance?' Bethesda asked, fluttering her eyes.

The concierge was lost for words. In place of a miserable brass band there now stood a group of gentle middle-aged women, all eager to shop – gentle that is except for the eccentric Amazon standing in front, a frightening figure of womanhood with knuckles like gobstoppers and biceps so large they could pass for coconuts. It was a battle lost from the start.

'Welcome to Percival Brothers,' he said, stepping back to let them through. 'Ground floor perfumery, stationery and leather goods…'

Fred Barnes, Yorkshire's own Tarzan, laughed and nudged his equally jovial partner in the ribs. 'See Mabel, I told you I was popular,' he whispered to the Pudsey Carnival Queen. 'Bigger than Eccles cakes I am. Stick with me, love, and I'll get you into pasties.'

Mabel Fletcher wobbled, giggled, and pinched him in the bum. 'It's not pasties I want to get into,' she said in a sultry voice so laden with innuendo that even caterpillars had trouble crawling. Their chaperone, for that's how Evaline Bamforth saw herself after three streets and a coffee shop of this nonsense, groaned and urged them forward.

'For heavens' sake, give it a rest you two. You're not in Hollywood now.'

None of them had been to the USA, let alone Hollywood, but Evaline's rebuke served to maintain the pretence. All three were climbing the steps leading to the main doors of the Alpine Palace Hotel where fifty or more ladies waited in line. Fred turned to Evaline and winked. 'Thanks for organising the "troops"' he said and waved at the crowd as he approached. Evaline blushed. The 'troops' were none of her doing. Perhaps news of Tarzan's visit had made the morning papers, but then perhaps not. Many of the ladies were happily ignoring the young man and clutching copies of sugary sweet romances to their chest, books with titles such as 'Summer Knights,' 'The Lilac Cavalier,' and 'A Whimpering in the Willows.' Evaline sighed, only one author produced such drivel and how typical of her luck that the dreaded woman was staying at the Alpine Palace; Felicity Merryweather, the Queen of Romance – or as was now painted in big red letters on a banner above the main desk of the hotel, "Felicity Merryweather in Person. Signatures: One shilling and sixpence."

Poor Elsie sat in the foyer of the Alpine Palace and tried her best to look calm and in control. In front of her and stacked as high as her publisher dared were numerous piles of books - prison bars in paper and print.

'Just "From Felicity" will do; otherwise, we'll be here all day,' her publisher said, a matter-of-fact looking lady in twin set and pearls who seemed to have an inexhaustible supply of Elsie's latest masterpiece "The Regency Rascal."

'There is no more Felicity!' Elsie snapped causing mild panic in the queue, then wrote in slow, laboured copperplate 'With best wishes to you and your family, from Elsie Tapp and Poodle,' on the next book she opened.

'It's your funeral, dear. But while you're still Miss Merryweather, and still under contract, I suggest fewer words and more full stops. You can be Elsie Tapp as long as you like after we've sold these books, but not before.'

Elsie gritted her teeth and signed the next few books simply 'Felicity,' much to her publisher's relief.

'That's the spirit! More books to the minute – well done!'

Elsie felt trapped. The monstrously matter-of-fact Marjorie Whippet had been travelling all night and showed no signs of fading. She'd arrived at the hotel demanding tea, bacon sandwiches and a porter to deliver the boxes of books from the station, and the ease at which she'd assumed command was frightening.

'This way dears, don't be shy. Felicity won't bite.'

Felicity might be lacking teeth, but Elsie wasn't. It may have been the fiftieth book or the fortieth; she didn't care. Her wrists were getting sore, her handwriting more deplorable and if Marjorie didn't cry 'stop!' soon there'd be trouble - 'bottle of ink over the head,' kind of trouble and possibly tears.

'Yes, she'd love to. That's very kind.'

'I'm sorry?'

Someone was speaking to Marjorie Whippet, and whatever the nice voice had asked, Marjorie had accepted on Elsie's behalf - too eagerly, the beleaguered author thought, and without consultation. She turned her head to see a soft, care-worn gentleman with a red face.

'This is Mr Percy Bamforth, dear,' Marjorie explained. 'He's run all the way from the high street to invite us to a party. Not any old party, but THE party. They'll be photographers!'

'Gentleman of the Press,' corrected the kindly looking man.

'Posh People…'

'Town Councillors and their wives.'

'And lots of grub…'

'Pork Pies and Egg sandwiches,' insisted Percy Bamforth, as though the promise of anything else would be unthinkable.

'Best of all, Elsie dear, the party's in the local cinema, and we'll get to watch "Dracula"! Isn't that kind of Mr Bamforth? We'll be guests of honour - extra, special guests of honour!'

Percy seemed embarrassed. 'Aye, well – I'd be delighted if you could come. My wife has nearly all of your books, Miss Merryweather, and those she hasn't she gets from the library. Evaline would never forgive me if I didn't invite you to the party. There would be war.

'Oh, and it's fancy dress,' Percy added, as way of explanation.

Marjorie's eyes lit up. 'How wonderful!' she cried.

'Not that you two ladies need bother with costumes.'

Elsie stared suspiciously at the gentleman. She'd read about people like him before, naturists – not to be trusted at parties, especially when reaching for the olives.

'Just come as you are.'

Elsie sighed with relief. The human body, never at its best after fifty something years, looked even worse devoid of fabric, and positively ridiculous when stepping out of a bath. Nature, she thought, should be constrained at all times, and naturists shot. She beckoned Marjorie close and whispered in her ear.

'Thank the kind gentleman for his invitation, but tell him "no".'
Marjorie shook her head.
'I'm sorry, dear, but we're going. It's publicity Elsie, my life and blood. Trust me, I know what I'm doing. You'll never guess who's coming, none other than Fred Barnes!'

There was a brief pause as both Marjorie and Elsie struggled with the name.

'Never heard of him,' Elsie said.

'And neither have I, but then I'd never been north of Enfield till today, so what do I know? According to this nice, kind gentleman, Mr Barnes is famous – North of England famous, whatever that means.'

Elsie tried to hide her annoyance but scribbled her name roughly and with much feeling into a copy of 'Three Cheers for the Hussar,' not as rough though as the voice that now said 'You couldn't possibly add "To George, with best wishes", could you?'

Elsie nodded, scrawled the extra words and handed the book back to what could only be described as Hercules in a headscarf. 'Here you are,' she said, smiling as the gruff woman in the large trench coat and wellington boots mumbled a gruff reply and shuffled self-consciously out of the hotel.

'Bye Mr Simpkins,' called out a very worldly gentleman behind the reception desk, and the gruff woman in the trench coat nearly stumbled on the steps in her hurry to get home.

'Now, where were we?' continued the receptionist. 'Oh yes, the honeymoon suite for a Mr Barnes. Oh dear, Mrs Bamforth – there seems to be a problem. Our honeymoon suite is booked out to a Mrs Pricklewood. There's no mention of a Mr Barnes.'

Evaline Bamforth stood impatiently at the hotel desk, her two guests somewhere in the foyer and no doubt giggling or worse.

'There's no problem at all,' she said looking around the room. 'That would be me, I made the booking. I'm Mrs Pricklewood.'

'But you're Mrs Bamforth.'

'Not today, I'm not. Today I'm Mrs Pricklewood.'

The worldly receptionist raised his eyebrows and looked knowingly at Evaline. 'Of course – and would sir and madam be wanting breakfast and a morning newspaper?'

Evaline was about to answer when she noticed her husband skulking behind a pillar.

'Percy!' she cried. 'What are you doing here? Why aren't you at home putting on your makeup and costume?'

If the worldly receptionist's eyebrows could move any higher, they'd be a wig.

Percy Bamforth shrugged his shoulders and walked over. 'I just wanted to see if everything was alright, and…'

'You have your guilty face on, dear. What's happened?'

'Nothing's happened, well, nothing in the way you mean "happened". It's just that I've invited another guest for tonight.'

'Really?'

'I know I should have talked it over with you first, I'm sorry – I acted on impulse. But you'll understand when I mention her name.'

'It's a "Her" is it?' Evaline asked.

'Does the name Felicity Merryweather, ring a bell?'

Evaline stared at her husband in surprise. 'DONG!' she said, trying not to laugh, then hugged Percy and kissed him on the forehead. 'You've invited Miss Merryweather! That's brilliant, what a clever man you are! Tarzan and the Queen of Romance, it's almost a title for a film!'

The man behind the desk coughed politely and asked his question again. 'So, would sir be wanting breakfast tomorrow and a morning paper?'

Percy looked confused. 'I expect so, but I'm not sure what it's got to do with you.'

'Oh dear,' giggled Evaline. 'It's not my husband you should ask but Mr Barnes.'

'My apologies, Mrs Pricklewood.'

'Mrs Pricklewood? Who's Mrs Pricklewood? This is my wife you're talking to - Mrs Bamforth.'

While the man behind the desk scratched his head in confusion, a clearly delighted Evaline hugged her husband even tighter. 'It appears we'll be entertaining another queen this evening, too,' she said. 'Our amorous Mr Barnes has brought a friend. That's her over there. Mabel Fletcher, the Pudsey Carnival Queen.'

The receptionist considered himself a man of the world, but apparently of a very different world from the likes of Mr and Mrs Bamforth, or was it Mr and Mrs Pricklewood, or Mrs Pricklewood and Mr Bamforth?

'So how many breakfasts for tomorrow should we say? Two, four, eight?'

'Oh, who cares about breakfast!' laughed Evaline. 'Just hand over the keys and let the fun begin!'

The receptionist did as he was told; puzzled, shocked and slightly in awe.

## Chapter Eighteen

The sisterhood were happy, the staff of Percival Brothers' Department Store were delighted, but most important of all Bethesda Chubb, scourge of the seven seas or whatever the number was back home, was smiling - she'd discovered chocolate, and lots of it. 'Heaven in a paper bag,' she whispered and popped another truffle into her mouth.

The women had shopped for hours and were now standing outside the main doors of the store, no longer ladies in tweed but ladies of fashion - exotic sirens dressed in all manner of finery with no hat too large, no dress too colourful, and in the case of those partial to tobacco, no cigarette holder too long. It was as though Vogue had arrived in Grubdale, but having being dropped in a puddle and with all its pages mixed up.

The more narcissistic of the women twirled around in front of the vast store windows, entranced by their new clothes, while the more generous complimented each other on their appearance. 'Your shoes, dear – too lovely, too divine. And your coat - so big and fluffy, so flattering to your figure.'

Those less sure of their appearance dashed back inside then reappeared shortly after holding more bags and draped with even more stoles and accessories.

'What do you think? Are these all too much?'

'Maybe the birds, dear. You look like a roost.'

Even Bethesda had succumbed to the call of fashion, not so much the fabric of her dress as the cut of the cloth, chocolate-stained but robust, pleats and belts aplenty, and with riding boots and a crop to complete the transformation.

'Crikey Bethesda, that's some outfit you have there. I don't know whether to shake your hand or salute.'

Bethesda wasn't listening. She was lost in her own world as yet another truffle followed the last, her smile brown with confectionary as the deliciously addictive chocolate melted in her mouth.

Someone squealed; someone or something, a high pitched screech that failed to stop.

'Ouch! What a horrid noise!' cried Miss Roach, putting her fingers in her ears and looking accusatively at the sister with the feathery hat. 'Are those bloody birds up there dead?'

'They most certainly are!'

'They sound pretty lively to me.'

'Don't be ridiculous; they're stuffed!'

'Can't you give them a knock on the head, to be sure?'

'No I could not, my hat's a work of art, not an aviary! Dammit all, Cecily, I reckon that noise is coming from your wrap. Why don't you give that a slap instead?'

Horrified at the suggestion her fur stole was anything but dead, Cecily Roach pointed to another high queen of fashion, this one boasting a large hat with lobsters and seashells attached.

'Don't you point your finger at me!'

The high pitched squeal continued, not deafening but annoying, like a score of fingernails on a blackboard with a choir of screeching owls practising their scales as accompaniment. The ladies covered their ears and blamed each other in turn, everyone that is who wore a feathery hat, a fur stole or had anything remotely animal pinned to their clothing.

'It's you! That awful noise is coming from you!'

The circle of ladies stepped back, leaving the only member of the sisterhood without a new hat, coat or fashion accessory, guilty as charged.

'Miss Cod!'

The accused sat on the steps of Percival Brothers' Department Store engrossed in a game of paddle bat. 'One, two, three, four, five, six, seven…' she counted as she tried to keep the rubber ball bouncing on the wood, then swore as the damn thing hit her on the nose again. Seemingly unaware of the commotion, Miss Cod unwrapped the string of elastic from around the bat and tried once more. 'One, two, three, four, five, six…Damn it!'

'Miss Cod, are you deaf?'

'Not now, dear. Can't you see I'm busy? That nice man in the store made it look easy.'

'Elizabeth, please! That infernal noise is coming from your pocket!'

'But I've nearly got the hang of this toy. Look – one, two, three, four…'

The small rubber ball on the elastic bounced back and forth, and for once Miss Cod managed to count past ten.

'…eleven, twelve…'

'Thirteen!' shouted Bethesda Chubb catching the ball in her hand.

# A TOUCH OF SPLEEN

Miss Cod stared angrily at Bethesda. 'Spoilsport! I didn't pinch your chocolates!' She was about to say more but realised her mistake. Her expression changed from annoyance to horror.

'Oh my, it's the sphere!' she cried and jumped to her feet. 'I forgot about the sphere!'

Miss Cod fumbled in her coat pockets and pulled out the offending object, now screaming like a steam kettle and hot to the touch, the arrow hardly visible as it spun around at alarming speed.

'It's Spleen! Oh crikey, he must be so close he's treading on our toes!'

'WEAPONS!' shouted Bethesda, and in a blur of green magic, a large bass drum with the picture of the good ship Emily P on its skin appeared strapped to her front.

The rest of the sisterhood followed suit, their various instruments pointing in every direction, each trombone, tuba and cornet hissing with green steam.

'Christmas carols already?' mumbled an old gentleman as he made his uncertain way past the band. 'Don't know where time goes nowadays,' he said as he dropped a couple of pennies down the end of a tenor horn. 'Only yesterday it was breakfast.'

Miss Cod struggled with the sphere. It glowed hot and passing it from one hand to the other like a baked potato burned her fingers. 'Ouch!' she cried, letting it drop to the floor, except instead of falling from her hand the sphere hovered in mid-air like a giant, noisy beetle.

'Goodness, I didn't know it could do that!'

'Well don't lose it now, not after all the trouble we've been through.'

Miss Cod bit her lip. It was best not to argue with Bethesda, especially when armed with the big bass drum. The only 'trouble' they'd had was trying to find dresses in a right size and choosing which dessert to go with which pie. 'Trouble' was hardly a word Miss Cod would choose to describe a day spent shopping. 'Bloody good fun,' and 'about time too,' were far better.

'What's happening now? That sphere has a mind of its own!'

The sphere had more than a mind; it had wings and a voice, and not content with either, the sphere lit up like a glow worm and made the shape of a big star in the sky to catch the sisterhood's attention.

'I think it's trying to tell us something!' cried Miss Roach in amazement.

In the absence of a convenient well and stupid children who should know better, then yes, the sphere was trying to tell them something. It was trying to point to a strange caped figure in the shadows carrying a body in its arms. Four of its arms, at least, with two left over.

'Or make pretty pictures.'

'Pretty pictures? Damn, I should have read the manual. I never realised the sphere could do half this stuff.'

'Manual? What manual, are you telling me there's a manual?'

'Everything has a manual, Bethesda. It's one of the professor's pet topics. Science is just the search for the right book.'

'Well right book or not, the sphere is telling us something; it's telling us to head over to that building. What do the lights say above the doorway? Your eyes are better than mine.'

'I think they spell out the word "Galaxy" There, you see – that's why the sphere drew a star! I'm not sure about the smaller lights though; I can read the word "Dracula" if that makes any sense.'

Bethesda sighed. '"The Galaxy Dracula." Funny name for a department store. Mind you; it seems the place to be – look at all those people queuing outside. Are you sure that sphere of yours isn't just interested in shopping? It's just a thought.'

Miss Cod bit her lip.

'FORWARD!' shouted Bethesda, banging her drum. 'FOLLOW ME!'

The sisterhood struck up a lively tune and marched along the high street, the perfect disguise but for their unfortunate choice of music, Oh Come, All Ye Faithful.

'Steady on, Constable. You didn't see a thing.'

'But Sharge, itsh them bashturds who shtole my teesh. You can't jusht let them walk away!'

The sergeant had every reason to let the sisterhood walk away; not wanting a fight with the big, bad drummer lady being one, and being fond of his dentures in situ being another. He pulled PC Drudge back into the shadows and tried to calm him down.

'You said "ladies in tweed," not ladies of fashion. We wouldn't want to arrest the wrong women now, would we?'

'But itsh them, Sharge! The brash band! It'll be the Marshaleish necsht!'

'Nonsense, they're guests of Mr Bamforth, and in fancy dress too, just like us.'

'Shept they're not. They're witchesh!'

'And we're ballerinas. It amounts to the same. We're working undercover. I'm sorry men, but these were the only costumes left. Now come on, hold hands and do what I told you – le pas de quatre!'

If only the sisterhood had played The Dance of the Little Swans, then perhaps the four policemen in tutus and uniform would have won a prize. As it was, they deserved hardly a footnote in fancy dress history as they danced out from the shadows, into the light and up the steps to the Galaxy cinema.

Anyone who was anyone seemed to be at the party. It was as though the streets had been swept clean of people, the shops all closed for the evening and with not a single soul anywhere to ask for directions. The great and the good of the town gathered in the foyer of the Galaxy cinema, some happy with their fancy dress costumes, others most definitely not.

'Good evening, Sergeant. So glad you could come!' shouted Percy Bamforth over the heads of his guests. 'Please, you and your men help yourself to drinks and sandwiches!'

Percy smiled at the Grubdale constabulary in their blue uniforms, tutus and big black boots; at least his wasn't the only ridiculous costume at the party, a point of view shared by the sergeant who, appreciating the full splendour of the poor man's gorilla costume, nodded in sympathy.

'Thank you, we will!' shouted the sergeant, and helped himself to a sausage roll and a meat paste sandwich.

Percy returned to the task in hand, being photographed for the Grubdale and District Advertiser by a theatrical gentleman with a waxed moustache and brown suede shoes.

'Now, if Mr Gorilla wouldn't mind beating his chest and snarling at the camera? That's the spirit, Mr Bamforth, well done! More menace in those eyes, perhaps? Imagine wanting to tear a man limb from limb – go on, you beast, let your imagination run wild.'

Percy's imagination did just that, flicking through the pages of every butcher's manual in the county; but whatever the violence stirring in his breast, Percy's eyes spoke more of indigestion than blood-crazed slaughter.

'Oh well, I suppose it will have to do,' said the photographer, his dreams of the Daily Mail Photographer of The Year vanishing with a single press of the shutter. 'Beggars can't be choosers, as they say. The show must go on.'

'Absolutely!' agreed Percy, and offered the disgruntled gentleman a plate of sandwiches before he could utter another pointless cliché.

'Egg and cress! My favourite!'

Somewhat cheered up by the food, the photographer glanced around the room, trying his best to decide who next to grace the social pages of the Grubdale and District Advertiser. It was a poor catch at the best of times, but where were all the celebrities promised?

'So tell me, where are the special guests? Has the delightful Mr Barnes arrived?'

The delightful Mr Barnes had arrived, and in an animal fur leotard that covered just enough of his body to ward off terminal goosebumps. He was being made a fuss of by a small group of middle-aged women who, considering they were supposed to be on the lookout for an evil sorcerer with a bent for world domination, should have known better.

'Did you knit it yourself, dear?' joked a very naughty Miss Roach, her cheeks more red than usual from drinking two large cocktails, one after the other. 'I'd give it a saucer of milk and put it out for the night if I were you,' she said, pulling at his leotard. 'Puss! Puss! Puss! Come to Mummy!'

'Oooo, look Cecily! He's got hairs!'

Fred Barnes tried to protest, smacking away a variety of hands intent on heading south.

'Now then, ladies, behave! I'm supposed to be giving autographs!'

'Then scribble your name on these, jungle boy!' laughed an even naughtier Miss Haddock, three cocktails the worse for wear and pretending to rip open her blouse.

Bethesda Chubb was not impressed. She pulled the woman back by her ears and stabbed at her with her riding crop. 'Behave yourself! You're acting like a drunken tart! Whoever that young man is-' Bethesda pointed towards the harassed figure of Fred Barnes, now defending his modesty with a potted palm. '-he's no evil sorcerer. Remember, it's Spleen we're after, not a bit of slap-and-tickle!'

'Speak for yourself, dear!' cried Miss Haddock, wagging her finger in Bethesda's face. 'It's been an age since my tickle was slapped. The trouble with you, Miss Bossy-Britches, is you've forgotten how to parr-tay!'

Cecily Roach wobbled over and wagged her finger at Bethesda too. 'Why can't we have parties like this? That last one you threw was rubbish. You should take notes. We're having a whale of a time here, and listen…'

Miss Roach put her hand to her ear in an exaggerated fashion. 'You hear, no seagulls!'

'Well said, Cicely! It's about time someone told Miss Chubb here the truth. We don't like your ship, we don't like your parties and we can't stand your bloody birds! Other than that though, you're lovely, so give us a kiss!'

Bethesda pushed the drunken Miss Haddock away and stared angrily at Miss Roach, who, with more than her share of Dutch courage, put her tongue out and blew a raspberry.

'You need a man, dear,' she giggled and pinched Bethesda's cheek. 'And the sooner, the better, if you don't mind me saying. Oi! Drinkies-on-tray person!' she shouted as Sid Bottle limped past in an ill-fitting dinner suit and shoes. 'I'll have another one of these delicious concoctions, whatever they're called.'

## A TOUCH OF SPLEEN

'Mersey Knee-Tremblers, ma'am.'

'Really? What a peculiar name, well give us two more and we'll call it a wobble.'

'Mr Pricklewood! Mr Pricklewood!'

Fred Barnes was in urgent need of help. The drink-fuelled sisterhood had fallen for his manly charms, intent on examining them in every detail.

'Mr Pricklewood, please!'

Percy nudged the photographer and winked. 'Not much of a Tarzan if he's scared of a bunch of ladies. I'd better do something I suppose.

'Coming, Fred! Never fear!' Percy assumed the manner of a wild beast, beat his chest and ran up the foyer stairs with as much noise and flapping of his arms as was decent. He was a great success. The party guests cheered and thought him a terrific sport as he took tight hold of the young Fred Barnes and lifted him to safety.

'That's the spirit, you two! Now hold that pose for a second!'

Fred Barnes tried his best to smile, but being carried down the stairs by a fat man in a gorilla suit was hardly Tarzan and his Mate.

'Ooooh, this is wonderful!' cried the photographer. 'You've never looked lovelier! Your fans will be cock-a-hoop!'

What fans these were, Fred could only imagine, and as Percy carried him down the stairs, it was impossible not to think of his film career taking a sudden, unwanted change in direction.

'Ahhh! Miss Merryweather! What an honour!'

Fame it seemed was as fleeting and flimsy as the safety pins on Fred's leotard. All eyes turned to Elsie Tapp as she stepped into the foyer, her poodle in her arms and with her publisher, the shrewish Marjorie Whippet in tow.

Evaline Bamforth beamed with happiness, Percy's mayorship all but guaranteed.

'May I present my wife, the beautiful Evaline,' Percy said, dropping the Yorkshire Tarzan on his feet.

Elsie Tapp nodded.

'And Mr Fred Barnes, who I'm sure needs no introduction.'

Elsie waved a few fingers in the poor man's direction.

'And Miss Mabel Fletcher, the Pudsey Carnival Queen.'

It was a red faced and angry Carnival Queen, having been elbowed aside by the sisterhood in their quest for jungle delights. Elsie smiled at the young woman then shook her head kindly as Miss Fletcher tried to curtsy.

'No need for that dear,' she said. 'I'm just a silly writer.'

Percy stepped forward. 'Here, let me get you a drink before the show begins. I'm not sure what they're called, but everyone finds them delicious.'

'Knee Tremblers,' said the ever-knowledgeable Sid Bottle.

'How quaint. I don't mind if I do,' Elsie said and helped herself to a small glass of the orange and green layered cocktail. 'Here's to a lovely evening.'

'Goodness,' she said, coughing and spluttering. 'Very original! Not sure if drinking these would help my enjoyment of the film. Perhaps something a little less adventurous? A cup of tea would be nice. Oh look, pork pie and sausage rolls, now there is a spread! You can't beat simple fare, that's what I say. Do you know, I was offered a prawn cocktail once. I wasn't sure whether to eat it or feed it. But this,' she said, looking appreciatively at the food on offer. 'Now this is simply splendid.'

Percy looked lovingly at his wife as Elsie chose a small slice of ham and egg pie and popped it in her mouth.

'Interesting costumes. Don't tell me, young man, let me guess. You're dressed as?'

'Tarzan.'

'Really? Edgar Rice Burroughs?'

'Just pie and chips for me, love.'

Elsie Tapp wasn't sure what to say, so she smiled and helped herself to a large sausage roll.

'Well, we might as well take our seats, don't you think?' Percy said, breaking the awkward silence.

'Oh no you don't,' interrupted the photographer. 'Not without a few more pictures for the paper, you naughty boy. Felicity Merryweather in Grubdale? I'd be strung up if I came back empty-handed.'

Percy sighed; it was all publicity and publicity was good, but did the awful man have to call him 'boy?' The smile froze on his face as he imagined the theatrical gentleman with the suede shoes swinging gently by the neck.

'Books!' shouted Marjorie Whippet. 'No photographs without the book!' She rummaged in her handbag and brought out a copy of Elsie's latest romance, pushing it firmly into the author's hands. 'And make sure you hold it up to the camera. I want everyone to read the title.'

Princess Peaches growled.

'Do we need the dog? Can't you hand it to someone?'

Elsie glared at her publisher and gave away the book instead. 'No photographs without my poodle,' she said, cutting the conversation dead. 'Now, where do you want me?' she asked the photographer. 'By the aspidistra?'

There was more awkward silence as the camera did its work, Elsie Tapp smiling sweetly as though butter wouldn't melt.

## A TOUCH OF SPLEEN

'DRACULA! Brrrr!' Percy said after the photographer had taken his last shot. 'Are we ready to be scared?'

'I suppose so,' Elsie muttered. 'I'm getting quite used to it by now.'

The other guests were ready to be scared too, laughing and chatting as they made their way through the doors to the auditorium; cowboys and Indians, jesters and kings, all the fancy dress costumes the town could offer, and with one other in addition - a solitary bandaged figure moaning softly to himself as he was wheeled carefully to his seat.

## Chapter Nineteen

Bethesda Chubb and the rest of the sisterhood found themselves swept out of the cinema foyer and up the stairs to the dress circle, and still holding their drinks.

'This is posh, Bethesda. Not like those pokey picture houses back home. These seats are almost new.'

'And comfortable,' added Miss Roach, sitting herself down and taking off her shoes. 'Be nice to rest the toes for a bit. I've been on my feet all day.'

'Yes, well we're not here for entertainment, are we, we're here to find Spleen. These new boots are killing me.'

'And these shoes. Martyrs to fashion.'

'And for the drink,' said a very tipsy Miss Haddock, realising her glass was empty. 'Elizabeth dear, please tell me you're not looking at that bloody sphere again? Why not be a pet and ask for a tray of those trembler thingies instead, much more useful.'

'And some sandwiches, there's a love. This partying's hungry work.'

Bethesda collapsed into one of the cinema seats and undid her jacket. 'Well, I suppose Spleen can wait. It's not like he's going anywhere soon. We have him surrounded, wherever he is.'

This peculiar logic seemed just and reasonable, and one after the other the sisterhood flopped down into the comfy seats.

'Oooh look, is that the young Mr Barnes down there? Yoo-hoo! Tarzan! Don't be running away, now!'

'Honestly Roach, you should be ashamed of yourself. You're twice his age.'

'And what if I am? I can still raise the Titanic - and speaking of ships, why can't we have a few sailors like our young Mr Barnes? I hate to say this Bethesda, but the deckhands you recruit are complete dogs. They'd be hard pressed to win a bag of biscuits at Crufts.'

## A TOUCH OF SPLEEN

Elsie Tapp thanked the kind gentleman showing her to her seat and congratulated him on his costume. She'd never met a cowboy before, but the man's dress seemed to tick all the boxes; check shirt, leather chaps and a ten-gallon hat. She was impressed; everyone it seemed had entered into the spirit of the occasion although some costumes were less convincing than others. Her host's for instance which was about as gorilla as a dormouse.

'I hope you like our cinema,' Percy said, with obvious pride. 'It's art deco.'

'It's very modern - lots of curves and smooth surfaces; rather like sitting inside a giant jelly mould, don't you think.'

Percy wasn't sure what to think. He'd never had his cinema compared to a jelly mould before. 'Well, I suppose it's not to everyone's tastes…'

'Don't mind me,' Elsie said. 'I'm stuck in the 1800s.' She tapped the back of his hand reassuringly. 'Your cinema is lovely. I'm sure it's the talk of the town.'

Elsie gazed around the large auditorium and noticed a few members of the Grubdale constabulary taking their seats. 'Oh look, Marjorie. I do believe we're being followed, and by police officers in fancy dress. I hope you're not expecting trouble, Mr Pricklewood. There's enough of that outside.'

Percy laughed. 'Trouble, in this town? This is Grubdale, Miss Merryweather. Nothing exciting happens here.'

'Grubdale isn't without its surprises. I met one last night.'

Before Elsie had a chance to explain, the lights dimmed, and the chattering and fidgeting stopped. The show was about to start. There were the usual coughing, flashes of light as cigarettes were lit, and then peace – a momentary peace broken by the whir and swish of pulleys as the curtains to the giant screen drew back.

Percy sat back in his seat and sighed with relief. The party was proving to be a great success. 'Here we go, Mrs Mayor' he whispered to his wife, and squeezed her hand. 'Love you.'

'Love you, too,' laughed Evaline pulling his arm over her shoulder and nestling close against his side. 'Shall we "snog,"' she joked. 'I hear it's what young people do when they go to the pictures.'

'Not in the Galaxy, they don't. We unleash Sid Bottle with his coal tar drench. One whiff of that and its goodbye Sodom and Gomorrah.'

'Do you think he'll mind? I quite like this furry side to your character,' Evaline whispered, stroking Percy's gorilla costume.'

'Well, there's a coincidence. I quite like this new jodhpurs and jungle boots side to yours too. Shall we brave Sid Bottle for a kiss?'

'Only if you beat your chest and promise me a pineapple. A girl likes to be wooed, don't you know.'

The two of them snuggled close and watched the opening credits, all their work finished and with the entertainment about to begin; a short jungle adventure followed by the main treat of the evening, the deliciously scary Dracula.

There was a loud cheer from the audience as the image of an elephant raising its trunk flickered on the screen, accompanied by the familiar opening bars to 'On Ilka Moor Bah't at.'

'Wheear 'as ta bin sin ah saw thee,' sang the audience, then laughed and stamped their feet. MGM could keep their lion and their 'Ars Gratia Artis'; Yorkshire Films had Nelly the elephant, Ilkley Moor and 'We Ain't Posh, We're Popular,' a well-loved motto with no need for translation.

The music changed. The cornets and trombones of the Brighouse and Rastrick Brass Band gave way to the string section of the City of Leeds Orchestra, with jungle drums provided by a very energetic Mr E F Bunting from No. 12, Zulu Gardens. 'Yorkshire Films presents...' appeared in big white letters as the music swelled to a crescendo, 'Fred Barnes and Dolores Del Monte.'

The audience cheered. 'Well done that man!' someone shouted as a spotlight shone onto the front row of seats where Percy, Evaline, and their guests of honour sat.

'Give us a yodel!' shouted somebody else.

Fred stood up and waved to his adoring public, ignoring the more lewd comments from the Miss Haddocks of this world. Sid Bottles' cocktails had loosened more than just tongues, and a shower of the best silk underwear Percival Brothers could offer fluttered down from the upper circle like giant moths shot from the sky.

Fred bowed low in mock appreciation, then sat back in his seat laughing. 'It's a rum job, this 'ere film business,' he whispered to Elsie Tapp. 'I could get to like it.'

Elsie's poodle was getting to like the film business too, if Fred Barnes' costume was anything to go by, for despite her small size Princess Peaches was attacking the animal fur as though her honour depended on it.

'Leave the nice young Tarzan alone!' Elsie cried and tapped the poodle briskly on the snout. 'I'm sorry, I don't know what's the matter with her. It's like the call of the wild some nights, and she was such a good little girl.'

Mabel Fletcher, the Pudsey Carnival Queen, seemed to find this funny and burst into giggles. 'I'm a good girl too,' she said in a Betty Boop voice and had to be pinched to stop.

'Yes dear, I'm sure you are, now let's watch the film, don't you think? I do so love a jungle adventure.'

# A TOUCH OF SPLEEN

'So do I,' whispered the Betty Boop voice, and the giggles started again.

Perhaps 'jungle adventure' was overly optimistic. From the opening shots of the film where the camera tracked through a surprising number of potted palms and surprised a disappointing number of budgerigars, one thing was certain - Yorkshire Films had risked nothing in bringing the story of Tarzan in Trouble to the screen, with jungle vines owing more to old rope than botanical insight; not that there was much swinging through the trees, the narrow confines of the Palm House, Harrogate putting paid to any of that nonsense. Jungle fauna seemed in short supply too and mainly limited to budgerigars, an African grey parrot and a glimpse of a giant python - only a glimpse mind, as not even the cameraman had dared pick up the snake and wrap it around a branch.

The story seemed to concern a romantic tug of war between Jane, Tarzan and some hot piece of Spanish tapas played by the seductive Dolores Delmonte. There was the added complication of slave traders, buried gold and stock footage of lions licking their lips, not to mention Juma the killer gorilla – a more realistic costume than Percy could ever dream of. It was all hearty, rip-roaring stuff with Nelly the elephant saving the day, and Tarzan renewing his affection for Jane in a tasteful fadeout at the end of the picture, but it was over far too soon.

'Is that it?' whispered Bethesda Chubb to the others of the sisterhood seated right and left. 'Hardly time to stretch my legs and the film's over. What happened to the gorilla?'

'I think he was squashed.'

'Really? That's a shame. I thought he was the main star of the film. I liked the budgerigars though, and the parrot.'

The rest of the sisterhood disagreed, but were lost in thought, their imagination fuelled by alcohol, the young Mr Barnes and which bits to nibble first. It was enough to make the snake in the Garden of Eden have second thoughts and hide the apple.

Whatever the drama on screen, a more devious script played outside the two large doors to the cinema, owing more to The Perils of Pauline than Tarzan in Trouble. Two shadowy figures had chained the doors together and were struggling to press a ridiculously large padlock shut.

'Got them!' whispered the smaller of the two.

'We certainly have!' whispered the other, putting a ridiculously large key to the ridiculously large padlock down the front of his shirt. 'What next?'

'Next, my dear Hilary, we march back to the police station and inform those idiots there we've trapped every last witch in Grubdale.'

'A genius plan!'

'It is, rather - though I say it myself!'

The two figures laughed, shook hands then, short of twirling their moustaches and flashing beetle-browed eyes at an imaginary camera, stepped down into the street.

'Good evening, boys!' greeted the fashionable Rowena Carp. 'I'd recognise you two anywhere!'

The vicar and the captain stopped dead in their tracks.

'You pair haven't changed a bit!' she said, but Rowena had - she'd changed into a lovely blue riding habit with matching feathers, and the yellow wyrm had changed too. Rowena had disguised the poor creature as best she could, which wasn't saying much. From snout to backside he was pantomime horse, but from backside to tail he was wyrm.

'You haven't by any chance seen a tall man dressed in yellow and with a face like a bluebottle?' she asked, sweetly.

Fred Barnes was on his feet and bowing to everyone, milking the applause like a professional. Tarzan in Trouble was a success although, considering the potency of Sid Bottle's cocktails, even a hand shadow of a rabbit would have reaped the same response.

'Come on Fred, sit down,' pleaded Mabel. 'I want to see the main feature.'

'You're staying with him tonight,' he joked, waving to the raucous women in the dress circle.

'And don't I know it. You're making a fool of yourself. Half the audience are drunk.'

'Well, drunk or not, they like my film.'

'But I want to watch Dracula, and you promised me I could. Come on Fred, the sooner you sit down, the sooner they'll stop clapping. There won't be time to watch the film if you don't.'

Fred did as he was told, but was not happy. 'Dracula,' he mumbled. 'It's just cobwebs and a bloke in a cape. I dunno what the fuss is about.'

It was all about the fuss. Dracula was one of the biggest hits of 1931 and had made Bela Lugosi a star. People had fainted from shock during the film's Hollywood premiere, but Derbyshire folk were a hardier breed. Still, there was a thrill in wanting to be scared, and safety in wanting to be scared together – not 'scream-like-a-baby' scared, but with sufficient shock and horror to make you snuggle close to your partner. Mabel snuggled close to Fred Barnes, and Evaline snuggled even closer to her husband. Whoever snuggled close to Marjorie Whippet received a loud slap for his trouble and a business card thrust in his hand.

# A TOUCH OF SPLEEN

'Shall I bite you now, or later?' Percy whispered to his wife, trying not to laugh.

'Later dear, when we're mayor and mayoress. Now be a good boy and eat your ice cream. See, I think of everything.'

Evaline passed her husband a small cardboard tub of vanilla ice cream and opened one for herself as the lights dimmed, and a murmur of excitement rippled through the auditorium.

Dracula had taken a year to reach Grubdale - more time than it took for a voyage to Whitby - but then the Count had the services of Thomas Cook and Sons of London at his disposal, and not the Acme Film Distribution Company, Cheadle Hulme. Expectations were high, the audience eager to be transported to the Carpathian Mountains and hear the immortal words: 'I am Dracula,' and 'Creatures of the night - what music they make.' But what music was this? Elsie Tapp shook her head. The titles on screen were reassuring enough - the name of the world's most famous vampire projected over the design of a bat - the music though was all ballet tights and feathers.

'Swan Lake?' Elsie whispered to her publisher. 'Now there's a surprise. Are there blood-sucking birdies too?'

Marjorie Whippet snorted with laughter, a loud unforgiving snort due more to being tickled than to Elsie's sense of humour. She slapped the gentleman to her left and pressed another business card into his hand.

Percy's muscles tensed; not those of his arms but the ones in his stomach. The ones in his bowels decided on an opposite tack. The music had changed and not for the better. The wooden ice cream spoon fell from his fingers as the familiar chords to My Old Man Said Follow the Van rang out from below the stage. Someone had sneaked into the basement, climbed aboard the Wurlitzer organ and was now pounding the keys and foot pedals to great effect. A gobbet of ice cream fell from Percy's mouth as Evaline squeezed his arm and leant close to whisper in his ear.

'You are the best, my darling. That's Mrs O'Reilly playing the organ, isn't it? What a wonderful idea. You've thought of everything.'

Percy was about to say 'But it's nothing to do with me,' when his wife kissed him gently on the cheek.

'What a kind, considerate man you are.'

Percy was feeling anything but kind and considerate. Confused would be a better description.

Confused and just a tiny bit frightened.

## Chapter Twenty

The giant Wurlitzer was Percy's pride and joy – a white and gold theatre organ, which, employing a lift and necessary gears, could emerge slow and majestic from beneath the stage. Artistes as famous as Esme Fingers and Bobby Thrush had been booked for the summer season, but as for the dreadful Mary O'Reilly getting her grubby little fingers on Percy's Wurlitzer, the answer was 'No! Definitely not! No, not ever!'

Except the truth was 'Yes!' The indefatigable Mrs O'Reilly had bested Percy again.

'Try not to eat with your mouth open, dear. It's not nice,' Evaline said, catching a glimpse of her husband in the light from the screen.

Percy grunted a reply and dropped the tub of ice cream at his feet. My Old Man Said Follow the Van, had finished and the opening bars to I Do Like To Be Beside the Seaside had the audience smiling, clapping and remembering the institution that was Mary O'Reilly. It was a favourite tune of hers and one she'd used to great effect accompanying custard pie fights or wobbly dance girls on screen. Percy sat upright as though the gobbet of ice cream had slipped down beneath his vest.

'How wonderful!' Evaline whispered and pinched her husband's cheek. 'Such a clever man. We love Mary!'

Percy didn't. Percy disliked Mary O'Reilly with a passion - a passion born from weeks of dodging vegetables thrown from the shadows.

'Mind you,' Evaline continued. 'She could have chosen something more appropriate, don't you think?'

Percy didn't know what to think. He only hoped the horrid woman was sober.

'…and perhaps play a little quieter? I can't hear what's happening on screen.'

The action on screen had little to do with sand, sea or platefuls of cockles. Various characters were huddled together in what appeared to be a stagecoach, discussing the dangers of travelling further that evening. There were dire warnings for one particular gentleman, much rattling of the rosaries, and whisperings of dreadful goings on in the Borgo Pass. It was a key scene, not that you would have guessed from the audience, fuelled by alcohol and intent on a sing-song. 'Beside the Seaside! Beside the Sea!' they sang as the trap door to the basement opened. 'Hooray!' they cheered as the lights from the giant Wurlitzer lit up the auditorium, and the marvellous theatre organ rose up from the depths. The scene was more Phantom of the Opera than the Tower Ballroom, Blackpool, for whoever sat at the keyboard, thumping out note after note of Roll Out the Barrel, appeared covered from head to toe in...

'Cats?' whispered Evaline, confused. 'What have cats got to do with the evening?'

Percy smiled awkwardly and shrugged his shoulders. He knew nothing about cats – not a clue.

'I see what you've done. They're singing to the music! What a brilliant surprise – a cat choir! You're a genius!'

Percy was beginning to feel more a fraud than anything else. He smiled and squeezed his wife's hand. The cats were singing in perfect harmony, but there was something sinister in their appearance, something not quite right; their peculiar shape, the bedraggled fur – the way their eyes glowed as powerful as the coloured lights on the organ.

'Vampire cats,' whispered Evaline, jokingly, then snuggled down in her seat to enjoy the film.

Percy dared not take his eyes off the cats. It was as if they were sewn together as a cape, hiding whoever sat at the keyboard, their bodies somehow deflated like so many punctured balloons. Evaline gave him a playful pinch.

'Just to warn you, dear. If you do buy me a fur coat – make sure it's mink.'

Percy tried to laugh but was beginning to feel distinctly unwell. 'Damn this bloody costume,' he thought as the sweat ran down his chest and back. 'I'll smell like a tramp by the end of the film. Damn this costume, damn this evening and damn that bloody Mary O'Reilly!'

'What was that?' Evaline asked. 'Did you say something?'

Percy shook his head and tried to look pleased, but it was difficult to appear anything other than a fool in the gorilla headgear with the large pink ears. He was worried, nervous about what might happen next. The music had gone on too long, and the strange appearance of the cats had unsettled the audience. The singing had stopped, and now Percy could hear complaints and murmurs of unrest.

'Enough with the music!' someone shouted. 'Let's watch the film!' and as if on cue, Roll Out the Barrel faded to silence as an unfortunate gentleman on screen set off for Castle Dracula. The organist had a sense of humour. A few bars of In the Monastery Garden rang out, and the cats, now casting their evil eyes over the audience, made the necessary birdsong accompaniment.

'Ah come on! Shut up or get back in the basement!' shouted the lone voice of protest, and Percy felt his stomach churn. It was a brave man who could take on the dreadful Mrs O'Reilly - a brave man or a fool.

The music stopped, abruptly, and with a whirl of arms, the organist cast off the cats and sent them flapping and screaming back below the stage. Percy sighed with relief. Murmurs of unrest gave way to silence as the film trapped the audience's attention and drew them in.

The story on screen progressed from a village tavern drenched in garlic to a menacing drive through the night. It had reached the point at which the stagecoach had arrived at Castle Dracula. There was a giant staircase, enough cobwebs to curtain a cathedral, and at one end of the room a very nervous gentleman carrying a suitcase.

'There he is,' whispered someone in the audience. 'He's standing at the top of the stairs.'

A few of the audience, those a little worse for wear from the hospitality, tried to turn around in their seats and look behind until common sense and a fierce nudge made them realise their mistake.

'On screen, silly. Look.'

The elegant figure of Bela Lugosi appeared, making his way slowly down the giant staircase. 'I am Dracula,' came the immortal words, drenched in a Hungarian accent so thick you could dip your bread in it, and the audience swooned - those of a romantic disposition that is, those who weren't flicked their Woodbine cigarettes on the carpet and swore the man wore lipstick.

'He wears lipstick,' whispered Fred Barnes to Mabel. 'And he's not foreign, he just forgets to put his teeth in.'

'Well, I think he's handsome. You should try taking your teeth out too,' giggled Mabel and tickled her Tarzan on the thigh.

There was a crash of noise from the giant Wurlitzer as the organist thumped the keys.

'Bloody hell! I was only tickling my boyfriend!' Mabel shouted.

'Listen to them. Children of the night, what music they make,' proclaimed Dracula on screen.

'And you can keep your bloody thoughts to yourself too!'

The audience laughed, Mabel slunk down in her seat, embarrassed, and Percy's stomach tightened into a knot.

'Please don't play the organ again,' he mumbled to himself. 'Please, just climb off the stool and go home.'

# A TOUCH OF SPLEEN

Whoever sat at the keyboard was in no mood to leave. Various buttons were pushed, knuckles cracked and fingers stretched.

Percy groaned: 'Oh God, What now?'

Now was something new. Now was not your usual music hall tune but something special. Now was a call to arms.

Percy hid his head in his hands. 'I don't believe it,' he moaned as the first cluster of notes sang out from the organ. 'Not The Flight of the Bumble Bee! She'll bloody ruin it, like she bloody ruins everything!'

Far from being a disaster, the figure at the keyboard could actually play, and the music matched the action on screen. Dracula had climbed the stairs leaving his unfortunate visitor to fight through curtains of cobwebs. There was even a giant spider scuttling up the wallpaper.

'Heaven help us!' Percy said, peering through his hands. 'There's bloody two of them!'

'Two of what, dear?' Evaline asked. 'And try not to curse. No one wants a mayor who swears.'

'Two people playing the organ, look!'

Elsie did as her husband asked and sure enough, there they were – a white-faced Mary O'Reilly playing the top register for all she was worth, and a green-faced, dehydrated Harry Renfield sat to her left. Happy Harry Renfield, as dead as a pork chop but with marvellous footwork on the pedals. They both turned to face the audience, their eyes shining like fog lamps as the giant Wurlitzer began its slow descent to the basement.

The sisterhood were uncharacteristically silent, sucking sticks of liquorice as they tried to make sense of the film. Miss Gulper and her companion, Miss Dab – shy and retiring, and with not a bad word to say about anyone – found the plot particularly hard work.

'So those young ones floating about in the mist are his wives?'

'Whose wives?'

'That chap with the white face and the candle climbing the stairs.'

'I think so.'

'The poor buggers, it must be thin pickings where they live. That bloke looks the wrong side of a century, and that's being generous. The stairs will kill him.'

'I think the secret is he's already dead.'

'Really? How peculiar. The honeymoon must've been a complete flop. He'd need more than a stiff whisky there. My Jeffrey was only good for sucking soup.'

'My Jack was only good for trimming the privet. He could rattle the dinner plates but nothing more. If you ask me, all that nonsense is over-rated.'

'What nonsense, dear?'

'Human nature nonsense - the call of the wild. My ears have been deaf to it for years. Give me a bag of lemon bonbons any day.'

'Well, I wouldn't go as far as that – a sherbet fountain, perhaps.'

Bethesda Chubb coughed loudly. She was never sure if the Gulpers and Dabs of this world were either delightfully innocent or dustbin filthy, but they were chattering too much and ruining the film. She tapped the back of Miss Gulper's chair with her foot and shushed them to be quiet.

'Hark at her,' whispered Miss Gulper to her friend, then mouthed the words 'dungarees,' and 'diesel oil.' Miss Dab, who seemed to know what Miss Gulper meant, nodded in agreement and mouthed the phrase 'a martyr to the carrots.'

Bethesda, understanding nothing, sat back in her chair content that she'd made her point.

The two continued.

'So why the couple on the church organ?' Miss Dab whispered, peering over the balcony at the slowly disappearing Wurlitzer. 'Do you think they've got the dates mixed up and they're here for a wedding?'

'Don't ask me. They may be ugly, but they can hold a tune. All those busy notes and not a sheet of music to read from.'

The audience was less impressed. The Wurlitzer continued its slow descent with the two musicians showing no sign of giving up. Not even a chorus of boos and catcalls made them stop, The Flight of the Bumblebee now giving way to the opening bars of Bach's Toccata and Fugue in D Minor, or as aficionados of the silent cinema knew it, that spooky bit of music before the mask's ripped off.

It had been a long time coming, the coconut – months to be exact; a convenient missile of retribution armed with as much hatred as Percy could muster. The perfect pitch, the perfect spin, and after a perfect trajectory, the perfect hit - bullseye on that dreadful O'Reilly woman's head, except heads weren't supposed to do that, fall from their shoulders and bounce on the floor.

The silence was deafening; a giant intake of breath that ruffled the cobwebs and stirred the cigarette smoke – a collective gasp of horror as the now headless Mary O'Reilly continued to play the organ as it sank below the stage.

Evaline Bamforth screamed. The whole cinema screamed – even the sisterhood lent their voices to the panic.

'Was that meant to happen?' Evaline asked, grabbing her husband by the arm. 'Please tell me that was a trick, that it wasn't real!'

The look on Percy's face told a different story. 'Oh God!' he shouted. 'I've just killed someone with a coconut! How on earth is that possible?'

'Darling, look at me! Tell me that was a joke!'

# A TOUCH OF SPLEEN

'Of course it's not a joke! How can someone's head falling off be a joke!'

'Because if it isn't a joke, then we're in big trouble! Her head! Look at the horrid thing! It's singing!'

It was Percy's turn to scream. Mary O'Reilly's head had rolled to the front of the stage, and to the horror of everyone in the cinema, was belting out the words to I Ain't Got Nobody! at the top of her voice.

'Arrrrggghhhh!' screamed Percy.

'Arrrrggghhh!' screamed his wife

And then it happened, suddenly and without warning – people dragged from their seats and pulled high in the air like marionettes, jerking and screaming above the audience's heads. Mabel Fletcher, Pudsey's Carnival Queen, was one, kicking and spinning as she hung 20ft from the floor, her elbows pinned to her sides by what felt like loops of sticky rope. She cursed loudly, joining the chorus of other frightened voices. 'What kind of stupid party is this!' she cried. 'You cut me down this instant, or they'll be hell to pay! I'm a good girl I am! I'll tell my dad if you don't, and we'll see who's king of the bloody jungle then! And stop pointing at my knickers! It's rude!'

Fred Barnes was innocent of all charges, his outstretched arm pointing at something entirely different, and with his mouth wide open in horror.

'I said stop pointing at my knickers! And what's that face for? Ohh, don't say there's a bloody hole!'

There wasn't. What there was made quick work of sliding down the rope towards its victim - a nightmare creature with eight legs, eight eyes and a body the size of a beach ball.

## Chapter Twenty One

Beetles are sensible; six legs, two eyes and a shiny carapace – the sort of creatures you can take home to your mother. Add another pair of legs and some extra eyes, though, and you'd be hard pressed to get past the front door. No one likes spiders - not even spiders like spiders; too many legs, too many eyes, and with hair so thick you could crochet knuckledusters from the fur, and that's just the small ones.

Mabel kicked her legs and screamed. 'Small' was not a word her spider understood; 'humongous, terrifying and bigger than bagpipes' maybe, but most definitely not 'small.' The creature edged itself slowly towards her and pounced.

'Oh, good shot, that girl! Smack bang wallop on target!'

The remains of the giant spider dripped from poor Mabel like thick pea soup. It was as though the girl had been dunked in a barrel of the stuff and pegged out to dry.

'Well done, Cynthia!' shouted Bethesda Chubb, and one of the sisterhood, her trombone still sparking and dribbling green magic on the floor, smiled and waved back.

'There's a big bugger to your left, Marjorie! Give it the full euphonium and all the trimmings!'

Marjorie Spratt turned to see a nightmare of a spider a full 5ft high swing down from the ceiling. There was a deep reverberating B♭, and a jet of green magic spewed from the euphonium, stopping the spider mid-flight and splattering the eight-legged monstrosity across the back wall as though it were paint.

'Good heavens!' cried a voice from the back row. 'Can't a girl enjoy a quiet vanilla tub without being covered in muck?'

The voice belonged to one of the lazier sisters who, now awake and drenched in gloop, had only a few seconds to wipe her eyes before reaching under her coat, pulling out a flugelhorn and letting another spider have three bars of I Got Rhythm right between the spinnerets.

'Excellent shooting, Bridget! Glad to see you're still with us!' shouted an excitable Bethesda Chubb, now in full brass band gear and laying into the spiders with a pair of drum mallets. 'Come on, Penelope; you're blowing a tuba not kisses to your favourite nephew! Put your back into it!'

The sisterhood was having fun, climbing over chairs or else leaning over the balcony to get a better shot - blasting away with their musical instruments at anything big, hairy and with far too many legs to be decent. But not everyone was enjoying the sport - not those unfortunate enough to be sitting downstairs in the stalls; Evaline Bamforth was having a miserable evening.

Evaline prided herself on being sensible and matter-of-fact – the sort of woman who'd shed a tear peeling an onion, but that was it. No quivering lips for her when thumbing through Little Women – she considered herself strong, rational and above all a rock to Percy's limpet. Throw in a Bosch-ful of hellish creepy crawlies, though and all bets were off. Even the most logical of women could leap on a table and scream the house down, and poor Evaline was no different. In as many minutes as it took for a head to fall off, giant spiders to appear and a coven of over-dressed witches to start blasting jets of green magic around the cinema, Evaline's emotions had run the whole gamut from horror to hysteria. She held her husband's face close to hers and stared into his eyes. 'Make it stop!' she screamed. 'I don't care what you do or how you do it, but make it stop!'

Percy was having a terrible evening too, with some guests dangling helplessly from the ceiling and others rushing and fighting with each other to escape. He nodded his head, desperate to reassure, the large felt ears of his gorilla costume flapping pathetically between Evaline's fingers. 'Don't worry my love,' he shouted above the cries and screams of the audience. 'I'll go and get the police. They'll know what to do.'

Evaline had every reason to worry. The police were already here and dressed in tutus. It was time for decisive action, time for a hero to step forward, and who better than the Yorkshire Tarzan himself, Mr Frederick Samuel Barnes. The young athlete had managed to climb into one of the 'royal boxes' either side of the screen, although why any member of the royal family would want to stay in Grubdale, let alone go to the Galaxy Cinema, was a mystery as yet unresolved by the great detectives of the age.

'I love you, Mabel Fletcher!' Fred shouted, then, standing on the edge of the box and holding a spider's rope for support, he made the cry of the jungle, clenched a Bowie knife between his teeth and took a giant leap to rescue his girl.

Physics can be a swine.

Geometry too - especially when applied to jungle vines, leopard skin briefs and the rainforests of the Belgian Congo. The Yorkshire Tarzan swung far too fast, far too wide, and in letting go of the rope fell far too hard right into the Dress Circle and the arms of the sisterhood.

'Ooooh goody,' came the happy cry. 'Here, hold my teeth, he's mine!'

'This is too much!'

Elsie Tapp gathered her coat from her lap and stood up to leave. 'I enjoyed the jungle film, Mr Pricklewood, but this gruesome pantomime is in poor taste.'

She indicated the chaos all around with a sweep of her umbrella. 'A good showman should tease his audience, not send them to hospital. Now out of my way before you hoist me to the rafters too.'

Elsie pushed past Percy and his wife and marched up the aisle to the foyer doors, forcing her way through the crowds with the tip of her umbrella. She was made of sterner stuff than the silly fools here. Cheap party tricks, that's what the evening amounted to; cheap party tricks and nothing more.

'For heaven's sake!' she cried as another giant spider blocked her way. 'I've seen bagpipes more convincing. Marjorie dear, are you coming too?' she shouted to her agent. 'Oh well, suit yourself.'

Elsie turned back to the spider and stabbed it quickly in the stomach with the point of her umbrella. It burst like a balloon, as Elsie knew it would. 'Even a ten-year-old could make something better than this,' she said, angry at being splashed with green goo. 'I've seen a dragon, Mr Pricklewood,' she shouted. 'Yes, that's what I said, a dragon. It takes a lot to scare me!'

Such fateful words and rashly spoken. What Elsie had never seen was Sid Bottle wearing his British Army gas mask, sporting a large tank of Tobacco Jones' Coal Tar Drench strapped to his back, and with a pump action greenfly sprayer in his hands. It was the stuff of nightmares. The doors to the foyer slammed open as Sid barged his way through. 'Leave those bastard spiders to me!' he shouted, before being beaten to the ground by a terrified Elsie Tapp swinging her umbrella like a poleaxe.

Elsie stormed out of the auditorium and into the foyer, muttering under her breath. 'Ridiculous party! Trying to scare everyone half to death! Oh, for goodness sake, what's the matter now?'

Another scene of chaos presented itself. People were banging on the large glass doors to the street, screaming to be let out. Elsie pushed her way to the front and tried to open the doors, but the tell-tale padlock and chain prevented her escape.

'I don't believe it!' she cried, rattling the doors. 'That horrid man has locked us in! What sort of party is this?'

'This is a great party!' Bethesda laughed, twisting a large spider the size of a small pig into all manner of shapes. 'Look, a poodle!' The general opinion was that her latest attempt looked nothing like a poodle - a giant hairy spider tied in a knot maybe, but not a poodle.

'Oh well, suit yourself,' she said, flinging the unfortunate creature over the balcony to join the others.

'STOP!'

It was the voice of authority – an iron fist wrapped in an iron glove, tied off with a barbed wire bow. Bethesda was furious.

'What do you mean "STOP"?' Who said "STOP"? Nobody tells me to "STOP"!'

The voice appeared to come from the stage where the face of Dracula filled the screen. Or was it Dracula? Dracula's face was black and white; the entire film was black and white, but this face was yellow and looked more like a grinning skull than anything else - a mask of a skull covered in jewels and gold embroidery.

'Oooh, colour!' whispered a few of the sisterhood. 'That's pretty!'

'It'll never catch on,' muttered a voice of dissent from the back.

The image on the screen changed, the camera now zooming in on two eyes staring out from the mask – two angry, red eyes filling the screen.'

'Oooh, red!'

The eyes looked around the cinema, searching for the audience; looking at every person in turn.

'Oh dear, the film's a bit boring isn't it? This bit I mean. Goes on forever.'

And then the penny dropped. The eyes had stopped on Bethesda and were changing colour, this time a vivid shade of purple that shone out from the screen and lit up the Stalls and Dress Circle.

'Oooh, purple!'

'Shut up with your "Ooohs" and "Ahhhs."' Bethesda hissed. 'Can't you see who it is?'

The sisterhood were more interested in the purple light and how peculiar they all looked in the dark. 'Terrible case of dandruff there, Petunia. Here, let me brush it off your shoulders.'

'Damn it all, girls! It's Spleen!'

At the mention of Spleen, the sisterhood sprung to attention, their musical instruments now pointing at the flickering image on the screen, an image that had changed from the giant mask to the familiar figure of the evil sorcerer himself, Tarantulus Spleen.

'Oh no you don't, sunshine!' cried Bethesda. 'Let him have it, my lovelies!'

All hell broke loose, the brass band instruments spewing out great snakes of green magic that raked and tore across the screen, burning through the fabric and showering the back wall with fire and sparks.

'My cinema!' cried Percy. 'What are they doing to my cinema!' But the image of Spleen remained, laughing through the green torrent and making all manner of dramatic, evil-genius-in-a-gown poses, all of them condescending and all of them an insult to Miss Chubb.

'Wait!' shouted one of the sisterhood, the bookish Miss Elizabeth Cod - she of the thick black spectacles, polo neck jumper and knitted knee-length socks. 'We're silly! That's not the real Spleen. It can't be, it's just an image projected on a wall! That's where the real Spleen hides, up there!'

The sisterhood turned around and brought their jets of magic to bear on the projection room window, filling the small room behind with fire and smoke.

'Noooo!' cried Percy Bamforth, struggling to understand what was happening. 'Don't! You'll burn the place to the ground!'

The image of Spleen laughed and jeered at the sisterhood, bending and twisting in the smoke but still clearly visible.

'Elizabeth Cod, you're a fool! Image on a wall be damned, he's down there!'

Back turned the obedient sisters, drenching what remained of the giant screen with more fire and brimstone, burning through the spider ropes that held a few of Percy's guests hanging from the ceiling. 'Ouch!' they cried as they fell to the ground. 'Ouch!' or words to that effect.

'Perhaps he's below stage?'

It was worth a try. Anything was worth a try - the sorcerer had to be in the building somewhere, and wasn't that organ music again?

'No! I won't have it! Not more bloody organ music!' cried an increasingly hysterical Percy Bamforth. 'Will someone please tell me what's going on?'

'ISN'T IT OBVIOUS?'

The voice had spoken.

'THOSE WOMEN OVER THERE WANT TO KILL ME.'

'Yay!' cheered the sisterhood from the Dress Circle, waving and leaning over the balcony to get a better look.

'AND THOSE SPIDERS OVER THERE WANT TO KILL THEM.'

'Boo!' jeered the sisterhood, and let fly with a few more bolts of magic.

'AS FOR ME, I'M STUCK IN THE MIDDLE.'

'What?!'

## A TOUCH OF SPLEEN

There was a clatter of brass as the sisterhood heaved their musical instruments over the edge of the balcony and rested them on the ledge, all pointing at the giant Wurlitzer.

Up rose the theatre organ, its lights flashing red, white and blue, and its keys playing the chorus to Ta-ra-ra Boom-de-ay.

But there was no one on board.

'Hey, I know this tune!' whispered one of the sisterhood. 'I used to sing it years ago!

'Ta-ra-ra Boom-de-ay, Ta-ra-ra Boom-de-ay.'

A few more of the sisterhood joined in with the chorus, tapping their feet and shaking their bottoms in time to the music.

'Ta-ra-ra Boom-de-ay, Ta-ra-ra…

BANG!

Something more substantial than the flickering image of a man in yellow robes kicked the stage from below, splitting the planks of wood and sending more beams of light up through the smoke.

'Ta-ra-ra…'

BANG! BANG!

A gigantic claw appeared through the hole in the stage, and then a second, each as big as a chest of drawers.

'Please Percy, let's go!' screamed a terrified Evaline Bamforth, dragging her husband with her.

'But my cinema! My beautiful cinema!'

'Your cinema's on fire, my love. We need to escape!'

'FIRE!' screamed the audience as they pushed their way out of the auditorium to the foyer. 'FIRE!'

'LADIES AND GENTLEMAN, PLEASE!'

The sergeant shouted again, trying in vain to bring some peace and order to the proceedings. 'STOP PUSHING!'

'THANK YOU! NOW IF YOU WOULDN'T MIND STEPPING BACK, PC WIGGERY HERE CAN TAKE ANOTHER SWING AT THE DOORS WITH THE CHINESE VASE!'

The police had taken charge and were attempting a plan of escape. It wasn't a bad plan – to break the two glass doors at the front of the cinema and run home to Mummy - just that their truncheons were in the wash, and the large pile of broken crockery on the floor was evidence of a slight miscalculation. The denture-less PC Wiggery urged the crowd to stand clear as he attempted to lift another ornamental vase from the floor and swing it like a hammer at the glass.

'Bollocksh!' he cursed. The outcome was the same: Brassingtons' Reinforced Windows – 6, Percival Brothers' Oriental Crockery – nil.

'Bloody hell, Sharge, thish is bullet proof glash, thish ish. We'll never get through.'

'You could always telephone for help, or use your whistles,' suggested Elsie Tapp, standing close behind the sergeant. 'Not that I'm interfering.'

The sergeant took a deep breath and tried to control his temper. The damned woman was worse than a fortune cookie, offering little nuggets of advice with every Chinese vase broken.

'Madam,' he said. 'If we'd found a telephone we wouldn't be doing this now, would we? And the same can be said for our whistles; our costumes being whistle-less on account of them being tutus.'

'You could always ask. I'm sure Mr Pricklewood has a telephone somewhere in the building.'

'But that would mean going back in there.' The sergeant indicated the foyer doors and shivered. 'And that would be silly now, wouldn't it, on account of all the giant spiders and whatnot?'

Elsie refused to be thwarted, whatnots or not. 'Then I'll go,' she said, and before the sergeant could explain his case, Elsie had turned around and was pushing her way through the crowd, back towards the foyer doors and the screen.

'There's a name for people like that, PC Wiggery.'

'I know Sharge, but I can't shay it without shpittin'.'

There are many unspoken rules in biology, two so obvious they're taken for granted: what comes out of a chrysalis is far prettier than what goes in, and never trust an animal without a backbone. It's just a pity no one had whispered these to the creature now emerging from the basement.

'Holy crap!' swore a horrified Sid Bottle, ripping off his gas mask and seeing the monstrosity for the first time. 'We need more drench!'

'Forget the drench!' shouted Percy as he ran up the aisle. 'Not even a Tommy gun will stop this bugger! Run for your life!'

It was excellent advice. The creature was a travesty of the black arts and about as big as a double-decker bus with muscles.

'You great, ugly, beetle-bastard bugger!' Sid cried, then rather wished he hadn't, on account of his perfectly innocent words being misconstrued, tied up in a knot and used against him. 'Bye!' he said, pushing the foyer doors open and escaping into the crowd, just as the indomitable Elsie Tapp stumbled into the auditorium.

# A TOUCH OF SPLEEN

'You there!' she shouted trying to catch Percy Bamforth's attention as he ran past. 'Is there a phone in the building? We need to call the police - some idiot's chained the two glass doors together, and we can't get out.'

'What do you mean we can't get out? We have to get out!'

'Unless you have a telephone or a sledgehammer big enough, none of us are getting out... Oh my God! What in heaven's name is that?'

Elsie's brain, ordinarily quick on the uptake and a demon with the Sunday crossword, had taken its time in sending out the necessary warnings that the gigantic puppet in the room was not a puppet but something worth avoiding at all costs.

'How do I know?' Percy screamed before shaking off Elsie's grip and falling back into the crowds on the other side of the door. 'I'm just a bloody gorilla!'

The creature stepped out of the shadows and looked down at Elsie, but this time her brain was ready. She screamed. A few of the sisterhood screamed too.

'Now then girls, no need to be afraid,' whispered Bethesda as loud as she dared. 'It's just a big lump of magic with claws. We've faced worse, remember?'

The sisterhood shook their heads. As far as big lumps of magic with claws went, this was the worst. It had the look of a hungry mantis about it– a 20ft tall mantis crossed with a 10ft wide crab. The fact that it answered to the name of Spleen seemed hardly worth a mention.

'It's big!' they whispered. 'It's very big!'

'Nonsense, we've sunk dinghies bigger than that before. Come on my hearties, heave-ho! Let's give the ugly bugger what for!'

But the brass band could hardly raise a squeak. No matter how hard the sisterhood blew, only the faintest dribble of magic appeared.

'Matilda, dear! What's happened to you sousaphone?'

The unfortunate woman shrugged her shoulders. The giant brass trumpet had uncoiled itself and fallen to the floor. Miss Spratt was next, her tuba now nothing more than a loop of shiny pasta.

'Has everyone lost their puff?' Bethesda whispered, trying to understand why her bass drum resembled a giant bowl of rice pudding.

'It's not our fault; it's the instruments. Look, they're melting.'

Bethesda stole a quick look and bit her bottom lip. This had happened before, many years ago, all this 'flopsy-ness.'

'It's bad magic, that's what it is,' she said. 'Dirty, bad trickster magic with Spleen's name all over it!'

The creature laughed, if you could call it laughter. His head thrown back, and with his shoulders shaking, but all the sisterhood could hear was an insistent clackety-clack as pairs of giant mandibles rattled against each other.

'Castanets?'

'Mouth parts dear, but as far as we're concerned, they're just another set of dentures.

'What do you say, girls, are you with me?'

The sisterhood muttered to themselves, their courage fading rapidly as their instruments puddled on the ground. Bravery was all well and good if you could spit fireballs and roast a hippo, but throw away the spell book and what was left – house bricks in a handbag and a pension worth tuppence.

'Mabel!'

A disorientated Fred Barnes - tampered with, traumatised and covered in love bites; stumbled down the Dress Circle steps looking for his girlfriend.

'Mabel! Is that you?'

Unfortunately, it wasn't. Fred had reached out in the smoke and found more than a gentleman should in the dark.

'Hands off, lover boy!' shouted a surprised yet intrigued Miss Trout. 'Can't you see we're busy?'

The only thing Fred could see was the mental image of his gorgeous girlfriend dangling from a spider's web. 'Where are you!' he cried, elbowing his way past Miss Trout and her friends. 'Talk to me!'

He stopped at the balcony, the flames from the projection room window cutting through the smoke, and there below, tall on stage and illuminated like a statue, stood Spleen.

# A TOUCH OF SPLEEN

## Chapter Twenty Two

Fred had never considered himself a coward. Giant spiders were scary right enough, but he'd seen one pop like a blister so maybe not so scary after all. This new nightmare was different; bladder-loosening, stomach-churning and bone-chilling, and with all permutations in between. It was enough to make a jungle hero throw away the leopard skins and take a job in the city, but Fred Barnes was in love, and the leopard skins, what was left of them, were staying on.

Someone took hold of his hand – a rather formidable-looking woman trying her best to smile and appear reassuring.

'What say we do this together?' she asked.

'Do what?'

'This!' she said, and drawing a cutlass from somewhere under her clothes, she waved it in the air. 'Let's show that giant cockroach who's boss!'

It said a lot for Bethesda's charisma that Fred, far from running away and having nothing more to do with women of a certain age, drew out his knife and waved it around in the air too. He smiled back.

'You take the head, and I'll take the tail, and we'll meet up somewhere in the middle.'

'For Mabel!' he cried.

'For the sisterhood!' added Bethesda, shaming her compatriots as she sat astride the balcony. Then with a final shout of defiance, Fred and Bethesda dropped over the edge and down onto Spleen.

Fred landed with a loud 'thump' astride Spleen's back and trying his best to ignore the sudden pain from his jungle regions, shouted 'Yee-Ha!' as best as he could. Feeling himself start to slip and fearing a helter-skelter slide into the second row, Fred plunged his knife into the creature's wing case and like Douglas Fairbanks in The Black Pirate, sliced himself to a stop.

'Oh, well done!' shouted the sisterhood.

Bethesda Chubb, having no jungle regions to bother about, shouted 'Yee-Ha!' in a deeper voice and head-butted Spleen full in the face.

'That's our girl! Now take him down!'

Spleen moved – a simple twist of the body but sufficient to throw his attackers hard against the floor.

'Ouch!' cried a sympathetic Miss Trout. 'That must've hurt!'

Spleen turned quickly, his giant tail ripping great swathes of plaster from the walls and the sisterhood, deciding silence was the better option, retreated into the smoke with only an occasional cough and splutter to betray where they were. Fred and Bethesda had no such choice. They were exposed – bruised and winded and lying on their backs like a couple of helpless turtles as Spleen stumbled forward and raised his claws.

A dog barked – a high-pitched yapping with delusions of royalty; Elsie Tapp's poodle had had enough.

'No Princess!' Elsie shouted, but it was all too late. There was a new wild side to Princess Peaches' character and one that thought itself invincible. No one, not even a gigantic clothes horse, was going to attack her Miss Tapp. Princess Peaches leapt out of the carpet bag with the speed of a greyhound. She was a poodle possessed; a fluffy pink slipper dipped in teeth, snapping and snarling as she ran headlong towards Spleen and glory.

'You get him!' shouted a bruised and winded Fred Barnes as Princess Peaches launched herself into the air and bit deep into Spleen's leg, her grip as tight as a plumber's wrench.

Spleen's giant insect eyes burned red with anger, their pupils nothing but pinpricks as the pain set in. The poodle's teeth were needle sharp, and there was nothing Spleen could do to shake the animal off. Princess had attached herself to a back leg only an expert in yoga could bend down and reach. Spleen roared with frustration, stamping and kicking his feet, smashing his two large claws on the floor, but short of rolling on his back and attempting the 'Fat Man Tying Shoe Laces On a Bed' position, the poodle was there to stay, gnawing and worrying Spleen's leg as though he'd stepped on a bear trap.

'Don't you dare try and kick my Princess! You leave my dog alone!'

Spleen felt the double pain of being stabbed in the shins with an umbrella and hit in the stomach with a steel re-enforced carpet bag. Elsie Tapp had come to the rescue and short of four more hands and a brace of swords, was attacking Spleen's underside like a Hindu god.

'Crikey! Look out for those legs!' Fred cried, then pulling himself up from the floor the Yorkshire Tarzan stumbled half-dazed back to the fight.

## A TOUCH OF SPLEEN

To the casual observer with one eye on the fight and the other on the odds for a knockout in the first round, Spleen's performance must've seemed like a great disappointment. Despite waking up as a giant insect ('evens' at best considering Kafka thought of it first), and flushing the sisterhood's magic down the pan (1 to 4, odds-on favourite), Spleen was hardly playing true to form. Where were the fireballs? Where were the thunderbolts and lightning and the very, very frightening? It was as though the evil sorcerer had run out of magic or even the ability to hold a decent conversation.

The truth is, Spleen was tired. It had taken all his energy to come back from the dead, that and more than a score of cats from the local neighbourhood. A couple of crows and the unfortunate Mr Renfield had seen him healthy enough to stand, but draining Mary O'Reilly of every last drop of blood had come at a cost; a 60% proof, monster of a hangover cost, and with the tremors thrown in as a mix. It was a wonder he could walk at all.

Bethesda was beyond walking. She'd been thrown against the back wall and bounced, neither experiences she could recommend. She'd had the wind knocked out of her sails, and despite leaning on her cutlass for support, could only shout insults to her companions above.

'Cowards, the lot of you! Call yourself sailors? You're nothing but a bunch of yellow-bellied sea dogs!'

Bethesda couldn't help but notice Princess Peaches gnawing away at one of Spleen's legs. 'No, I take that back,' she cried. 'You're not fit to be considered sea-dogs! You're jellyfish, that's what you are – spineless, blobby jellyfish!' But not being stupid, spineless blobby jellyfish, the cowards stayed where they were.

Nobody likes to be called a coward, particularly cowards themselves, and a fair few of the ladies were teetering between 'not so sure' and 'maybe.' Miss Florentine Trout, less jellyfish than most but still spineless in the dark, felt the insult 'a trifle harsh.' 'But we've no magic!' she shouted. 'What do you expect us to do?'

'I expect you to come down here and bloody well help!' came Bethesda's curt reply.

'Well, if you put it like that!' Miss Trout shouted, hitching up her skirts to jump. 'Are you with me, girls?'

A few were, those that had come 'tooled' for the job.

'Heavens above, Elizabeth! What do you call that?'

Miss Cod looked both embarrassed and a little sore. 'A cricket bat with nails,' she muttered, re-buttoning her coat. 'And don't ask,' she said in answer to a few questioning looks.

'I won't,' whispered another sister, a similar pained expression on her face and with a bed sock stuffed with billiard balls in her hand..

Miss Tench, an otherwise shy and retiring member of the sisterhood, swung a large, two-handed machine out from beneath her evening gown, pulled hard on a piece of thick cord, and smiled as what looked like a giant tin-opener spluttered and spat into to life. 'Timber!' she whispered, the look in her eyes enough to frighten a grizzly. Miss Trout was impressed. 'That's the spirit!' she cried, sliding a brass knuckle-duster over her fist. She looked down from the balcony, trying to make out the figure of Bethesda Chubb below. 'Hang on in there!' she shouted. 'Here we come!'

A more substantial sister appeared by Miss Trout's side. 'Liber-tay!' the woman cried. 'Liber-tay! Egali-tay!...'

'And you can put those away!' interrupted Miss Trout.

'What?'

'You're flopping out dear – like a Jersey cow. Your silk blouse seems to have sprouted a sow's ear.'

The substantial lady giggled. 'Oops!' she said, making no attempt to adjust her dress. 'I'm like that big painting in France – "Liberty leading the People."'

'If you say so. But if by any chance you're trying to catch the eye of young Mr Tarzan down there, I wouldn't bother. Miss Haddock's scarred him for life. He's good for nothing but a monastery garden…'

'Says who?' the infamous Miss Haddock cried, pushing her way to the front and making little secret of dismissing her rival with the flick of a finger. 'Scarred, my foot! He's ready for seconds!

'Geronimo!' she shouted and vaulted over the balcony.

'What she said!' shouted the substantial lady leaping after Miss Haddock.

'And wait for me!' cried another of the sisterhood.

A few more of the women came to Bethesda's aid - a row of brave sisters falling over the the balcony like so many synchronised swimmers elbow dropping a whale. 'Aaaargh!' they cried, then cried 'Aaaargh!' again, but in a shrill, harsher key - more flattened fifth than a perfect fourth, as with a flick of its tail the creature that was Spleen tossed the women back over the balustrade to smash themselves against the wall. It was like a Busby Berkeley musical in reverse.

Bethesda tried to close her ears to the 'thump,' 'thump,' 'thump' of soft, upholstered bodies hitting brick and plasterwork. 'Typical,' she muttered, then pulling her cutlass out of the carpet, Bethesda dragged herself across the floor to join Fred Barnes and Elsie Tapp. 'All for one, and one for all!' she whispered, half-heartedly.

Elsie had no intention of playing D'Artagnan. Her nerves were all shot, and the only thought in her head was to rescue her beloved poodle. Let the fire take the monster and the whole bloody town, Elsie was past caring. 'Take that, you brute!' she cried, finding a far better use for her hat pin than fashion allowed. 'And as for you, little madam; you can come here this instant!'

Princess Peaches, the little madam in question, was having too good a time to simply trot back to Elsie's side. She was gnawing and worrying Spleen's leg like a beast possessed, the sorcerer's ankle taking on many identities in the poodle's wild imagination, most of them 'rabbit.'

Elsie was not impressed. She was trying her best to rescue her dog, but Princess Peaches was having none of it. 'Dammit, you ungrateful cur!' she shouted in between wild sweeps of her arms. 'Do as you're told!'

You could have heard a pin drop if the pin hadn't been thrust like a dagger through Spleen's tail. Princess Peaches shook her head, hardly believing her ears. For a purebred poodle with as many 'best in show' rosettes as flowers in a vase, being called 'a cur' was the worst possible insult. It was the 'C-Word' in the language of human-canine interaction – almost as bad as being shouted at by the one human in the world Princess Peaches adored. How dare she, how very dare she, Princess Peaches thought, then considered the insult again and barked twice in protest. Once was enough, the second bark was like the sisterhood's cry - a sudden key change followed by a long howl as the poor dog found herself flying through the air, kicked rudely aside by Spleen as soon as Princess Peaches had opened her mouth. Elsie feared the worst and ran out from under Spleen's legs with her arms outstretched. 'Got you!' she cried as she managed to catch her beloved poodle, which out of mere coincidence were the exact same words spoken at the exact same time by Spleen as he scooped Bethesda up in his claws.

'No!' cried those of the sisterhood still able to stand, but it was a 'Yes!' from Spleen - a quiet, soft-spoken 'yes!' that along with Elsie's footsteps as she escaped to the foyer, seemed the loudest noise in the building.

A mantis is a messy eater. It prefers its victims head first, chewing the top off its prey then splashing around the ketchup as good as any drunk with a fish supper. Fred Barnes - part-time butcher, part-time Tarzan but full-time sex symbol to the over-forties - knowing nothing of entomology but knowing only too well how many buckets of ketchup constitute a reasonable-sized pig, took one look at Bethesda caught in the creature's claws, and chose to be loudly and spectacularly sick. Mabel Fletcher, full-time, good-time girl, but part-time eel-straightener at Mac Fisheries, was spectacularly sick too, not on account of any ketchup, just that she hated seeing anyone throw up.

'Mop and Bucket in row B!' laughed Bethesda Chubb, trying to be brave, but those sisterhood still conscious and looking over the balcony knew different. The sisterhood had lost. Without magic they were no match for Spleen, not this giant of a monster. 'Leave the poor woman alone!' they shouted, as though the evil sorcerer would take the slightest bit of notice.

Bethesda refused to scream. She refused to do anything but struggle – a mad few seconds of kicks and thumps, a pause, then a blur of arms and legs - but Bethesda Chubb, Pirate Queen and Scourge of the Seas, found herself held fast. There was nothing she could do except swear, and this she did with all the words she knew from A to Z, then back again to F.

'You tell him, girl!' shouted the sisterhood; impressed, newly educated and trying not to cry.

Miss Elizabeth Cod cried the most. 'I can't look,' she whispered to her friend, Miss Trout. 'I just can't. I'll faint.'

The more resilient Miss Trout elbowed Elizabeth hard in the ribs. 'You will look!' she whispered. 'And you'll smile at Bethesda too. Not like that, not like you've been waiting for years to see her come to this!'

Elizabeth tried to smile, but the very act of being told made her self-conscious, the best she could manage falling halfway between 'hello' and sucking a raspberry pip from between her teeth…

…and then she was sick.

'Sorry!' cried Elizabeth. 'It's not you, I promise. It's just that awful smell.'

Miss Trout had noticed it too, and fumbling for her handkerchief succumbed to the same, all down the balcony and onto the floor. Other sisters followed - a gurgle and splash of sensitive stomachs.

Bethesda Chubb, her arms crossed and eyes closed, sighed heavily and waited for death. 'So this is it,' she thought, 'the end, oblivion; one bite and then nothing.' 'Oh, for heaven's sake!" she cried. 'I'm trying to die with dignity here! Can you all stop being so bloody ill!'

But it was impossible, some terrible smell had the sisterhood as leaky as sieves, and those not rushing to the balcony took off their hats to wave and cheer their leader, then had second thoughts and used them as buckets.

'Ungrateful swines!' shouted Bethesda as she found herself lifted high off the ground. 'And as for you!' she said staring into the face of Spleen. 'Make it quick! One big bite and to hell with you all!'

Bethesda closed her eyes tight shut and mumbled a prayer, a few hastily remembered words from when she rubbed the runes and danced naked in the snow, but not being the most conscientious of witches, all she could think of was pain, more pain, and how it would hurt. She shivered. She could hear the giant insect jaws open, feel the hot breath of Spleen on her face, and then…

…nothing, just a single drip of saliva on her cheek. Bethesda waited for a few heart-stopping moments, then opened her eyes. 'Oi! I'm not a box of bloody chocolates!' she cried, but Spleen seemed distracted, his right eye on

# A TOUCH OF SPLEEN

Bethesda and his other staring at the sisterhood being violently ill on the balcony.

The reason for the sickness was obvious, someone stank – not the usual heady mix of cigarette smoke, beer and stale armpit, but a smell so nasty it would shame a skunk.

'I hope that isn't you,' Cecily Roach managed to say in between reaching for her handkerchief and swallowing hard.

'It most certainly is not!' snapped Miss Carp.

'Then who is it?'

An empty wheelchair bounced down the central aisle of the Dress Circle and collided into the balcony.

'I'd say it's him over there!'

All eyes turned to stare at the figure of a man in bandages; loose bandages that fell away with each uncertain step.

'Oh my God! Will you look at the poor man's face!'

The sisterhood recoiled in shock, unable to comprehend the full horror of the man's appearance. There were sores, and there were holes, and then there were these sores and holes. There were bits of metal, and levers too, and string and safety pins – but most of all there were…

'Maggots! Yuck!'

'You don't catch that from sitting on a toilet seat!'

'For heaven's sake Cynthia, listen to yourself. The poor chap might hear us!'

'And what if he does? Someone needs to tell him, even if his best friend forgot.'

'You can be heartless at times – a real bitch. I mean look at him. If the poor sod hadn't enough to worry about, there's that tail…'

'What tail? Where?'

'That one there!'

The tail was plain to see, a rat's tail dragging across the floor; a tail that had seen better days, but a tell-tale tail none the less.

'I don't believe it! I'd recognise that tail anywhere! Oh my God, it's him! It's Vermyn bloody Stench!'

'STENCH!'

A crash of glass and a chorus of screams provided a suitable accompaniment, even if the noise came from outside in the foyer. The creature acknowledged his name with a sneer, what was left of his lips pulling back to reveal what was left of his teeth, and with what was left of the sisterhood stepping back as far as they dare. Here was their old nemesis, the terrible rat-thing that was Spleen's proud creation; Vermyn Stench - head of the sorcerer's secret police.

'I thought he was dead!' shouted Miss Cod, trying to make herself heard above the screams and roars coming from the foyer. 'Wasn't that circus freak burnt to a crisp all those years ago?'

Stench had been burnt to a crisp, and more. Lesser beings would have died and turned to kitty litter, but not Stench. Spleen had shaped his rat-thing from hardier stock and cursed the creature with long life. Nothing, not even the voracious cave squid that had shredded his troops to jam and ribbons, could kill him now, but immortality had come at a cost. Stench's spirit was willing, but his body was weak; and it was difficult to see which bits were Stench, which bits were straw stuffing and which pieces of Meccano fitted where. What was Stench and what was flintlock pistol was easier to see. The terrible creature glared menacingly at the sisterhood, silencing the gossips with a single look, then lifting the double-barrelled weapon from his side and resting it with difficulty on the back of a seat, Stench pointed the business end of the pistol over the balcony.

'Oh, that's just brilliant! I'm going to be shot too, am I?' shouted Bethesda. 'As though being chewed to death isn't enough. Well, bullet or bite, it's all the same to me., so make up your mind!'

Which Stench did, and pulled the trigger, and with the tremendous 'crack' of the pistol firing, Bethesda fell to the ground like a stone.

Silence – the calm before the rage; those few seconds of disbelief as the sisterhood's ears buzzed and rang out with the noise of the shot.

'Did he just…'

'He most certainly did!'

'The big, hairy, stinking bastard!'

Other words followed, much more of the same and equally as colourful. But words were not enough. The sisterhood pounced, thumping and kicking Stench, jumping on his back and pulling at his ears, until with sheer weight of numbers the terrible rat creature fell to his knees. And then the rage took hold - a bloodlust with no quarter given, the sisterhood tearing at the creature's fur with their hands and teeth, ripping out fistfuls of hair and stuffing, cracking tired bones with their boots, and throwing streamers of guts in every direction. It was like the search for a winning ticket in a drawer full of junk.

'Hey! You lot up there! I'm not dead yet!'

Someone was shouting from the stalls, a very loud and familiar voice. Miss Roach spat out one of Stench's toes and looked over the balcony to where a prostrate Bethesda Chubb was waving back at her.

'Missed me?' laughed Bethesda. 'Cos' mouldy old Egyptian mummy has. Talk about a rotten shot - big gun like that, and Stench misses the bowl completely. Typical!'

## A TOUCH OF SPLEEN

But Miss Roach wasn't sure, neither were the other sisters looking over the side of the balcony and spitting out more of Stench's personal belongings. Perhaps they'd been too quick to judge, a little too accepting of the evidence. Maybe Bethesda wasn't the target after all. Maybe, just maybe mind, they'd made the teeniest, tiniest mistake…again. Miss Roach pointed slowly towards the giant figure of Spleen leant uncertain against the cinema screen. 'I don't think Stench missed at all,' she said as Spleen sank slowly to the floor, his face all jam and broken biscuits, and with two large eyes now black holes leaking goo. 'Pretty good shot, to tell the truth.'

The reason for all the screams and breaking furniture in the foyer, burst through the swing doors.

'NEVER FEAR, THE CAVALRY IS HERE!' shouted a very regency Rowena Carp riding the most peculiar yellow charger imaginable, and with a very frightened Elsie Tapp holding on to her for dear life. 'TALLY HO!' Rowena cried, swinging a large parasol around her head as the yellow wyrm reared up on its back legs. 'CHARGE!'

There was hardly room to trot let alone gallop, but the collapsed figure of Spleen was target enough.

'GIVE HIM BOTH NOSTRILS, MCTAVISH!' Rowena shouted, and the yellow wyrm dutifully obeyed, blasting the giant body of the insect with two jets of white flame, and setting fire to the entire building in the process.

'Well ladies, I don't expect much but a thank you would be nice.'

The sisterhood stood around the smouldering remains of Stench and Spleen, with a triumphant Rowena Carp brushing ash from the gold braid of her hussar's jacket.

'Something along the lines of "Darling Rowena, you were right all along. Thank you for saving the sisterhood and winning the war, and here's a gazillion gold ducats and a tiara." That sort of thing.'

The sisterhood were unimpressed, but mostly sodden and dirty, for unlike the sparkly clean Rowena, the unfortunate ladies appeared to have been the main means of putting out the fire.

Rowena continued, putting up her hand as though showered with praise. 'Enough,' she said. 'You'll only make me blush. Just make sure I'll never sail in one of your ships, or eat another one of your ship's biscuits again. No cheques mind, just the good, old fashioned shiny stuff.'

Something stirred in the ashes.

'Oops, McTavish, we've missed a bit,' Rowena said, jumping down from the wyrm and pinching Elsie Tapp's umbrella from her hand. 'Fore!' she shouted and hit the 'something' a hefty swipe, shattering it to dust.

'That was Stench you just clobbered there,' Miss Cod said, in passing.

'Really? Well, he's nothing but soot and cinders now, is he - and good riddance.'

'It's what he would have wanted, I suppose – a final rest. He came good in the end.'

Rowena studied Miss Cod closely, her face puzzled. 'I have no idea what you're talking about, dear.'

'I said Stench came good in the end. It was Stench who killed Spleen; two shots to the head with a duelling pistol. Bang! Bang!'

'Now you're being spiteful. Stench? Are you kidding me? A mere pistol?' Rowena kicked a small pile of ashes to make her point. 'Don't make me laugh. What has a lady got to do around here to be appreciated, save the world? I thought winning the battle was enough.'

'It was Stench, I tell you. Some hocus pocus of his – a magic bullet. And because Spleen died, then so did Stench. It's obvious when you think about it. Perhaps we should say a few words? Pay our respects?'

Rowena shook her head in disbelief. 'Well it's too late for that now, isn't it,' she said as Demetrios jumped off the back of the wyrm and used a fresh pile of ashes to good effect. 'Burial at sea; is that respectful enough?'

Demetrios completed his 'ceremony,' shaking each of his hind feet in the air to get rid of the dust. 'Well, that's that then,' Rowena said, climbing back on the yellow wyrm. 'Show's over, job well done and all that. Nothing more we can do here, is there, except pose for photographs – and to be honest, you all need a bath. I'm not one to complain, but really girls…poooeee!'

'That would be Stench,' Bethesda said, taking hold of the wyrm's bridle. 'Stench by name, stench by nature.'

Rowena looked unconvinced. 'If you say so, my dear, but be a lovely stinky-poo and let go of my 'horse.' I want to go home.'

'Not so fast, Rowena. You're forgetting something.'

'Am I? Soap and towel? Tweezers? A razor for your chin?'

'You're forgetting Grubdale.'

'Really? Well don't worry your little head about that. I'll never forget Grubdale. This horrid town is engraved on my memory like a tattoo.'

'And Grubdale will never forget us and that's the problem. The Professor made me promise. We have to put things right, as though we didn't exist – remove any trace of memory.'

'Surely you're not suggesting…'

Bethesda took out a handful of cigars from her coat pocket and nodded slowly.

## A TOUCH OF SPLEEN

'Struth, Bethesda! Do you realise how many cigars we'll have to smoke for the whole town to forget? I'll be spitting tar! Surely there's an easier way? Can't we put something in the water like that silly little village with the rats?'

Bethesda wasn't listening. She put the cigars in her mouth, lit them one by one and was now blowing thick, purple, smoke rings that billowed and churned, and formed small clouds high above their heads.

'Oh well, if it's to be the old purple smoke treatment, I might as well try a cheroot.'

Rowena grabbed a cigar and lifting Demetrios back on the wyrm, blew the perfect smoke ring around his head. Demetrios' eyes opened wide, his pupils sparkling with all different colours, then the poor Jellico fell fast asleep. Rowena stroked him lovingly on the head.

'Serves him right for being a gigolo. I don't know, all that money I gave the vet and he goes and cuts off the wrong bits. He won't remember a thing when he wakes up, and by thing little madam, I mean you.'

Rowena aimed her barbed comment at Elsie's poodle, who poked her head out of the carpet bag and sniffed the air. 'Hussy!' whispered Rowena, blowing purple smoke over Princess Peaches, and just to make doubly sure, she thrust three lit cigars into Elsie's mouth and thumped her hard between the shoulder blades to make her inhale. 'Suck, you silly woman!' she said, and Elsie, surprised at herself, did.

Percy Bamforth sat up in bed, his heart racing and with his face covered in sweat. Something terrible had happened, he knew that, but for the life of him he couldn't remember what.

'Are you alright, my love?' his wife asked, daring to open her eyes and greet the morning light. 'You look...'

She was going to say 'hairy.' She was going to say a lot of things, but for the life of her she couldn't remember what.

Fred Barnes knew exactly what to say, but couldn't for the life of him think how to start. He was sitting up in bed, the sheets held tight under his chin, and staring in disbelief at Percy and Evaline.

'You're dressed as a gorilla!' he managed to cry.

'And you don't seem to be dressed at all!' shouted Percy

'Anyone for eggs?' came a voice from the kitchen as Mabel Fletcher tried to remember the recipe for Omelette a la Pudsey.

## Chapter Twenty Three

Autumn had arrived and with it the promise of knitted scarves and the first snuffles of the season. It was a time of nuts, berries and scurrying squirrels, and at Number 8, Wellington Gardens, it was almost the hour for crumpets and hot, rum tea.

'Come on my little darlings,' cooed Elsie Tapp as she trotted along the pavement to her London apartment. 'Cook has promised us something nice for supper!'

Her 'little darlings' leapt and barked in excitement. 'Supper' was such a delicious word; not as marvellous as 'squirrel' or 'rabbit', but more snuggly and tummy-filling. They dragged Elsie the last few yards, then pulled her through the gate and up the steps to the front door. 'My but you're getting stronger,' Elsie commented, with pride.

Someone had left a large envelope on the top step - an envelope that had seen better days, better postmen, and from the look of what was stuck to the outside, better mail bags too.

'Hello, what's this?' Elsie said as she bent down and rescued the object from the excitable puppies before they could tear it to shreds.

'Miss Tapp, Somewhere in London, England,' she read, amazed at the ingenuity of the Royal Mail, but catching a faint whiff of regurgitated fish, Elsie held the envelope aloft as she opened the door. 'We're back, Mrs C,' she called, then dropped the four leads on the floor and let her darling Princess and the three puppies scamper off in the direction of the kitchen.

Elsie looked at the envelope with a fresh eye. There was a triangle of green paper stuck to the top with a drawing of a seagull and the word 'airmail' scribbled in red ink. Elsie was familiar with stamps, she'd been a keen philatelist for years, but this looked more like a doodle on gummed paper than anything worth collecting. 'How very odd,' she muttered, before opening the envelope and pulling out a number of sheets of small, closely-spaced handwriting that

## A TOUCH OF SPLEEN

were sufficient to tell a tale if not a chapter in a book. 'Tea, Mrs C,' Elsie called before taking off her coat and sitting down in her favourite chair in the drawing room. The letter deserved careful study, but she would need her spectacles. The handwriting was so small it was as though the author had a lot to say but too few sheets of paper to say it on. Elsie searched in her handbag, ignoring the small bar of chocolate she had saved for later. 'Here we are,' she said, opening a pair of lorgnette glasses and holding them close to her face. 'Now, let's see what all this fuss is about.'

'Dear Miss Tapp,' she read. 'Please accept our sincere apologies for calling you a witch...'

'Well really, of all the cheek!'

'...but, as I hope you'll understand after reading this letter, Grubdale is no ordinary town.'

Elsie thought better of throwing the sheets of paper in the fire and read them through, word by word. She read the letter that evening, then re-read it before getting into bed, and not being able to sleep, switched the bedroom light on and re-read it from start to finish. It was fantastic; beyond fantastic. It was the most extraordinary and thoroughly odd letter she had ever received. It was an apology, a very long letter of apology written by a certain Mr Cross - a peculiar gentleman who appeared to be a galley hand on a ship called The Emily P. Another gentleman, a Mr Dashing seemed equally guilty and wretched, and had also signed his name to the confession.

'The fact is, Mrs C,' said Elsie the next morning as she dipped a finger of toast into a soft boiled egg, 'forgetting all the silly bits, some of their stories seem strangely familiar. It's maddening, like a distant memory whispering in my ear. Grubdale, for instance; such a peculiar town with a peculiar name, and for some peculiar reason, I think I've been there on holiday. It's ridiculous I know. Dammit, have we ever been to Derbyshire? I'm not sure about anything anymore.'

'You sent me a postcard from Buxton, once.' mumbled Mrs C, her mouth full of fruitcake as she read the letter. 'And a souvenir pork pie.' The way she pronounced 'pork pie' was as though the very idea of posting meat products as presents was unthinkable.

'Did I? Well there you are then, no wonder Grubdale seems familiar.'

'Meet many witches and dragons there?'

'I don't think so.'

'And giant spiders that snap you in two?'

'I most certainly did not.'

'Then it's all rubbish,' said Mrs C, chasing a stubborn piece of fruitcake around her bottom teeth with her finger. 'Just two old fools on the drink.

There's no such place as Grubdale – I've checked in the A to Z. I'd throw the letter in the bin and think no more of it. Remember what the doctor said? You're not to get excited. You're still the wrong side of delicate.'

There was comfort in Mrs C's no-nonsense words. Elsie smiled and squeezed the cook's hand. Of course, the letter was rubbish. Witches, dragons and rat-things in bandages? She'd be on the front seat on the fast bus to the 'funny farm' if she believed all of that. Still, a pink poodle that breathed fire; why was the idea so difficult to dismiss?

The telephone in the hall rang and Elsie, guessing who it was, groaned and pushed her breakfast plate away.

'The "mistress" calls,' joked Mrs C. 'Should I answer?'

'Please, I don't think I can face the terrible Marjorie Whippet, this morning. She probably wants to pay a visit, stink up the house with those awful purple cigars of hers, and squeeze me for another book.'

'Yes, dear. Well, it's not my place to say, but I think she's an addict. Not even that Mr Churchill smokes as many King Edwards as her. She'd be better off with a pipe.'

Elsie poured herself a cup of tea and looked out of the breakfast room window. 'Tell her I'm ill, and I'll phone back next week,' she shouted, hearing Mrs C pick up the phone.

Later that morning, with breakfast finished and a log fire burning nicely in the grate, Elsie Tapp sat down at her writing desk, smiled at the sleeping puppies tucked up in a basket by her feet, and threaded a single sheet of paper into her Remington typewriter. It was time to begin a new adventure, a new sickly-sweet romance full of crinoline, domino masks and villains called Ralph, but ideas were thin on the ground. Her muse, never short of words or storylines before, had disappeared on holiday for the season.

Elsie muttered to herself. 'All I need is a good title,' she said, but her mind was as blank as the sheet of pink paper. She typed the words 'HOSTAGE TO LOVE,' smiled, frowned then ripped the paper out of the typewriter and started again. 'PASSPORT TO PASSION' seemed a marked improvement, yet promised an intimate knowledge of something, that for all of Elsie's years, remained a mystery as peculiar as the Mary Celeste. Her nom de plume, Felicity Merryweather, was the queen of romance, and where romance was concerned, there was no passport to anything. Miss Merryweather's characters were happy where they were, frolicking around in a perfumed garden of stolen kisses, squeezed waists and promises of undying love and doing the dishes.

'THE PIRATE QUEEN.'

## A TOUCH OF SPLEEN

Elsie considered the title, then dismissed it with the others. She doubted a female pirate would stay innocent for long, certainly not as long as 50,000 words, including title and chapter headings. New ideas were so tricky to find.

Elsie stared at the shelves, at the numerous copies of numerous editions of her numerous books, and groaned. Felicity Merryweather had run out of steam, and her Regency novels had run out of history. There wasn't a stately home left she hadn't stuffed to the rafters with cads and heroines. Even her 'rolling meadows' were so heavily sprinkled with shepherdesses and handsome young gentlemen out for a stroll, if she tried to write anymore they would have to join a queue. Short of ditching the crinoline, there was always Victorian Britain, but what a difference a few decades make. Victorian Britain was all satanic mills and eligible gentlemen far too old. Romance in Victorian Britain ended the day top hats grew tall, dresses washed dark and whiskers could be tied behind the ears when slurping the soup. 'Impossible! I might as well write about those women in tweed in that wretched letter.'

There should have been an orchestra, a crescendo of strings, a suitable climax to mark the birth of an idea. Now that Elsie thought of the letter, of the ridiculous townsfolk and their funny ways, and the weird and wonderful creatures described, the more plausible the idea seemed. Of course, she would have to add to the story, to flesh out the characters with thoughts of her own, but one thing was sure, there would be no romance. Her days of writing sugary nonsense were over.

Elsie tore the pink paper out of the typewriter and threw it to the floor. 'Bye-bye Felicity!' she cried and reaching for the second pile of foolscap, threaded a fresh sheet of green paper into her Remington.

'LAVENDER & HADDOCK,' she typed, thinking the title suitably silly and suggestive, then with a flurry of fingertips continued with the words 'Part One of "THE TROUBLE WITH WYRMS" Trilogy – A COMEDY IN THREE WRYGGLES" by Dame Agatha Prodd.'

Elsie smiled and hugged herself. For some ridiculous reason, this new pen name made her giggle like a schoolgirl. She spun the chair around and smiled at her darling poodles asleep in their basket. 'Wakey, wakey!' she cried. 'Mummy is going to write a silly little book!'

Her confession was met with snores of indifference, the three puppies snuggled against Princess Peaches and all four were fast asleep.

'My darlings,' sighed Elsie, and leaning over the basket she tickled the largest and cutest of the puppies gently under the chin. 'Snuggle-wuggles,' she cooed and gave the pink poodle a soft tap on its big wet nose. The puppy opened its eyes and gave Elsie a knowing look, as if to say 'Once, but never again,' then sneezed and burnt a small hole through the basket.

# MIKE WILLIAMS

# A TOUCH OF SPLEEN

## List of Characters

Commander Crillock – Commander of the SS Behemoth, the jewel in Tarantulus Spleen's navy.

Lieutenant Flume – unfortunate sailor with a weak stomach.

Emperor Tarantulus Spleen – Usurper, bully, evil-sorcerer, all-round nasty bloke with a face like a blue bottle. Far too many arms for a cardigan.

The Sisterhood – last bastion of decency in the kingdom of Wyrm, which doesn't say a lot. Argumentative, middle-aged witches given to drink, shopping and dressing the same in tweed and sensible shoes.

Bethesda Chubb – Pirate queen, and commander of the flag ship Emily P. Argumentative, charismatic, bulbous and pugilistic.

Rowena Carp – elegance personified, if not wrinkled in all the wrong places. A senior member of the sisterhood, but not necessarily wise with age. She is the only member of the sisterhood to keep a familiar - Demetrios the Jellico, from the forests of Tweeb.

Florentine Trout – shrill-voiced member of the sisterhood, not overly fond of the perfumed and fashionable Rowena Carp.

Petunia Mullet – sporty member of the sisterhood. Likes to row the boat and shout 'hallelujah!'

Cecily Roach – amorous member of the sisterhood, desperate for a bit of 'slap and tickle', but not as desperate as Miss Haddock or Miss Spratt

Miss Haddock and Miss Spratt – two excitable members of the sisterhood, neither of them to be trusted with young men in leotards

Elizabeth Codd – studious member of the sisterhood. 'Good with gadgets' as Miss Roach would say after too many drinks.

Miss Gulper and Miss Dabb – elderly but quiet members of the sisterhood. Are either very innocent or dustbin filthy.

Demetrios - a Jellico from the forests of Tweeb. Beloved companion of Rowena Carp. Resembles a fat, pink poodle but breathes fire and would bite the hand off your arm if you offered him a biscuit.

The Yellow Wyrm – the last surviving great wyrm of legend. Male – probably, adolescent - most certainly.

Mildew, Squint and Pursglove – ex-pupils of Grubdale Towers, and now reluctant pirates on board the Emily P.

Silas Churn – a man of some importance in the tiny, coastal village of Fish Gut Bay. Master of the Watch, and Keeper of the Tinderbox.

Percy Bamforth – manager of the Galaxy cinema, Grubdale. He has three passions in life – his beautiful wife, the Wurlitzer theatre organ installed in the cinema, and getting elected as mayor of Grubdale. He has two major headaches too – getting elected as mayor of Grubdale, and his nemesis the terrible Mary O'Reilly, ex-pianist from the old picture house.

Evaline Bamforth – graceful wife to Percy, worldlier and far cleverer than her husband. She has two passions in life – her slightly paunchy husband, and getting her slightly paunchy husband elected as town mayor.

Mary O'Reilly – ex school cook and frustrated pianist, dying to get her fingers on Percy Bamforth's Wurlitzer organ. Far too fond of the drink for her own good, but an excellent shot with a cabbage or cauliflower.

The Reverend Ainsley Cross – meddlesome pensioner, still suffering nightmares from 20 years ago when witches came to town, the dead walked and dragons burned down the school. Has found solace in brandy and pickled eggs.

Captain Hilary Dashing – meddlesome pensioner, still suffering nightmares from 20 years ago when witches came to town, the dead walked and dragons burned down the school. Has found solace in whisky, and ham and cheese sandwiches.

Elsie Tapp – formidable woman of a certain age. The kind of lady who'd break the heart of a Turkish wrestler, but mostly with her fists. Author of more than a dozen sickly, sweet romances, using her pen name, Felicity Merryweather.

Princess Peaches of Pontefract – Elsie Tapp's beloved, pink-dyed poodle who's more desperate for a bit of slap and tickle than any of the sisterhood.

Happy Harry Renfield – a jovial, red-faced gentleman, although not so jovial now since a certain ornate chest washed up on a beach in North Wales. Purveyor of jokes and novelties.

Fred Barnes – Yorkshire Films' one and only Tarzan, also a pork butcher in his spare time.

Mabel Fletcher – Fred Barnes' girlfriend. Pudsey Carnival Queen, 1931.

# A TOUCH OF SPLEEN

Bob and Jesse Furness - land lord and land lady of the Cheddar Cheese, Grubdale , one of the more respectable pubs on the high street.

The Desk Sergeant – the calm voice of authority in the police station in Grubdale.

Constables Wiggery, Drudge, Jones and Smith – the thin blue line.

Sid Bottle – caretaker and general handyman at the Galaxy cinema. Convinced there's something big and nasty in the basement.

Marjorie Whippet – Elsie Tapp's publisher in London

Mrs C – Elsie's no-nonsense cook in her London flat.

The Bandaged Man – ?

## About the Author

Mike Williams (1959 to one day when he's not looking) was born in the town of Market Harborough and due to a mix up with a local fortune teller was photographed for much of his first year in a dress. After moving to the Derbyshire Dales to escape the shame, he took to farming like a duck to liver pate and for many years seemed perpetually doused in manure, mostly from slipping on the cobbles or walking too near the cows at milking time. Educated at Buxton College, Chesterfield Art College and Trent Polytechnic, he threw away the wellington boots for a briefcase, was awarded a doctorate in 1986 and since then has lectured and published widely in plant physiology. He can be found waxing lyrical to students on the intimate contents of a leaf at Trinity College, Dublin or running around a park in an attempt to lose weight. He is married with two goldfish and an overdraft.

For more information on other books by Mike Williams then visit www.facebook.com/Grubdale

Printed in Great Britain
by Amazon